W9-BOC-368

Running Scared

BOOKS BY LINDA LADD

A Love So Fine
A Love So Splendid
Forever My Love
Lilacs on Lace
White Orchid
White Rose
White Lily
Dragonfire
Midnight Fire
Frostfire
Christmas Romance Anthology
Dreamsong
Silverswept
Fireglow
Moonspell
Wildstar
Broken Promises
On Wings of Desire
Bittersweet Temptation

LINDA LADD

Running Scared

BOOKSPAN
GARDEN CITY, NEW YORK

Book club edition published by BOOKSPAN,
401 Franklin Avenue, Garden City, New York 11530

ISBN: 0-7394-1175-6

Design by Paul Randall Mize

Printed in the United States of America

For Bill, my husband and best friend—
thank you for 29 wonderful years of marriage.

And for our two beautiful children—Laurie and Bill.

With heartfelt appreciation to my literary agent, Richard Curtis.

Running Scared

One

KATE REED opened her eyes. It was still early, well before dawn. The drapes were open and she could see the stars in the night sky, blinking, twinkling, beautiful. She turned her head to the green glow of the digital clock on the nightstand beside her. Just before five o'clock. She had a few minutes yet to come awake. Above Pop's oak bookcase bed, the ceiling fan cut the air slowly, lazily revolving and throwing whispery waves of cool air over her bare arms.

Her husband, Michael, was already up, which surprised her. She could hear him moving around, probably in the kitchen because of the faint light in the hallway outside their bedroom. She tugged the soft quilted blanket up to her chin, comforted by the fragrance of Downy clinging to it. She didn't want to get up yet, especially since Joey was still sleeping soundly in the bassinet beside her. At the thought of her beautiful baby boy, she shifted on her elbow and looked down into the portable crib. They'd only gotten him a month ago, after two years of trying to adopt, and she already loved him as much as if she had given birth to him herself. He slept peacefully, and she peered through the dim light a few more seconds to make sure his tiny chest was rising and falling.

He was fine, so she lay back and let her mind stray until she began to wonder why on earth Michael was fooling around in the kitchen at the crack of dawn. Good grief, he'd managed to beat the sun up! Not like Michael at all.

Beside her, Joey grunted, coughed, then began to stir around, kicking his arms and legs and working himself into a good, hungry wail. The digital numerals on the bedside clock blinked to 5:02. Eager to pick up the baby and cuddle him, she swung her legs off the bed and slid her feet into house slippers. Yawning, she pulled on the embroidered robe that matched her black silk pajamas, the outfit Michael had brought home from his last business trip.

Sleepily she shuffled across the room to the dressing table and switched on a small lamp. Her reflection loomed in the mirror, looking a little worse for wear after the first month of motherhood. She combed her fingers through the long, honey-blond hair tousled around her shoulders, liberally sunstreaked with lighter shades from recent weeks on the river. Yawning, she leaned close enough to examine eyes the color of rich brown sable, but at the moment a bit bleary and bloodshot from so many middle-of-the-night feedings. But it was little price to pay for all the joy Joey had brought into her life, she thought, smiling as she turned back to the crib. Joey was just about the best thing that had ever happened to her.

"Good morning, sweetie," she crooned, lifting the squirming baby up against her with the doting tenderness she'd learned since becoming his mother. He seemed so small and fragile but the truth was that he was a big baby for his age, healthy and strong. She sighed with contentment. There was nothing else like it, this bond forming between them, strong and irrevocable, mother and child.

As she'd expected Joey's diaper was sopping wet, so Kate sat on the bed and changed him, then got him all snug and comfy in a brand-new drawstring sleeper gown, one from Baby Gap, no less. Michael had become quite extravagant with his new son and made enough purchases from Neiman Marcus to outfit ten newborns. She smiled, pleased that her husband loved their son the way she did. Carefully she lifted him, raising him and cooing to him while he kicked his feet and made funny little gurgling goos back at her.

She took a moment to tuck him into the quilted sling Michael had also picked up for her, a lifesaver she'd soon found, because she could keep him lying contentedly against her chest while her hands were free for work. Sort of like a papoose but worn across the front instead of the back. She wondered if Joey liked it so much because he could hear her heartbeat and feel her warmth, kind of the same principle as putting a ticking clock in a puppy's basket. She'd found the device worth its weight in gold since it allowed her to keep Joey with her when she ran the bait shop and canoe rental on the riverbank behind the cabin.

"Okay, sugar lamb, time to eat, huh? You're a hungry boy this morning, I know you are. You want your bottle, don't you?"

Murmuring soothingly to Joey, who was getting a little riled up about her taking so long to get his bottle ready, Kate walked down the hall and into the brightly lit kitchen where she found Michael down on one knee, lifting the hem of the curtains and peering outside at their detached garage.

"What are you looking at?" she asked curiously, pausing in the doorway. Somewhere far out on the river she could hear the low buzz of an outboard motor, no doubt an early angler wanting to beat everyone else to his favorite fishing hole.

Michael dropped the curtain and spun around as if she'd caught him peeping into a bedroom window. What on earth was his problem lately? He'd been so nervous.

"I heard Bubba barking's all. It woke me up so I thought I'd see if anyone was around."

Bubba was a bluetick hound who lived with Maude Cecily at her cabin, about two miles downstream from them. As far as Kate was concerned, Bubba was a good dog that caused trouble for no one. Her grandfather and his friends used to feed him leftovers from their lunches down by the river. Kate smiled when she remembered how Bubba used to sit up and beg if anybody opened a bag of barbecue potato chips. He wouldn't touch any other flavor.

"Bubba doesn't usually come up close to the house," Kate told Michael, moving to the refrigerator and pulling out a couple of Joey's bottles that she'd prepared the night before. "He's always chasing something. No reason to get so uptight about it." She turned and leveled an inquiring look. "You sure are jumpy lately, Michael."

"I'm not jumpy. Just being careful. It could be a prowler out there, for all you know."

Kate couldn't help laughing. "Here? Who'd want to burglarize us? All we have is live bait and the soft drink change. If I were you, I'd be more concerned about our new house sitting empty up in Clayton."

"You don't have to worry about that with the alarm system it's got. Down here, it's a different story. We're out in the boondocks where anything could happen. I'm just thinking about you and the little guy there."

Kate smiled as he came over and took Joey out of her arms. He shifted him into one arm and chucked him under the chin with his knuckle. "Hi there, tiger. We're gonna have to get you a dog one of these days, too, you know. A watchdog, maybe. A beagle like the one Pop used to have?"

Michael's innocent remark brought up all the grief she'd fought daily since her grandfather had his fatal heart attack about six weeks ago. Pop had raised her since she was four after her parents had died in a fiery crash outside the air force base in Tokyo where her father had been stationed. Pop had been the only family she'd had left, until she'd married Michael, and now they had Joey. Having the baby was helping her cope, though. "Try not to worry so much, Michael. Pop was never broken into, and he lived in this house for nearly thirty years. By himself, since Grandma died."

"Yeah, and he was the sheriff, too, for most of that time,

with a shotgun he kept loaded and ready. Everybody for miles around knew it. That's why nobody bothered him." Michael sat down at the kitchen table with Joey. "Now we've got a son to worry about. Can't let anything happen to him, now can we?" Kate stopped shaking the bottle in her hand and watched him gaze fondly at the baby. He'd grown to love Joey, too, she had no doubt of that. They'd had their troubles in the past, but Joey was going to make their marriage strong again, she knew it.

"Is the bottle about ready? Joey wants some breakfast, and right now."

Kate nodded, hardly able to believe they were actually living at the cabin together instead of up in St. Louis. Once they'd moved up there, they'd grown apart, but maybe down here along the river, they'd be happy again, as happy as they'd been at the beginning of their marriage.

"Put him up against your shoulder and pat his back. He likes that."

Michael stood up and transferred the baby to his shoulder, his handsome features absorbed with his son. At five foot eight she was almost as tall as he was, and she smiled, pleased at what a good father he'd become. He'd never shown much interest in children but he was certainly showing his willingness to help care for Joey. But he'd been very apprehensive, too, and she didn't know if that was because of his inexperience with the baby or the fact that he wasn't yet used to the quiet life along Current River.

Turning, she switched on the gas underneath a small saucepan of water, then put a bottle on to warm. She stuck the other one in the zippered pocket on the outside of Joey's sling for later, along with Joey's pacifier and a couple of clean disposable diapers, so she wouldn't forget them later when she took him down with her to open the bait shop.

"You sure that dog's not barking at somebody out there?"

Michael suddenly asked, twisting around to look out the windows.

"I don't think so. He's just on the scent of some animal. Why are you so worried about it?"

"I guess I'm just on edge," he said then. "I can't help it. This place just seems so isolated after living in the city so long."

Michael still looked a little sleepy as he raked one hand through his short, wheat-colored hair. He was an extremely good-looking man with classic, movie-star features, fair of complexion though his face was very sunburned at the moment, and very fit from lifting weights and working out on the Stairmaster. When they'd wed, everyone had thought them the perfect couple, both young, blond, and athletic.

"We're safer down here than in the city. I never got used to all the crime up there."

She poured herself and Michael cups of coffee but only got a sip or two before her son let her know in no uncertain terms that he was not happy. He was ready for his breakfast, and he was ready for it *now*.

"Okay, okay, precious, it's coming," she murmured in the ridiculous singsongy baby talk she often found herself using with the baby. But it made Joey smile and screw up his face until the double dimples under his right eye deepened, and Kate loved that. "Now let me test it, sweetie cakes, so it won't burn your little mouth."

Joey would have none of her delay tactics this morning, and though he usually was an incredibly content and quiet baby, he didn't mind fussing and squirming around in Michael's arms as she tested the temperature of the formula inside her wrist. Just right, thank goodness. She picked him up and tucked him carefully into the sling before she touched the nipple to his lips. He shook his head in a frantic attempt to get it, then took to it like a hungry bass to a spinnerbait. Kate chuckled as he began to suck greedily, his bright dark eyes glued to her face.

"At the rate he's going through these bottles, he's going to be a twenty pounder before the fourth of July," she murmured more to herself than to Michael, who sat watching her where she leaned against the kitchen counter.

"He's getting big, all right," Michael said, sipping his coffee. The note of pride Kate had sensed so often in him revealed itself loud and clear again, as his eyes lingered on the infant in her arms.

Kate had caught him on occasion all alone in the nursery, bending over the cradle, smiling at Joey and letting the baby hold onto his forefinger. He'd taken part in caring for him, feeding him, even changing his diaper, though Kate liked to keep Joey with her for the most part. In the sling against her heart. He was her heart, had already filled some of the empty nooks and crannies left by Pop's passing.

Yes, she had to say that Michael had been good as gold the past month, taking care of all the grocery shopping and trips into town. Kate hadn't been anywhere but home for over a month, but that was fine by her. At the moment Kate could truly see the affection in Michael's gray eyes, and was pleased he was bonding with their child, too.

Unfortunately, Michael's tender expression disintegrated as Bubba erupted in an insistent yapping somewhere down in the backyard near the riverbank. He got up and peered out the window into the darkness.

"I'm telling you something's out there. I wish this fog would lift. I can't see a thing past the dusk-to-dawn light."

Kate shook her head, nonplussed by his uneasiness. She'd never seen him so nervous and on edge. Back home in St. Louis, he was usually so confident, secure about himself and everything else, but maybe that was because they had a child now, a child to love and protect. She knew she had become much more protective now that she was responsible for Joey, but she really didn't share his concern about being burglarized. Nearly everyone along Current River knew everyone else, and besides that, one of Pop's best friends, Gus Shelter, was the county sheriff and often dropped by the bait shop to check on her. Nobody was going to rob them.

"Bubba barks all the time. He's a hound, and they're always trailing rabbits or squirrels."

Michael still didn't look convinced. As her husband continued to peer out the window, Kate shook her head at the way he was dressed. Even down here on the river, where everything was supposed to be informal and laid-back, he was still a lawyer at heart. He wore creased Calvin Klein jeans and a black-and-white–striped Perry Ellis sweatshirt, and though sockless, he wore a pair of expensive tasseled loafers. Yes sir, a regular river rat, he was. Kate laughed to herself, knowing that his poverty as a boy made him appreciate such things. Her indulgent smile quickly faded, however, and she gaped at her husband in complete astonishment when he suddenly whipped out a great big, chrome-colored pistol from somewhere behind him and held it pointed up in front of his shoulder like Sonny Crockett used to do on *Miami Vice*.

"My God, Michael, where did you get that thing?"

"I carry it with me sometimes. It pays to arm yourself these days."

"Or when you represent sleazeballs who'd just as soon shoot you as give you the time of day?"

Kate really hadn't meant to say it that way; it'd just slipped out. She'd meant it sarcastically and that's the way it had sounded. She'd much preferred it when they'd first married three years ago and he was a district attorney in St. Louis. He was making only a fraction of what he pulled in now but he'd been proud of his work then and talked to her about his cases. Since he'd become a criminal defense attorney he'd become secretive about his clients and unwilling to discuss the people he dealt with.

"That's right. Sometimes they get pissed off at me so I have to be ready for them."

Kate glanced down as Joey squirmed and pushed the nipple out of his mouth with a disgruntled sputter. Time for one of his gigantic belches, she supposed. She took him out of the sling and placed him upright against her shoulder, gently patting him on the back. Bubba was barking his head off again, and Michael looked really alarmed now.

"I'm gonna go down and see who's out there. Stay here and don't come out till I get back."

"I really think you're overreacting, Michael. . . ."

"Maybe so, but I'm still going to check it out," he said in the stubborn tone that meant she wouldn't be able to dissuade him. She watched as he opened the door and eased cautiously across the rear sundeck. He had definitely been cooped up down on the river too long. She made up her mind to encourage him to go back to the city for awhile and get a fix of police sirens and traffic jams. Otherwise, he was going to drive her crazy, too.

When Joey gave a long, hearty burp, Kate smiled, always amazed how loud they were, more like a teenage boy than four-week-old tyke. Now he was ready for more, and she shifted him back into the sling and put the nipple back into his greedy little mouth. She secured it to the elastic loop that held it in place and freed her hands. She picked up one of Joey's silky black curls and caressed it between her thumb and forefinger, hoping Michael wouldn't get so excited when he came across Bubba that he'd shoot his own foot off. He'd never been one to handle guns before, certainly wasn't a hunter like Pop had been.

Once the baby was settled in the sling and sucking happily, she carried her coffee mug to the sink and stood looking outside. Good lord, it was so foggy. She hadn't realized it was so bad, man, a veritable London soup. She took another much-needed sip of coffee and admitted yet again what a complete caffeine fiend she was. She wondered why the fog was so dense this morning. There were always mists over the river this early in the spring but this looked thick and dank, the kind that rolled low and spookily over the ground.

Kate could see Michael halfway down the sloping backyard now, still on the concrete flight of steps, up to his knees in swirling smoky clouds so that it seemed he descended into a boiling cauldron of water. He really wasn't much more than a silhouette against the eerie yellowish glow thrown out by the tall vapor light mounted high on a utility pole. He was holding his gun out in front of him with both hands, straight armed. Yeah, he was definitely a would-be Don Johnson, she decided.

She listened for Bubba but the dog had hushed up his racket, probably munching on a chicken bone he'd dragged out of the bait-shop trashcan. Maybe Michael would finally admit they were all safe now and come back up and eat some breakfast.

Michael had stopped now, directly underneath the yard light. He was advancing slowly, looking from side to side like a member of a SWAT team, and she suddenly remembered that she needed to thaw out something for dinner. A roast would be good, she decided, since she could put it on frozen in the crockpot before she and Joey went off to work.

Still watching her husband make everything safe and secure for his family, she readjusted the bottle, tightening the elastic band so it'd stay put, then sneaked another swig of java. Joey was settled comfortably and would fall asleep soon. She glanced out the window, coffee mug in hand.

Oh, God. Who was that? Someone else *was* out there. A second figure was moving out of the shadows into the smoky light right behind Michael. Michael didn't see him, and Kate hit her palm frantically on the glass trying to warn him but could only watch with horror as Michael suddenly whipped around. The other man's arm was extended, and a shot cracked, the report strangely muffled underneath the low-hanging fog bank.

"Michael!" she screamed, panicking, but both men had disappeared now, hidden by the thick swirls of fog. She wasn't sure if he'd been hit or not. Her shock faded as she realized she had to call 911. She ran to Pop's old rotary-dial phone, grabbed the receiver and held it between her ear and shoulder, her fingers fumbling at the numbers.

"Put the phone down."

Shocked to hear a voice so close behind her, Kate whirled around, losing her grip on the phone. It fell hard, clunked against the wall, then swung erratically back and forth by the cord. Kate stared at the complete stranger standing in her kitchen, disbelieving in that first stunned instant that he was actually there.

"That's a good girl," he said in a voice that was strangely subdued, almost casual in tone, but very thickly accented. "Now put kid on floor and back that way." He gestured toward the sink with the automatic weapon he held in his black-gloved right hand, a deadly dark-blue steel pistol aimed at her head.

Sheer, unadulterated horror engulfed her, and she couldn't make herself obey, couldn't make herself believe this was really happening, that it wasn't some kind of terrible nightmare. Fear jerked a knot in the back of her throat, and she put both arms protectively around Joey in his sling and stared wordlessly at the intruder. The man was tall, at least six feet, deeply tanned with faintly lighter circles around his eyes such as a lifeguard or an alpine downhill skier would have. Long white-blond hair was bound back at his nape. He wore a tiny diamond stud in one earlobe, and looked young, in his twenties most likely, lean and strongly built. He wore some kind of black windsuit and black Nike hightops. His eyes were black frozen ice. He watched her unblinkingly out of them, completely calm.

"Do it. Put boy down so you and me can have little chat." He pronounced the last as *lattol shot*, and she suddenly recognized the accent. It was Russian. Like some of the Olympians from Moscow she'd met when she'd been running in marathon competitions. Oh, God, what was a Russian doing here? What did he want?

Kate finally forced her lips to move, but her knees were trembling violently inside the legs of her black silk pajamas. So was her voice when she got her mouth to work.

"Who are you? What do you want?" It had to be a robbery, she realized then. Michael had been right, after all. "We don't have any money here, but take the cars, they're expensive models, there's a Lexus and a brand-new Ford Explorer, take them both, take whatever you want. Just don't hurt us."

The blond kid smiled, revealing straight, extremely even teeth as white as his hair. "I know of you, Kate Reed. You win bronze medal. You gutsy woman, I think, but not so stupid. Put boy down so he won't get hurt."

For a fleeting instant Kate held to the hope that this was a bad dream, a *really, really* bad dream, but when she looked down at Joey, he was still sucking happily at his bottle, his round eyes latched adoringly on her face. He stopped a moment to grin, his lips curving around the nipple in his mouth. Oh, God, she couldn't let anything happen to him. No matter what else happened, she couldn't let them harm him.

"Do it," the man ordered sharply. "Don't be stupid."

Kate stared at him, her mind racing, trying to come up with a plan. He wasn't wearing a disguise. She'd seen his face, could identify him, and everybody, especially the granddaughter of a lifelong law officer, knew what that meant. He meant to kill her. There was no compassion in those weird obsidian eyes either, nothing but cold, merciless power. And now as she continued to balk, a sliver of anger appeared in him, disrupting his unruffled demeanor.

"Do it!" he said, louder this time, but he was getting impatient because his alien accent became even thicker.

"All right," she hedged, her heart thumping so hard that she shook with each beat. "Please, don't hurt us. We'll do what you want."

The pan of water was still boiling on the stove. Out of the corner of her eye, she could see steam rising in wisps, though she didn't look at it. An idea began to form, and she slowly obeyed the man with the gun, lifting Joey out of the sling with both hands, then turning slightly as if she meant to lay him on the linoleum floor in front of the dangling telephone.

As she bent over with him, she suddenly darted to the left instead, slapping her palm hard atop the push-button light switch. The room plunged into darkness, and Kate grabbed the handle of the pan and flung the boiling water at the intruder. The scream of pain that followed told Kate she'd hit her mark.

Clutching Joey, she dropped to a crouch behind the counter and crawled toward the bedroom as he stumbled around in the darkness, yelling in his own language and knocking over kitchen chairs in his search for the light switch. She didn't have much time, and she scrabbled quickly on hands and knees into the hall. A shot went off behind her in a strobe flash of black and white. The acrid odor of burning cordite filled her nostrils. Oh, God, he was going to kill her! Joey wailed as Kate tightened her grip on him and took off for the sliding doors in the bedroom. Struggling desperately, she finally forced the lever up and slung back the heavy glass door, just as the light flared on in the kitchen.

Frantic, heart thudding wildly, she ran across the small side deck and jumped down into the grass, losing one house shoe in the iris bed. She had to get away from the house, into the woods where the fog and darkness would hide her! She could hear the blond kid yelling again in Russian words she couldn't understand as she gained the forsythia hedge at the edge of the yard and scrambled headlong into its thick, low-lying branches.

Throat clogged with a solid lump of terror, she rocked Joey back and forth, trying to muffle his scared cries against her breast. He wouldn't stop, getting more and more furious and frightened as she tried to get him to hush, and she fumbled desperately for the bottle in the elastic band. She found it and gave it to him the best she could with hands shaking uncontrollably, praying he'd stop crying, her whole body quivering. He took the nipple, and Kate held him tightly. Oh, God, they already had Michael. They shot at him. Oh, God, oh, God, what was she going to do?

Two

FOR THE FIRST chilling moments Kate sat carved in stone, on her knees, every muscle rigid. All she could hear was the pounding of her heart—hard, fast thuds that filled her ears and drowned out everything else. Frozen with the most utter, complete fear she had ever known, she clasped Joey tightly against her breast and struggled for the presence of mind to search the darkness for Michael. He had to be out there somewhere, probably hiding as she was. Oh, God, he had to be. He couldn't be dead, he couldn't! None of this could be happening.

But it was happening. Somewhere out in the black foggy night she heard another man call out. This one shouted in Russian, too, the deep voice drifting eerily through the cloying dampness. Disembodied, hostile, excited with blood lust. They'd come to kill them, her and Michael both; somehow her instincts told her that. The big blond man, his eyes had told her that, too, cold, lethal, eager to spill blood.

Oh, God help them. Why was this happening? She rubbed her face with one hand, found her skin sweaty and hot despite the clammy air. She couldn't stop trembling, no matter how hard she tried, and she clamped her teeth tightly together and heaved in a lungful of cool air through her nostrils. She had to pull herself together, she had to, if she and Joey had any hope of getting out of this alive.

Two men were down at the riverbank. She could hear

them shouting back and forth at each other, and it sounded as though they were speaking Russian, too, but she couldn't quite tell for sure. She raised her head and strained her ears as they came closer, running up the concrete steps that led from the river to the rear sundeck.

This is absurd, impossible, she kept thinking but knew she didn't have time to dwell on that. It *was* happening, and armed men were out there, searching everywhere for her. She had a chance to evade them so long as it was dark, but when dawn broke they'd find her. She had to get away, now, before the sun rose.

Shutting her eyes, she swallowed hard and tried to reason. Come on, Kate, suck it up. You're the only one Joey has. She wasn't sure if they would hurt him, but if they were ready to shoot Michael and her in cold blood, Joey wouldn't have a chance against them. She wasn't about to let them get their dirty hands on her baby.

Okay, think, think, think. Reaching either of the cars was out. Her Explorer was locked up, out front, and she didn't have the keys anyway. Michael's Lexus was inside the garage, and that's the first place the blond guy with the gun would expect her to go. All the lights were on inside the house now, and the shadows flickering across the windows told her that somebody was in there searching for her. It dawned on her then that her only chance was to try to escape on the river. Pop's jon boat was still tied up at the concrete landing, gassed and ready to go. All she had to do was get to it.

Her mouth went dry at the thought, her lips stiff, and she moistened them with her tongue as she peered toward the river. Rolling fog obscured everything, shrouding the trees, wisping and swirling upward in columns in some spooky, macabre dance. She could hear the distant soft rush of the current behind the harsh grate of cicadas. She had to get past the men, and she had to do it while it was still dark. She could make it to the boathouse blindfolded. She knew the yard and riverbank better than anyone. More importantly, the men after her didn't.

You can do this, you can, she told herself firmly, ignoring the goosebumps sweeping up her spine and pebbling the flesh of her arms and legs inside the thin silk of her pajamas. Thank God they were black and would blend with the night, but Joey's sling was white. She'd have to bend over to keep the men from seeing it glowing in the darkness. She put her hand down and found the top of Joey's head. His curls were silky under her fingertips, and God bless him, she could hear him sucking contentedly on the bottle. Maybe he'd be good, keep quiet for awhile. He was used to being inside the sling while she went about her work at the bait shop. Maybe all this jostling wouldn't seem so strange to him. She settled him securely inside, adjusting the strap more tightly so that he'd ride snugly against her chest. Thank God for the elastic band that held his bottle in place. Listening intently, she slipped off the other house slipper, waited a moment, then took a deep breath and inched deeper into the overhanging bushes, angling away from the yard toward the woods behind the forsythia hedge.

She wished she had a gun. She was a good shot, a very good shot. Pop had made sure of that when she was growing up. She had scoffed at Michael, but he'd been right to be concerned. She had a bad feeling about him. He was dead, she felt sure of it; the gunman had been too close to miss him. In her mind she saw him dead—lying on the ground, blood all over him, a black bullet hole between his eyes. She shook off that awful image. She couldn't think about that now. She had to think about Joey and getting him to safety. Michael might have escaped, he could have; she had to hope he had.

Slowly, cautiously, every nerve ending taut and quivering like plinked piano strings, her legs like bags of jelly, she inched along on her hands and knees, Joey secure against her chest. Every instinct told her to hurry, hurry, move faster, faster, get away, get as far away as you can, but she could hear the small sounds she was making, the rustling of dead leaves, twigs snapping beneath her weight, no matter how hard she tried to keep quiet. If she could hear them, they could hear them.

She stopped again and listened. Thank God for the fog. She wouldn't have a chance without it. The moist gray clouds were protecting her, distorting sounds with their rising columns and rolling, stealthy creep across the grass. The coolness of it surrounded her, filled with the fishy odor of the river, the earthy smell of wet grass. She realized that she'd begun to shake again, couldn't seem to stop, and a terrible taste fouled her tongue, sour, bilious, sickening. The taste of fear.

Her breath caught at the sound of running footsteps crossing the grass, muffled into dull, quick thuds. She backed more deeply into the wet foliage, afraid they were getting ready to beat the bushes for her. Someone ran past her hiding place, and after a godawful eternity of building up her courage again, she took off, quickly this time, toward the woodshed off to the right of the circle thrown from the security light.

Michael had been accosted just below where she was now, and she tried to pick out a dark form lying on the grass but couldn't see anything. The woodshed was built of red brick, about ten feet square. She got to the rear of it undetected and pushed herself to her feet, her back pressed against the wall. Entirely enfolded in the mists, she rocked back and forth with Joey in a lame attempt to keep him calm, or maybe she was trying to keep herself calm. She strained her ears, trying to find out where the men were before she struck out for the boat.

Gasping, she pressed back as a figure emerged under the lamplight and headed swiftly up the hill toward the cabin, swirls of fog trailing out in his wake before he was swallowed up again. It wasn't the guy who'd accosted her in the kitchen, but a shorter man with a close beard, a goatee. His clothes were dark and he had a flashlight in his hand, one with an intense white illumination like those carried by cops. The bright beam of light slid back and forth, aimed up the yard toward the house, trapped under the fog like a lantern inside a pup tent.

Her heart began to pound again. How many of them were there? She was so scared that she had to force herself to move again when his footsteps finally faded. She crept, crouched over, to the big cottonwood tree, knowing that once she was there, she was within feet of the riverbank. Keeping down, she felt around until she reached the low concrete wall that edged the landing built about twenty yards upriver from the bait shop and boat ramp. She hunkered down and strained her ears. The gush of the river drowned out everything else now, gurgling and splashing in eddies around the concrete landing steps.

She was close now but she still had to be careful. She peered up at the cabin and saw the faint glow of flashlights under the mist. Feeling more confident now that all of them were up there looking for her, she stepped over the wall and hurried across the concrete pad and down the steps where the boat was moored to an iron ring.

Except for the rushing water, eerie silence held the night. Heart in her mouth, she made her way to the jon boat rocking in the current at the base of the stairs. The familiar odor of the river was welcome, and she embraced it like an old, dear friend. Current River looked black and deep in the strange gray light, foreboding as daylight began to dispel the darkness. Across the water on the far bank she could see the beginning of the faint pearly glow over the trees that heralded morning. She didn't have much time left before the men could see her.

Joey was beginning to get restless, no longer nursing but squirming around inside his quilted bed. Please, please, don't cry, she said over and over to herself, stepping down into the fifteen-foot aluminum boat and feeling it dip beneath her weight. The sky was festooned with a few pink streamers over the horizon, and the mist was already beginning to dissipate. Fumbling with fingers that seemed glued together, she managed to jerk loose the knot and pull the tether free from the mooring ring. She climbed over the middle seat and safely settled in the stern. She sat down and put her hand on the motor. Still no outcry. They hadn't seen her.

Picking up the paddle lying in the bottom, she put the end of it against the steps and shoved hard, propelling the boat out into the stream. When she floated free she sat still, allowing the current to take her away from the dock, her fingers curled over the handle of the start-up cord. Please, please, start, she thought, then jerked hard. A whine first, then a loud buzz as it caught, but then Kate's heart sank as it gave a couple of halfhearted sputters and died. The sudden loud noise frightened Joey, and his high-pitched scream echoed out over the water, telegraphing their location as surely as a giant pointed finger.

"The river! The river! Get her before she gets away!"

That floated to her loud and clear, one of the foreigners speaking in English. They weren't at the house as she'd thought, but closer, down in the backyard. She jerked the cord again, able now to see dark figures running down the steps. Oh, God, God, she had to get it started. The boat was floating slowly downstream toward the boat ramp where the men were headed.

Frantically she jerked the cord again. Again and again. Joey yelled louder, his voice muffled somewhat by the sling, and she sobbed with growing despair as the motor wouldn't catch. Then she realized she hadn't pulled out the choke. She jerked it out. The men were almost to the bottom of the hill, well within gunshot range. Grinding her teeth together she yanked one last time, giving it all she had. The motor fired, the buzz-saw roar music to Kate's ears. She grabbed the handle and thrust it down full throttle, veering the bow out to midriver, then upstream.

Her nearest neighbor was downriver as was the town of Van Buren, but her only choice was to head the boat straight up the channel where the river was deep and swift, away from the men with guns scattering out along the bank behind her. The speed of her flight broke up the fog and sent feathery patches up into the gradually lightening sky. She peered back over her shoulder and saw a man on the landing firing a gun at them. She ducked down but when she looked back a second later, she saw the others piling into a boat pulled up on the launching ramp. Oh lord, they'd come in by boat. She pressed the throttle harder but the ancient motor was already at full capacity.

Kate wasn't one to kid herself. Their boat was bigger and a lot more powerful. Pop had bought his old Evinrude at least twenty years ago, maybe more. It was on its last legs, good for lazy days of fishing but not for life-and-death chases with killers. She didn't have a chance to escape them once they opened their throttle; she'd be done for in minutes.

The sun glinted on the river now, burning off the last vestiges of fog. Her pursuers were out in the channel behind her, and their boat was at least an eighteen footer, probably rented from The Landing down by the Van Buren bridge. Two men huddled in the stern; another was in the raised bow, still taking potshots at her. She kept her head down and protected Joey whose terrified cries were barely audible over the roar of the motor.

When a sandbar rose in the distance, Kate suddenly knew what she had to do. The river channel was treacherous in places but she knew it by heart, every twist and turn, every gravel bar, and more importantly, every underwater snag. Kate sped on, following the main channel until she reached a gravel bar covered with thick bushes and weeping willow trees. Like so many in the Current River, it lay at midstream and she cut to the left of the narrow island, a course that took her out of sight of her pursuers. In a second they'd enter the shallow stretch of river behind her, but that's all she'd need. She veered hard left toward the trees on the bank, well aware of the exact position of the gigantic rootwad hidden just underneath the surface. The tangled roots jammed with logs was the most dangerous place in the entire river, with half a dozen collisions and boat accidents there within the last year.

By the time the other boat rounded the gravel bar and roared after her, Kate was back at midstream as if she'd been in the channel all along. Gripping the throttle hard, she looked over her shoulder, watching as the bigger boat bore down on the underwater barrier. The boat's hull cleared it easily but the big motor rode deeper and didn't fare so well. The spinning props hit the deadly snag at thirty miles an hour and the boat stopped on a dime, slinging everything and everyone forward with the velocity of pebbles from a slingshot. She watched the man with the gun hit the glittering water ahead of the boat, bouncing head over heels across the surface like a skipped stone just before the boat upended with an awful crash and rending of metal and fiberglass. The disabled craft began to sink, the transom torn off, the motor gone.

Her whole body sagging with relief, Kate faced forward and held her speed steady, comforting Joey the best she could, trying to control the trembling in her limbs while putting as much distance as possible between herself and the men trying to kill her.

Three

DMITRI IVANOVICH KAVUNOV squatted on his haunches at the bottom of Kate Reed's boat ramp. He was an attractive man, especially to the ladies, some indefinable aspect of his scholarly, quiet nature holding innate charm for the women who met him. During summer classes at the small academy on the outskirts of Moscow where he lectured in art appreciation from time to time, young female students were drawn irresistibly to his good looks and intellectual refinement, attention he was well aware of but neither wished for nor encouraged.

Dmitri was fairly tall at five eleven, trim, fit, comfortable with his easy agility, his athleticism giving him a masculine grace whether walking to class or jogging woodsy campus paths. He wore his dark brown hair cropped short on top but thick and wavy at the nape. The glint of silver at his temples, along with a neatly manicured goatee, lent him the look of the sophisticate he was. His eyes were large, the color of charcoal ashes, but with an uncommon warmth and luminous quality when focused on someone or something he found intriguing.

At the moment, Dmitri's gaze contained little such warmth as he fixed his attention at center stream where swirling eddies splashed and gurgled in the swift-running, appropriately named Current River. He sorted through the gravel beside him and chose a small, flat rock, which he sent expertly skipping and skimming over the rippling blue-green surface. This rural setting and the Ozark Mountains surrounding it were surprisingly peaceful now that the report of gunshots and roar of outboards had dwindled to a faint whir somewhere upstream.

The woodsy banks and remoteness of the place was almost primeval in its untouched natural splendor, reminding him of the small river village outside St. Petersburg where he was born almost forty-five years ago. That stream, too, was swift and treacherous, rampant with rapids, and crystal clear to the rock-strewn bottom. His father had taught him to fish in those meandering undercurrents, as his father had taught him. Even his great-grandfather, who'd been a watchmaker in the Moscow shop of the famous jeweler, Peter Carl Fabergé, had enjoyed the pristine water, many years before the Bolshevik revolution.

God, how he had missed it and everything Russian during all the early years when he'd lived in the United States, but now that the Communist regime was dead he traveled freely back and forth, often visiting his brothers and sisters in the North, but more often than not acting as courier between his Moscow boss, Ilie Kafelnikov, and Ilie's American business partner, Vince Saracino. Dmitri didn't enjoy working for Saracino but he respected Kafelnikov enough to put his personal feelings aside. They went back a long way, he and Ilie, to the time when Ilie recruited a young, impressionable Dmitri into the KGB. Now Kafelnikov had turned to a darker path and reigned as the most powerful crime boss in Moscow. Two years ago when he'd asked Dmitri to gather a few good men to act as bodyguards for his daughter, Anna, when she married Vince Saracino and moved to America, Dmitri had agreed out of loyalty and respect.

Still, he missed his homeland and wished he was there now, fly-fishing waist deep in that icy stream, listening to the whispering currents and warm summer breezes. Instead, here he sat, deep in the boondocks of Missouri, bogged down with this dirty business he had gradually come to despise. He would not remain with Kafelnikov's daughter much longer;

he'd had enough of Vince Saracino and his uncontrollable rages.

Behind him he heard Michael Reed scream with pain as Misha tried to force him to talk. Reed must be a complete and utter fool to have crossed Vince the way he had; Dmitri had not trusted Reed when he'd first met the man a year ago in St. Louis. But Dmitri never would have suspected him to be stupid enough to do anything this self-destructive. Vince wanted Reed stone-cold dead, as an example if nothing else, but Reed's woman's unexpected flight was complicating what should have been an easy contract hit for Dmitri and his team.

Now Reed was interfering with Dmitri's personal schedule as well, which was even more annoying. Dmitri had first refused Vince's demand to take out Reed, instead wishing to return to Russia to teach and run the small antique shop he owned there, but Vince Saracino had pulled out a trump card, one he knew Dmitri could never resist—a genuine, mint-condition Fabergé egg. Even though it was not the most beautiful of the priceless masterpieces wrought by Fabergé, the miniature gold charm the jeweler had fashioned to hide inside it was intact. More importantly it was one of the lesser-known imperial eggs commissioned by Czar Nicholas himself. Kavunov had hungered for it since Saracino had obtained the prize off the Russian black market while in Moscow courting Anna. Saracino had dangled the gilded, diamond-and ruby-encrusted masterpiece in front of Dmitri's coveting eyes as enticement to take on the contract hit, and Dmitri could not bring himself to refuse that bait.

To his never-ending pride, Dmitri already had three Fabergé creations, exquisite watch fobs designed to decorate the chains of old-fashioned pocket watches. Two of these ornaments his great-grandfather had passed down as heirlooms within the Kavunov family. The other one, of considerably lesser value because of a crack in the lacquer, he'd managed to purchase in Rome five years ago. His true pride and joy was the lapis lazuli pair of cuff links set with a circle of tiny diamonds.

Behind him, under the covered boat pavilion, Reed screamed like a pig under the butcher's blade. Dmitri frowned, glancing behind him at Misha and their prisoner. Misha's long, lanky blond hair was pulled back into a ponytail, held low on his neck with a rubber band. Dmitri thought the boy looked like a damn fool sissy, especially now with one of his ears pierced. He could not understand what young men were thinking these days, adorning themselves as vainly as harlots. At the moment, Misha's face was stretched tight with fury, his teeth clenched, his left cheek and jawline bloodred and blistered from the boiling water the Reed woman had flung at him. The burns would worsen, the pain becoming more excruciating later. Misha had been careless and was paying the price.

Dmitri shook his head, irritation flooding him again. It was completely daylight now. If anyone else ventured into their midst he'd have no choice but to kill them, too, and that's the last thing he wanted to do. He was tired of killing people, though he'd made it his livelihood for some time now and had become quite adept at quick, quiet assassinations. To prevent their discovery at the river behind Reed's cabin, he'd already ordered the chain strung across the gravel road that led customers from the log house down to the riverside bait shop. The woman's black Ford Explorer had been hidden in the woods until he could catch her and get the hell out of there.

Thanks to Misha's bungling, they didn't have much time left, should have been long gone while it was still dark and foggy. He hoped Yuri and the others caught the girl and baby quickly and brought them back. He had no doubt they would. They were all well trained and hand-chosen by Kafelnikov to ensure his daughter's safety, something Anna sure as hell needed now that she was married to a psycho like Vince Saracino. Yuri was the best operative of Dmitri's team, and Dmitri trusted the veteran of the Soviet-Afghanistan war implicitly.

Kafelnikov's other picks for Anna's team were former Moscow police officers, corrupted by American dollars and the privilege of living in the United States. Both were so obsessed and delighted with the rich Western lifestyle, he doubted they'd ever again set foot on Russian soil.

The third time Misha caused Mike to scream for mercy, Dmitri grimaced and stood up. His older sister's boy was dear to him, but he was still a hotheaded punk. Marina had been worried about her son, for good reason, and Dmitri agreed to take him in hand after the boy had shot and killed one of Russia's hottest young hockey stars because the player wouldn't agree to go on the take for Kafelnikov. Unfortunately, he did it in plain view at a busy intersection on Gorky Street.

Kafelnikov had recruited too many young Russian thugs to wreak havoc on their own people. They were a joke, a violent, savage bunch of losers with not an iota of the finesse Dmitri and Kafelnikov had acquired in the KGB. They were reckless, and though Dmitri loved his nephew dearly, Misha was probably the worst of the lot. But under Dmitri's tutelage he would learn. Somehow Dmitri had to teach him restraint and instill in him at least a modicum of honor. Misha had a cruel streak, seemed to enjoy the suffering of others, while Dmitri did not. To him, such a lifestyle had been a necessity, an evil required to serve his beloved Mother Russia. He'd accomplished his missions exceedingly well, but now that he performed for money alone, the job had become distasteful. His only consolation was that the people he hit were unsavory characters at best, mostly deserving of death at his hands.

His nephew had the American lawyer bound with silver duct tape under some kind of roofed pavilion that Dmitri assumed was to shelter boats during the winter months. Andre had managed to wound Reed in the shoulder and subdue him, while Misha totally screwed up getting the girl and the baby up at the house. Now the boy was embarrassed he'd let her escape in the course of his first mission with his uncle, and in so doing, complicated Dmitri's carefully laid plans and put them all in danger of discovery. It should have been an in-and-out procedure, simple, clean, leaving both the man and woman dead in an apparent robbery. Now Misha was soothing his wounded pride, and the painful scalding he'd received, by torturing their one captive. Indeed, Marina's boy had a lot to learn. But he was only eighteen; wisdom would come to him in time.

At the moment, Misha was stomping down brutally on Reed's injured shoulder, which was little more than a flesh wound, a mere slice of the biceps. Reed was squealing again, shrilly, like a terrified woman, and Dmitri called out, ordering his nephew to stop in a burst of Russian that readily revealed his impatience. Misha obeyed instantly as he did with all of Dmitri's commands, but Reed kept groaning and rolling his head from side to side. The lawyer knew enough about Dmitri and his handpicked team to know he was a dead man.

A shout floated off the water and Dmitri turned quickly, hoping his men had managed to return with the girl. Instead he caught sight of Yuri jogging along the rocky riverbank; Andre and Nikolai were behind him, one supporting the other as they struggled along. When Yuri reached him he spoke rapid-fire in their own tongue.

"The bitch tricked us, Dmitri. Led us straight into some kind of hidden snag that tore off the motor. Sank us and dislocated Nikolai's shoulder."

Dmitri cursed inwardly, irritated beyond belief. Though Andre and Nikolai were good men, he and Yuri should've come alone. The two of them could have done the man and woman silently and efficiently and been halfway back to St. Louis by now.

"See to Nikolai, Misha. You know what to do. Yuri, get another boat in the water."

Both men scurried to do his bidding. Dmitri stared down

at Michael Reed, lying prone and moaning on the ground at his feet. The man was weak, had no backbone, a begging, writhing worm. "Yeller," as they used to say in the old American westerns he enjoyed during his early days in the United States.

Heaving out a heavy, put-upon sigh, Dmitri pulled out the 9 mm Beretta he wore in a shoulder holster underneath his black nylon Nike windsuit. It felt good in his hand, a constant companion for at least twenty years. More comforting than any wife. His own thoughts struck him as pathetic: What man would consider his weapon more valuable than the company of a good woman? But he'd needed or wanted very few women since he'd lost Alina. He'd mourned her with deep, abiding anguish for many years, only until recently when he'd been plagued inexplicably by a loneliness and need for female companionship that cut almost as deep.

"You're a very stupid man," he said to Reed, hunkering down and speaking conversationally. His English was flawless, and he prided himself that few could tell he was not a natural-born American. In the early days in the KGB he'd been stationed at the Soviet embassy in Washington, D.C., where he'd worked undercover as a diplomat and mastered the slang, the popular music, the pop culture, until he'd fit in like any other man on the street.

"Your wife got away with the kid, Reed. You've caused me a hell of a lot more trouble than you're worth."

"Please, Kavunov, please, just listen, listen. This is all a mistake. I can make things right. Give me the chance, I swear to God I can."

"Time's up, Mike. Tell me where she's gone, or you die, right here, right now." Dmitri did not intend to waste any more time, could not. Reed had been aboard Vince's outfit long enough to know that. He placed the barrel of the Beretta flush against Reed's flaring nostril and watched the man's eyes bulge and grow wild. "Tell me where your wife's gone."

Reed was still hesitating, playing hero. Dmitri wondered briefly if the lawyer actually had the guts to give up his own life to save his woman. Dmitri would bet he did not. Few men he'd encountered had enough gumption when it came right down to it. He wondered how he'd react himself with a gun barrel jammed into his nose but knew the answer very well. He would have died for Alina, if he'd been given the chance. Overcome with despair at the news of her death, he'd come close to hanging himself in his apartment in Washington, just as she had done inside her cold, dank cell in Lubyanka Prison. Michael Reed, on the other hand, only had a second or two to make up his mind. As Dmitri had expected, Reed shut his eyes and revealed his true character by gasping out words of betrayal.

"You'll never find her without me. . . . I can show you the way. She'll go to the police if we don't stop her. The sheriff down here's a friend of hers. . . . Oh, God, please, Kavunov, don't kill me, I can help you. . . ."

"What lies upriver from here? A town where she can get help?"

"No, no, it's all wilderness upriver from here, government land. Nobody's allowed to live out there. Everything's downriver at Van Buren. She won't find anyone who can help her but there's a cabin . . . one she takes care of for some people . . . you know, through the winter. That's the only place she could go. . . . It's well hidden so you'll never find it without me showing you how to get there. I'm telling you Kate knows this river and the woods like nobody else. Her grandfather taught her to hunt and stalk deer, shoot guns and all that stuff. She'll get away if you don't let me help you, please, please."

Reed's wife shared Dmitri's mother's name, Katya, and some of her strength as well. Kavunov already admired this woman named Kate, more than this sniveling piece of garbage ready to betray her. Misha had known of her accomplishments, shown them pictures of her when she'd won a medal in the Olympic marathon in an unbelievable show of courage. She was a beautiful woman, Nordic blond, obviously strong-willed, and at the moment showing herself more than resourceful. She was extraordinary, all right; she'd proven it without a doubt, but what Reed pointed out was the truth. The surrounding forests were thick and impenetrable even here near this cabin and fishing camp. Dmitri knew how to track her but he didn't know the area well enough to find her first, and it was only a matter of time before the authorities would come snooping around to check out the gunfire echoing downriver. He didn't have time to waste in beating the bushes.

A guttural scream shattered the stillness of the dawn, and he glanced down to the riverbank where Misha held Nikolai down with one foot while trying to jerk his arm back into the socket. Misha was laughing while poor Nikolai yelled Russian curses and rolled around like a wolf in a trap. He was a weight lifter, bulked up and corded with muscle, as was his partner, Andre, both hardened from a decade policing the dingy streets of Moscow's worst districts. They wanted to be called Nick and Andy now, were saving their money for white Ford Rangers and big-screen television sets.

Dmitri returned his attention to Reed. At the moment, he must think only about the job at hand. Vince Saracino had offered Dmitri a masterpiece over which the art world would drool if he would teach Mike Reed a very hard lesson, and teach it Dmitri would.

"We'll see how helpful you are, my friend. Don't even think about making a run for it or I'll give you over to Misha to play with. He's pissed off as hell about what your wife did to him."

A terrible expression flared in the bound man's eyes, but underneath Dmitri caught the glimmer of hope. A false one, because Reed was going to die as soon as they found the woman and the baby. Dmitri almost felt sorry for the guy, but the truth was inescapable. Reed had only himself to thank for getting into this ugly mess with Vince.

The prow of the jon boat cut through the shimmering water of Current River like the point of an arrow. Long chevron wakes streamed out behind Kate as she motored slowly up a remote stretch of the river. It was calm and beautiful, with giant oaks and sycamores and leafy elms hanging over the shoreline, tranquil and serene with little sense of the gun battle that had echoed downriver not thirty minutes before.

The water was crystal clear, revealing rocks of myriad shapes and sizes lining the bottom and schools of gray fish darting away from the noise of the boat. The lush vegetation reflected in dark green water along both banks, and Kate rode through them, feeling numb and wrung out, unreal, as if she were a painted figure gliding through a Monet painting.

A blue heron suddenly took flight from a half-submerged log and Kate jerked in alarm, trembling from nerves still ragged and scraped raw. The big bird flapped its wings in a slow majestic bank to the right before disappearing over the treeline. Kate tried to shake herself out of her stupor. She gripped the throttle so tightly her knuckles were white and clutched Joey close against her with her left arm. They would come after her. She didn't know why, or when, or how, but these men, these killers, wanted her dead and wouldn't stop until she was.

She shivered all over, then forced herself to think straight because she didn't have time not to. There were other boats at her own boat dock for the killers to board, and very few other boaters hazarded this dangerous stretch of the Current—no one she could turn to for help. It was too swift for good fishing, for the most part completely remote and uninhabited with no hint of civilization, the terrain rough and mountainous. All around her the Ozark National Scenic Riverways stretched for miles, with any and all commercialization against federal law. She could count on no one to protect her.

She tried to think, reason, stop looking behind her, and concentrate on what had to be done. Her goal had to be to find a way back downstream to Van Buren and alert Gus Shelter, the county sheriff. But the killers were behind her, blocking her way, just as they'd been when she fled the cabin. She couldn't risk going downriver by boat without running into them again. Her best bet, her only choice, really, was to hole up and hide until she could think of a way to contact the sheriff's office. She could motor upriver all day until she ran out of gas and encounter no one, and no matter what course she chose it was going to be hard on Joey.

Miraculously he lay quietly curled in the crook of her arm, finally having given up on crying when she'd gotten the pacifier out of the zippered pocket of the sling. He was sucking on it, staring up at the sunny blue sky passing overhead as if fascinated by the puffy white clouds. His face was red and blotchy from bawling so hard. He was so little to be out here, going through this nightmare. She snuggled him closer, kissing the top of his head, trying to decide the best course of action.

She really had just one option. The Picketts' cabin. It was back off the river, up a hill concealed by the trees. She could probably hide there without being found. John and Betty Pickett were old friends of Pop's, a couple from Kansas City who'd had the place for decades, before the government had bought up all the riverfront land. They wouldn't be down until the end of the month, late May when the smallmouth bass season opened, but their cabin would be hard to find. The men chasing her weren't woodsmen, and they wouldn't know such a place existed. She'd be safe there for awhile, she felt fairly confident of it, at least until she got a grip on her shredded nerves and trembling limbs and could decide what to do next.

The A-frame cabin was not too far away now, and she

kept her eyes ahead, peeled for the distinctive grove of cedar trees fronting the Picketts' place. When she finally rounded the last bend, she motored straight for one of the many creeks that fed the Current. Thank God she knew about the cabin because she didn't know where else she could go.

Relieved, now extremely anxious to get Joey out of the boat and hot sun and into a safe haven, she guided the prow of the boat straight into the bank and underneath the drooping fronds of a pair of low-lying willows that half-hid the creek. She maneuvered the boat as far into the inlet as she could, lifting the prop and cutting the motor.

Silence descended like a dropped drapery. Kate sat still, watching, listening, still so shaken she quivered all over. A robin chirped somewhere in the trees above her with a cheerful, top-of-the-morning trill. Cheet, cheet, cheet. Nature back to normal. No gunshots to send wildlife fleeing from danger. She was the wildlife now, she thought, a sick feeling congealing like cold grease in the pit of her stomach. Joey's low, unhappy whimper brought her back to the job at hand, and she scooped him out of the tight sling.

"It's all right, punkin, I've got you. You're gonna be all right now, you'll see."

God, she hoped that was true. She stood, the boat rocking under her weight, and she steadied herself, then stepped barefoot into ankle-deep water so cold that chill bumps raced up her leg. Suddenly she felt exhausted, now that she was hidden in the foliage, and her muscles seemed to lose their mass, dissolve into flimsy rag-doll padding. She sank to the ground, cross-legged, suppressed emotion clogging the back of her nose and making her eyes burn. She heard herself making strange choking noises against Joey's curls. Strangled, helpless sounds, despair, delayed reaction to the adrenaline still surging through her blood.

In the water beneath her toes she saw the glint of minnows darting through the shallows like silver flashes of light. Normal. As if nothing horrible had happened. Joey started squirming, and Kate realized she was holding him much too tightly, in a veritable death grip. She loosened her hold, her face crumpling, her mind awash with the sheer disbelief of it all. Oh, God, what was she going to do? She didn't have any clothes for him, no blankets, no formula, nothing. She was still dressed in her pajamas, for God's sake, the black silk wet and clinging coldly to her skin. No shoes. No money.

Kate put her hand over her eyes and tried to force reason. These men had something to do with Michael's criminal defense work, that's all it could be. She'd done nothing wrong, never broken the law or associated herself with criminals. Suddenly anger streaked through her, slashing through the paralysis. They were after her husband; it had to be that. He'd gotten into some kind of terrible scrape with the hoods and drug addicts he defended. Her rage soon died and pain filled her heart when she realized Michael could very well be dead. Heartsick, she squeezed her eyes shut and caught her trembling lower lip. If only he'd remained a district attorney none of this would've happened. Instead, he'd surrounded himself with criminals and thugs and brought this horror down on their heads.

She felt so sick for a moment she thought she'd throw up. Her body felt tight and empty as if some giant had jerked her up and twisted her as mercilessly as a pair of soaked socks. Forcing a deep breath, she wearily pushed to her feet. She had to keep on, couldn't let them get Joey. No matter what she had to do, she would protect him from them. She looked down at him and his dark gaze touched her heart, and she felt a hot rush of tears she didn't want or need. She had to get a handle on her nerves, her fears, but then Joey grinned at her, his double dimples deepening underneath his eye. Determination flowed up strong and fast from some gut-deep wellspring inside her, and she jutted her jaw. By God, he'd be all right, both of them would. She'd get them out of this mess somehow, no matter what it took.

The path up the hill wound through thick cedars and undergrowth, a circuitous, steep, rocky ascent. Slipping once or twice and cutting up her toes, she tried to tred on the soft, springy green moss that clung to the slope. After a quarter of an hour's climb, she made the clearing that led to the house, another five-minute walk that would alert her to anyone approaching the house once she was safely inside the small A-frame cabin. Simple, rustic, the place had a living room, kitchen and a couple of bedrooms. Lots of plate-glass windows overlooked the front, where just a glimpse of the distant river could be viewed from the screened-in front porch. The Picketts had enjoyed the isolation, roughing it with neither phone nor television. An extremely devoted couple, they came down to fish and relax, to meditate, to enjoy each other's company. Thank God they enjoyed creature comforts enough to have a running well and a gasoline-driven generator for electricity.

When she finally reached the house she took a moment to glance down the trail behind her. Just barely through the leaves she could see a shining white strip that was the river, glistening and flashing in the bright morning sunshine. A beautiful May day. A day of death and destruction. Exhausted, she realized her bad knee was aching, the one she'd nearly wrecked at the last Olympic games, the tendons behind it burning as if she might have pulled them loose. She hadn't noticed it until now and she tried her best to ignore it. She could rest here, at least for a little while, maybe an hour, two perhaps, before she pushed on in search of help.

Climbing the battered wooden steps, she walked across the small back porch. A wide deck ran all the way around the house, with dozens of mounted antlers from the deer John Pickett had bagged over countless fall hunting seasons. The screen door opened easily at her touch but squeaked shrilly from want of oil. She rose on her tiptoes and ran her fingers along the nearest ceiling rafter in search of the key. The extreme silence was beginning to unnerve her, and she kept glancing around, afraid she'd see her deadly pursuers surging out of the trees after her and Joey.

Inside it smelled musty, closed up, all the drapes and miniblinds shut for winter, except for one in the kitchen that sent a rack of slanted sun rays across the linoleum floor, the brightness dancing with golden motes set alive when she'd opened the door. She crossed the living room and picked up the odor of stale ashes from the grate of the Shrader woodburning stove. Two old recliners, brightened by floral chintz slipcovers, flanked the hearth, and an old, navy blue pull-out couch was positioned across from them. A table held a reading lamp, a couple of John D. MacDonald's Travis McGee paperbacks, and Betty's sewing basket with the balls of yarn she used for her colorful afghans.

Humming softly in an attempt to keep Joey content a few minutes longer, Kate entered the bedroom. An ancient brass double bed was set against the interior wall, a spotless, white, old-fashioned chenille bedspread covering the stripped feather mattress. Several of Betty's bright afghans were folded over the ornamental footrail, one in a red-and-green zigzag pattern, the other blue and yellow striped. There was a cane-backed rocker covered with a blue and white star quilt, an oak bookcase with more Travis McGees, and a bedside table with a white Bible on top of it. One small window overlooked a nearby sycamore tree and the trail from the riverbank.

Gently lowering Joey on the bed, Kate watched him kick his little legs for all he was worth and wave his arms as if he were flagging down a taxicab. He was tired of being held, and he worked on the pacifier until it wiggled in his mouth as if alive and trying to get away. She tugged the two feather pillows from underneath the cover and placed one at either side of him. He was too little to turn over by himself yet, but Kate never took chances. He was growing fast, learning fast. According to her baby book, some babies squirmed their way onto their stomachs by five or six weeks. She tucked a finger into the leg of his diaper and found him dry, and once he lay calm and quiet again, she scooped him up and held him close to her breast, taking comfort in his warmth and sweet baby smell.

Sitting down in the rocker, she propped him against her shoulder the way he liked best. He settled down against her, making little slurping sounds on the pacifier, and Kate shut her eyes and tried to relax muscles drawn up into tight balls. She felt relatively safe here, at least for the moment. No one could find this cabin without help, and it'd take the men time to reorganize, especially if any of them had been injured when their boat rammed the rootwad. She couldn't delay long; she had to find some dry clothes, some supplies for the coming trek downstream. No telling how many days it'd take to find her way to Van Buren on foot, unless she got lucky and ran across some road leading out of the woods to a farm or inhabited cabin.

It was likely, too, that a friend of hers would come by the bait shop to see the baby and realize she was missing, and once Gus found that out, as sheriff he'd leave no leaf unturned until he found her. She just had to lie low and keep out of sight until he came looking for them. She'd make it, and so would Joey. She patted his back, her heart softening as he nestled his little face tiredly into her neck. At that moment she vowed on her life that she'd never let anyone hurt him. Never. She'd die first.

Kate sucked in her breath, eyes widening as she realized again that that was exactly the fate her pursuers had in store for her.

Four

IT'S NOT MUCH FARTHER, I tell you, ten, fifteen minutes tops. I swear, it's the only place I can think of that she'd go this far up the river."

Dmitri said nothing, watching the cowardly bastard give up his wife to save his own life, a woman who showed ten times more guts than Reed ever had. He was beneath contempt, undeserving of a man's respect. It was one thing to tell them where she might have gone, but to lead them to her himself! God, what kind of husband would do such a thing? He supposed Reed was out to save his own skin but that wasn't going to happen. Vince wanted him dead, so dead he was going to be.

"Please listen to me, Kavunov," Reed begged, twisting around in the seat in front of Dmitri, his hands still bound behind him with duct tape. Misha was in front of the small fishing craft, gun resting on his knee, and Yuri sat in the stern, controlling the throttle. Dmitri had left the other two behind to clean up any mess Misha'd made inside the cabin. Reed had to yell his betrayals over the bleat of the motor.

"The cabin's hidden from the river, way up high, with a real good vantage point. She'll see anyone who tries to sneak up on her. She'll take off if she sees you. Trust me on this, Kavunov, I'm telling God's holy truth, so help me. We'll never find her if she spooks and disappears. Let me go up first by myself and explain what's going down. All I need is a few minutes to make her understand and cooperate. You'll lose her if you try to storm the place. I'm telling you, I know Kate like a book. I know the way she thinks. If she sees you coming, you'll never catch her." He paused, licking blood from the corner of his mouth where Misha had punched him. Dmitri could see wet, shiny blood where the striped sweatshirt clung to his upper arm.

"It'd be better if we killed the motor pretty soon now before we get too close to the cabin. She'll hear us if we don't, and then she'll run if she suspects anything at all. She's smart, I'm telling you."

Kavunov needed no one to tell him the woman was intelligent. Reed, on the other hand, was another matter. He was clearly a fool and obviously considered his captors of the same ilk. Reed wanted time to flee for his life, of course, but his caution did make sense. Dmitri glanced out at the thick, forested banks with endless tangles of undergrowth choked with weeds. If the woman took the baby and hid in the wilds, it could take them days to find her. He was going to have to trust Reed to approach the woman at this cabin he talked about, or at least make him think he did.

Sighing at yet another complication and inwardly chagrined by so many unexpected delays, he set his gaze out over the beautiful blue-green river. It was very peaceful here in the state of Missouri. Strange that he'd never heard of the Ozark Mountains until a few weeks ago. Perhaps he would come back here one day, once this job was done. To fish, perhaps. He did love to fish.

Once Joey was sleeping peacefully in her arms, Kate rose slowly, never having realized how truly resilient infants were. Good God, why wasn't this baby completely traumatized after she'd dragged him around, jounced and jogged him, not to mention the eardrum-shattering blare of gunfire and roaring motor boats. She supposed he was used to the sound of motors, from time spent with her at the bait shop every day, but in any case Joey had been good, wonderful through it all. She just hoped to God neither one of them had to go through anything else so harrowing.

Lowering him gently onto his back, she fluffed the pillows around him, just in case. She smiled, love for him building up until it filled her chest like some kind of soft and fuzzy balloon. Tears rushed to her eyes, and just as quickly she blinked them back. She didn't have time to give in to maudlin thoughts or emotional breakdowns, to worry whether Michael was dead or alive, or worst of all, lapse into the delayed shock that kept nibbling at the edges of her sanity. She had to think coherently and be smart enough to get herself and Joey to safety. That's all she could let herself think about.

She moved to the window that faced the trail leading to the river and raised it an inch or two. She strained her ears for the sound of boats but heard only the distant whisper of the current. She relaxed a little bit more, but not much. Surely the guys in the boat had been injured, perhaps not seriously but enough to seek medical attention. If that were the case, the nearest doctor was in Van Buren, and they'd stick out in that small town like sharks in a motel swimming pool. Maybe Gus would get them before they could get her. But she couldn't rely on that. The big blond, the young guy who'd known her name and Olympic past, might be more resourceful than she expected. He looked like somebody who wouldn't give up easily.

The bedroom closet had sliding wood doors, and she opened one, pleased to see that Betty had left behind plenty of suitable outdoor clothing. Betty was nearing sixty and medium sized but Kate wasn't going to be particular about fit. She grabbed a pair of indigo denim Wrangler jeans and one of John's white T-shirts, as well as a heavy, dark green sweatshirt. Stripping off her robe and silk pajamas, she slipped both shirts over her head, then stepped hurriedly into the pants. They were too big on her but she could make them work with a belt.

Down on her knees she rummaged around among the shoes thrown into the bottom of the closet until she found a soiled but sturdy-looking pair of white sneakers. They fit her relatively well, too, especially when she tugged on a pair of John's thick white athletic socks. She crouched by the window as she tied the laces, her eyes glued to the path leading up from the riverbank. There's no way they could find her here, no way, she told herself again, no earthly reason they'd choose this particular bend in the river to strike out through the woods in search of her. She was safe unless, and until, they found where she'd hidden the boat. Even then she would be forewarned by the buzz of their outboard.

Checking Joey, she found the baby sound asleep, poor angel. As unfair as it all was, he was going to learn how to rough it the next few days. As she made her way to the kitchen, she wondered again who the men were. There could be no explanation except that they were after Michael for some reason. It occurred to her, with a ray of hope, that if they already had him, they wouldn't pursue her. Oh, God, even if Michael was in their hands, even if they'd already killed him, she was a witness, had seen the Russian guy real well, had seen the ruthless look of anticipation in his eyes. He wanted to kill her, had been looking forward to it. Shaking again, she hurried to the kitchen window and peered through the blinds at the trail through the cedars. No one in sight. No sound of a boat.

In front of her, the old pump was bolted to the sink, and she primed it from the gallon milk jug of water Betty always left for that purpose, then worked the handle vigorously until the first sputter of water emerged, brackish and brown with lime deposits. It gushed clear within seconds, and she leaned down and splashed some up over her face. It felt good, braced her, and she filled the glass and gulped it down quickly, not realizing until that moment how unbelievably thirsty she was. She took a bright yellow-checked dishtowel from the wall hanger and rubbed her face dry. She listened for the sound of a boat again, her eyes locked on the place where the woods ended below the cabin's rocky front yard. She couldn't let up on her vigil, not for a minute.

Now she had to find enough supplies to last them through the night, through several days if she could find a way to carry them. She went to the freestanding white metal cabinet and pulled open the doors, well aware that the Picketts had come down in late March and replenished their stock of canned goods and nonperishables. Thank God they liked milk in their coffee, she thought, grabbing up the small tins of Pet Milk in one arm. It wasn't Joey's formula but, mixed with water, she could probably coax him to drink it. There were six cans of the stuff, and she set them down on the brown-and-white–speckled counter.

She had to have diapers. There were two clean ones in the quilted sling, but she'd probably have to use one of them when he woke up. The Picketts sure weren't going to store any Luvs or Huggies in their kitchen. Her eyes swept the kitchen, a throwback to a thirties diner with its yellow gingham curtains and an old metal breadbox with a hinged door adorned with a faded picture of a puffy-topped loaf of bread. A two-tier yellow utility cart was pushed into one corner, and Kate was relieved when she saw the five large rolls of paper towels wedged into the bottom shelf. Bounty, the quicker picker-upper. What better brand to use for diapers? She searched the junk drawer beside the sink for masking tape to hold the paper towels around Joey, and also fished out a can opener for the condensed milk and a red rubber band she could use as a ponytail holder.

Peering anxiously down the trail from the kitchen window, she pulled up her hair as well as she could and secured it in place. After checking to make sure Joey was all right and stooping to listen at the bedroom window, she stood up, poking around in the closet for a bag. She finally fished out an old tan knapsack, one made of sturdy-enough canvas to do the trick. She could strap it on her back where it wouldn't interfere with Joey's sling across her chest.

In the kitchen cabinets she found a flashlight and some new batteries, both in plastic Ziploc bags. As she searched through Betty's cabinets she found Ziplocs the woman's favorite way to store things. There was a pocket-size portable radio atop the bread box, and she flipped it on to make sure it worked, then off again when she heard a crackle of static. She might be able to pick up a station once she was on the move, Poplar Bluff, maybe, when she was outside and higher up on the ridge that rose behind the cabin. She stuck it and a box of waterproof matches she'd found on the stove inside another Ziploc, then checked the window, growing more confident as the minutes passed. She filled up an old Boy Scout canteen, then tied it and a couple of warm, rolled-up patchwork quilts to the bottom of the knapsack.

She tried to gauge the time. At least an hour had passed since she'd embarked on her narrow escape up the river. Maybe closer to two hours. She couldn't linger much longer, not if she wanted to be on the safe side. Putting the canvas bag on the counter, she pulled open the top and piled in the Pet Milk and a thick roll of the paper towels, the tape, can opener, a couple of cans of Vienna sausages she found, some crackers, and a package of dried apple rings. Not exactly gourmet meals, but it'd keep both of them alive until she got them to Van Buren.

The pack was fairly heavy but she was strong enough to carry it. She was glad now that she'd kept up her daily workouts despite her bum leg. She would do whatever it took, and she'd never been afraid of the woods. Pop had taught her to stalk deer, to recognize signs that would bring her out to civilization if she ever became lost. She'd make it to Van Buren and when she did, she'd make sure the filthy animals who'd shot Michael ended up behind bars where they belonged.

Kate drew up and stood very still, her hands still on the knapsack, as something suddenly occurred to her. There *was* someone who lived up in this area of the Current. She'd forgotten all about it until now, but she'd heard her grandfather mention him a couple of times. Pop hadn't told her much, just said he'd seen the kid again, or something to that effect. When she'd asked questions, Pop had seemed a little secretive and uncomfortable with the conversation. She racked her brain, trying desperately to remember. He said the guy was a little strange and lived off the land, had some problems to work out. John, his name had been John. If he was a friend of Pop, he'd help her. Her heart raced for an instant, spirits buoyed at the thought of finding an ally. Maybe she could search for him, beg him to take her down to Van Buren. That hope flagged almost at once when she realized that she didn't have a clue where to look for him. He could live miles farther up the river for all she knew, or even have left the area for good years ago. She wouldn't know him if she saw him anyway.

Before she left the kitchen she paused in front of the stove, then picked up John's razor-sharp filet knife in its leather scabbard. Wishing he'd left one of his guns behind, too, she strapped it to her belt, then picked up the heavy knapsack and headed to the bedroom. All was clear, so she carefully felt Joey's diapers again and found them wet this time. She changed him with a fresh Luvs, handling him very gently, wanting him to sleep as long as he could. He only fussed a little as she retied the drawstring at the bottom of his gown.

She froze at the sudden cry of a startled bluejay just outside the window. Her breath caught and she ran to look. A man was climbing the trail, swiftly, almost running up the steep pitch of the hill, and she recognized him at once as Michael by the black-and-white–striped sweatshirt he wore. Thank God, he'd gotten away, too!

He was heading for the back porch, and she raced to meet him, jerking open the door, very relieved he was all right, but angry, too, that he'd dragged them into such a dangerous mess.

"Michael! What's going on? Those men are trying to kill us!"

"Shhh, be quiet, Kate," he told her, pushing her aside and shutting the door behind him. He twisted the lock and peeked out through the closed miniblind. "Listen to me, Kate, just listen. They're down at the river and they'll be up here any minute so we've got to move fast."

Kate stared at him in unbridled horror. "Down at the river? Did you bring them here? My God, Michael, did you lead them to us?"

"I had to, Kate, God, I'm sorry about all this, but they were going to kill me. They had a gun at my head, I didn't have a choice. You've got to get away, do you understand, Kate? You've got to take Joey and make a run for it."

"But who are they? What do they want? I don't understand any of this!"

Michael grabbed her shoulders, his fingers biting into her flesh, his eyes frantic. His face was swollen and beginning to bruise. "Dammit, Kate, listen to me. They're going to kill us. We've got to run, get out of here while we still can. It's our only chance. It's a miracle Kavunov let me come up here by myself."

"Kavunov? Who's he? What did you do to him?"

"For God's sake, Kate, we don't have time to stand around arguing like this. They want Joey back, that's what they want. He came off the black market, cost me two hundred grand, and I never paid it. I thought I'd have it by now but things didn't work out like I expected. I'm telling you they aren't playing games with us, Kate, you've got to take Joey and find someplace to hide. I'll go out the front and try to lead them away from you. It's our only chance. They'll kill us both if we don't."

Kate stared at him, trying to absorb what he was telling her until Michael grabbed her again and shook her furiously, panic rising in his eyes. Blood trickled from the side of his mouth.

"C'mon, Kate, move! You've got to get Joey out of here before they get impatient and come up here after me. It's the only chance we've got! They're bad news, Kate. Killers, for Christ's sake! We're both dead if they catch us. Go on, do it, get Joey." Michael opened the door and headed out, flinging back over his shoulder, "Quick, take him out the other way. I'll try to lead them downstream!"

"Wait, Michael, wait!" Kate cried, but he was already gone. She could hear the hollow sounds of his feet clomping across the back porch. She had to get away, too, before they came. She slammed the door, throwing the lock and heading to the bedroom for Joey. Her heart pounded with renewed danger, and trembling all over, she grabbed Joey off the bed, putting him into the sling as a shout sounded outside on the trail. She bent and looked out, just as three men in dark clothes appeared at the bottom of the clearing.

"Reed's running! Get him, Misha!"

The voice floated clearly to her in perfect English, and she didn't wait to watch but clutched Joey against her, grabbed the knapsack, and fled for the other side of the house. She ran for the door off the front screened porch that opened into the edge of the woods. She jerked it open and burst outside, crossed the side sundeck and dropped down into the tangled bushes below. Heart in her throat, she kept low, Joey pressed against her breast, the mind-numbing terror back, threatening to overwhelm her as wild shouts broke into the quiet morning air, followed by the loud crack of a single gunshot.

Five

PANTING HARD, heart thudding, Kate dropped to her knees halfway up the steep ridge rising behind the Picketts' cabin. Her lungs burned like acid, and she grimaced, holding the knee she'd cracked in her frantic scramble to get away. Joey was furious and fussing, and she tried to soothe him in a raspy, scary voice that wasn't her own.

Sucking in deep breaths, she fumbled with his pacifier, hands shaky and uncooperative, but Joey latched onto it eagerly and she rocked back and forth, holding him in the sling and trying to calm down. She kept herself hidden behind a thick mulberry bush, struggling to get her arms through the straps of the heavy knapsack and balance it between her shoulder blades. She could hear the men yelling down below, their movements in the yard filtered through the fluttering green leaves of saplings and undergrowth covering the steep slope.

Kate's breath caught as a man brutally kicked open the back door and charged inside. Then she froze to stone as a terrible bloodcurdling scream echoed distantly from the path Michael had taken. Oh, God, no, they'd caught him. Instincts told her to take off again, hide, get Joey away, but she couldn't make herself move when she caught sight of the blond man with the ponytail dragging her husband across the backyard. She stifled a sob with her palm as the Russian dropped Michael at the bottom of the steps and began to stomp his chest. Oh, God, how could this be happening? How could they have gotten involved with these awful people?

The woods grew still, so quiet she was afraid to run now for fear they'd hear the rustling bushes as she crept through them. A bluejay shrieked nearby, making her jump, but her eyes were riveted starkly on the scene below as a third man walked across the back porch and descended the steps. He was of medium build, fairly tall, and moved gracefully with a slow, erect stride, the man with the goatee, she realized, as he turned where she could see him better. Something about his bearing told her that it was he who called the shots. Kate's black silk pajamas were clutched in his fist.

Another man trailed him outside, smaller and quicker moving, and the three killers stood in a circle around her husband's prone body. The bearded guy hunkered down beside Michael's head, and though Kate couldn't hear what was said, she could tell Michael was pleading for his life. He kept shaking his head, trying to get up, only to be shoved back down when suddenly without a moment's warning, the blond man bent down and put a gun to Michael's temple. A shot rang out, jerking Michael's head to the side.

Kate sat paralyzed with horror for an instant, then was overwhelmed by pure and utter panic. She tore mindlessly up the hill, no longer thinking about the noise she was making, no longer thinking about anything but getting away from the men who'd just murdered her husband in cold blood. Wild-eyed, desperate, blinded by tears, heedless of Joey's frightened screams, she crested the hill and took off headlong down the other side, knowing they would follow, that she had nowhere to hide, had to get away, lose herself in the undergrowth before they got her.

Clutching Joey's sling with both arms, she stumbled on loose shale and half fell, half slid on her back down into a clump of thorny brambles, sharp needles jabbing into her cheek and ripping her sweatshirt. She tried to protect Joey, barely cognizant of the pain. Hysteria threatened when she turned back and saw a pursuer high atop the hill just above her.

Jumping to her feet she took off at a run toward the river. She veered off onto a game trail that wound its way through thick tree trunks, ducking under low-hanging branches, trying to avoid the vines tangled everywhere. She thrashed down into a ravine choked with sumac, hoping the leafy tunnel would hide her flight. She ran hunched over low, fighting her way through spider webs and ducking her head to avoid the stinging whiplash of branches until she emerged breathlessly into a sandy creekbed.

Splashing through ankle-deep water, she sprinted harder, aware most creeks drained into the Current. Constantly checking over her shoulder, she was gulping down air so hard and fast that her throat burned and pain jabbed her lungs. Her foot slid off a wet rock and she went sprawling, landing hard on her right hip and striking her head on the rocky ground when she tried to protect Joey. A slash of pain imploded inside her temple, and she felt warm blood running down her cheek.

Dizzily she forced herself to her feet again, light-headed, weak in the knees, limping, her bad knee ready to collapse. Joey was wailing uncertainly, as if confounded over her wild behavior, but she couldn't worry about that. Oh, God, they were going to kill her, execute her, shoot her in the head the way they did Michael! She had to get away, hide somewhere, she had to! A moment later she burst out of the brushy creek about thirty yards up from a small gravel island in the middle of Current River. She knew the course of the stream well enough to realize exactly where she was and the depth of the water, and she headed straight for the island, slogging as fast as she could through the knee-deep, swirling currents, her goal the thick willows covering the sandbar.

She could feel sweat rolling down her face, stinging her eyes, or maybe it was blood from the gash on her head, and she sobbed with sheer relief when she finally sloshed into the shallows at the sandbar. If she could hide among the waving willow fronds, stay out of sight, she could crawl to the other side and strike out for the opposite bank of the river.

Dragging herself into the lush, deep shelter of the willow trees, she collapsed on her back in the cool shady haven, her labored lungs wheezing for air. Joey bawled at the top of his lungs but the rushing torrents drowned him out. Seconds later, she watched helplessly as the blond youth burst out of the creekbed in her wake, gun in hand, peering up and down the riverbank in search of her. She ground her teeth together and squirmed frantically through the wind-tossed willows toward the bottom end of the island. The river ran deeper in that area, with treacherous currents boiling around submerged rocks and snags, but the killers wouldn't be able to see her if she forded stream there.

The third killer had come into view now but none of them had seen her. She caught sight of the man with the beard, directing them downstream with a pointed forefinger. His two minions took off at a run along the rocks and driftwood lining the shoreline, and Kate held her breath, terrified he'd turn toward the island and realize where she'd escaped, but he didn't, oh, thank God, he didn't. He drew a pistol from underneath his jacket and moved upriver alone, scanning the woods as he walked.

Thank you, God, thank you, God, she muttered over and over, forcing herself to go on, out of the safety of the willows into the swiftest part of the current. This was the worst place she could attempt a ford, much too dangerous with a baby in her arms. But the willows blocked her from view here, and she'd be as good as dead if they saw her. She waded into the river until she was waist deep, hoping it didn't get much deeper, holding Joey up as high as she could. The frigid river was a welcome shock to her hot, sweaty body, and she fought onward, trying to keep her footing, but Joey was squirming restlessly in her hands, the roar of the water drowning out his cries.

She proceeded slowly and cautiously until she was chest deep in the river, but there the swifter current took hold of her, causing her to lose her footing and step off balance. The velocity of the water hit her like a hard shove in the back, and she went under, the backpack taking her down like an anchor. She floundered desperately to regain her footing as they were swept downstream a few yards, frantically trying to keep Joey's head out of the water. Lunging with all the strength she had left, she caught onto a log jutting out from the bank and braced her feet against the current. They'd only gone under for a few seconds, and Joey was screaming and red in the face as Kate pulled herself into the shallows and crawled through cold, slimy black mud into the refuge of a stinking, stagnant canebrake. Shivering and shaky from the dunking, she strained to see if the killers had spotted them.

Groaning with relief that no one was in sight, she kept her focus riveted on the island that blocked her flight from the opposite bank and quickly pushed her way through the nasty water and thick stalks of cane. This side of the river was even more rugged, and if she could fight her way farther into the wild terrain and hole up somewhere, they'd never find her.

For perhaps twenty yards she backed away through the foul water until she found a beaver's slide down into the cane. There she pulled herself up onto the firmer bank, her eyes still searching behind her for the killers. Joey's screams had weakened into frightened whimpers, and once she was sure they couldn't see them, she dragged herself back to her feet. She staggered on, exhausted, her feet heavy as anvils with caked mud until she finally had no choice but to sink down on her knees and rest.

"Shhh, Joey, baby, it's okay," she got out somehow, but she realized she was sobbing and couldn't make herself stop. But she couldn't disintegrate now, couldn't give in and let the men find them. Joey was all right. He was cold and he was wet but he was okay, and he was still with her. She sat still a moment, calming him, calming herself. She was trembling all over, aching, sopping wet and filthy but she was alive. She forced herself to move again. She couldn't just sit and wait for them to cross the river.

She kept low, her back aching as she trudged on hunched over and moving as fast as she could. Deeper and deeper into the woods she pressed on, tearing down spider webs and swatting at the tiny gnats and mosquitoes that swarmed off the forest floor and buzzed in her ears and worried her nose and mouth. Only when she was unable to see more than ten yards through the wild, overgrown forest did she feel safe enough to walk upright. Joey had quieted some but she wasn't sure how much more he could handle as she moved on, afraid to stop until every muscle, joint and bone in her body screamed for mercy. She was nearly dragging her injured leg now, but she had to put more space between herself and the river.

When a man stepped out in front of her and blocked her path, Kate couldn't believe her eyes at first and blinked hard, thinking she was imagining him. But he was still there when she opened them again, huge, dirty, bladed with bright sunlight streaming through the heavy canopy of oak trees. His face was smeared with mud, and so was his long, scraggly beard, a Bible-prophet beard that hung against his chest. His hair was just as long and filthy, stringing out of a jungle hat. He was dressed all in camouflage, and she stared at him in disbelief, shocked he'd gotten so close without her seeing him. Her eyes fixed finally on the long rifle he held, the barrel pointed at her heaving chest.

Oh, God help her, he was one of them. They'd spread out on this side of the river, too. Some of her inner fortitude snapped like rotted rope, and she felt her heart give way. She sank slowly to her knees. She had nowhere else to run, nowhere to hide, was so totally, completely exhausted she wasn't sure she could anyway. Oh, God, she was going to die now, she was going to have to hand Joey over to them, her darling baby, to these awful, horrible, murderous men. Still unwilling to give up the son she loved with every fiber of her being, she clutched Joey stubbornly against her heart, lifting her chin and vowing never to give him up willingly.

The man in camouflage stared at her, his eyes very pale and vivid blue, piercingly intense in his filthy face. For an instant their gazes locked as if fused, and Kate felt the tingling electricity in that moment, the terrifying tension that built to a breaking point until she could not draw a breath as she waited for him to pull the trigger and shoot her dead. Then, suddenly, without warning, without a word uttered, he was gone as magically as he'd appeared, melting into the verdant cloak of the trees, leaving Kate staring after him, the distant rushing of the river the only sound in the deep silence of the woods.

Six

KATE WAS AFRAID to move. She kept her eyes shut tight, every nerve taut. She banded Joey against her breast with both arms, waiting for the man to change his mind and come back to kill her. Was he really with the others after her? If he was, why would he let her go so easily? Why would he let her keep Joey? In God's name, he looked more like Jeremiah Johnson or some kind of Ozark mountain man. She swallowed convulsively, thinking about what they'd done to Michael. He couldn't be dead, he just couldn't, none of this could be real.

Kate opened her eyes when a bird fluttered onto a leafy branch a few yards distant. It was a bright red cardinal, and he cocked his head and watched her out of one beady black eye. His scarlet feathers were a startling contrast to the gray-green foliage choking the forest landscape. Nothing else in the forest seemed willing to move.

When she realized that Joey was wriggling in her arms, his cries plaintive and pitiful inside the wet sling, she realized she had to get going again. She couldn't just sit there and wait for one of them to find her. She peered around anxiously, saw nothing, heard nothing. The strange apparition was gone. She braced one hand on the ground and forced herself to her feet again, wincing and groaning with effort. Holding the baby tightly she began to walk rapidly, her eyes darting around from one tree to another, one tangled thicket to the next, stopping often to listen and watch. It was only a matter of time before her husband's killers realized she'd crossed the river, and they'd come after her. They wouldn't be as merciful as the bizarre mountain man, whoever he was.

It dawned on her then that he might've been Pop's friend, the one named John. But, no, he couldn't be. He was much too old to be the kid Pop had known. It didn't matter who he was anyway, just that he'd let them go. He apparently meant them no harm, so now she had to concentrate on finding a place where she could lie low and rest her throbbing leg and take care of Joey. She kept her eyes glued to the wooded ridge she was approaching, feeling the extra effort of the ascent when she started the climb, but she had to get higher, up where she could see them coming.

Half an hour later, scratched up and so tired she couldn't think straight, she fought her way out of the scratchy, insect-infested brambles to an elevation that made her feel a little safer. She chose a spot under some dense branches thick with leaves and backed inside the cool darkness, rustling the limbs first to drive away nesting snakes and spiders. For several moments, she examined the forest stretching out in the distance, still so uptight she couldn't relax. Terrified she'd detect figures moving stealthily through the white dogwoods and pink redbuds scattered among the loftier oaks and sycamores, she saw nothing except a million green leaves stirring in the soft, spring breeze.

Another pathetic little whimper came from Joey, and Kate's heart twisted with compassion. She lifted the baby out and laid him on his back on the ground in front of her. She shrugged out of the knapsack and stripped the sling from around her neck. She wrung out the wet fabric, watching Joey kick his feet inside the soaked sleeper. He waved his arms vigorously, his face turning red as he slowly built up to outrage at the way she'd been treating him. The bottle was still snug inside its elastic holder, a miracle in itself after all they'd been through. She pulled it out and touched it to his lips. He gave one last angry sputter, then grabbed at the nipple. Sucking intensely, his shiny black eyes searched her face accusingly as if demanding an explanation for being dragged through the woods and shot at.

"You're a tough kid, know that, Joey?" she said, then cut off her words in dismay, afraid even a whisper would carry through the quiet woods. She searched once again for their stalkers. Only the distant roar of the rapids filtered through the morning. The killers weren't in sight and neither was the bizarre man in camouflage, but that didn't mean he wasn't lurking around somewhere, completely invisible in his green and brown forest garb. She didn't see him now but she hadn't seen him the first time either, not until he'd dropped into sight right in front of her. The songbirds had begun a symphony of chirps and cheeps and warbling whistles, cheerful woodland creatures going about their business as if killers weren't out there among them, hunting down Kate to kill her.

Okay, you've survived till now, Kate, use your head, be smarter than they are. Outwit them somehow. She had to force herself to think calmly, regroup her thoughts, control the panic that kept threatening to engulf her. She stretched out her leg and massaged her swollen knee, shivering, then realizing how cold and clammy she felt despite the warming of the day. Joey was probably cold, too. Immediately she stripped off the clinging infant sacque. His diaper was heavy with river water, so she removed it and squeezed it out the best she could. All her supplies were wet from the plunge in the river, except for those things in plastic bags, but the dancing shafts of smoky sunlight pouring through the tree branches would dry Joey's damp skin, and the diaper, too.

A bird called stridently, as high pitched and anxious sounding as Kate felt. His mate came back with a less elegant, throaty *chuck-chuck-chuck*. She straightened out her other knee and tried to stretch her aching muscles, grimacing when pain streaked to her toes. She rotated her leg side to side as her orthopedic specialist had shown her, wishing she had on the brace he'd ordered custom made to fit her knee. She'd worn it faithfully when exercising since her fall at the Olympics. Despite the pain, she felt strong enough to go on. She jogged several times a week and practiced the gymnastics she'd mastered as a child, but she'd never pushed this hard without her brace. But she could do this, *would* do it. A little rest was all she needed. Then she'd get going.

Focusing her attention on the trees below, she grappled with everything that had happened, trying to make sense of it. Everything was about Joey and had been from the beginning. Michael said Joey was a black-market baby, that he'd bought him. But that simply could not be true. The adoption had been a private one, out of the Philippines, the contractual agreement made with the mother before Joey was even born. And Michael had promised, sworn to her on all that was holy, that everything was legal and aboveboard.

Good God, how many legal forms had she filled out on the kitchen table with Michael sitting at her elbow, helping her? Every detail of their lives since they'd married—their pasts, health records, financial status—all for the mother's peace of mind. Kate had done everything required of her, signed the legal contract, read all the fine print. My God, had the entire thing been a scam? Had Michael been able to trick her so thoroughly? But why, why would he do such a thing?

Desperately she tried to remember everything he'd said from the first moment he'd brought up the idea of adopting a baby from overseas. It had been on the day Pop was buried, the day she'd been so hurt when Michael hadn't shown up for the funeral service after promising he would. She'd even considered asking for a separation that day, give them time to sort out their problems. They'd grown apart during the last year, Michael spending more and more time at work, telling her less and less about his clients.

Pressing her fingertips against her aching temples, she leaned back against a tree trunk and forced herself to recall everything he said and did that had led up to this terrible nightmare. Michael knew his killers; he'd admitted it. Why hadn't she realized he was in such serious trouble? Surely he'd said something that should have given her pause, but how could she ever have expected him to be involved in something as awful as this, something that would take his life?

Lifting Joey against her, she fought a rush of tears, seeing him die over and over, the way his head had jerked on impact, how quick and cruel it had been. She cradled the baby against her shoulder and scanned the trees while she cuddled him, gently rubbing his back in circles the way he liked. He burped a moment later, a dainty one compared to most, but he had calmed somewhat from their wild run, and so had she. Wearily he laid his head down on her shoulder, and she realized he was probably ready for his nap. The Luvs she'd set in the sun was almost dry, so she quickly diapered him.

When he was back in her arms and content, eyelids drooping, Kate let her mind return to the day of her grandfather's funeral, trying to recall precisely what Michael had said when he had finally shown up. She had been alone down on the riverbank, wondering what she should do about the sorry state of their marriage.

Kate could remember that day two months ago so clearly. It had been a beautiful afternoon in late March, clear and breezy with fresh-smelling air, when trumpets of daffodils glowed pure gold in the sun and newly budded oaks along the riverbank fluttered vivid green against gray tree trunks. Current River had rushed along its cold-blue, crystal-clear torrent, but even now, weeks later, she could still feel the loneliness that had been inside her heart when Michael had finally shown up, his first words soft with apology.

"I'm so sorry, Kate. I tried to get here in time. I really did."

Kate jerked her head up from watching the currents eddy

around a submerged log, startled to see Michael standing a few yards away. Anger came quickly and she didn't try to disguise it. "You promised you'd come, Michael. I was all alone. I needed you."

Michael glanced out over the river and stuck his hands in the pockets of his trousers. He was still dressed up, must have come straight from his office, in a navy blue double-breasted suit worn atop a crisp white shirt with his monogram on the breast pocket.

"I tried my best to make it in time for the service. I swear to God, I did. I got held up arguing a motion. I drove as fast as I could. I'm sorry. Please try to understand."

Kate didn't want to talk about it. She looked down at her bare feet and swished them back and forth through the cold water. She didn't answer. She was tired. Tired of Michael spending so much time at work, tired of being alone all the time.

Michael moved closer and sat down on a flat rock beside her. "I saw all the food Pop's friends brought over. Everybody's going to miss him a lot."

"Yeah, especially me."

Her voice choked some, and Michael put his arm around her shoulders. "You going to be okay, sweetheart?"

Kate laid her head on his shoulder, her anger fading because she was glad he was there. She needed somebody to hold on to. "I guess. It's really hard. You know how close I was to Pop."

"Yeah. He was a good guy, even if he didn't care much for me."

At the moment, she was too emotionally drained to get into that with him. Pop hadn't liked some of the people Michael dealt with or how often he left Kate alone. Something was wrong between them, even Pop had sensed it, something she couldn't quite understand. Maybe they needed time apart to think things through. Maybe she ought to discuss it with Michael now, when her nerves felt so dead.

"How long do you want to stay down here? I took a couple of days off to be with you. You've got a lot to think about, with Pop's house and business to take care of." He reached out and lifted a strand of her silky blond ponytail and she leaned against him, wishing things weren't quite so complicated.

"I love it down here. I feel good when I'm on the river. Free."

"It's a pretty place. Peaceful. That's probably what you need right now. Some peace and quiet." Michael was trying to make it up to her now, being so sweet, she knew that, but she welcomed his kindness. They used to be so close, Michael so attentive. Why had they grown apart? How had it happened?

"Michael, I've decided to stay on here for awhile."

"That's okay. I think you should. Tie up all the loose ends, put the place up for sale. I'll handle the realty contracts when I get some time, then I'll invest Pop's money for you."

"No. I mean I want to live here. All the time."

For the first time, Kate turned to look at him, her eyes searching his handsome face, and she could see the shock in his eyes. He stared at her, openly dismayed, as if he had no idea of the strain their marriage had suffered over the past year. They hardly saw each other, much less had a meaningful conversation.

"Kate, listen to me. I know you're upset today. You're fed up with me, and I know it. It's my fault. I've been neglecting you. I haven't kept promises when I should have, wasn't here today when you needed me. I've hurt you, but I don't want to lose you. Please, let's try to work things out. I know we can."

Kate was truly surprised that he even cared, but heartened that he wanted to make a go of it. "I never see you, Michael. What kind of marriage is that? We used to do things, go places, laugh and have fun together. Now all you do is work. I feel like a housekeeper instead of a wife. We'd both be bet-

ter off if we split up for awhile, think about what we really want out of life."

"No," he said, his voice sharper now, "no, we won't." He took her hand, and she looked down as he sandwiched it between his palms. His skin was deep brown from a two-week business trip to Los Angeles. Her fingers seemed very white.

"Look at me, Kate. I mean it this time. I'm going to do better, I promise you. I want us to start over. I'm tired of the grind I've been in. It's time for us to begin again, rebuild our marriage."

Kate's eyes narrowed at his earnest appeal, trying to plumb those pale gray depths, wanting to believe him but not sure she could. His work had gradually become everything to him. She had hoped for a day when he would say these things, look at her the way he was doing at the moment, but they'd been trying so long. She was tired of new starts. She wasn't sure about anything anymore. She wasn't even sure she loved him anymore. Her own inner admission stunned her, and she glanced away, hiding her dismay.

"I like it here, Michael. The quiet life. I want to stay and run Pop's business. He left it to me, along with the cabin. It's enough for me. I have lots of high school friends who still live in Van Buren. I can be happy here. I hate living in St. Louis."

She heard him heave a deep sigh, but he always did that when he didn't have a pat answer. He was turning arguments over in his mind, trying them out, the way he did in court when he was grilling some poor, helpless witness on the stand. When he spoke, she was utterly astonished by his words. She turned her body and watched his face as he continued, not sure she could believe her ears.

"All right, sweetheart, if that's what you want, I'll come back here and live. I can set up a practice in Van Buren, or maybe down in Poplar Bluff. It'd be worth it to me to get you back. I mean it this time, Katie, I swear to God I do."

Something moved inside Kate, some little squirm of joy

she'd thought was dead, or was it hope? She felt her mouth respond, curve a little, though she was afraid he'd change his mind before the sun went down.

"Why are you saying these things now? You like it in the city. Lord, how many times have I heard you berate everything you went through when you were a boy. Why would you agree to live here now?"

Michael resorted to his most winning self, lifting one corner of his mouth in the sexy half grin she used to love. She thought she'd gotten over that weakness, but there were times, apparently still were, when she couldn't resist him, when he became all boyish and vulnerable, and she remembered the shy, bashful kid he'd been when they'd first met in junior high. She waited, wondering what on earth had come over him to promise something so rash. He'd been acting strangely in the last six months, edgy, easily irritated, overly concerned with his work.

"I wanted to surprise you when I was sure, but I guess I'll tell you now. Maybe then you'll understand why I want us to try harder." He leaned back on his palms but his gaze remained on her face, studying her eyes as if wanting to savor her reaction. "I think I can get us a baby, Kate. A little boy."

Kate felt herself go weak as if all her muscles had collapsed at once. They'd tried so long to have a baby, failed miserably no matter how many specialists they'd seen. For the first two years of their marriage, conceiving had been their primary concern since they'd both hit thirty, but they'd failed. She was barren, and she felt guilt flood over her, as it always did. The doctors had told her that her ovaries had just stopped producing eggs, some physiological reason caused by years of constant physical training and pushing her body to the limit. She'd stopped ovulating, unnaturally, years ago, and she hadn't even known it. Sometimes she felt that was what finally drove them apart. The constant pressure to conceive, making love by ovulation charts and basal thermometer readings. In-

timacy had finally become a chore for both of them, all spontaneity and tenderness gone from their lovemaking.

"How? The adoption agencies have all turned us down because of your possession charge."

"That charge was dropped and expunged from my record, you know that. I had one of my clients in the car. The stuff was his. But this isn't through an agency. It's an unwed mother. From the Philippines. I heard about her through one of my clients."

"An unwed mother?" It occurred to Kate that Michael's term was a bit archaic for the times, but she wanted to know more. "Who is she? Why would she want to give up her baby to us?"

"I think her family's forcing her to. She's real young, but they want to make sure it goes to a good home." He paused. "Her father's a lawyer in Manila, but over there it's a disgrace if a woman of her station gets pregnant before she's married. He and I can handle it legally. She's pregnant now and we'd get the baby as soon as it's born. It's all real hush-hush, you know, that kind of thing. They want the girl to marry some other guy, one her father picked out for her."

"My God, he can't just take her baby away from her like that, can he? That has to be illegal. If not by law, then morally. How can she bear giving up her son?"

"The girl's just turned fourteen. She made a mistake and has agreed to obey her parents. She's due soon, so we might be able to get him within the next couple of weeks. It's not definite yet, but I'm pretty sure I can work out contractual terms and make sure everything's legal."

"But, Michael, I'm not sure I could, under these circumstances. God, I feel so sorry for the mother. It's just wrong to make her give him up, like this. I can't imagine how terrible it would be . . ."

"Listen, Kate, the baby's going to go up for adoption, one way or another. I'm almost positive I can get him for you if

you want a baby, but I don't want to hear these misgivings about the mother. It's her decision, not ours."

Kate turned her eyes from his face and stared out at the river. Michael was right. The choice was up to the girl and her family. Maybe the mother wanted to give the baby up. After all, she was just a child herself. She tried to remember when she was fourteen. She'd been running track in junior high under Coach Caputo. Hadn't had her periods too long. Good God, how young that was to become pregnant.

She perused the nearby bank where a cluster of daffodils was bobbing in the wind. She and her grandma had planted them there when she was around ten. They were spreading up the bank now, under a huge elm tree. A little boy would love it here on the river, fishing and swimming, and he'd keep Kate company when Michael was working all the time. Despite the vow he'd just made, Kate knew full well that Michael would never completely give up his career, not for her, not for anyone.

"Well, sweetheart, what do you say? Let's try to be a family this time, a real one. I swear I'll be a good father, and a good husband. I want that, too. I do, you'll see."

When Michael took her hand and lifted it to his mouth, she surprised herself by being completely unaffected. The physical part of their relationship was for the most part dead, and she wasn't sure they could ever revive feelings withered up for so long. But a baby might change things for the better; maybe if they had something so precious to share, to love, they could learn to care about each other again. A terrible thought occurred to her.

"You're sure this is completely legal, aren't you, Michael? It's not some kind of scam, is it?"

Michael gave her a look filled with injury. She wasn't sure if his reaction was real or not. "Of course, it's legal. I'm handling everything myself. We'll both have to sign the papers. It's just a private adoption, is all. They're being really careful about us, too. They want to make sure he'll be all right, that we have the money to take care of him. We've got to answer a bunch of questions, show we're responsible people. It'll take awhile since they're in Manila, but we should have everything ready by the time the kid's born."

Kate still hesitated. "You know how I feel about things, Michael. I don't want to be a part of anything that isn't completely on the up-and-up."

"For Christ's sake, you act like I'm some sort of criminal. I just represent them. I'm not one myself. Give me some credit, will you?"

Kate wanted to believe him; his eyes seemed indignant enough. "Is the baby healthy? I've heard about crack babies, and babies with AIDS. Some of the Romanian children brought over here were mentally impaired. . . ."

"It's perfectly healthy and so is the mother. She's having regular prenatal care, I know, because I checked all this out with her doctor. They're going to send me her medical records, and I can probably get a picture of the mother, if you want one. Why are you so suspicious all of a sudden? I thought you'd be thrilled about this."

Kate stared at him, not finding it nearly so hard to understand her misgivings. She didn't try to argue with him anymore. "Let me think about it for a few days, Michael. I'm tired now, and still awfully upset about Pop. This is all so sudden. I just feel numb, I guess."

"Sure, sweetie, think about it. It's all I've been thinking about for weeks. I wanted to make sure I had a good chance at getting the baby before I mentioned him to you. Think about it, Kate. A month from now we can be living here together with our son. It's your dream, sugar. Please let me give it to you."

With that, Michael rose and helped her to her feet. She allowed him to drape an arm around her shoulders as they started back together toward Pop's log cabin. Weary of disbe-

lieving him, she began to consider that he just might possibly be telling the truth. Why else would he want a baby if he didn't want their marriage to work? Maybe it would be possible for them to redeem their relationship, if they both tried hard and compromised the way they'd done in the early months of their marriage. Maybe, though, she just wanted to trust him again, wanted to believe things could be the way they had been in the beginning. She missed that, missed being a couple, wanted their life together back, because with Pop gone, she had never felt so alone in her life.

Now, Kate thought, shaking her head, she knew Michael had been lying about Joey. She looked down at the little boy, asleep in her arms. A black-market baby, Michael had said. Oh, God, where had Joey come from if not from a good family in Manila? Who had given him up if it wasn't the unwed girl Michael had described, had shown her a picture of? Oh, God, what if it wasn't legal? What if Joey really wasn't hers at all? She couldn't bear to even think about it. She loved him so much, adored him, more than anything else in her life. She couldn't give him up, not to anyone, especially the kind of men who were after him. She'd have to find a way to keep him, a legal way; she'd have to get out of the woods and find a lawyer, find someone who could make things right again.

Anxious now to move on, she quickly gathered up the supplies she'd spread out to dry and found most of them barely damp. She stuffed them into the knapsack and slung it over her shoulders, then settled a newly contented Joey into the sling. She held the sleeping baby tightly against her for an extra moment, a new determination setting her jaw firm. No matter who Joey was or where Michael had gotten him, she wasn't going to give him up without a fight, a custody battle if need be. Right now, though, she needed to find shelter for the night, a safe, warm place where no one could sneak up on them.

Lingering a few minutes to watch the woods for any sign of her pursuers, she stood up and pushed her way out of the tunnel of bushes. Choosing a direction that slanted away from the river and south along the ridge, the way to Van Buren and the way the prophet-bearded guy hadn't gone, she forced herself to move on. Stepping carefully, she remembered all Pop's lessons about tracking deer, putting each foot down carefully between fallen branches, choosing footfalls on hard ground and rocks, so nothing was left disturbed. She'd leave no trail for the killers to follow. She straightened up as an idea formed in her mind, glancing behind again. Still no sign of the armed men. Maybe she should leave a few false trails now and then as she moved along. It wouldn't take much work, and if anyone did manage to follow her, it might buy her some time.

Chewing her bottom lip in indecision, she wondered if she should take the time to do it now. She had to assume mountain man was long gone. He'd already had the chance to accost her, and for some reason had left her alone. Her primary concern had to be the men gunning for her. The blond guy with the ponytail had murdered Michael without blinking an eye. Oh, God, how could Michael have done this to her? To himself? Had everything he'd told her about Joey been lies?

Well, she couldn't think about that yet, couldn't take time to figure out what was true and what wasn't, couldn't even take time to mourn his death. Later on, after nightfall, holed up somewhere safe, then she'd try to figure how to get out of this horror he'd brought down on their heads. Once she reached Van Buren, Gus would help her get to the bottom of it. Right now, she'd better concentrate on making it out of the woods in one piece.

Seven

AROUND NIGHTFALL Kate found a series of caves in a limestone bluff that jutted up like a stone guard two hundred yards from Current River. A trickle of fresh water cascaded down from the caverns and pooled into a tiny creek that meandered toward the riverbed. Concealing herself in the thick brush at the base of the rocks, she listened for pursuers, afraid to put herself in plain sight on the ledges.

Clutching Joey tightly in one arm, she took a deep breath and climbed the stone shelves until she was about thirty feet above the forest floor. In the still, cool late afternoon, the first dusky wave of twilight crept stealthily over the woodlands. Not even a breeze stirred in the leafy thickets below, and she felt certain her pursuers could not track her after dark. She'd be safe until morning.

Relieved she could finally rest her weary bones, she bent low and peered into the pitch-black opening of the nearest cavern. There were few black bears left roaming the Ozark foothills, but in this remote stretch of federal wilderness, they had been sighted on occasion. Kate wasn't about to disturb one in its den. Loosening her backpack, she set it down and fumbled inside for the flashlight. The bright beam swept through the darkness inside, revealing a dirt floor strewn with loose shale. The cavern was small but the ceiling high enough that she could stand upright. She bent and carried Joey inside where it was dry and habitable, with enough ventilation to start a fire.

Kate could hear a quiet tinkle of water somewhere and searched until she found the narrow crevice from which it trickled. She bent and scooped up a handful, smelling it, then tasting it with her tongue. Cold and clean. She retrieved her pack from outside, then descended to the ground with Joey to gather enough firewood to last them through the night. After several trips she got the matches from the Ziplock bag and patiently worked until she got a blaze going with some dry kindling and wadded-up paper towels. She felt like celebrating when the branches caught and she held her cold hands up to the warmth.

Thinking the hellish day would never end, she spread out a quilt, sank down and freed Joey from the sling. He'd been unbelievably good throughout the afternoon trek as she'd trudged on and on, exhausted but afraid to stop too soon. But now the poor little thing had had enough. He was hungry and tired, and tired of being good. He let her know it with a shrill wail that echoed off the stone walls until it seemed that a dozen angry babies filled the cave.

Unzipping the pocket of the sling, she got out a bottle of formula, pleased beyond all reason that she'd stuck in an extra one. Could it really have been only that morning that the Russians had burst in on them? It seemed an eternity. She shuddered, remembering the cruelty in the blond man's black eyes. Not wanting to think about the men after her or worry about how close they were, she concentrated on Joey, checking his diaper and finding it soaked.

The paper towels had dried out, so she quickly fashioned a makeshift diaper and held it together with a strip of masking tape. Joey gazed up at her while she worked, stopping his sucking once in awhile to form his mouth into a smile around the nipple, showing off his double dimples.

"Oh, Joey, how can this be happening to us?" she muttered, but her voice cracked, and she had to swallow down a fierce surge of despair.

Joey's answer was a kick and a string of gurgles and goos

before he went back to sucking for all he was worth. She remembered the first day they'd gotten him, how happy she'd been, how beautiful she'd thought him. As she sat cross-legged beside the fire, with Joey nursing happily in her arms, the images flooded back, as indelible as a newsreel. She'd been painting Joey's crib that day, waiting on pins and needles for Michael to call, when the telephone rang.

"Kate, it's me."

Michael's voice was excited, not quite his own, higher pitched, nervous sounding, and she hoped, shut her eyes and prayed, that things had gone as they'd planned.

"Is everything all right?" Still anxious, she clutched the receiver more tightly, terrified the adoption had fallen through, though Michael had assured her there was little chance of anything going wrong.

"You bet it is. I've got him. He's right here with me, in the back. Sound asleep in his car seat."

"No way, Michael! You said we couldn't get him until he was at least two weeks old. I was supposed to go with you to pick him up."

"Things moved too fast for that. The birth was easy, went real well. He's big and healthy, over nine pounds at birth. The mother's parents didn't want her to get attached to him, so they went ahead and sent him out with the nurse we hired."

Again sadness for the mother touched Kate, though she was more than relieved nothing had gone wrong. "Is that all right? Did the doctor say it was okay for him to be taken on a plane so soon? He made the flight all right, didn't he? He's not sick?"

"No, no, nothing like that, quit your worrying. The doctor didn't have a problem with it at all. He's three days old and doing great."

"Three days old! I can't believe you didn't tell me all this! I've been going crazy down here."

"Didn't want you to get your hopes up in case something did get screwed up." The cellular phone crackled slightly, interrupting them a moment, but she heard his next words loud and clear. "He's all ours, Kate, we've got ourselves a bouncing baby boy."

Kate stared out the window over the sink, down at the deserted bait shop, fighting tears of joy. Sheer relief, gratitude, all that and so much more mingled inside her, making words impossible; the back of her throat was clogged too tight.

"Kate? You still there?"

Swallowing hard, she forced herself to answer. "Yes, yes, I'm just trying to absorb all this. When will you get here? I can't wait to see him!" Suddenly she laughed and blurted out, "I can't believe it, Michael, we've got a baby, a son, just like we always wanted! When will you be here?"

Michael's laugh was cut off with another buzz of static, then he came through clearly again, his words astonishing her. "Try five minutes. I'm on the county road right now, just above Pop's mailbox."

"No! You're lying to me! You can't be that close!"

"Oh, yes I can. Go outside on the porch. We'll be there in five minutes."

"You should've called! I'm not ready. Everything isn't exactly right yet!"

"He won't notice, believe me. Hurry up, go outside and wait. It's time to meet your new son." The line went dead, and Kate found herself staring incredulously at the receiver in her hand, feeling shell-shocked and numb, but then she laughed with pure exhilaration. She slammed the receiver back into its cradle and went running to the front of the house.

Outside she watched the road for only a few minutes before her black Explorer came into sight. Michael had insisted on taking it instead of the Lexus, and she'd thought it strange at the time until he'd admitted he needed the extra room for all the stuff he was going to buy for the baby.

Clutching her hands together, she stood at the end of the side-

walk where the gate stood open and watched Michael pull the car around with a delicate crunch of gravel. The baby seat was in the back on the left side, just the way they'd read in the instruction booklet, and she ran to the window and stared through the tinted glass, gazing upon her son for the very first time.

"Oh, Michael, he's beautiful!"

Michael was already out and coming around from the driver's side. He was grinning, seemingly as proud as if the boy were his own. Kate opened the door and leaned over the sleeping infant, her heart bursting with pleasure. He really was beautiful, so tiny, just a little bundle in a blanket, his face round with a ruddy complexion, lots of dark curls, lots more hair than any newborn she'd ever seen.

"Just look at all that hair."

"Yeah, thank God he wasn't bald, and he's not even that wrinkled up. Some newborn babies look like little old geezers."

Kate laughed at Michael, hearing the immense pride in his voice and looking up at him. "I just can't believe he's truly ours. They can't change their minds and take him back, can they? Tell me they can't do that, Michael."

"Of course not. Stop thinking that way. C'mon, let's get him inside. He slept nearly all the way down here so he's probably wet his pants."

For the first time Kate realized how jittery her husband was acting. He'd probably been terrified the whole drive down, afraid the baby would cry or want a bottle. That's why she'd wanted to go along to get the baby. Michael was so fidgety that she smiled, deciding she'd better take charge. "I told you to come get me before you went to pick him up. Besides, he doesn't wear pants yet," Kate murmured, carefully unbuckling the strap and lifting it off. Suddenly she appreciated Michael's apprehension; she was almost afraid to touch the tiny baby herself. Neither one had had an iota of experience with newborns.

"What if we wake him up? He's sleeping so peacefully."

"We've got to get him in the house sometime. Hurry up, just pick him up and let's take him inside," Michael urged anxiously, showing his frayed nerves again.

When Kate slid her hand underneath the infant's bottom, he opened one eye and squinted up at her. Her heart melted like grease on a griddle. His other eye opened when she cupped the back of his head in her other hand, marveling at how small he was.

"He's going to have brown eyes, I'll bet. Look how dark they are, almost black," she whispered, then wondered why she was whispering. She found out why when the baby began to fuss and wave his little arms around. Kate lifted him out of the infant carrier, still holding him with both hands.

"Don't drop him, Kate, watch out, he's squirming around." Michael looked ready to pace the driveway as Kate settled the baby in the crook of her left arm.

"I've got him, Michael. Stay calm." She smiled at her husband a moment and he took a deep breath.

"I just want to get him inside and settled before anybody comes."

"It doesn't matter if anyone comes," Kate told him, but they really should get him in out of the sun. Still smiling, she watched him as he made angry little sputtering sounds and jerked his arms up and down a mile a minute. Kate rocked him gently, back and forth in the cradle of her arms, stunned that she knew what to do, that her own maternal instincts had come to their rescue, as surely as if she'd raised a dozen kids of her own.

"There, there, sweetie pie," she crooned softly, reaching out to touch his soft cheek. "Don't you worry a bit, little one, you're home now. I'll take good care of you, I promise, yes, I will."

The baby grunted and tried to kick, then let out the most awful belch she'd ever heard. She and Michael looked at each other in shocked silence and then laughed together when the baby followed with a contented sigh.

"Well, that apparently made him feel better," she said, gazing down at him, awed by the tiny little fingers, now clutched into tight fists the size of walnuts.

"He's a man's man, that's for damned sure," Michael agreed, then moved around the back and opened the hatch. "I picked up a portable crib at the Neiman Marcus baby department because the saleslady said it's better to keep him in the same room with us for awhile before we put him in his own baby bed."

"You're becoming quite an expert on babies," Kate said, but she was pleased he had taken the interest. Every such remark made her feel as if he were truly determined to make them a family.

"I got some books on child raising at Barnes and Noble, too. And a bunch more clothes for him, some in bigger sizes, too. I figure we won't be getting back up to St. Louis anytime soon." That was music to Kate's ears. Michael seemed to have come back from whatever distant journey to fame and fortune he'd been on for so long.

He retrieved a huge teddy bear from the front seat, one about ten times bigger than the child Kate held. "That thing'll scare the wits out of him."

"I got some smaller ones, too. This one's for later."

Michael rushed to the back and started unloading as if he were in a race, and his unstrung attitude was beginning to infect Kate, too. Suddenly the immensity of their responsibility concerning this helpless child hit her. She hoped they could take care of him the way they were supposed to, and she was very glad Michael had picked up those baby books. "I hope we don't do anything wrong."

"I think he's gonna be a pretty good kid. He hardly made a peep all the way down, I'm telling you, barely a sound the whole way."

Kate held him securely and walked slowly up the front walk, Michael behind her, toting the portable crib under one arm and the diaper bag in his other hand. She opened the screen door with one toe and entered the house, sitting down in Pop's brown rocker-recliner. She put her knees together and laid the baby down atop her lap, unable to take her eyes off him.

"Hello, little precious," she cooed, and he blinked his dark eyes as if still blinded from the brightness outside. "You are so little, you know that. Barely big enough to fit on my lap."

"He's really pretty big for a newborn, at least that's what the nurse said. Nine pounds and ten ounces." Michael had set the bed upright and was arranging the padded bumpers around the edges. He got down on one knee beside Kate. Both of them stared down at the baby.

"He's a good-looking kid, all right," Michael said. "He looks a little like his mother."

Kate nodded. "He has dark hair like hers. Remember, in the picture she sent you it was braided into long pigtails."

Michael suddenly seemed reluctant to get into that subject, no doubt afraid Kate would dwell on the birth mother's sorrow. "Let's not talk about her. He's ours now, nice and legal."

Nodding, Kate reached down a forefinger to touch the child's tiny fist. Immediately the baby curled his little fingers around the tip of her finger and squeezed so tightly that Kate was startled. "Look at that grip, would you? Oh, Michael, I can't believe we finally have him. I just can't believe it, not after all those years wanting a baby."

"Believe it. He's ours, forever. There are bottles in the diaper bag ready to feed to him. The nurse got everything ready for us. And I've got a bunch of cans of the right kind of formula, you know, the kind for newborns. They said we'll have to change it to whole milk eventually but we can figure that out when the time comes."

"Of course we can. We'll figure out everything."

"I've got more stuff outside in the Explorer. I'll be back in a minute."

"Okay, I'll sit here and hold him."

Kate was very content to do just that, and she admired their son as Michael disappeared outside again, banging the screen behind him. She unwrapped the pale blue blanket and saw that he wore a white terrycloth gown that had a drawstring at the bottom. Again she marveled at his teensy arms and legs but he was fully awake now. He didn't fuss but kicked his legs and waved his arms in a jerky fashion as if he was startled they were attached to him.

"We're going to have to learn all about each other together, now aren't we?" she crooned, giggling at herself for adopting the ridiculous baby talk. How easily it had come to her!

"You are such a handsome boy," she told him, tenderly caressing one of his silky dark curls. "With all this black hair and those cute little ears. You're going to be the best-looking boy in high school someday, you know that?"

He gurgled, and she saw for the first time that he had a double dimple in his cheek, high, just under his eye. She smiled tenderly at him, then looked out through the picture window when she heard Michael's voice. She could see him beside the Explorer, pacing back and forth as he spoke into his cellular phone. His voice was muffled enough so that she didn't know exactly what he was talking about, but he didn't look happy. She hoped his office wasn't calling him back to the city on some emergency. Surely he wouldn't do that, not on their son's first day home.

The baby kicked harder, and Kate picked up one of her grandmother's knitted afghans from the arm of the chair and carefully spread it out on the floor. She leaned down and laid him on his back, then got on her knees beside him.

When he kept fussing and twisting she feared he might be wet, so she carefully untied the drawstring. The plastic diaper looked very white against his bare skin, the tender flesh mottled and bluish in color. "Oh, my little love, just look how fragile you are. Well, let's just see if you're wet, or not."

Intruding one forefinger down the front of the diaper, she realized that he was indeed. Soaked, as a matter of fact. Reaching out to the diaper bag, she dragged it toward her and pulled out a newborn Luvs, thinking it incredible how small it was. She knew how to diaper a baby because she'd been practicing for the last week on one of her old dolls. The baby lay still for her, watching her every move as if he thought her quite fascinating.

Lifting his bottom with the utmost care, she dragged off the diaper and dusted him with a little Johnson's Baby Powder she'd found in the bag, then positioned a clean diaper underneath him. She had to stretch it nearly double to fit him at the front, but he only kicked and made little grunts that delighted her.

Once she had the sleeper back on him she sat back and just stared down at him. The most terrible wave of tenderness began to build inside her, and she knew how blessed she was to have gotten such a child. She felt her heart expand with a love that she knew would only grow stronger as each day passed. She wanted to cry, and laugh, and dance around the cabin, all with pure joy.

"See, changing diapers wasn't so bad. I haven't done it yet, but I watched the nurse. Those tapes make it easy. Remember when they used to use safety pins?"

Michael had come back inside, watching as Kate rewrapped the baby inside the soft receiving blanket and lifted him to her shoulder. She rocked back and forth, smiling. "He's so good. He hasn't cried yet."

"Yeah. I was afraid he'd get crazy on me on the way down but he slept like a baby."

Kate shook her head, but he didn't seem to notice his pun. Wanting to see her little darling again she laid him in the crook of her elbow. "It's time we gave him a name now that he's here." Kate hadn't wanted to do so before, for fear something would go wrong, but now she was eager to christen him.

"What do you have in mind?" Michael asked, sitting down beside her. "I know you've been thinking about nothing else since I left."

Kate gazed up at him, not sure how he'd react to the name she'd chosen. "I want to name him after Pop. You know, Joseph, and I thought we'd name him after you, too, Joseph Michael, maybe."

"Joseph Michael Reed," Michael repeated slowly. "Sounds good, if we can call him Joey for short. I've always liked that name."

"Joey," Kate murmured, gazing down at the tiny baby. She smiled. "That fits him perfectly. Welcome to your new home, Joey. The three of us are going to be very happy together."

"Let me hold him," Michael suddenly demanded. Pleased that he wanted to, Kate waited for her husband to get settled into the rocker, then carefully lowered Joey into his lap.

Michael was smiling down at Joey, obviously as besotted with him as she was. "Who was that on the phone? Your office?"

His smile faded somewhat. Michael nodded. "Yeah, they wanted me to come up and sort out a problem they had on a deposition but I told them I wasn't about to miss my son's first day at home."

More than anything else he could have ever said, his words filled Kate with pleasure. Happily, she watched him rock their new son and felt for the first time that they were going to make it together. Michael was finally ready to be a husband to her and a father to Joey, and that was all she had ever wanted from him.

Eight

THE IRONY of her thoughts of the day Michael brought Joey home was not lost upon Kate. She had discarded her initial wariness over Michael's sudden interest in adoption and fatherhood, had fallen in love with Joey right off the bat. Now after a month of holding him, diapering him, feeding him, she loved him so much that the thought of giving him up was inconceivable. She couldn't even think about doing it without getting sick to her stomach. There had been signs, of course; she knew them now, in retrospect. Michael's secrecy, his nervousness and constant pacing and checking at the windows. He'd feared all along these men would come for Joey, and he'd been right. He'd paid for his deception with his life.

Her throat constricted, tears threatening as she relived the moment of Michael's death. She shook her head, forcibly pushing the ghastly image out of her mind, unable to think about it anymore. She was safe at the moment, but she had to get on the move early tomorrow. She had to get to Van Buren and contact Gus at the Carter County sheriff's office. She'd leave at dawn before the killers got started again. But why were these men Russians, if that's what they were? Who were they? Why would they be involved, she asked herself, until a possible answer suddenly occurred to her. Unless Joey was from Russia instead of the Philippines! Could that be it; could he have come off the Russian black market? She'd heard of Americans adopting babies from Romania and Bosnia, and she supposed Russian orphans could be obtained the same way. She looked down at Joey, wondering if he could have come from one of those places, smuggled into the country like some kind of exotic bird.

Appalled at the possibility that Michael had been a part in any such hoax, Kate felt weak again. She ought to eat something; she had to keep up her strength. The thought of food revolted her, but she dug in the pack anyway. Maybe she could stomach some crackers. She ripped open the top and forced herself to eat one. It had little taste.

Joey was not having the same problem. He was slurping happily, his eyes half closed in the ecstasy of peace and quiet. He interrupted his enjoyment to watch as she stood up and stripped off her damp sweatshirt. Shivering in the chilly air, she got on her knees and rinsed some of the mud off it in the tiny stream, then laid it out beside the fire. She did the same with her jeans, then built up the fire to a good hot blaze to warm up the cave.

Wearing T-shirt and panties, she picked up Joey and snuggled him close as she leaned against the wall, covering her bare legs with the other quilt. Her mind revisited her dire predicament, detailing everything she'd been through, and her first inclination was to disbelieve any of it. She couldn't quit thinking she was trapped inside a horrible dream, that she'd wake up soon in her own bed, with Michael safely beside her.

Maybe she should just stay put for awhile, here in the cave where it was unlikely the killers could find her. Good God, she was miles out in the wilderness, away from any road. There was no way Michael's killers could find her. The forest was too rugged, and she'd hidden her trail too well.

It stood to reason they'd realized she'd crossed the river. Still, they couldn't be familiar with this terrain. Unlike the peculiar man in the jungle fatigues. He might still be slinking around, watching her, waiting for her to come out into the open. Or waiting for her to sleep. Kate felt a shudder start at the base of her spine and undulate with hair-raising dread all the way to her scalp. She stared through the mouth of the cave into the dark night. Afraid of what might be out there, she pulled on her damp jeans, just in case he did come, then withdrew the filet knife from its scabbard and laid it close beside her leg.

She had to move swiftly. Get to the authorities. Gus might already be looking for her. Surely someone had heard the barrage of shots the men had fired on the river. She lived a good distance from her neighbors but the gunfire would echo for miles over water. Van Buren and its environs weren't used to violent gun battles. She contemplated about what might be going on with Gus and his deputies. Surely Gus knew by now she'd disappeared since he made a habit of checking on them before he went off duty.

It dawned on her that she still had the portable radio. She shifted Joey to her left arm as she searched in the pack for the radio, found it and shook it out of the plastic bag, hoping the batteries hadn't gotten wet. She laid Joey on the ground between her legs for a moment as she fiddled with the dial. Nothing for a few seconds, then to her relief a buzz of static. Rolling the wheel with her forefinger she found no stations, then realized that she probably couldn't pick up the signal from inside the cave.

Rising, she ducked out the opening and squatted where she could keep an eye on Joey. Working with the dial, she finally hit a station playing hard rock that blared so loudly she cringed in dismay. Desperately she fumbled to shut the thing off, then sat frozen. If her pursuers were still out there, or the man in camo, they could've heard it echoing through the trees. They could be up and moving again right now, coming toward her. She stared fearfully out into the dark trees and listened. All she heard was crickets and cicadas but now she was nervous again, afraid to relax.

Turning the volume very low, she finally found KWOC

out of Poplar Bluff. The disc jockey was hosting the Oldie Goldie hour. Fats Domino was crooning, bringing back memories of Kate's childhood when Pop let her stand atop his shoes and danced her around the cabin's living room. *I found my thrill-oh on Blueberry Hill-oh.*

She propped the radio on the rocks, went inside and picked up the baby. She didn't want to let Joey go for a moment, even though he needed to stretch and squirm after being cooped up all day inside the sling. She felt the blue receiving blanket by the fire and found it dry and toasty. She wrapped him up, and with belly full and content, he slept against her shoulder almost at once.

Outside again, she sat cross-legged beside the radio, patting Joey's back. She closed heavy eyes, thinking about the grueling chase, incredulous now that she'd escaped with only scratches and bruises. But she had come very close to death that day, she and Joey both, so close it terrified her.

Her eyes snapped open as the radio newscaster came on, a woman with a soft, alluring voice a lot like Marilyn Monroe's, and began a rapid summary of the top-of-the-hour news. What time was it? Kate wondered, as the woman went on in her fawning, dulcet tones.

"*Our top story continues to develop.*" The woman sounded a bit more animated now as though she was growing excited: "*A Van Buren couple is now being sought by the authorities in connection with the kidnapping of a baby from a wealthy St. Louis family. Although our reports are sketchy at this time, the Missouri State Highway Patrol has identified the female accomplice as Kate Reed, a woman well known throughout this region as the winner of a bronze medal in the marathon nearly three years ago at the Olympic games. . . .*"

Astonished, Kate bolted upright, startling Joey awake. He fussed a little but Kate hardly heard him as she stared down at the radio.

"*. . . Kate Reed's husband, Michael Reed, a former Van*

Buren resident and well-known criminal defense attorney in St. Louis, is also on the run from the authorities. The kidnapped infant is purportedly still in their possession. If anyone should sight either of these individuals, the Van Buren police is asking that you call 911 without delay or contact the Carter County sheriff's office or the Missouri State Highway Patrol. Both kidnappers are considered armed and dangerous, and the public is warned not to approach or try to apprehend them. In other news, the Missouri Senate voted in favor of repealing . . ."

Kate couldn't believe her ears. Kidnapped? Now they were accused of kidnapping Joey? Who had come up with that absurd charge? Good God, had Michael lied to her about that, too? She stared down at Joey in stunned disbelief. Could Michael have actually had a hand in something that terrible? Obtaining Joey off the black market was one thing, but kidnapping him? Oh, God, surely he couldn't have done such a thing.

In her heart she admitted that he could have done it, probably had done plenty of illegal things through his practice. Had the men chasing them been his accomplices in the abduction? Was that why they wanted Joey? To hold until his parents paid the ransom?

She squeezed her eyes shut as *Moon River*, the smooth version from Henry Mancini, began to play on the radio. If Michael had done it, the police would think she'd played a part in it, too. And the killers thought she'd double-crossed them. That's why they were so determined to murder Michael and her. Oh, God help her, she was in worse trouble than she ever could have imagined.

Nine

KATE CAME AWAKE with a start, heart hammering. She lurched upright and grabbed the knife, instinctively aware something was wrong. Rigidly straining to hear any sound outside, she stared at the dusty shaft of sunlight slanting across the cavern floor, fearing armed men would burst in at any moment. A few seconds passed without attack, and she forced herself to relax a little, wondering if she'd been dreaming the danger. Then she heard it, a strange, low-pitched buzz very close beside her. The hairs on the back of her neck quivered and stood up as she slowly turned her head and looked down at Joey.

A snake lay close beside the baby, a huge one, so near that its flat, triangular head nearly touched his blanket. Oh, God, oh, God, the orange and black bands were unmistakable in the dim light. A timber rattler, the biggest one Kate had ever seen.

Sheer, unmitigated aversion shook her to her bones. Timber rattlers were the largest poisonous snakes in Missouri, and this one was five feet long and as big around as a grapefruit, its head alone as big as Kate's doubled fist. It was stretched out close to the fire, drawn by the warmth. And she'd already disturbed the deadly pit viper enough to make him flick his rattle.

Kate's heart thudded harder inside her chest, every muscle tensed tight, her instincts telling her to snatch up the baby, get him away, now, now, before it's too late. Her stomach rolled with helpless horror. She'd never been so close to a venomous snake. She forced herself to remain still, knew she could not make a quick movement that might cause the rattlesnake to strike. But she had to get Joey away! She couldn't stand it, it was almost touching him! Oh, God help her, a timber rattler was so deadly. If it bit either of them, they'd die in agony.

Swallowing hard, trying to subjugate the rising panic, she clenched her fists and forced herself to think rationally. She had to drag Joey to safely, slowly, carefully, without disturbing the viper. She inched her left hand toward the bundled baby. The snake lifted its head. Its black, elliptical eyes focused on her. Kate stopped moving. The rattler twisted nervously, its rattle brushing Joey's legs as it began to coil. Its tail rose very slowly and loud rhythmic clicking filled the quiet cave.

Kate's stomach dropped. It was coiling to strike. She could remember Pop's warnings about how snakes could lunge at people, but only for about a third of their length. Joey was much closer than that, and now the rattlesnake's neck was undulating into the deadly "S" curve, probably thinking her prey. Or, oh, God, what if it thought Joey was the prey? Snakes that size could disengage their jaws and swallow small animals whole—squirrels, chipmunks, even rabbits.

Gooseflesh rippled her skin, making her tremble like a leaf. The snake twisted its head side to side and drew its tail into a tighter coil. She'd never be quick enough with the knife. It'd get her before she could kill it. She had to do something, distract it, throw something, a stone, anything, to make it strike away from Joey.

Kate groped the ground beside her for a rock, then caught her breath as Joey began to rouse. He whimpered and kicked inside the blanket. Oh, no, no, the snake was twisting toward the baby and finishing its coil. Thinking only that it was going to bite Joey if she didn't do something, she lunged away from the baby, yelling and clapping her hands. The timber rattler turned and struck, launching its long, heavy body at her.

Screaming, Kate jerked back to evade the bared fangs,

then panicked completely as it fell writhing near the fire. She snatched up a handful of burning coals and hurled them as hard as she could at the twisting, rattling serpent. The snake recoiled under the rain of fire and slithered like a sidewinder into the shadows. Kate grabbed Joey and fled the cave, scrambling hysterically down the ledges, sobbing and shaking, taking to the trees and not stopping her flight until she heard Joey making strangling sounds against her breast.

Afraid he was choking or bitten, she dropped to her knees and jerked open the blanket. Joey lay on his back staring up at her, and she frantically examined his arms and legs, but when she looked into his face again, she realized that he wasn't hurt at all. He was laughing. She couldn't believe it at first. She'd never heard him laugh before, not the giggling, gleeful little sound he was making now. She stared at him, stunned, then he did it again, the same funny little chortle. He thought this was all amusing, their mad scramble down the cliffs, the way she was panting and sobbing, all done for his entertainment.

Joey smiled, kicking and gooing, as if nothing had happened, and Kate buried her face against him. She felt his little fingers tangle in her hair and hang on, and she wept hysterically, the sound muffled against his body. She had to get him to safely, she had to, before something terrible happened to him.

After a good, hard cry, she forcibly pulled herself together, sat up, looked around, and realized she was making too much noise. For the first time she felt the sharp burning sensation inside her palm. She opened her hand and found the skin red and throbbing. It hurt like hell and she cradled it against her chest. She had to get going before the men came. She had to have her backpack. Oh, God, she had to go back inside the cave.

It took several minutes to dredge up enough courage. The rattler's long gone, she told herself as she reclimbed the cliff, then repeated that reassurance a few more times outside the cave's entrance. Joey was crying now, hungry for his morning bottle. She had to feed him, had to get the canned milk and the rest of the supplies. She bent and peered into the opening. She didn't want to put Joey down on the ground, but she didn't want to take him inside either.

"Okay," she said, "Okay, suck it up, do it."

She still didn't go inside.

"Okay, the rattler's a mile away by now. You probably scared it as much as it scared you."

Kate didn't believe herself.

Finally she forced herself to edge just inside the mouth. She searched the darkness but didn't see the viper. Her pack was against the wall where she'd used it as a pillow. She began to react with long, awful shudders that crawled up her back like wakes behind a boat, and she heard herself make a low, repulsed moan at the back of her throat. Inhaling deeply, she held the air inside her lungs and stepped carefully, watching the darkness where the rattlesnake had slithered, listening for its lethal buzz. When she got close enough, she grabbed the strap of her knapsack and jerked it toward her. Nothing moved, so she pulled her sweatshirt, quilts, and baby sling away from the fire where she'd spread them to dry, then backed warily to safety.

Outside she took a moment to get a grip. She hated snakes, even the little green garter snakes she often found in her backyard. Her hand felt on fire now, and she didn't know what to do for it, had no medicine, nothing to doctor it with. She tried to remember what she'd heard about treating burns, any plants or natural forest remedies, thought of aloe, then remembered something about plunging burned skin into cold water. She took a moment to get Joey settled across her chest in the sling, but he was throwing a screaming, twisting fit. She had to get out of there, now, before someone heard him, but she did take a moment to submerge her injured hand in the creek.

Shivering all over, she realized her hand was the least of her problems. Her knee hurt more, brought on by the abuse of the day before. Her whole body was stiff and sore. She wasn't used to running for her life, falling down hills and floundering through frigid, rushing rivers. This life-or-death struggle was far different from jogging or riding a bicycle. She looked around, listening for any kind of threat each time Joey stopped wailing long enough to take a breath. She heard nothing but her own distressed breathing.

For the first time since she'd seen the snake, she put Joey down but only long enough to pull her sweatshirt over her head. The sun was up but hidden by a thick bank of rain clouds that grayed the day to dreary. She wasn't sure what time it was. She hadn't gotten much sleep, tossing and turning, and startling awake every few minutes from one terrorizing nightmare after another.

Going down on her knees, she set about taking care of Joey's needs. She had to quiet him before they could move on. Otherwise, his cries would bring their pursuers down on top of them. Praying the killers weren't close enough to hear him, she lifted him, grimacing and trying to support him with the back side of her scorched hand. When she cradled him against her shoulder, he felt very tiny and helpless.

Briefly she wondered about his real mother, whoever she was, especially if he'd been abducted, and it took no imagination to envision how frantic the poor woman must be. But she didn't want to think about Joey belonging to someone else, couldn't conceive how horrible it'd be to have your baby snatched away. She didn't want to think of her husband lying dead either, a bullet lodged in his head.

Thrusting the terrible thoughts aside, she went to work, crooning to Joey about how much she loved him as she quickly removed his soiled diaper and cleaned him with water from the stream. She quickly wrapped him in a fresh Bounty diaper and put his gown back on, and then he was happy as a lark, gurgling up a storm. Kate was glad he didn't understand about big, poisonous rattlesnakes and maniacal Russian killers. Her nerves quivered as she glanced up at the caves, and she hoped she could find a safer shelter next time.

Despite her resolve to keep her mind blank, thoughts of Joey's real family haunted her, and she wondered who they were, how Michael had become involved in stealing their baby. Had he hired killers to do his dirty work? But why would Russians be involved? Where had he met such men? None of it added up. Joey's mother must have gone crazy for the last month, wondering if her baby was dead or alive.

Michael's story about the unwed Filipino mother must have been an out-an-out lie. How many deceptions had Michael fed her, after all his reassurances that everything was aboveboard? All the legal documents she'd signed, the medical records proving the mother was healthy; everything must have been a sham. She'd believed every word her husband had told her, had swallowed it all because she'd wanted a baby so much. How gullible she'd been! How could she not have seen through the deceit? Probably because Michael had played her like a fine-tuned fiddle, as he had so many other times during their marriage. Now because of him, she was being hunted down like an animal.

Even worse, if she did make it out of this ordeal in one piece, she might have to give Joey back to his real parents. God help her, she wasn't sure she could. It wasn't fair, none of it, but she had to concentrate on getting help, then letting the authorities handle the legalities. She'd never been in trouble before. Maybe she could convince them of her innocence. At least they weren't trying to kill her as Michael's Russian accomplices were.

A sense of urgency streaked through her. She didn't have time to sit back and figure out how she'd gotten into this predicament. She wasn't safe yet. She had to feed Joey and get on the move again. She rinsed out a baby bottle, struggled with her burned hand to use the can opener, diluted the milk with clear spring water and prayed Joey'd take it. Thankfully he did, and she secured it in the elastic band and took off, stepping carefully, now on the lookout for snakes. She had another long walk ahead of her today, but even if she pressed hard, didn't stop often, she couldn't make it to Van Buren for several days. Once there, though, Gus would protect her. Until then her primary concern was to evade her Russian stalkers. She was under no illusions about them. They were probably in the woods now, hot on her trail.

The morning was becoming more overcast, with a stiff breeze pushing smoky clouds across the sky like an eraser cleaning a blackboard. It looked like rain, and she hoped to God it didn't pan out. Her journey was going to be hard enough without plowing through sucking mud and driving rain. If the thunderstorm that was threatening materialized, they'd have to hole up somewhere again. Possibly inside another cave. She wasn't sure she could bring herself to do that, but she would have little choice if she didn't find a logging road or trail that would take her out of the woods.

After about an hour of walking, Kate's knee ached worse and her burned hand throbbed unbearably. She stopped when she heard a muffled *thut-thut* of helicopter rotors beating somewhere downriver. She wondered if the State Highway Patrol was searching the sandbars and forested banks for her. Maybe Gus had found her missing and put two and two together about the St. Louis kidnapping. He knew they'd adopted Joey about the same time; he'd been out to visit him countless times. Or had the authorities found Michael's body and deduced he'd been involved somehow?

The awful moment when the young Russian shot him in the head had been running like a rewinding video tape inside her head. She was next. Maybe she'd get lucky; maybe the police would capture Michael's killers before they got her. Even as she hoped that would happen, she knew it was unlikely. The men chasing her were professionals; it was a miracle she'd gotten away the first time.

Kate set her jaw, anger rising. Mentally she stiffened her backbone, surveying the thick forest tracts stretching in every direction. They'd come after her, all right, there was no doubt about it. They would kill her and take Joey. God only knew who'd get him after that, but it was unlikely it'd be his real family now that the abduction had gone so wrong.

"I won't let them take you, Joey, I swear to God I won't," she whispered to Joey.

Her pursuers were not close at the moment or she would have heard them shuffling through the dead leaves littering the forest floor. Not so the strange bearded man, who could tiptoe around without a sound, but if he'd wanted them, he'd had them in his gun sights. He was probably miles away now. She thought again of Pop's friend, John, wished he'd happened on her instead of the hermit, wished she knew where to find him, but she couldn't depend on that long shot.

What she had to do was throw her pursuers off her trail, trick them, send them on wild goose chases while she made good her escape. Pop had taught her how to track, and part of that was to recognize false trails. If the men after her weren't trained trackers, and she doubted they were, by God, she'd leave them a few calling cards to remember her by. She had to use her wits, outsmart them. There were things she could do to delay them. She'd be damned if she'd make it easy for them.

For almost an hour she did just that, nerves constantly on edge, eyes and ears alert for any movement in the quiet woods. She backtracked her own footsteps, doubled back over her trail, crisscrossing several times and making dead ends in the middle of sticky briar patches. She broke branches and twigs leading away from the trail atop the ridge on which she intended to walk into Van Buren.

When she happened upon a nest of swarming yellow jackets hidden in a leaf-choked depression in the ground, she smiled coldly and set a trap that the men following her wouldn't soon forget. She worked hurriedly but took enough time to do the job right. It would pay off in the long run, and while she meticulously laid a trail straight into the lethal mass of buzzing yellow jackets, she enjoyed a pleasurable vision of the big blond with the earring who'd accosted her in her kitchen blundering into that particularly nasty surprise.

By the time she was done, the sun had come out briefly and lit the forest like a new-car showroom. She was sweating profusely and took another moment to stoop beside a creek she'd been following. She dipped her burned hand into the water and bathed her flushed face, drank thirstily, then filled Joey's empty bottle with fresh water. Then she struck off in earnest, beginning to feel a little better about her chances.

Now they were on her turf, and they no longer had the element of surprise on their side. They'd find out that she wasn't quite the sitting duck anymore, not like she'd been when they'd burst into her home. And they sure as hell wouldn't take her baby without a fight.

Dmitri allowed young Misha to take the lead as they fanned out in the dense undergrowth where the woman had left a trail. The entire situation was completely out of hand. Kate Reed was making them look like greenhorn amateurs, vanishing into thin air, and none of his men, other than Yuri and himself, were adept woodsmen and trackers.

After she had given them the slip at the river, they'd returned to the cabin to dispose of Mike Reed's body. Dmitri had ordered Andre and Nikolai to ditch him somewhere no one would find him. While they'd weighted him with stones and sunk him in the river, he and Yuri had gathered supplies from the house so the whole team could head back upriver where the girl had escaped. Yuri had finally picked up her trail on the opposite bank of the river, and they'd tracked her until dark, then spent an endless night listening to Misha complain about the hardship. His nephew was a spoiled boy.

At dawn they'd struck out again and had been trudging through dense, impenetrable ground cover ever since. Andre and Nikolai walked behind him, talking about how they were going to visit Disney World after this job was done. They were debating whether to go in the fall or winter after the tourists had thinned out. They wanted to visit Pleasure Island where the nightclubs were, then fly out to Las Vegas. Dmitri wished they'd shut up and think about Kate Reed; he was sick to death of hearing about their love affair with America.

Off to the right, a little ahead of Misha who walked point on the left, Yuri moved swiftly along as if on a short stroll instead of an all-day hike. He was more than proficient in the woods, expert at tracking deer, and eventually he would find Kate Reed's trail. She was lucky to have escaped them the first time, but getting through this kind of untamed wilderness with a tiny baby was another story. Nevertheless, his admiration for her was growing by leaps and bounds. He found himself resisting the idea of executing her the way Vince had ordered.

Instead, incongruously, incautiously, he had been harboring the idea of finding her, interrogating her first to determine if she was as guilty as her husband. He had a feeling she was as fascinating in person as she was resourceful in evading them. He was actually looking forward to meeting her. The idea of capturing her, holding her against her will, had begun to excite him. He'd had women whenever he wanted them but never any kind of serious relationship. Mostly he'd contented himself with the expert services of high-class call girls out of Moscow, and he'd invariably choose strong, athletic women like his Alina had been. Like Kate Reed was.

Dmitri wondered how Kate Reed would act once he had

her under his control, if she'd beg as her husband had. No, he didn't think she'd plead for mercy. And he didn't think she'd last much longer out here in the wilderness alone. She was a clever woman for sure, but she had to be exhausted, couldn't have gotten much sleep, not after all she'd been through. They'd catch her before the day was out, and not a minute too soon, since he'd heard the sound of search helicopters since early that morning. No doubt someone had alerted the authorities to gunfire on the river.

"Over here, uncle," Misha suddenly called out from a distant stand of cedar trees. "She pushed through here not long ago. The bracken's bent over and broken where she lay down in it."

All of them, including Yuri, shifted course, moving at an angle toward his nephew's position. "Beat the bushes for her. She could be hiding somewhere in all these briars," Dmitri said in a low voice to the two men behind him. "Spread out and keep quiet."

Dmitri moved cautiously toward Misha, thinking the thick ground cover hid countless places the girl could use to ambush them. She might have gotten her hands on a gun somehow, perhaps from the cabin, but he didn't think so, or she would have fired on them a long time ago. They were getting close now. Her tracks were appearing more often, her trail easier to follow as she tired. His eagerness leapt, and excitement rushed through his blood. The time was at hand, he knew it; he could almost taste it.

"There, on the branch, Nikolai, a piece of her clothes," Andre said softly, pointing with his gun to a tangled thicket close to Nikolai's position.

As Nikolai pushed his way through the prickly thorns and tangled vines, moving cautiously, Dmitri thought it an odd path for the woman to choose. It didn't take him long to figure out why. When Nikolai let out a bloodcurdling scream, Dmitri crouched down and jerked the Beretta out of his shoulder holster. Andre already had his gun drawn as he approached his partner but began to shriek, too, as Nikolai ran toward him, his hands beating at his head and shoulders. It was then that Dmitri heard the ominous buzzing and saw the dark cloud of yellow jackets swarming after the two hysterical ex-policemen.

Dmitri and Yuri quickly backed away as the men tried to outrun the stinging horde in a headlong dash toward the creek they'd forded about fifty yards back. Both were yelling at the top of their lungs, and Dmitri cursed under his breath as Yuri joined him, his gun out and ready.

"She's begun to set traps," Yuri commented, pointing out the obvious. "Reed was right. She knows the tricks of the woods."

"Yes, she's quite a woman."

Yuri gave him a surprised look as Dmitri slid his pistol back into his shoulder holster. The woman was clever, all right, a fitting adversary. He wet his lips. He couldn't wait to get his hands on her.

Kate stopped and listened. Miles away, through the vast empty woods, she could hear a man screaming, maybe two men. She smiled coldly. They'd found one of her little surprises. She suspected they'd blundered straight into the yellow jackets, just as she'd intended. Good, she hoped they were stung so badly they swelled up like blowfish. In any case, the delay bought her some time. Time she desperately needed because now she knew for sure they were coming after her. If they were close enough to hear, they were close enough to catch up to her.

Trudging on, she made good progress, keeping to the ridge where she could peer down over the forest floor where they'd have to come after her. Occasionally she'd climb outcroppings of rock or wade for awhile down one of the small creeks meandering toward the river. Joey had slept for the most part, but when he was awake, she'd take him out of the sling and hold him backwards against her chest so he could kick and look around. She kept up an amazing pace, considering the condition of her knee and seared palm, but the cloudy day made the grueling hike cooler and less exerting.

A long time after she'd heard the men yelling, Kate stopped and sat on a large flat rock to rest her leg. She rubbed her aching knee. If only she'd had on her leg brace when she'd been surprised at the cabin. Some mornings she did put it on when she expected to have to load and unload the canoes at the bait shop. Without it now, her knee was beginning to feel as bad as it had that first time she'd gone down on it, during her last competition at the Olympics. She'd been almost to the finish line when she'd fallen.

It had been a day like today, cloudy and windy, but extremely hot with a thunderstorm brewing. She could remember the taste of ozone in the humid air. She had been ahead from the start, and she'd kept her lead. But as she'd neared the stadium where the race ended, the sky had darkened to the color of charcoal briquettes and a veritable floodgate had opened on the marathon runners. She could remember distinctly how the thunder had boomed suddenly, rolling like a giant's roar over the crowd. . . .

The fans, so cheerful and eager to root her on until the crash of thunder, took off like frightened rabbits for sheltering trees or bus-stop overhangs, as the dismal gray gloom spoiled their fun. The next bolt of lightning struck somewhere off to Kate's right, so violently that the ground shook beneath her feet.

Jerking her head, she expected to see a tree toppling to the ground. She never saw the oily puddle on the macadam, hidden by the mist and rain, until her right foot slid across it, turning her ankle and sending her off balance. She tried to stop her fall but couldn't, and went down hard on her bad knee.

Sheer agony ripped up her leg. Her vision blurred and her stomach knotted as shouts sounded in front of her. Somehow she saw a bunch of photographers running toward her through the downpour. Groaning with pain, she got herself up into a sitting position but she could feel her bone scraping against something. She held her knee immobile, grinding her teeth to stop from screaming. She looked behind her. No one else had crested the hill.

Kate clamped her jaw. She wouldn't quit, not when she was so close to the finish line. She managed to get up somehow, later she wouldn't understand how. Her kneecap felt as if someone had hammered a spike deep into the bone. She staggered and stopped as a young South African appeared at the top of the hill. When she saw Kate was struggling, she increased her pace.

C'mon, c'mon, try, you've got to try, Kate told herself. She attempted to run, and a sour acid bubbled up the back of her throat. A white-hot streak of pain shot from her knee to her ankle every time she put her foot down. She couldn't run, could not do it, but she could walk, she could limp, she could drag her leg, if she had to.

Rain beat down harder, sharp, chilling her, or maybe that was the pain, but she refused to give up. She trudged on. She'd make it, God help her, even if the street flooded and she had to swim. Time seemed to slow down, get on its knees and crawl the way she wished she could, and she glanced back over and over, watching the little South African. She could see her bright red hair now as she came closer and closer. Elsa, who was Kate's best friend among the competitors, was in sight now, too, and a girl from Spain was some distance behind her. Kate dragged on, half pulling her leg behind her.

The spectators were running back to watch the dramatic new development, despite the downpour, smelling blood, yelling encouragement, but all she could think about was the ancient gladiators and the way the Romans held their thumbs down when they wanted death. When her leg went numb, she began to worry about injuring herself irretrievably. It was heavy now, stiff as a pirate's peg leg, as if her knee joint was frozen.

When the South African passed Kate, the youngster didn't look at her injured rival. She didn't slow her gait or change expressions. What was her name, anyway? Something weird, a nickname that was dumb. Kiki, that was it, little Kiki was passing Kate up. Kiki was going to win the gold.

Kate set her jaw and dragged her dead leg onward, staring at the red, green and blue South African flag on the girl's back. Okay, Kate, there's still the silver, and that ain't so bad. Pop had said that a million times when she'd come in second in high school events.

The bone was grinding against something that hurt so bad, maybe a tendon, she didn't think she could stand it. She was maiming her leg by keeping up like this, probably killing her chances of ever running again, but she couldn't make herself stop. She was too close, inside the stadium now, thousands of fans cheering her on. She kept on, thinking how long, how hard, she'd worked for an Olympic medal.

Never give up, never, she thought, but gave up that weak mantra when Elsa came abreast of her on the last curve of the final lap. Her friend did look at her, and Kate saw the sympathy in her pale blue eyes. She, more than anyone, knew what this was costing Kate.

"Go for it, Elsa!" Kate hissed through gritted teeth, the rain pelting her face and muffling her words.

Elsa surged ahead, and Kate gave in to the urge and got down and crawled on her hands and knees like a baby. Behind her the girl from Barcelona was just entering the stadium but she was very tired. Kate was close to passing out. She bit the inside of her cheek, an old trick that hurt enough to get her mind off her knee. Pulling herself along as fast as she could, she kept on because now she knew she was close enough to actually win the bronze. Ten more yards.

Three guys with remote television cameras on their shoulders found her crippled plight and with great glee were determined to make Kate their own personal version of the agony of defeat. A youngish man with a blond beard and shaved head was walking backward in front of her so he could get a better shot of the excruciating effort twisting her face.

"Get the hell out of my way," she ground out, half expecting him to ask her to smile for the camera.

The photographer moved to the side but stayed in her face, probably hoping she'd faint so he could zero in on her eyes as they rolled back into her head. Angry with him, and her knee, and the storm that made her lose the race of her life, she reached down deep, deeper than she'd ever done before. She pulled out every shred of inner strength she had, every vestige of will.

She'd come to win a medal, and by God, she was going to get one. She forced herself up to a standing position and, incredibly, managed to run, limping heavily. But she didn't have to stand the pain for long. The finish line was five yards away. She'd stand beside Elsa again as she had in Munich. She'd win for all the folks waving American flags, for Pop, for her friends back home cheering for her, but most of all, she'd win it for her new husband, Michael.

Her leg gave out again two yards from the ribbon, now a broken, crumpled wad on the pavement. She began to crawl again. Elsa was on the other side of the line, apparently forgetting her own exhaustion as she jumped up and down and yelled Kate's name. Even Kiki was waving her on.

The press were having a heyday; in a shark frenzy over this painful little drama, even they, the vultures of the airwaves, wanted her to win the bronze.

A few more inches and she'd have it. The exhausted Spaniard was close behind her, running hard, her arms pump-

ing. Kate could hear her feet slapping against the wet pavement. With the last ounce of effort she had left, Kate threw herself forward, pulling herself bodily over the tape.

"You did it, Kate, I can't believe you did it!"

That was Elsa's voice; the Swede was on her knees now, giving Kate a hug. Kiki was there, too, smiling. Kiki reached down and took hold of Kate's hand, squeezing it and telling her how brave she was. Even the Spaniard said olé, or something that sounded like olé. Cameras clicked. Reporters gathered. Rain pelted. Thunder rumbled. Then Michael was there, her husband, the man she loved, the man with whom she wanted to share this final moment of triumph in her career. He was pushing the others away, leaning over her, and she clung to him, wanting the comfort of his arms.

"My God, Kate, you did it, you won! I'm so proud of you!"

Kate stared up at him and basked in the warmth and worry in his eyes as he knelt down and supported her. She lay back against him in the pouring rain and closed her eyes. Too tired even to smile, her body finally gave up the fight. Her mind shut down, and darkness rushed in like a cloud of liquid black ink, and all the shouts and rain and rolling thunder slowly faded to utter stillness. . . .

As the vision of that incredible day faded from her mind, Kate sighed and rocked back and forth with Joey in her arms. Now Michael was dead, and she would be, too, if she didn't find a way to keep going. She'd made it that day in the rain, she thought, and she'd make it now. She couldn't let herself give up, not because her leg was aching badly enough to fall off, not because she couldn't use her right hand, not for any other reason. She pushed herself upright and started off again up the crest of another hill, using flat rocks and mossy patches to hide her footprints. Never give up, never.

Ten

BY LATE AFTERNOON, the sun had come out and broiled overhead for hours. It was hot for May, especially the way Kate was exerting herself. Despite the thick canopy of trees shading the woods, she wasn't sure she could keep up her swift pace. Worse, she'd misjudged the distance to Van Buren. She wasn't anywhere close yet, and it might take days fighting through the tangled vegetation with its hordes of biting insects.

She was already fighting exhaustion, her limp more pronounced with each step, and Joey was restless confined in the sling so long, crying and fussy from the change in milk, and wanting out, wanting things back to normal. She finally stopped, each of his loud wails making her cringe. Sounds bounced off the woods like subterranean echoes; the killers would be able to hear him, even if they were still acres away.

Her stamina nearly drained, she dragged herself to the top of the next hill, to a spot where she could glimpse Current River glinting like a silver ribbon through the tree branches. She collapsed to the ground and leaned back against a fallen log, resting for a moment before she spread out Joey's receiving blanket and laid him on his back. She changed him again and buried the soiled diaper under some rocks, afraid he wouldn't be able to tolerate the Pet Milk.

She couldn't stop yet. Not this soon. There was still enough daylight to find a road or trail that led out of the woods. If she couldn't find one, she'd have to spend the night in another cave, and she couldn't imagine being able to shut her eyes for fear of snakes, no matter how desperately she needed sleep. Last night she'd startled awake a hundred times in a cold sweat. Tonight would be no different.

Stretching out her leg she massaged her sore knee for a few minutes, unwilling to get up. She kept trying to relax her muscles and forget her burned hand while Joey enjoyed his freedom. Once he got his fill of twisting and kicking he'd go to sleep. She couldn't complain; he'd held up better than she had.

Not too far distant a sound filtered through the peaceful twittering of the birds. Alarmed, Kate jumped up and scanned the trees. It wasn't a man's voice like before; it was the baying of hounds. Oh, God, the killers had dogs. Or maybe it was the police, the state patrol with their K-9 units, or even the FBI. She'd seen bloodhounds in action, and a woman with a baby didn't have a chance against them. Dread filled her as the shrill barking echoed through the trees, and her heart stopped when the first animal burst through the brush about fifty yards away.

Within seconds, half a dozen more dogs crashed through the undergrowth, snouts to the ground or high in the air sniffing out her scent. Their howls echoed eerily up through the trees as they zigzagged between saplings and tree trunks, unimpeded in their purpose as they jumped logs and crashed through tangled thickets. Not trained bloodhounds but a pack of wild dogs, unchecked by human handlers, running in a snarling, bloodthirsty pack.

Heart pounding, Kate grabbed Joey and took off. She'd seen deer carcasses ravaged by starving dogs, torn to shreds, devoured to hair and bone. These vicious animals bore no resemblance to tamed household pets but were scavenging beasts. The yelps of the pack filled her ears as she ran, shrill with bloodlust and the instinct to kill. Oh, God, what would they do if they got hold of a defenseless baby like Joey? She had to get up high, climb a cliff or a tree, get Joey off the ground where they couldn't get at him.

In the grip of full-fledged hysteria, she flew down the other side of the ridge, her eyes locked on the towering granite cliff rising before her. She had to get there, climb far enough off the ground to evade the excited dogs. She looked behind her and saw the leader of the pack about twenty yards behind her, a huge black and tan hound, roving back and forth across her trail, baying with the heat of the chase. A German shepherd was abreast of him, running hard, straight at her. Kate sprinted blindly, branches whipping her face and arms, Joey's frightened screams in her ears, her only hope reaching the bluffs before the dogs knocked her down.

Heaving in great clumps of air, she finally burst through the dense mulberry bushes that hid the granite face of the cliff, sobbing when she saw the sheer wall rising above her. No footholds, no rocks shelves, nothing to climb. Kate whirled around to fend off the attack but not quickly enough. The big shepherd leapt at her on the full run.

The hundred-pound dog slammed against her side, sending Kate sprawling. She twisted her body and protected Joey as the shepherd snarled with bared teeth, saliva dripping from his jaws. The hound went for her leg, and she screamed in pain as its sharp incisors sank into her ankle. Forgetting her burned palm, she jerked out the knife and slashed wildly at the growling animals. The hound yelped in pain and slunk off to the side, and Kate sobbed as three more of the pack formed a ring around her, snarling, feral, fangs bared, fur ridged high on their backs. Panting, terrified, holding Joey tightly with her left arm, she pressed away from them, screaming and brandishing the knife if one of them darted in at her.

"Get, get outta here," she yelled, letting go of the sling long enough to grab a heavy rock. She hurled it at the shepherd, glancing it off his snout. He retreated but another one took his place. Kate's fingers clutched the knife as tightly as she could, and she yelled at them again, knowing it was only a matter of time before several attacked at once.

A huge black mongrel inched around to one side of her position, his strange yellow eyes never leaving her. When he leapt, she swiped him with the blade but not before he got his jaws around her tennis shoe. She kicked as hard as she could, frantically stabbing at him, sobbing, slashing with all her strength, then almost as quickly as the attack had begun, it ended. Inexplicably the snarling, keening animals fell back.

Her lungs laboring for breath, Kate pushed herself deeper into a shallow aperture cut into the rocks. Her sock and shoe were bloody where the shepherd had sunk his teeth, but she ignored the pain and kept her knife ready. She knew it wasn't over yet; they'd come in for the kill.

"Hey, down there, you just about got yourself eat up, didn't you?"

Kate jerked bodily at the sound of the voice. Twisting her neck from side to side, she picked out a figure high atop the cliff and stared in disbelief at a little girl, maybe nine or ten years old. The child placed a couple of fingers to her mouth and sent an ear-piercing whistle out through the woods. The killer dogs came bounding up around Kate, tails wagging, menacing stances gone.

"They must've thought you was a coon," the girl called down to Kate. "Stay put, okay? I'll be down in a jiffy."

Drawing in great gulps of air, Kate tried to calm Joey's hysterical shrieks and keep a wary eye on the animals circling around and swinging their tails as if she was suddenly their best friend in the world. She couldn't quite believe her eyes when the little girl came striding along the base of the cliff, friendly as could be, smiling widely with the most beautiful white teeth Kate had ever seen. She had dark red hair, braided neatly into long pigtails secured with yellow ribbons to match her T-shirt. She wore blue-jean shorts and what looked like brand-new white Adidas tennis shoes.

"I bet you was scared of them dogs till I called them off, weren't you?"

"Yeah. Real scared." Kate cupped her forehead with her left hand, striving to regain control of her nerves. She wasn't having a whole lot of luck.

"They do look a mite fierce, I reckon. But they ain't bad when you get to know 'em some."

"Yes, they sure do." Kate eyed the seemingly docile dogs, then bent to examine the bite on her ankle.

"Uh oh, did Leech get you in the foot? He don't mean no harm but he's a big old thing. That bite deep?"

"It's bleeding but I guess it's not too deep." Kate was having trouble controlling her voice. She kept looking at the dogs, expecting them to metamorphose again into the murderous beasts of moments ago.

"My name's Millie Mae Jones. Who're you?"

Kate looked at the girl, disbelieving they were calmly having this discussion. The hounds had plopped down on their sides to rest now, their tongues lolling out the sides of their mouths. Tired from the hunt.

"Kate. Kate Reed."

"What're you doing way out here in the deep woods? You get lost, or something like that?"

Kate debated whether she should tell the child the truth, that she was being chased by men trying to kill her. She decided Millie Mae Jones wouldn't believe her anyway.

"Oh, look, you got a baby in that thing on your chest. It's so little, ain't it? Can I see it, Miss Kate? I love little babies more'un just about anything but my hound dogs."

Kate struggled up to her feet, keeping a firm grip on Joey. "I don't know. He's still pretty scared of the dogs."

"Oh, they ain't gonna hurt him. Don't you worry, Miss Kate, they're trained real well. The truth is they're my brothers' dogs, you know, for hunting and keeping people outta our cornfields. But I always take'um out on a run in the woods on days I don't have to go to school." She smiled her wide, movie-starlet grin, her teeth dazzling against her tanned, freckled skin.

"You live on a farm?"

"Yes'm, just up there, over that ridge." She pointed. "That next one, you can see it if you look real hard."

Kate nodded but her heart sped as she searched the little girl's face. "Do any of your brothers have a car that could take me into Van Buren, Millie Mae? I've got to get there as soon as possible." She hesitated. "There are some men after me, Millie Mae. Bad men. They shot my husband, I saw them. I've got to get to the sheriff's office before they find me."

"My brother Matty's got a big truck." Millie Mae's big blue eyes got even rounder. "Gee, some men shot your husband? That sounds like something straight off *America's Most Wanted*, don't it? That's me and my brothers' favorite TV show, that and *Cops*. They both come on together, every Saturday night. You seen them?"

That's a good sign. Maybe they're a law-abiding family, Kate decided, as she took Joey out of the sling and turned him around until his back was against her chest. Her foot was throbbing now, but the baby stopped whimpering and peered curiously at Millie Mae, who got up close in his face, smiling and talking baby talk.

"Why, look at you, you're just as little as a mite, ain't you? And pretty as you can be. Is it a boy or a girl, Miss Kate?"

"A boy. His name's Joey."

Millie Mae reached out and held Joey's hand, then grinned hugely when he clutched her thumb. "He likes me already, don't he? You just come along home with me, Miss Kate. My brothers are great big and strong. They won't let those bad men get you and little Joey, I promise. You'll come, won't you? It's not far, and I got some good salve I can put on where Leech got you on the foot."

Kate figured she didn't have much choice. After the wild flight from the dogs, she was dead on her feet. If the people after her were anywhere in the vicinity, they would have heard all the screaming and barking. If Millie Mae's brothers had a vehicle and would drive her to Van Buren's sheriff's office, Gus Shelter would protect Joey and her. Or a phone. Maybe they had a phone!

"You sure your brothers won't mind you bringing me home?"

"Oh no, I know they won't mind. They'll like you right off, I reckon, because you're so pretty. They like real pretty girls, every one of 'em do."

"How many brothers do you have, Millie Mae?"

"Four. All of them are older'un me. Mama died when she had me so Granny took care of us. She's gone now, too, just last June, but she was real old, almost a hundred years old."

"I see." Now that things were a little more under control and her heart rate was back to normal, Kate gazed out over the hollow and hill rising on the other side of it, fearing she'd see the blond man targeting her with a rifle's scope. "Have you seen anybody else in the woods today? Men dressed in black?"

"No, I ain't seen nobody but you all day. The hounds would've sniffed out their trail if they'd come through here. Hey, could I hold Joey for a minute, if I promise not to drop him?"

Relieved that the Russians hadn't made it this far anyway, Kate reluctantly handed Joey over but the little girl seemed to know how to hold a baby. She cradled him in her arms, then beamed up at Kate.

"He's just so pretty."

"Yeah, he sure is." Kate looked up into the deepening dusk. "It'll be dark soon. Think we better get going?"

"Yes'm. I ain't supposed to be out here in the woods after dark. It's the rules. Matty gets real put out at me if I wander too far off, even with the dogs along to protect me. You see, he promised Granny he'd watch over me and the pigs just before she died and went to heaven."

"The pigs?"

"Granny raised hogs so we'd have plenty of bacon and ham."

Millie Mae seemed to think that was explanation enough. Kate knew there were many hill families along the river who scratched out a bare existence on the hard, rocky ground, rough characters for the most part, but Millie Mae seemed all right. Her clothes were clean, and someone definitely had taught her manners.

"C'mon, Miss Kate, I'll show you the way. That sure is an ugly bruise you got there on your cheek. I bet it hurts something awful, don't it? We'll smear a gob of Granny's salve on that, too, if you like."

Kate nodded, then limped along beside the young girl. She could feel blood trickling down into her shoe but it wasn't terribly painful. Her hand throbbed like the devil, but things could be worse. At least the dogs were bounding through the trees in front of them, controlled by Millie Mae's whistled commands. If her Russian assailants did catch up to her, she'd have a better chance with Millie Mae and her great big, strong brothers than she would all alone in the woods. She listened to Millie Mae's chatter and Joey's answering goos, thinking the skinny little girl with the freckles and the pigtails might just turn out to be the best friend she ever had.

Eleven

BY THE TIME they reached the outside perimeter of Millie Mae Jones's farm, Kate was having serious misgivings about tagging along with the little girl. It had taken about twenty minutes of walking, or limping in Kate's case, to reach the hilltop dirt farm where Millie Mae lived. More disturbing, the well-tended patches they'd passed so far included not just the usual farmer's crops of corn and beans but plenty of healthy marijuana plants as well. Millie Mae's brothers obviously ran one of the lucrative marijuana farms that had become increasingly prevalent throughout the rugged Ozark Mountains.

The fields through which Millie Mae led Kate in a rather circuitous route were small in size, the illegal plants set inside newly planted corn that would eventually grow tall and screen the marijuana from casual observers. Pop and Gus both had been aware of this new, drug-driven culture among hillbillies who'd turned in their white-lightning stills and gone to more profitable endeavors. The sheriff had also mentioned that most of these hill marijuana growers were completely, utterly ruthless. Now Kate was headed straight into their hidden conclave.

As she ducked underneath camouflage netting strung up between trees as concealment for a small metal-roofed shed, she felt a sinking sensation—maybe because of the empty cans of ethylene alcohol tossed into a big pile—that a crude methamphetamine lab was being operated inside. It occurred to her that the weird guy with the long beard and camo fatigues could be one of Millie Mae's big brothers. If that turned out to be the case, she felt fairly certain he wouldn't shoot her down in cold blood. That's more than she could say about everybody else after her.

"Watch out now, Miss Kate," Millie Mae said, turning to look back at her, for some reason having decided to call her that from the first. "You have to watch your step and go just where I go or you might step into trouble. Matty and the boys, they've set a bunch of booby traps for the law so they cain't be giving us no ugly surprises."

Oh, God, Kate thought, there was no doubt now, though there hadn't been much to begin with. She was walking smack dab into a den of petty criminals who might just as soon shoot her as look at her. She stopped warily and glanced around but saw no booby traps or alarm systems. Through some cleared woods about thirty yards up the hill, she could see a long mobile home set in a grove of oak trees. There was one of those new, smaller satellite dishes attached to its roof, painted in a streaked green-and-brown pattern. Indeed, the entire trailer was painted with olive green and black camouflage. Camouflage was turning out to be quite the thing out here in the hills. Like it or not, she was about to associate herself with drug traffickers. On the other hand, these guys couldn't be any more lethal than the killers after Joey and her. She frowned, realizing they very well could be as bad, or even worse. She just hoped to God, they weren't.

The pack of dogs flew ahead, apparently pleased to be back home, heading in loping strides toward a tall, beefy man who'd rounded the back of the long, well-kept trailer house. It was a big one, set up on concrete blocks, also painted olive, with a dark green awning supported by rough-cut poles forming a makeshift front porch. He was wearing blue denim overalls with a black plaid flannel shirt underneath it. Unfortunately, he wasn't the man she'd met in the woods the day before.

"That's Matty up there," Millie Mae informed Kate as she halted long enough to tickle a forefinger underneath Joey's chubby chin. "He's the oldest of us all. And he's the biggest, too. He's strong enough to pull his truck with a rope held between his teeth. He's got real strong teeth. We all got 'em. That comes from our Granny. Matty's been thinking of getting in that strongest man in the world game, you know, the one they're always showing on that ESPN sports channel. He'd win it, sure as shootin', I know he would. Why, I've seen him throw empty whiskey barrels all the way up to the barn loft, that's before Luke accidentally caught it on fire. But Matty's almost got it all built back good as new now. We keep the dog pens up there where the horse stalls used to be." She gestured at a large, weathered barn farther up the hill behind the trailer.

Millie Mae seemed proud of Matty's accomplishments, and Kate wondered why Matty had felt the need to pull a four-wheel drive vehicle around with his teeth. The future strongest man in the world watched them approach. Some kind of assault rifle stood propped against the side of the mobile home, the kind the army used, near enough for him to grab at any moment. With each step that brought them closer to the man, Kate's apprehension grew. She clutched Joey a little tighter.

Matty was looking bigger by the minute, in fact. She wasn't sure she'd ever seen a man with such a powerful, barrel-chested physique. He wasn't real tall but his arms were absolutely massive, his biceps the size of large hams. His hair wasn't red like Millie Mae's but lemon blond, his skin florid, apparently the kind that burned easily in the sun. He had a sunburn now. His sleeves were rolled up, and she could see homemade tattoos on each forearm. One of them said MOMMA. She couldn't see what the other one said, and wasn't sure she wanted to know. As they crossed the last patch of sunlight filtering through the giant oak trees, she saw he held a can of Budweiser in his right hand. On his left hip he wore a very large pistol in a black leather holster. Please, please, don't be drunk, Kate thought, as Millie Mae greeted her scary-looking brother.

"Matty, look here what I found out in the woods. The dogs sniffed her out," Millie Mae called out happily, as if she'd been on an Easter egg hunt and come up with the coveted golden egg. "Ain't she pretty? Got big, brown eyes just like Granny's."

Oh God, don't say things like that, Millie Mae, Kate thought, stomach plummeting. She waited nervously for the beefy man's response. Up close she could see that he really wasn't very old, probably early thirties at the most, around Kate's age, maybe. She watched Matty squeeze the aluminum beer can until it was flat as a pancake, then toss it aside. It hit with a metallic clink on a bunch of other beer cans. She hoped he hadn't drunk them all at once. He scratched the blond chest hair showing at the open throat of his shirt. He didn't say anything, just stared at Kate. Kate gave a tentative smile, hoping that if he was drunk, it was the passing-out kind.

Millie Mae was chattering on like an excited little bird. "And she has a little baby with her, too, Matty. Cute as a shiny new button, ain't he? She let me hold him in my arms for a minute. Some bad men are chasing her so I told her we'd be glad to help her get away from them. You won't let 'em hurt her, will you Matty? I like her and I promised her you wouldn't let nobody hurt her."

Millie Mae's voice had grown a trifle worried, no doubt because of Matty's continued silence, and that worried Kate, too. She could feel her heart thudding against her breastbone. The man was immensely strong, she noticed again, broad shouldered and as muscled as Paul Bunyan, or even the Blue Ox. He wore a short, unkempt beard and looked like the most dangerous, ignorant redneck Kate had ever laid eyes on.

"How do you do, ma'am?"

Kate nearly sagged in relief, her hold on her baby relaxing a little. Then a tiny bit more when he smiled broadly, displaying the biggest, whitest set of truck-hauling choppers Kate had ever seen. Even on Los Angeles television news anchors.

"How do you do," she answered with the same absurd courtesy. As if they'd run into each other at the afternoon Bible Study at the Baptist Church Missionary Society. A dreamlike torpor was seeping over Kate again, making her feel as though she was still slogging her way through the living nightmare she'd been in for the last forty-eight hours. He seemed civilized, so Kate decided to tell him the truth, or most of it. "I, well, I appreciate your sister bringing me home with her like this. Some men broke into my house yesterday morning. They killed my husband." It was the first time she'd verbalized Michael's murder, and she swallowed down the enormous lump that came into her throat. "I ran into the woods with my baby but they've been chasing me. I couldn't have made it much farther on my own."

"Probably DEA." Matty Jones nodded with sage assurance. "Them guys're always busting in on people's private property. They ain't found us here yet, and they won't without being real bad-assed sorry they messed with us four Jones boys."

Kate stared at him, left speechless by his comments. Finally, she said, "Well, I'm not really sure who they are. They might've been some enemies of my husband. I saw them kill him." Michael's dead, she thought, still unwilling to believe it. How could something so awful be true?

"Those fucking bastards," Millie Mae said reassuringly, patting Kate's arm.

Kate turned astonished eyes on the child. Matty was quick to reprimand his little sister.

"You watch your mouth, Sissy girl. You know good and

well you ain't allowed to talk like that until you get to be twelve."

Matty was smiling at Kate again, so she shook off her shock and forged on as Joey began to squirm inside her arms. Her voice sounded a little shaky. This place made her nervous. "If you could just take me down to Van Buren to the sheriff's office, he'll help me, I know. He's an old friend of my grandfather's." She cut off abruptly, hoping to God that Gus hadn't arrested Matty for anything.

"You talkin' about Gus? Gus Shelter? He's the one what put my baby brother in jail for drunk and disorderly t'other day. But Little John needed to dry out a spell, anyway, I reckon. He likes his Bud, just like the rest of us." Matty shook his massive, shaggy head. "Gus's a good ol' boy, I guess, even if he has to arrest us, and whatnot. So he's a friend of yours, huh?"

"Oh, yes, for years and years," Kate answered, nodding cautiously but encouraged, now that she and Matty Jones had a mutual friend. She wondered if Gus knew the Jones boys were harvesting weed up here. "He took over from my grandfather. You might've known him, too. His name was Joseph Macon, but everyone called him Pop."

"You kin to Pop Macon? Well, I be damned and tarred black. He arrested me my very first time. For bustin' up the Coke machine down at the IGA store." Grinning, Matty shook his head as if that was his fondest memory. Apparently it was. "Those were the good ol' days back then, but Granny tanned my butt with her rug beater for gettin' in trouble so young. I was just nine, no older than little Sissy here. That's why I don't want her usin' swear words till she's of the right age."

Not surprisingly, Kate couldn't think of anything to say to that, either. Nodding agreeably, she told herself that she and Joey were still better off here than alone in the woods chased by murderers. And luckily, Matty Jones wasn't one to hold a grudge against his arresting officers. She smiled, hoping that would be enough.

"Do you think you might be able to take me on into town, Mr. Jones? I'd be mighty obliged." Kate realized she was lapsing into hillbillyese but felt it was the right thing to do under the circumstances.

Matty's response was a hearty laugh that seemed to roll up from somewhere deep inside his beer gut. "Nobody's called me that in a coon's age, I reckon."

His teeth shone remarkably white against his ruddy face, just like Millie Mae's. It was amazing out here in the hills, without fluoride in the water. The rest of him didn't match up so well. He was pretty dirty, especially around his fingernails. She tried not to notice the greenish line at the base of his bull-like neck. She watched him pull out a dirty handkerchief and blow his nose.

"Well, ma'am, I don't suppose I can get you there tonight. I got a man I gotta meet later this evenin' but I can probably carry you down there first thing in the morning, if you want. The truck's not here right now anyways. My brothers had to run up Eminence way, then they was gonna swing back and pick up Little John out of the jailhouse but they'll be back before dark." He noticed Kate's bloodstained sock for the first time. "Hey now, you might want to bind up that ankle before it gets some infection to it. Here, you can use this." He offered her his soiled handkerchief as a bandage. Kate was circumspect enough to take it.

"Ol' Leech bit her before I could whistle him off but it ain't deep," Millie Mae explained quickly.

"It's nothing, really," Kate managed weakly, certainly not wanting to offend him, but not comfortable holding his filthy handkerchief either. "I'd sure appreciate that ride into town first thing in the morning. I can pay you for your trouble once we get there."

Matty nodded. "Sissy, take her on inside and let her rest a

spell while you cook up some supper for the boys. I have to say you do look a tad weary, ma'am."

Kate had to laugh a little. "I'm tired, all right. I've been walking for miles."

"You're safe enough now. We don't cotton to strangers snooping 'round. We shoot first, then ask them what their bidness was."

Kate didn't know whether he was kidding or not, so merely nodded until he gave his big radiant smile. She returned it obligingly, as if she thought he was Robin Williams all over again.

"You wouldn't have a telephone, would you? So I could call Gus?" she asked hopefully.

"Nope. Them phone lines don't come up this far in the hills. I got one of them cell phone gadgets hooked up in my truck, though, but it don't work good unless you take it up on the ridge. You can try it, if you want to, when the boys get back with the truck."

"That's very kind. I appreciate it."

Matty nodded and grinned at her until she felt a little uncomfortable. Please, please, let me and Joey make it through till tomorrow, she prayed silently, following little Millie Mae into the camouflaged mobile home. She turned back at the door, just in time to see Matty pick up his automatic weapon and stroll off toward his marijuana patch.

Inside the trailer Kate's eyes latched first on the gigantic big-screened, color television set that took up most of the living room.

"Ain't that a beaut?" Millie Mae said, nearly convulsing with pride. "And it's got surround sound and a little baby picture up in the corner so Matty and Mark can watch the Nascar races while Luke and Little John and me watches the *Dukes of Hazzard*. Since we put up that little antenna thingy outside on the roof, it works real good."

"How many channels do you get?" Kate asked, trying to

be polite as she examined the dim interior. No lights were on, and most of the curtains were drawn.

"Fifty-four, and some of 'em even got people speaking in Mexican and that language they use up in Paris, France, you know, that place where Princess Diana got killed in that car wreck with her boyfriend named Dodi. Can't make heads or tails of that, though. None of us can, not even Matty."

Besides the gigantic TV set there was an old couch that made into a bed, one that was still pulled out and piled with lots of rumpled blue sheets and a blue-striped feather pillow without a case. Three old vinyl recliners repaired with silver duct tape sat in a row under a gun rack that held at least nine guns. Dozens of boxes of ammunition were stacked on the bottom shelf. The kitchen was to the right and looked fairly clean enough, except for a sink full of dirty dishes. The whole place smelled strongly of scorched hog fat.

"Luke left the bed pulled out again. He's the biggest slob of all my boys," Millie Mae was informing Kate now. "Granny used to whup him regular for making messes. Now he don't get in no trouble unless Matty's in a foul mood and slaps him up the side of the head." She grinned tolerantly.

Kate followed her around the edge of the sofa bed and down a narrow hallway, listening as the child gave her the fifty-cent tour, pointing out the rooms as they walked by. "That's Matty's room, he shares it with Little John when he's not in the county clink for drunk and disorderly. I'm glad he's coming home today, though. Mark and Luke share this one here. This's the one we keep the pots in till the seedlings get big enough to grow outside."

Kate peered into a room filled with marijuana plants set underneath about a dozen portable fluorescent lights. Most were about a foot high. Millie Mae had stopped at the end of the hallway.

"I got this one all to myself now that Granny's gone to meet her Maker. We used to share it. Being as I'm the only girl and all, Matty says I'm special. Do you think I'm special, Miss Kate?"

Kate looked at the little girl, wondering what on earth would happen to her in the future, living out here in the middle of nowhere with brothers who were hard-drinking criminals. "I don't know what Joey and I would've done if you hadn't come along," she said truthfully.

"Oh, now, I'm just glad I ran into you. We never get any company, except for when the truant officers come around if I go to missin' too much school. Now let me see, I guess we need to get some salve on that dog bite. I keep it cool in the icebox so it won't go to smelling too rank. It'll help heal up all those cuts and bruises of yours. That's the bathroom. It's got running hot water and all." She grinned, proud again. "Matty got us all this stuff selling weed. Granny wouldn't let him do it while she was living, but now he does whatever he wants cause he's the boss of all of us. Hey, you want me to take care of Joey while you get washed up?"

Kate couldn't help but clutch the baby more tightly but she tried to hide it. "No, I guess I better give him a bath, too, while I'm at it."

Glad when Millie Mae nodded agreeably and headed for the kitchen, Kate carried Joey into the bathroom. She was very glad to see the lock on the door, and she felt better the minute she pushed the button in the door handle. She laid Joey down on the counter and felt tears burn as he looked up at her out of his luminous black eyes.

"We're going to make it through all this, Joey, I promise you," she whispered. "Just hang in there a little longer." The thought of his being kidnapped, of possibly having to hand him over to the authorities hit her like a punch in the jaw, and she thought for a moment that she couldn't bear it, couldn't do that, no matter what happened. It couldn't be true, could it? That he was abducted, that he had a family waiting and worrying to get him back safely?

Carefully she scooped him up and cradled the back of his head tightly against her neck. "Oh, Joey, I love you so much."

Joey fought her tight hold, so she blinked back her emotion. She couldn't worry about that now anyway. She had to get to Gus first, then she'd deal with whatever happened next.

Joey was content to lie atop the counter and watch the round lights above his head while Kate opened the taps and held her injured hand under it, then splashed cool water on her face. She lifted her head and stared at her reflection. She hardly recognized herself. Her blond hair was filthy, most of her ponytail pulled out of the rubber band. She had a purpling bruise on her left cheek and a deep scratch across her right one. She looked as though she'd just been dragged off the battlefield at Shiloh. And she felt as bad as she looked. She gazed yearningly at the shower stall, wanting a bath more than anything. She jumped when Millie Mae's voice sounded just outside the door.

"Hey, I got one of Granny's dresses out here in case you want to wear it. I think it'll fit if you want to. She was real skinny like you."

Kate opened the door. Smiling, Millie Mae handed Kate an old-fashioned sundress made of red-and-white–striped cotton. Circa 1940, by the looks of it. "It's a pretty old one, but I like it the best. It's too big for me so far but I'm gonna wear it someday when I get older. Matty got a picture of Granny wearing it when she was young like you." She shrugged. "I reckon you can wear it, if you like, or not, since you got your own stuff so dirty. Got a pair of sandals, too, if you want em."

"Thank you, Millie Mae. You're really very sweet, you know that?"

"Oh, that's okay, Miss Kate, you'd do the same for me, wouldn't you now? Here's that salve, and if you want to, you can wash yourself up real good before dinner. You can use my towel, if you want to. I only used it since Tuesday past. Mine's the bright yellow one. Each of us have a color and we can't use no other. I get them washed now and again when I got the time. I'm pretty busy taking care of the boys and doing my homework."

"Where do you go to school, Millie Mae?"

"Down in Van Buren. Mrs. Berry's third grade class. I make really good grades. I've learned lots of stuff since I've been watching that Learning Channel on television. That, and Discovery, too. I saw all about them originals, you know, the black people way down there in Australia. Boy, they sure do live hard. We all have a lot to be thankful for, don't we, Miss Kate, livin' here in the U S of A?"

Kate nodded, realizing she meant aboriginals, trying to absorb the sheer absurdity surrounding her.

"I'll be getting back to the kitchen now. Bye."

Millie Mae ran off down the hall, and Kate shut the door, carefully locking it again. Breathing more easily, she stared at herself. Only until tomorrow, she thought. Make it through the night, Kate, and they'll take you in to Gus's office. She would just have to be vigilant and watch her every move. And *their* every move, especially Matty's. He seemed harmless enough, but she had a bad feeling that he wasn't harmless at all, and neither were his three brothers who would no doubt show up any minute, armed and dangerous, and exhilarated from their latest drug run.

Twelve

KATE STOOD in the shower stall for a long time, warm water sluicing gently over her bruised, aching body. She held Joey securely against her chest, and the baby seemed to enjoy the soothing bath as much as she did. She tried not to think what would happen next, afraid to see into the future. Everything had gone crazy, her calm, predictable world upended into chaos. She hoped fervently that Matty and Millie Mae would come through for her. She felt relatively safe with them; at least she wasn't being hunted through the woods like Bambi in deer season.

After awhile she forced herself to step out of the shower, wet hair streaming down her back while she swaddled Joey inside Millie Mae's bright yellow towel. She quickly dried herself and wrapped the towel around her head. Joey was doing fine; only a couple of scratches to show for their harrowing ordeal. Kate, on the other hand, looked like Mike Tyson's punching bag. She remembered how nervous she'd been the day Michael brought Joey home. Despite all the baby books she'd read, she'd been leery of handling him or giving him a bottle.

Now, after two days fighting for survival, Kate knew that infants were hardy little creatures, a lot hardier than she, whose emotions were as battered as her poor abused body. But she would make it, God willing. She'd come too far and been through too much to give up now. If she could last one more night with these strangers who promised to help her, she and Joey just might make it.

Joey was squirming around on the vanity in front of her, jabbering in his secret language. She retrieved the paper towels and masking tape from the knapsack, vowing the first thing she'd buy after hitting town tomorrow was Luvs, packages and packages of them. She hoped to heaven that Millie Mae and her big burly brother kept milk in their refrigerator, but had a feeling they drank more Bud than anything else. Even Millie Mae, she feared. Joey caught hold of the paper diaper she was fashioning and hung on, his eyes latched on it.

"Now you let go of that, you little stinker," she whispered, laughing softly. Her heart warmed with love, she scooped up the baby and held him tightly. She loved him like her own, more than anything else in the world. She wondered if he really did have a family out there somewhere, frantic with worry. She shut her eyes, her lip trembling. He was all she had, now that Michael and Pop were dead. She couldn't let anyone take him away from her.

Her throat ached with sorrow. All her life she'd lost the people she loved, one after another, beginning with her parents. She couldn't bear giving him up; she had to cling to the hope that she wouldn't have to. After all, she didn't know for sure he'd been kidnapped. Michael's deceptions had permeated everything; maybe the kidnapping accusation was a lie, too. Maybe an infant had been abducted but it wasn't Joey. It couldn't be Joey; Joey was hers.

Determined to believe that, to think positively so she wouldn't lapse into despair, she hurriedly diapered him and pointed his tiny arms into the sleeves of the soiled sleeper. She tied the drawstring at the bottom, wishing she had one of the clean, downy-soft sleepers in his closet at home. Leaning against the counter to keep him from rolling off, she unwound the towel on her head and let her hair straggle around her shoulders. She stared in the mirror as she finger-combed the tangles, deciding against using the hairbrush lying on the counter—one that had enough red and blond hairs caught in the bristles to construct a Dolly Parton wig.

Other than the family's obvious propensity to use a communal hairbrush, the bathroom was very clean. Millie Mae was well groomed, but Matty, well, Matty was a different story. He could use a long, hot bath, several of them, in fact. On the other hand, there were five brand-new toothbrushes in the wall hanger, each one replete with a personal box of Rembrandt toothpaste. If nothing else, the Joneses valued dental hygiene.

Joey had been googling as she babytalked him, but now he was beginning to get sleepy. Thank goodness he had a place to lie still, without being jostled around. He deserved a long, peaceful nap. She thought of how close the timber rattler had come to biting him, and shivered with renewed revulsion. She needed to get dressed quickly. She'd had to work up enough courage to take a shower and only ventured *that* because of the lock on the door. She hoped Millie Mae's bedroom door was similarly equipped.

Millie Mae's old-fashioned sundress with its matching red sweater still hung on the wire hanger. She'd seen pictures of her own grandma in similar garb, and realized the outfit probably dated from the Second World War. She lifted the full skirt and examined the fabric, finding it in remarkably good shape for vintage forties.

Kate stepped into it, thinking it odd the zipper was on the side, but the dress fit her tolerably well, only tight across the bustline. Ruffled straps crisscrossed in back but had adjustable button holes, and she struggled to make them fit. The skirt hit her slightly above the knee because she was tall, but she was only glad the dress was clean and dry, and not caked with river mud. She slipped on the short sweater and felt like a normal human being again.

The jelly jar of salve looked rancid, but when she unscrewed the lid, it smelled all right—not good, but not rotten. She dipped her forefinger in the oily gunk and gingerly smoothed it over her burned palm and bitten ankle, then dabbed some more on the cuts and bruises covering her face and arms. The deepest wound was on her temple and still throbbed if she turned her head too quickly. She hadn't had time to worry about it, but now she parted her hair and eyed a raw scab about the size of a quarter. Now she wasn't even sure where she'd gotten it, but thought it might be during her mad scramble to get across the river. That terrifying flight seemed an eternity ago but was only yesterday morning. She winced with loss, eyes burning with tears when she thought of Michael lying on the ground, shot to death. They'd finally begun to get their lives in order, their dreams of renewing their marriage, raising Joey, all dead with him, destroyed forever. Kate forced the horrible pictures from her mind and concentrated on doctoring a long, ugly scratch down the back of her arm.

A short time later she heard the sound of tires crunching upon gravel outside the mobile home, followed by a distinct roaring sound, more like a farm implement than a family vehicle. Her pulse quickened, not sure who to expect, fearing it might be the Russian killers or even the Highway Patrol now that she was accused of kidnapping. She didn't want to turn herself into anyone but Gus, or they'd surely take Joey away from her.

Cautiously she raised the tiny window above the commode. She breathed easier when it appeared to be Millie Mae's wayward brothers who'd arrived home. The throbbing idle came from a jacked-up black Dodge pickup truck with big chrome pipes all over it. The three boys inside seemed to be enjoying the jet-engine roar until the ignition was suddenly cut, dropping total, complete silence over the farm. The Jones boys piled out of the cab, all smaller versions of big brother, Matty. She could see him now, too, striding up to the truck from the shack she feared housed their meth lab. What if it occurred to Matty that Kate might turn him in to the sheriff? They'd never let her leave if they thought that, at least not alive.

"Where the sam hill have you guys been? I thought you mighta run into the law again."

"Nah, Matty, we stopped at the Dairy Queen and got us one of those big sundaes called Peanut Buster Parfaits, with the peanuts and stuff in it, after we picked up Little John at the jailhouse. Um, um, they put cherries and whipped cream on top if you ask 'em to, and man, oh, man, it was serious good eatin', scrumpdilicious, right, Mark?"

The speaker who liked his ice cream appeared to be a younger member of the motley-looking group. He stood a little shorter than the others and was probably still in his teens, fourteen or fifteen, maybe. He was dressed in a black Harley Davidson T-shirt and dirty denim jeans with a ripped-out knee. Kate didn't think the hole was a self-inflicted fashion statement such as the college kids liked to do. His hair was long and carroty red, held back in a ponytail low on his neck. All the Joneses had various shades of red hair, most of which were displayed in the hairbrush on the vanity.

"I don't give a shit about cherries and whipped-up cream. Did the deal go down without the fuzz showing up?"

The ice cream lover looked suitably chastised. A different brother came to his defense and faced Matty's fierce scowl. "Yeah, ain't no reason to get down on Luke. Monty showed up and said he was gonna run things by hisself now that his brother's doin' eight to ten in the Jeff City pen. Said he had a big deal going down in a couple of days with some biker gang up north and wants you in on it."

"Did he bring the dough?"

"Yeah. Cash. Luke, open it up."

"Did you count it?"

"Yeah, it's all there."

Luke quickly obeyed, setting a tan duffel bag down on the truck's hood. Matty unzipped the bag and sorted through stacks of bills held together with rubber bands. Obviously overcome with exuberance now that he'd gotten his loot, he ruffled his kid brother's bushy hair. "Attaboy, Luke. Next time don't be stopping for no snacks. You know how I worry about you and the boys." He turned to another brother, the one who'd not had much to say. He was the tallest, but not by much. "Hey, Little John, how'd you like the pokey? Did anybody make you their woman?"

The men guffawed, appreciating his witty quip, and Kate shut her eyes and felt sick. Little John vociferously denied any such dalliance, citing his fists and his big brothers' collectively vicious reputations enough to keep other prisoners at bay. When Kate slid the window back down, he was showing off the black eye he got from a deputy. She didn't want to hear any more. Maybe she should stay in the bathroom until morning with the door securely locked, or maybe she should sneak out the back door with Joey and make a run for it. On the other hand, she didn't want to make any of the big hillbillies mad at her. She shouldn't ever have come here with Millie Mae, but now that she'd made that mistake, she had to trust the little girl to control her scary redneck brothers.

"Miss Kate, you 'bout done in there?" Millie Mae's voice filtered in from the hall again. "I just about got the chicken all fried up crispy and ready to eat. And guess what else, the boys are all here now and dying to meet you. I already told them how you're as pretty as a picture."

Great. Kate hoped to God none of them were wife hunting.

"I'll be out in a minute, Millie Mae." She tried to make her voice sound pleasant and eager but feared she sounded terrified.

"Okay. I'll just leave you some sandals out here by the door, okay?"

"Okay, thanks."

"Did Granny's dress fit you okay?"

"Yes, very well."

Kate listened as the child moved off down the hall toward the other end of the trailer, heard some of the men, maybe all of them pile into the living room with a flurry of loud greetings and clomping boots, and lots of teasing for their baby sister. Kate's trepidation mushroomed as their conversation dwindled to lots of hushed whispers.

Kate had a sudden vision of them kicking down the bathroom door and dragging her out, for God knew what horrendous purpose. Oh, please, Lord, please let me make it through one more night, just one more night's all I ask. She lifted Joey, who roused enough to sputter and fuss a couple of seconds. She placed one hand on the doorknob. Still she hesitated, not wanting to leave her sanctuary. Setting her shoulders, steeling her resolve, she took a deep, fortifying breath. Okay, this is it, crunch time. Just go on out there, go along with whatever they say, do what they say, make any promises you have to. Survive through the night.

The hallway felt cool after the steamy bathroom, and as she slipped into the sandals, the delicious aroma of pan-fried chicken hit her. Her mouth watered and her stomach growled like a starved puppy. She realized then how hungry she was, how little she'd had to eat in the last two days. She hadn't even thought about food until now. She'd had a cracker or two, a handful of dried fruit, water, but that was about it. She needed to eat something, keep up her strength, in case the boys turned out not to be as friendly as their kid sister.

The entire Jones family was waiting for her in the living room. The men were all lounging around in their respective recliners. Millie Mae stood in the kitchen area, grinning from ear to ear, as if she were a magician and Kate was her best trick. All she needed was a top hat and cane.

They all stared at her as if she were something rare indeed.

"Hello, everyone," she said as brightly as she could muster with her heart beating ten miles a minute. She felt herself getting all tensed up, ready to run for the bathroom.

Then all four boys rose in tandem, even Little John, who looked a little worse for wear after drying out in one of Gus's cells. He was the closest to Kate, and she could smell him big time. The odor of unwashed underwear and urine. She smiled real friendly-like at him. One of his eyes was swollen shut, but he grinned back and nearly blinded her with his teeth. Movie-star teeth was indeed a family trait with the Joneses, all right, she thought, her eyes moving from one gleaming white mouth to another.

"This is my new friend, boys. Miss Kate's her name, and her little baby's name is Joey. She's in trouble and Matty says we can help her, didn't you, Matty?"

"That's right, sweet pea." Matty was looking Kate up and down with a good deal of interest, and Kate prayed he didn't find her the least bit attractive. She should never have taken a bath and cleaned up. That was stupid, stupid, stupid. "You clean up real good, ma'am, now that you got all the blood and dirt off you, even with all them bruises and bite marks."

"You're very kind to say so," she said carefully. "I want you all to know how very much I appreciate your help. I don't know what I'd have done if Millie Mae hadn't found me."

"Millie Mae's a good girl. Always bringin' home strays and whatnot." Matty seemed to remember his manners then, maybe because all his brothers were staring at her as if she was a Peanut Buster Parfait. "That one, there, standing by the new Magnavox, he's Luke, he's the third brother Mama bore. He got all the way to the tenth grade so he's the brains of the family." He guffawed, and poked said brain in the ribcage.

Luke was slighter of build and the only one who had on eyeglasses. They were old-fashioned rimless granny-type glasses that hooked over his ears. Kate had a feeling they might have belonged to the same grandma who had owned

Kate's dress. Luke grinned, and seemed as though he might be a bit shier of nature than the others, despite the red and blue swastikas tattooed on both his forearms.

"How do you do, ma'am?" Luke politely took off a filthy white baseball cap emblazoned with JOHN DEERE in fluorescent orange letters. A smudge of motor oil blotted out the J and the O. "Don't you worry none now about them men that be wantin' you dead and all. Nobody's gonna mess with you while we're around." To prove his mettle, he pulled up his navy blue T-shirt heralding MURPHY'S TEXACO AND BAIT and revealed a huge pistol stuck down inside his pants. Kate was not relieved but tried to appear thus.

"Thank you, Luke. But these men are dangerous. I wouldn't want any of you to get hurt because of me."

Everyone seemed to think that was extraordinarily funny. They laughed and laughed, even Millie Mae, so Kate grinned, too, very pleased to find them in such jovial moods.

Matty was the one who chose to explain. "Don't reckon nobody's ever gonna mess with the four of us together here on our own place. People 'round here know better. Pa always said, 'take no prisoners, boys, take no prisoners.' We never forgot that and it's done us to good stead, ain't it, boys?"

There was solemn nodding of heads all around, and Kate paused but knew they had no idea what kind of men they were dealing with. Michael's killers were professionals, totally merciless. "These men, they aren't from around here. I think they might be foreigners down from St. Louis—"

"I hate them foreigners and city folk worse than water moccasins," said Mark, who wore a waxed red mustache. He politely introduced himself. "I'm Mark. The second one."

"Hello, Mark." They exchanged smiles, and she was startled to find that one of his front teeth was slightly crooked. But still very white. But she was beginning to feel a bit more secure in their company, her rock-hard muscles loosening to the consistency of concrete. They obviously intended to play

Galahad to her damsel in distress, and she was all for it. "A couple of them sounded like they spoke in Russian accents, but I can't be sure. I know one of them did, a young blond guy who tried to kill me."

"Ruskies? You mean like in *The Hunt For Red October?*" demanded Luke, obviously impressed.

Kate nodded.

"We seen that movie on HBO a couple weeks back," Matty informed her, nodding. His eyes narrowed suspiciously. "What are they doing way up here in the hills?"

"I don't know who they are but I think they want my baby. That's what my husband told me before they shot him." Her voice choked a little on the last. Michael couldn't really be dead, could he? "Haven't you heard anything about this on television or the radio?"

Kate tensed, hoping they hadn't heard her portrayed as a kidnapper, pleased when everyone shook their heads.

"We ain't ones to watch much news," Matty informed her. "Too many sports channels with racin' and wrestlin'. We like to watch movies, too, when we ain't out on runs."

"So you're a widow lady now?" Mark seemed pleased about it. Kate stiffened up again.

"Can I see that little baby?" Little John came over, bringing his cloud of jailbird body odor with him. Kate was glad there was a working shower just down the hall.

"Sure," she said with extreme and utter reluctance.

"He's a little fella, ain't he? How old is he?"

"About four weeks."

"Lord have mercy, imagine that. I like babies," Luke shared with her, smiling to prove it.

"Yeah, me, too."

Millie Mae was beaming, apparently pleased by Kate's warm welcome into the household. "See, I told you she was all right. She ain't gonna rat us out, are you, Miss Kate, and tell the sheriff about the weed we grow out here?"

Everyone froze, very interested in her answer.

"No, of course not, absolutely not. I can't tell you how grateful I am for your hospitality. I'd never say a word to cause you any trouble, not after you took me in like this."

"That's okay, I keep telling her that," Millie Mae deferred, shaking her head. "We're sort of known in these parts for helping out needy folks. Granny taught us about helping your neighbors and that Golden Rule and all the Commandments in the Good Book. Ma named the boys after the apostles, I guess you noticed that, though. Not me, though. I'm named Millie 'cause my grandpa was in the military." More nodding all around and proud looks directed at Kate for her approval. "Now let's go eat before the mashed potatoes gets cold. Let's all just fill up our plates off the stove and go outside on the picnic table to eat. It's nice and warm out there. I got some milk for Joey, Miss Kate, if he's getting hungry, too."

"Yes, he'll want a bottle any time now."

"Millie Mae's a real good cook," Luke told her as they followed the little girl into the kitchen. "She makes hotcakes just like our Granny did but sometimes she puts raisins in mine, just for me."

Kate nodded and kept smiling, standing back and watching the boys heap absolutely gigantic portions from various pots and kettles simmering on the burners. Mashed potatoes and milk gravy. Canned green beans seasoned with a hunk of pork fat. Creamed corn. Cornbread. Golden brown chicken draining on a paper towel. All perfectly prepared. Kate's stomach began to churn again and she fought the desire to snatch up a drumstick and devour it like locusts in a biblical plague.

The Jones family apparently did everything in the order of their births, so Matty was the first to pop open one of the Budweiser cans in the chilled six-pack waiting on the counter. Mark came next, then Luke. Little John actually offered his place in line to Kate, but she refused, citing the excuse that she had to prepare Joey's bottle. She did so and warmed it under the hot-water tap while Millie Mae fixed both of them a heaping plate.

"I like to cook a whole heap at once so we'll have plenty of leftovers the next day. That way I only have to cook once in the evening. The boys don't mind much. I just fix the things they like the best so they don't mind eating them twice in a row."

"Well, it all smells very good. I'm so hungry I could eat a horse."

Millie Mae found that highly amusing, as if she'd never heard the phrase before. "Well, c'mon, before they come for seconds and scrape up everything that's left. Gotta be quick as greased lightning 'round here."

The picnic table was under the wide, leafy branches of an enormous oak tree, the shade cool and comfortable. Two detached benches were set beside the table, filled up by two boys on each side. Millie Mae squeezed in beside Mark at the end of the nearest bench, and Kate dragged up a rusty green metal outdoor chair and sat at the end. She was a little lower than the rest of them, but it was the kind of chair that rocked slightly and she positioned Joey in one arm to feed him his bottle.

"Does he cry much?" Little John peered down at Joey, his black eye looking very painful indeed, now that Kate saw it close up. Grease from the chicken wing he was eating covered the sparse blond whiskers on his chin with an oily sheen. Actually, chicken grease covered all their chins in an oily sheen.

"Sometimes. He's a really good baby, though."

"Wonder what them Ruskies want him for?" Matty shook his head, befuddled.

"There was a story about that the other night on *Matlock*," Luke suggested, obviously the television aficionado of the family. "They was counterfeiting American money and stuff."

"No shit," said Little John. "Bet that one was a good episode, huh?"

"I really don't know why they're after us," Kate said. "That's why I'm so eager to get to the sheriff's office."

"Don't worry, we'll get you there," Millie Mae assured her as she got down off the edge of the bench. "You want me to hold little Joey so you can eat? It's real good. You look like you could use some food inside you."

Though reluctant to give Joey over to anyone, Kate finally agreed and let Millie Mae take her place in the rusty chair. She handed Joey down and Millie Mae took over the bottle with the expertise of a trained nanny.

Kate took a seat beside Little John, but not too close. The first bite of mashed potatoes tasted like manna from heaven, some of the best she'd ever tasted. She said as much to Millie Mae.

"Yeah, Granny always told me to add a pinch of rosemary sprigs to creamed potatoes. It just makes 'em taste better, don't know why, but that's all there is to it, right, boys?"

"Right."

"Sure does."

"That's right, gonna go inside and get me some more right now."

Millie Mae simply beamed.

The chicken was excellent as well, and Kate realized she'd never been so ravenous in her life. She was feeling a lot more comfortable now among the raw-boned hillbilly boys, thinking they were probably just poor hill folk who had been forced to sell drugs to make a living. She didn't think any of them would harm her, but she wasn't sure enough to let down her guard completely. Suddenly it occurred to her to ask them about the man she'd encountered in the woods. Maybe he was a cousin or something.

"Yesterday when I was trying to get away in the woods, I saw someone. A great big guy, dressed all in camouflage."

They all stopped eating and stared at her.

"He was real dirty with a long beard and hair. I thought he might be a man named John that Pop used to tell me about."

"That sounds like the one we call Bigfoot," Mark said. "But he usually stays on t'other side of the river. He ain't friendly, that's for damn sure."

"He's plumb crazy, Miss Kate," Little John added, voice muffled by the half cup of mashed potatoes he still had in his mouth. "We're all real careful to stay clear of him."

Luke put down his beer can and nodded. "Yeah, once, we started across the river to hunt down a buck Mark was tracking and Bigfoot shot at us. Never did see him but we knew who it was. Knocked the gun right outta Matty's hand without leaving a scratch on him. He can shoot like a sonofabitch. No, uh uh, none of us don't mess with that old coot. Matty's seen him a couple of times up the road at Jumbo's truck stop gettin' his grub and stuff, but we stay far away from him, he's nutty as a fruitcake, crazy as a loon, I tell you."

"He didn't try to hurt me, or anything. Just showed up out of nowhere and scared me to death."

"We think he escaped from the loony bin," Millie Mae confided in a low voice. "You sure was lucky he didn't haul off and shoot you dead for trespassing on his side of the river."

After listening to all that, Kate felt lucky she'd survived the encounter with their Bigfoot neighbor. After they finished eating, she and Millie Mae washed the dishes at the kitchen sink while Little John slopped the hogs. It was Mark's turn to be lookout for any lawmen who might be snooping about, and the other two boys retired to the living room to watch *The Dukes of Hazzard* with North Carolina drag car races rushing by in the picture-within-a-picture feature in the corner of the screen.

Millie Mae chattered on about all the important things in

her life, including her favorite television shows. Kate found out she was extremely partial to MTV, but the cartoon network was her "bestest favorite," that and the one that was always selling the most interesting things for people to buy up with their plastic credit cards. Why, all you had to do was call and they'd send stuff through the mail to you. Sure wished they had a telephone line and she'd make Matty get some of those shiny new pans they was always advertising, pans that browned meat real evenly and would never, ever wear out, no matter how many times you used them. Imagine that, never, ever, no matter how many times you used them.

At one point, Kate had Millie Mae show her the cellular phone in Matty's truck, but she couldn't pick up a signal. Matty said she could try again later after he got back from his evening drug run. Thirty minutes later he took the truck and drove off, and Little John, finished slopping, had taken his oldest brother's place in one of the recliners. When an episode of *Xena, Warrior Princess* came on, the two younger brothers were immediately smitten and vowed her to be the most beautiful lady they'd ever seen, especially when she was riding on a horse, and tough, too, as tough as nails. Unfortunately, they decided to light up a joint to pass around and Kate soon excused herself, pleading tiredness, as the pungent odor of marijuana settled in a cloudy haze around the television set.

Once in the back bedroom Millie Mae had directed her to use, Kate locked the door and opened a window and sucked as much fresh air as she could into her lungs. A nice breeze was blowing in from outside, so she lay down on the bed and got Joey settled beside her. At least she didn't have to worry about snakes tonight. She played with him for awhile, smiling as he grabbed at one of Millie Mae's red hair bows. After he went to sleep, she lay down beside him, fully dressed, even her shoes, definitely planning to stay that way. Just in case.

Millie Mae was going to sleep on a cot in the room where they kept the marijuana seedlings, and after an hour or so, she heard the child go inside and shut the door. She couldn't hear the boys but could still faintly smell the scent of cannabis. Kate lay back and tried to relax. She stared up at the ceiling tiles where rain had seeped in. Directly above her head was a rust-colored stain shaped like the state of Idaho.

Joey had soiled his diaper earlier and she'd changed him, but she was afraid the whole milk might disagree with him. Not yet, though, because now with his little belly full, he was sleeping peacefully. She made sure he was covered securely with a soft quilt, then tried again to relax enough to go to sleep. She was so tired, maybe too tired to rest well. But she was also on edge again, now that Millie Mae's brothers were getting high. She listened to the low murmur of their voices in the living room intermittent with bursts of giggling laughter. They were watching reruns of Johnny Carson now; she could hear the familiar theme song and the roar of the audience laugh track. She shut her eyes, hoping she would get enough rest to sustain her. The last thing she remembered hearing was Ed McMahon's booming gut laugh.

Thirteen

YURI HAD PICKED UP the girl's trail just before dark the night before. Thus far she'd been adept at hiding her tracks in thorny ravines or making them stumble into yellow jackets' nests. Now, apparently, there was a fresh ingredient in the soup. Something had sent her tearing headlong through the forest, leaving them a path to follow as wide as Red Square. Dmitri wasn't precisely sure what had spooked her to such a degree, having come to the conclusion nothing much *could* shake her. Filled with admiration for the woman's courage and ability to evade them, he was astonished to find himself secretly rooting for the escape of his own prey. Despite his perversity, Dmitri's role in Kate Reed's desperate little drama had suddenly become a good deal easier. This time luck was on *his* side.

When Yuri had first spied the bent saplings and broken branches of Kate's wild flight, Dmitri suspected another of her tricks, like the stinging yellow jackets. He glanced at Nikolai. The man's face was fiery red and pitifully bloated from insect venom. Occasionally the former officer would moan furiously how he'd make the bitch pay for his suffering. Misha's face, too, was painfully blistered from scalding water. Kate Reed had plenty of tricks she didn't hesitate to use. They'd kept on strict alert since they'd started earlier that morning around eight o'clock; they had to be getting close to her.

Dmitri moved slowly, placing each foot with care, his Beretta hanging loosely in his right hand. He'd learned to expect the unexpected from this Katya. Her resourcefulness and resilience were causing him a great deal of trouble, placing his team in jeopardy, especially now that the law was involved. As intriguing as he found her, as much as he coveted the chance to get her alone and find out if she was as smart and beautiful as he thought, he needed to concentrate on getting the baby and getting the hell out before the authorities launched an extensive manhunt. His men were like fish out of water among these redneck provincials, and it wouldn't take the State Highway Patrol two minutes to figure out they'd been involved in Mike Reed's murder.

About ten yards on either side of Dmitri, Misha and Yuri were combing the woods as they walked along the base of a granite cliff rising off the hilly forest floor. She had come this way, probably late yesterday afternoon, then inexplicably turned westerly, when she'd traveled south before, parallel to the river toward the nearest town. He wondered what had caused her to change her mind and conjectured she might be sick or injured. He didn't want her to get hurt, certainly didn't want to kill her. In his eyes she'd earned respect, and he found himself sorting through various reasons he could use to justify letting her go once they got the baby. He was not one to leave loose ends, but unless it was disastrous to his own success, he would not execute Kate Reed.

When they crested the next hill they found a neatly cultivated cornfield. There was no fence or wall, but the waist-high green stalks indicated a nearby farmhouse. Yuri searched the perimeter of the corn until he found the path Kate had taken through the field. Dmitri motioned Andre and Nikolai to take point. He'd already given orders to take her alive, and under no circumstances could they risk harming the child.

The long, straight cornrows reminded Dmitri of his grandfather's farm and the happy days he and his siblings had spent there in his youth. Those early days had been good, comfortable times, and he enjoyed visiting there where many of his brothers and sisters still lived. He regularly sent them money, American dollars, to insure that Kavunov lands survived the Russian political upheavals. Someday he would retire to the farm where he'd once been so happy.

Pregnant in the wind sluicing through the corn were barnyard odors, the well-remembered stink of hogs and perhaps chickens in a coop. Probably the home place of an old man and woman scraping out a bare subsistence as Dmitri's grandparents had done their entire lives inside their generations-old stone cottage by the river. Good-hearted folks who'd not hesitate to take in a frightened woman and her baby. They'd give her food to eat, a warm bed, anything they had. Once more the desire to quit this dirty business and return home to his Russian roots burned fiercely inside him.

"Hey, hey, aaaah . . ."

Andre's loud cry awakened a flock of nesting guinea hens that flapped and squawked in startled flight, raising more racket than an air raid siren. As Dmitri jerked his eyes around, the two Moscow cops dropped into the ground like rabbits in a disappearing act. He blinked, not sure what was happening as the earth gaped open like a hungry mouth, crumbling the earth under Misha's feet as well. The boy dropped his gun and grabbed frantically at the cornstalks, and luckily Yuri was close enough to grasp Misha's shirt and haul him back from the edge. Dmitri stepped back quickly from the yawning pit, realizing a sink hole had been covered with dead cornstalks.

"Kavunov, get us out of here!" Low, urgent, Andre's voice floated up from about twenty feet down.

"Keep quiet," Dmitri ordered, helping Yuri drag Misha farther away from the pit. More dislodged dirt rained down, extending the broken earth closer to his own position. He stepped back and scanned the field for a farmer with a shotgun welcome for trespassers.

Below, Andre and Nikolai were not trying to scale the fifteen-foot dirt wall, smart enough to know the dynamics of a sink hole. When the ground gave way, it gave way. It was only a matter of time before the edges cracked again and ate up more of the field. Someone had taken effort to disguise this particular surprise for unwanted intruders. Dmitri found it unlikely that Kate had had the time to fashion anything so elaborate, but if she hadn't, they had a new problem on their hands.

"Hashish, Dmitri." Yuri was gesturing with his gun across the gaping crater. Dmitri searched among the cornstalks until he found the cannabis plants. Illegal drugs on the premises gave a whole new dimension to the problem. He didn't have long to consider his options because the sound of howling dogs thrashing through the field grabbed all his attention. Dmitri motioned for Misha and Yuri to drop back and take cover.

Within seconds three dogs burst out of the cornrows and headed straight at Dmitri. As the German shepherd in the lead took a running leap at him, Dmitri raised his gun and fired once, the report muffled by the silencer. The dog yelped as the bullet struck him in the chest, the impact hurling him backward. He landed at the edge of the pit where he lay twitching. The rest of the animals circled the dying dog, slavering, growling, fangs bared, their attack spooked by the smell of fresh blood. Before Dmitri could melt into the woods, a voice rang out directly behind him.

"Drop them guns, you bags of shit, or I'll blow your heads clean off your shoulders."

Turning his head slowly, Dmitri locked eyes with a very big, dumb-looking hillbilly type, one with a lethal M-16 rifle pointed directly at his chest. He dropped his Beretta and raised both hands. A wary glance told him that Misha and Yuri had been apprehended in similar fashion, by what appeared to be clones of the beefy man prodding Dmitri in the back with his gun. One hard shove between the shoulder blades sent Dmitri into the pit, and he tried to jump and roll but couldn't block his fall. He grunted as he hit hard, numbing his left shoulder, dirt and cornstalks caving in on top of him.

Misha was disarmed and came down hard after Dmitri, pinwheeling his arms for balance. Yuri was tossed in headfirst, body slamming into Nikolai and knocking him flat. Dmitri counted four rough-looking hillbillies ringing the pit. All were young, sunburned, muscular and covered with tattoos. All looked extremely pissed off. He got up and raised his hands, riveting his attention on the big guy who was ordering them to toss their weapons out of the pit nice and slow. They all quickly obeyed, not ready to argue with four M-16 rifles zeroed in on their chests.

"Look, man, we don't want any trouble with you guys." Dmitri kept his tone calm and his hands high. "We aren't the police. We didn't mean to trespass on your land."

"Hey, Matty, I bet they's those damned Ruskies chasing Miss Kate and Joey," one of them said with a godawful redneck twang. He was younger, with smooth apple cheeks that still had pillow creases as if he'd rocketed out of bed just in time to kill a couple of trespassers. He continued, focusing his weapon between Misha's eyes. "We oughta shoot 'em up right now and kick some dirt in on them for what they done to her."

"Yeah, and they killed Sissy's favorite hound dog, too." That came from yet another one with orange hair and a stiff, waxed mustache. He had on overalls with no shirt. Dmitri could see that his sunburn ended at the collar line and halfway up his biceps.

They all seemed to know Kate Reed rather well. Seemed to consider her a good friend, which was very bad news for Dmitri. He wondered how greedy they were and if he could get to the pistol he kept strapped to his ankle. He discarded the idea at once. With four automatic rifles trained on them, it'd be like shooting fish in a barrel. He'd have to talk his way out of trouble. They looked as though they had brains the size of shelled peanuts. Surely he could outsmart them.

"You got to listen to me. The woman's lying to you. What'd she tell you? That *we're* the bad guys? That's bullshit.

She's lying to you. She stole that baby out of the hospital nursery right after it was born. Took it from its own mother. We're here to take it back home, that's God's holy truth."

"You shut your big mouth. Miss Kate wouldn't steal no baby, no way." That was the one with imprints on his face.

A sudden high-pitched scream startled them all, especially those down in the pit. The big guy named Matty swung his weapon around, then lowered it as heartbroken weeping came from the vicinity of the dead dog.

"They shot Ol' Pete, he's dead, ain't he, Matty? He's deader than a doornail."

Dmitri couldn't see anyone but it sounded like a child, a little girl, maybe.

"I know, Sissy, don't cry. It's okay," soothed Mister Waxed Red Mustache. "We're gonna make 'em pay for killin' Ol' Pete. Pay hard."

"And for what they done to Miss Kate, too. Poor Ol' Pete ain't done nothing to deserve to get shot dead," interjected hillbilly number four, who'd remained silent until now. He looked the most dangerous, and Dmitri kept his eyes on him an extra moment. Tears, genuine ones, were running down his cheeks, shed over the dead dog, Dmitri presumed. Who the hell were these guys? Farmers from hell? And where did they get state-of-the-art U.S. army–issue M-16's? He decided to concentrate on the oldest one, who seemed less affected by the demise of Ol' Pete than the others.

"Look, Matty, you've got to believe me. She's not what she seems. She comes off so sweet and pretty, so helpless, but she's not." He glanced around, latching on Nikolai's disfigured face. "Just look what she did to my friend here. Look at his face, if you don't believe me. Does that look like something some innocent little miss would do? Tied him up to a tree and beat the shit out of him, she and her husband did it. If we hadn't gotten there when we did, they would've beaten him to death."

The rednecks took turns looking at each other. Long, questioning, wide-eyed, dumb looks. No, smarts didn't exactly run in their family. The little girl's face suddenly appeared at the edge of the hole near Matty's black combat boots.

"You killed my dog, you fucker," she said, hurling a clod of dirt down on Dmitri. He turned his head and deflected it with his shoulder.

"Now don't you be cussin', Millie Mae, you know better," the big one said absently, gently pushing her back with the toe of his boot. Dmitri had a feeling the redneck was beginning to have a doubt or two about Kate's motives. It was time to push a little.

"There's something else you guys don't know. There's a big reward out on her head. The kid's parents hired us to come down here and get their baby boy back. That's all they want and they don't care how much it costs. Help us get her and I'll give you half the reward."

Matty hesitated, thoughtfully chewing the inside of his cheek. For thirty seconds or more he lunched on it while the rest of them waited and watched. The little girl was still crying over the dog's carcass and occasionally pelting Dmitri with clumps of dirt. Dmitri was glad she was not the negotiator.

"How much dough you talkin'?" Matty was very suspicious.

These two-bit marijuana peddlers were uneducated hicks; it wouldn't take much to make them roll over. "Three hundred grand. I'll give you half, a hundred and fifty thousand to split up any way you want. She's up at your residence, isn't she?"

"Residence?" repeated the one who'd been crying a minute ago, obviously tenderhearted despite the swastikas decorating his arms. "What the hell's that supposed to mean?"

"You took her in, didn't you? Helped her, right? Believed her cock-and-bull story. But she's lying, playing you guys for fools. She's bad news. She kidnapped that baby. Haven't you heard the copters flying all over the place? The cops are after her, and she'll bring the law down on you. The feds'll bust up your business and get you for harboring a felon. You don't want that to happen, do you, because of her?"

Matty raised his gun to Dmitri's head. The other rednecks followed suit like a synchronized firing squad. "What'd you know about our bidness?"

"We saw the marijuana plants growing out here but we don't give a damn. All we want is the girl. Hand her over and we'll take her back to St. Louis. That'll get the authorities off your back and out of here for good. The kid's parents are filthy rich. You'll get your half of the money, I swear to God you will."

"Why should I trust fereigners like you, who ain't even real Americans?"

Dmitri decided to lie a little, fairly confident he could control the quartet of dumb-ass boys once he was out of the hole and armed again. "You can keep one of us as hostage until we bring back your share of the money, if you want. Make it an even trade."

Everyone waited silently as Matty considered the deal. Slowly considered the deal. Dmitri could almost visualize the cogs and wheels winding laboriously inside the big hick's head, rotating slowly, inching notch to notch, like the inside of a worn-out alarm clock a few minutes from dying.

"Matty, we can't just sell out Miss Kate," said an overalled clone.

"That's a heap of money, ain't it, Matty?" said a second. "Enough even to move into town. In a real house and stuff?"

"Maybe we could all get us a truck, too, with that kind of money," agreed waxed mustache.

The rednecks all looked at one another, obviously losing some sympathy for Kate Reed's plight. Greed was indeed an amazing incentive.

"In different colors like our towels so we know whose's whose, and what not," said creases-in-the-face, becoming excited now.

Matty was listening, still thinking the hard thoughts.

"You willin' to shake on it?" Matty demanded at length, eyes narrowed shrewdly as he examined Dmitri's face.

At first Dmitri didn't know what he meant, then realized the hayseed wanted to cement the deal on a handshake. Christ, the boy was even stupider than he looked. "You bet I will. A gentleman's agreement is the best kind, that's what I always say, right, Yuri?"

Yuri nodded slowly, following Dmitri's lead and smiling like old friends, but his eyes were watchful. Yuri had been around the block a few times, served with the Soviet army in Afghanistan; he knew how dangerous these kind of men were.

"All right, we'll haul you out and go get the girl. I don't cotton none to baby stealing, not even for Miss Kate who seems real nice, and all. But you ain't gonna hurt her none, not without dealin' with me first."

Dmitri gave a warning glance to the others. If he could prevent it, he didn't want any bloodshed with the hillbillies. Yuri and the two cops would know that. He wasn't so sure about Misha. His nephew was still too unpredictable, rash and easily provoked. The hillbillies hadn't even patted them down for other weapons. It wouldn't take much to get the upper hand. Timing and persuasion would win the day, he thought, as a rope dropped down and dangled right in front of his eyes.

When Kate came out of the back bedroom still wearing Granny's sundress and her tennis shoes, Joey clean and changed, her knapsack was already packed for the drive into Van Buren. She had heard a commotion at the other end of the trailer as she fed Joey his morning bottle, lots of yelling, slamming doors and running feet. But the Joneses made a lot of noise no matter what they did.

The extreme quiet was unnerving, though, as she stood alone in the living room. Even the giant television was turned off. No one was in sight anywhere, not even Millie Mae. The living room door stood ajar and the wind was stirring up the tan draperies on the window beside it. She glanced at the gun rack. Some of the guns were missing. She wondered what had happened, where they'd gone in such a hurry. She hadn't heard anything except for dogs barking.

"Hello," she called, standing in the open door and searching the yard. "Where is everyone?"

No answer. She stepped outside, holding Joey and looking to see if the truck was still parked at the end of the trailer. It was. Frowning, she tucked Joey into the sling, hoping he'd doze off for awhile. Something was wrong, she felt it with the new sixth sense she developed since she'd had murderers hunting her down. It was too quiet.

They'd had biscuits and bacon gravy for breakfast. Their plates were still on the picnic table. A plate full of biscuits was covered with a screened picnic dome to keep off flies. She lifted it, chose one and took a bite. She took two more biscuits and absently stuffed them into her dress pocket. When she realized what she'd done, she knew she was still struggling to survive, foraging food wherever she could get it. Thank God, this terrible ordeal would soon be over. Within the hour she'd be in Van Buren at Gus's office.

Joey was getting fussy, and she worried that the milk was upsetting his tummy. When he finally took his pacifier, she sat down in the metal chair and rocked him, listening for dogs barking in the woods. She didn't hear anything but the flock of blackbirds chattering high in the oak branches. Occasionally wind would whisper through the cornstalks and make them rustle like silk petticoats.

As she stared at the souped-up Dodge truck, she had an almost uncontrollable urge to run to it, get it and take off for town, now, before anyone came back. The impulse was strong enough to bring her to her feet, but she couldn't just steal their vehicle, not after all their kindness. Her uneasiness was growing faster than her gratitude, however, and she walked out to the truck, thinking she could try again to get hold of Gus on the cell phone.

Inside, the shiny black truck looked like a disaster area. The seats were filthy, torn in places with lots of empty Dr. Pepper and Budweiser cans and crumpled-up McDonald's Happy Meal cartons. The truck smelled strongly of marijuana and motor oil. The keys weren't in the ignition. She looked under the floor mat and found a hole through which she could see the gravel of the driveway. Behind the visor she found a Penthouse centerfold of a bosomy blonde but no keys. She dialed the phone again but the signal wasn't strong enough to get the call through. She clunked the door shut and stood gazing out through the cornfields. She looked down at Joey and brushed a curl of dark hair off his forehead. It was then she heard a cry and jerked her head up in time to see Millie Mae running up the cornrow as fast as her bare feet could carry her.

"Miss Kate, Miss Kate! You gotta make a run for it. Matty's gonna give you to those bad guys after you. They shot Ol' Pete dead, and they're gonna turn you in for half of the money. You got to get away, they're comin' now, right behind me! Hurry, quick, I know a place you can hide!"

Kate wasted no time asking questions. She took off after Millie Mae, who was running full speed toward the barn. Kate kept looking back toward the cornfield, saw no one but could hear the yapping dogs getting closer. Millie Mae pulled open the barn door, gesturing wildly for her to hurry.

"C'mon, Miss Kate, they ain't never gonna find you up here in Granny's root cellar. The boys won't think 'bout it neither."

The little girl ran through the shadowy barn, past horse stalls converted into dog pens, and Kate followed her, anxiously clutching Joey. She could hear shouts now, could hear the men congregating around the trailer.

"Here 'tis, through here," Millie Mae said, pulling Kate

into a small room at the back of the barn. It looked as if it was being used as a moonshine still, with dozens of whiskey bottles affixed with handprinted labels, the walls hung with farm tools and mowing implements. When Kate shut the door behind them, the windowless room plunged to near darkness. The child dropped to her knees and frantically brushed away the dirty straw littering the floor. A moment later she pulled up a trapdoor and quickly scrambled out of sight.

Kate peered down into the black hole until Millie Mae jerked the cord on a lightbulb suspended from the ceiling, illuminating a long, narrow root cellar lined with shelves of home-preserved fruits and vegetables in mason jars.

"Hurry now, Miss Kate, you don't have no time to waste. Don't worry, nobody's gonna know you're in here but me, I promise."

Kate hesitated, feeling as if she were walking into a trap, but she could hear the dogs' excited barking and knew it was too late to run. Holding Joey tightly, she made her way down the slanted wooden steps.

"I'll take care of the dogs so they won't give you away," Millie Mae told her urgently, "then after them bad guys go off again, I'll come back and get you out. Just don't make no sound, stay real quiet, okay?"

Kate nodded, watching the child scamper back up the ladder. The heavy trapdoor came down with a soft thud, followed by scraping sounds as Millie Mae scattered straw over the opening. Light footsteps creaked on the dusty floorboards above her head; then all was silent. Kate looked around, estimating the root cellar to be about six feet wide and twenty feet long. It felt like a grave, dark and cold and dank, and she shuddered violently, realizing that if her pursuers found her, she was utterly and completely at their mercy.

Fourteen

BY THE TIME they converged on the rednecks' camouflaged trailer, Dmitri felt certain Kate Reed wouldn't be hanging around inside waiting for them to nab her. Her instincts were too damn good. Annoyed she'd given them the slip, Dmitri clamped his jaw as Yuri checked out the interior of the mobile home. His frustration aside, he did admire the woman's instincts for survival.

"She's gone," Yuri said, appearing in the front door and waiting for further orders.

"Well, she cain't be far. We ain't been gone long enough," offered the hick named Matty, scratching his head as if completely baffled by the lady's sudden disappearance.

"Then let's spread out and search for her," Dmitri said, taking charge before Kate could get a good head start. "Matty, you guys check out the cornfields and the woods behind them. We'll cover the road leading out of here and the adjacent fields. If you find her, fire a shot in the air, then bring her back here."

Matty Jones nodded, and his little herd of hillbillies flocked off without a word, whistling to their mangy mutts now barking and whining around the barn. Dmitri's eyes sharpened when the little pigtailed girl exited the barn and secured the door behind her. She had something caught up in her T-shirt, dog food, he realized, as the animals pushed and leapt for the nuggets she was tossing.

Some distance down the cornrows, Matty gave a shrill

whistle. The dogs bounded off obediently to do his bidding, but the child hung back and stared daggers at Dmitri. From thirty yards away, he could see the hatred on her face. She seemed determined to remain where she was, as if standing guard, only moving away from the barn door when Matty Jones yelled angrily at her. In that moment Dmitri felt positive Kate Reed was somewhere inside that barn. A sensation akin to euphoria flooded him. Fate was giving him a chance to approach her on his own, which was exactly what he'd hoped for.

He turned to Yuri. "You and Andre take the road out and see where it goes. Misha and Nikolai can search the pastures out to that grove of trees in the distance. Signal if you get her. I'll fire two shots to bring you back in. Nobody's to hurt her or endanger the baby, understand? I want her alive."

Nikolai didn't look pleased to be deprived of revenge over the yellow jackets, so Dmitri met his disgruntled gaze with a hard look until the other man broke eye contact and nodded.

"I'll check out the barn and stay here in case she doubles back. Get going, before she gets away again."

Dmitri watched his team move off, guns in hand as they spread out and beat the bushes for hiding places. If he was wrong about the barn and Kate had gone on the run again, odds were they'd flush her out sooner or later. When he glanced back at the barn, all his intuition told him she was there, and he'd learned a long time ago to trust his instincts. She was up there, he knew it, probably hidden away by the little girl. He grinned to himself as he climbed the rocky slope, savoring the moment when he'd finally have her under his control, to do with whatever he wished.

When he reached the barn door, he slid out his Beretta and held it up against his shoulder. Kate would not go down easily, and she might have a gun by now. Stockpiling lethal weapons seemed to be a pastime the hillbillies enjoyed. He pressed back against the wall and lifted off the bar, then nudged the barn door with his toe. He peered around the doorjamb and studied the shadowy interior, heavy with commingling odors of straw and dust, unwashed animals and dog manure. Nothing moved; the only sound was the insistent buzz of bluebottle flies.

Proceeding stealthily, determined not to underestimate Kate Reed again, he moved down through stalls nailed with chicken wire, slowly, carefully searching the gloom. But he suspected right away that the closed-off room at the rear of the barn was where he'd find her. A thrill rushed him. He wanted this woman, wanted to best her, to prove that he could, to get up close and personal with her.

Cautiously he eased open the door and found it a storage area for the hillbillies' abundant supply of homemade booze. There was a lawnmower and a carpenter's bench with lots of rusty tools, but no hiding places big enough for a woman and baby. He hesitated, frowning, so sure that he was on the right track that he wasn't ready to give up yet. He wondered then if she might be up in the loft.

Dmitri stepped back outside the storage room and lifted his gaze to the vaulted part of the barn. The roof had been damaged at one time, burnt, it looked like, but partially rebuilt. Raw pieces of lumber striped the ceiling over the loft. Another portion of the roof was open to the weather. He could see the wind skittering white clouds across the azure sky. He took a step toward the loft ladder, then stopped in his tracks when he heard the weak wail of a baby.

Dmitri stood very still, triumph rising inside him. He had her now. The muffled crying wasn't filtering down from the loft. It was coming from the room he'd just searched and eliminated. He turned back, smiling now with sheer, joyful anticipation. Stepping lightly, he entered and stood listening until he isolated the sound as coming from beneath the floor. Of course, there would be some kind of cyclone cellar or storage hole. Most barns in Russia were similarly equipped to store autumn apples and potatoes.

Going down on one knee, he brushed straw away until he uncovered the hinge of a trapdoor. Keeping out of the line of fire, just in case Kate did have a weapon, he grasped the iron ring and slowly pulled the door up. Instantly the unhappy sounds of the baby floated clearly to his ears. The wooden steps disappeared into utter blackness. Dmitri squatted to one side, gun held ready.

"You might as well come out, Kate. You're trapped down there, you know. You're awfully good, but your luck just ran out."

Silence. She would never give up without a fight. He already knew that much about her.

"Come now, Kate, you don't want to get the baby hurt, do you? Give yourself up. You tried your best, but it's over now."

The baby was growing angrier by the minute, crying hard. Dmitri would have to go down and get her but he wouldn't have expected anything less. Like him, she wasn't the type to surrender with a whimper and a sob. She'd fight tooth and nail to the end. He liked that about her. Liked lots of things about her. Only thing was, this was the end of the line for her, and she'd better accept it.

After a moment's hesitation, he decided that if she'd had a gun, she probably would have come out blasting the minute she'd heard his voice. Chances were she was totally unarmed. Helpless. Again, he felt that strange tingle of excitement, and he recognized it for what it was. It was lust, for her, to have her on her knees at his feet, utterly at his mercy.

"Okay, if that's the way you want to play it. I'll come down and get you."

Nevertheless he was more than alert when he started down, holding on to the steep steps and leading with his gun. It was too dark to see much, but he could tell by the loud cries that Kate had the baby somewhere at the deep end of the root cellar. He made it to the bottom, peering blindly into the pitch-black hole. He listened. The baby's cries drowned out everything else. He finally made out the single lightbulb dangling from the ceiling. He reached out for it with his left hand, keeping his gun trained in the darkness where the baby was screaming.

Before he could pull the cord, he felt a wave of air at his

left and managed to duck just enough for the glass jar she'd thrown to glance off his shoulder instead of smashing against his head. She attacked him bodily then, hurtling out of the darkness and grabbing his gun arm. It was a valiant effort; she was strong for a woman, but she didn't have a chance against his superior strength. She fought like a wild animal but he handled her easily, jerking her around until her back was against his chest, his left arm clenched tightly around her neck. She struggled and kicked, her breathing loud and panting until he flexed his biceps and cut off her windpipe. She jerked and clawed at his arm but he brutally increased the pressure until she choked and gasped for air. She gave up then and stood completely rigid, locked in against his body, the fingers of both her hands clutching his forearm.

"Got you," he breathed, his mouth pressed hard into her right ear. He licked her earlobe, and she struggled desperately until he cut off her air again. She quit fighting and he let her draw a breath. Her hair felt silky against his cheek, smelled of soap, clean and soft. He brought his right hand up, still holding the Beretta, and pressed his arm up against her heaving breasts. She fought the intimacy until he flexed his arm against her throat and brought her under control.

"Now, Kate, Kate, you've got to be good. The running's over. I win, you lose. You're mine now, to do with as I wish." He tightened his biceps a degree, just to show her he meant business, lifting her up onto her toes and making her struggle to breathe. He kept his voice low, very soothing. Her heart was racing hard now, her breasts heaving under his gun hand, exciting him even more. "You've got to listen now, do exactly what I say. Will you do that, Kate? Tell me you will."

She gave a slight nod and he relaxed his arm a bit. He gave her a hard shove, knocking her to her knees away from the steps. Dmitri reached out and jerked the light cord. The bulb flared, and Dmitri got his first good look at Kate Reed. She immediately scrabbled on her hands and knees toward the baby, but he stepped sideways and blocked her path, his shoulder knocking into the hanging bulb and sending it jerking wildly from side to side. He pointed his gun down into her upraised face.

"Uh uh, Kate, that's a no-no."

Kate Reed stared up at him, shadows careening over her face as the light swung erratically behind him, giving the dank cellar the flickering, strobe effect of a silent movie. She was beautiful, more so than he'd hoped for. She didn't really resemble his poor Alina, now that he saw her in person. Alina'd had raven black hair and eyes, a petite ice-skater's build, but Kate Reed possessed another of his beloved's qualities. She had Alina's fierce spirit. He saw it in the way she held her chin, stubbornly, defiantly, even now when he had her completely under his power. Alina had been the same way, obstinately proceeding along her own course despite all Dmitri's entreaties, attempting to defect at a skating competition in London, her ultimate plan to live with him in America. She had ended up imprisoned by his own superiors in Moscow, caught in a trap like Kate Reed now was. Alina had preferred to take her own life, rather than to live out the rest of her days alone in a prison cell.

He stared down at Kate, thoroughly intrigued by her spirit and will to survive, as he'd been all along, yet now he realized only too well that he desired her sexually as well; his body burned with it. But he wanted her to come to him willingly, enjoy the experience, give to him and take from him, and there was only one way to make her do that, to exert that kind of control over a woman like her.

Dmitri backed over to where the kicking, bawling baby lay on the dirt floor in some kind of white quilted pouch, but he kept his eyes trained on Kate. He didn't really worry about her dashing up the steps to freedom. She would never leave her baby behind. She proved him right seconds later.

"Please don't hurt him." Kate came up on her knees in alarm as he crouched down beside the squirming infant, as if she actually feared Dmitri would shoot a little baby.

Dmitri smiled. "Sit down, Kate. Behave."

Kate hesitated until he pointed the gun at her. Then she sat down on her heels, her eyes wide and frightened, but for her child, not for herself. She had brown eyes, rich chocolate, extremely expressive. She had on a red and white sundress, which surprised him, and his gaze moved to the ruffled shoulder strap which had broken loose in their struggle. It hung free, revealing the top of a naked breast. Her skin looked like pale, pale porcelain. He wet his lips. She was really something, this Kate Reed, this woman he had finally captured.

"Please don't hurt him. He's just a baby."

Dmitri clucked his tongue and shook his head, chastising her with an injured look. "Now, Kate, what do you think I am? You think I'd hurt a helpless, little baby like this? I do have my faults but I'm not a monster."

Kate stared at him, remaining silent, no doubt trying to figure him out, decide what she had to do to disarm him. She truly had the most revealing eyes, probably very warm when she wasn't so scared. Her face was pretty banged up, bruised and scratched from running away from him, but that only made her more attractive.

"Actually," he told her, picking up the baby and settling him into his left arm, "I'm pretty good with kids. I had eight brothers and sisters, so I had to baby-sit a lot." He lifted a brow at Kate as the child began to quiet. "There, you see, I have the magic touch. He likes me already."

Dmitri sat down on one of the lower steps where she couldn't get past him. Kate backed farther away, watching him closely without speaking. She was more frightened now, edging up on terror, wondering what he was going to do to her, all alone down in this dark, hidden hole.

"You're wondering why I don't just shoot you and take the baby, I suppose?"

Kate waited a couple of heartbeats, then nodded once, her big brown eyes never leaving his face.

"Well, you see, Kate, as hard as it is to believe, I sort of like you. Can't help it. You've shown a lot of guts to evade me the way you have. Not many people can say they got away from me. I'm too good at what I do. You're a spunky woman. I have to admit, I do like spunky women."

"Who are you? Why are you trying to kill me?"

"My name is Dmitri, and you know very well what I want."

"You want Joey, I know that, but I don't know why."

Dmitri shook his head and propped a foot on his opposite knee. He shifted the whimpering baby into a more comfortable position, rocked him a little, rested his gun on his thigh. "Now, Kate, don't start some kind of innocent act and ruin my high opinion of you. You know good and well why we're here. You were in on this whole thing from the beginning. You and your husband, go ahead and admit it. I doubt, though, that you came up with such a hare-brained idea. You're not that stupid, are you, Kate?"

"I'm telling you the truth. I didn't have anything to do with any of this. I don't know why you're here. Why can't you believe me?"

The woman was after his own heart, growing calmer as they talked, her mind working, trying to figure a way to get herself out of such a terrible dilemma. Annoyed by her denial, however, he made his voice harder. "Don't fuck with me, Kate. You're in no position to anger me with lies."

"It's true, I swear to God. Whatever happened, Michael must have done it on his own."

Dmitri wasn't sure that was true, but he did consider it for a moment. "Maybe the two of us can work something out, Kate, something we can both live with."

"What do you mean?" But she knew; he could tell by the flicker of realization that flared in her eyes, and the revulsion that followed it.

"The way I figure it, I only have so many options about how I should deal with you. Want to hear them?" Her strap had slipped some more, and his eyes focused hungrily on the satiny skin of her breast.

Kate saw his interest and brought her knees up against her chest and wrapped her arms around them, a self-defensive stance. She didn't know what to do, poor thing. She was trapped like a mouse in a bucket. And Dmitri was a very big cat with sharp claws and lots of time to play with her before he went in for the final kill. She didn't answer his question, only stared warily at him.

"Number one option: I can kill you right now, put a bullet between those big brown eyes of yours, and take the baby. That'd probably be the simplest way to proceed. And the smartest."

"Then why don't you?" she threw back, trying to sound less frightened than she was. She didn't like being toyed with. He truly did admire her guts. No begging from Kate, unlike her cowardly husband. Unless he put his gun to the baby's head, then he suspected she'd plead prettily enough. He didn't want to do that unless he had to. He had some scruples, after all.

"Number two option: I could make love to you, long and leisurely, to my heart's content, then kill you and take the baby."

"If you're giving me a choice, I prefer number one."

Dmitri had to laugh. Kate was dauntless. She amused him, he had to give her that. "Or I suppose there's a third option: I could make love to you, then let you go."

Kate was loosening up, he thought, beginning to realize that she might make it out of the cellar alive. "That sounds a little better than the first two. What about option number four: letting me take Joey and get the hell out of here?"

"His name is Joey? I like that. I have a brother named Josef."

Kate was frowning at him, shaking her head. "Who are you? Did Michael really kidnap Joey? Did you help him do it?"

There she went again, playing innocent, working on his sympathy. "I don't want to kill you, Kate, I really don't. Don't force me to."

Kate studied him a moment, glanced away, then back. Her eyes didn't waver. "You expect me to lie down and willingly have sex with you in exchange for my life? Is that the deal you're offering me?"

"I think that would be a pretty good exchange, something we both might enjoy. Afterward, I'll still have to take the baby but I'll let you live."

To Dmitri's surprise, Kate gave a short laugh, one that died instantaneously. "And you expect me to believe that after you finish with me you'll keep your word and let me waltz right out of here, free and easy, no questions asked?"

Dmitri put his hand holding the gun against his chest and assumed an offended posture. He was enjoying sparring with her. "Ah, Kate, you impugn my honor with such unkind remarks. I am an honorable man, in my own way. You deserve to live after the fight you've put up. I had to kill Mike, you understand, but I don't really have to kill you, not now that I've got little Joey here. I'm the only one who can save your skin. Any one of the others out scouring the woods would just love to shoot you down on sight. Unfortunately, they don't share my admiration for you. I'm trying my best to be the good guy here. I'm trying to do you a favor."

Kate's answer came without hesitation. "I'll do whatever you want if you'll let me keep Joey."

Dmitri actually found himself wishing that he could. He turned the idea over in his mind for a few moments, wondering if he could get her and the baby out of Missouri and somewhere safe, perhaps at his own place in Moscow, woo her a bit, charm her into living with him until they tired of each other. They would make a good team, he and Kate, if she would come around to his way of thinking. They probably had more in common than she thought.

"I'll go with you, do whatever you say, anything you want, if you let me keep Joey," she repeated, moving a little closer to him. "I love him. I've had him since he was born. Please don't take him away from me."

God, she was a tempting woman. He watched her take her hand and push some of her blond hair behind one ear. He'd really like to agree to her demand, take her back home with him, settle down, use his savings to provide them a good life. But Vince Saracino would kill him if he did that. The guy was a psycho; he'd find them, no matter where Dmitri took Kate and the boy. Dmitri wasn't sure she was worth dying for.

Kate held her breath, watching fearfully as the man considered her counteroffer. If only he'd put Joey down, then she could at least make a move against him. She didn't understand what he was trying to do. He was a handsome man, looked and acted intelligent, was well spoken, even sophisticated. He didn't have any accent but she thought he was Russian, although he seemed too normal to be the ruthless, bloodthirsty killer she'd first thought. There was a look that glowed inside his dark eyes, gentle almost, as if he felt sorry for her.

Why in God's name was he sitting around chatting with her like this? When he had her around the neck, she thought he was going to choke her to death or put his gun to her head and shoot her dead. That's what he'd done to Michael. Why was he trying to coerce her into making love to him when he already had her at his mercy, could throw her down and rape her, if he wanted to. Was he too fastidious a man for that kind of sexual violence? Was it possible she could use seduction to gain her freedom? To keep Joey with her? Did she have the stomach to do something so abhorrent?

"Do you know who Carl Fabergé was?"

His question was so off the wall that she could only stare at him. She tried to think what he was after now. She needed to play along with his game, whatever it was, but she didn't understand what he was getting at.

"The man who designed the jeweled eggs?"

"Yes." He seemed unduly pleased she possessed such knowledge. She racked her memory for more details.

"Didn't he make them for Czar Nicholas?"

"That's right. Which egg do you like the best? Do you have a favorite?"

Kate struggled with the bizarre turn of conversation but played along with him, hoping something she said would make him let her go. "I saw an exhibit once, at the St. Louis Art Museum. There was one made out of platinum and gold that had a miniature train inside it. I remember that you could wind it up and the wheels would turn."

"That's the Trans-Siberian Railway Egg. Nicholas had it commissioned at the turn of the century. My great-grandfather worked in Fabergé's shop. You see, Katya, we do have some interests in common."

The killer stared at her with seemingly new respect, and a deep, awful sense of unreality began to grip Kate. This man, Dmitri, had no choice but to kill her, no matter what he said, how long they talked, what they had in common. She had seen him commit murder. How could he let her go?

"Who's your favorite artist?"

God, what was he doing? Why was he asking these questions? She swallowed, wondering what he wanted her to say. Which artist would a man like him admire? She couldn't think of any Russian artists. "Van Gogh, I guess."

Kate jumped when he threw back his head and laughed. He shook his head, still smiling. "Leave it to you, Kate. Nine out of ten women will say Monet or Renoir, but I should have guessed you'd be more discerning."

Kate wondered if she could wrest the gun from him. Maybe if she could get him to put it down, put Joey down, maybe if she pretended she wanted him to make love to her, she could grab it and shoot him. She'd have to; she had to do something before he got tired of talking and finished her off. She felt her pulse begin to throb, and she was revolted at the mere thought of letting him touch her, much less enduring any intimacy with him. She swallowed down the nausea squirming up the back of her throat.

"Come over here, Kate."

Oh, God, she thought, God, she couldn't do it, couldn't let him touch her. She saw him bending over Michael and giving the order to kill him, saw Michael's head jerk backward. She bit her lip.

"I'm not as bad as you think. I have my good points like everyone else but unfortunately, I sometimes have to kill people. And I'll kill you, if you don't come over here right now."

Kate stood up. Dread crawled up her spine like a fat, slimy slug. He was smiling, holding Joey like a doting uncle would. Joey had quieted. Dmitri would have to put him down if he made love to her, put down the gun, too. She swallowed again, feeling so sick inside that she thought she'd throw up. She had to do it, had to; it was her only chance against him.

Forcing herself to act, she moved until she stood directly in front of him where he sat on the steps. He lifted the gun and her pulse stilled when she thought he was going to shoot her straight through the heart. But he reached up instead, still holding the gun, and caressed a long strand of her hair with his thumb. He kept his forefinger on the trigger.

"You're special, you're really special," he whispered, and she knew then he wanted to seduce her, show his male prowess; that had been his goal all along, to make her want him, not to fight his advances. She steeled herself and shut her eyes as his hand moved down the side of her face where his thumb could caress her cheek. The metal of the gun barrel lay cold against her ear. "So soft yet so strong. You remind me a great deal of someone I used to know."

Kate opened her eyes and stared at him. He was in pain, thinking about some woman he'd cared about, his eyes clouded with it. He came back from his past and focused on her as he dragged his thumb down over her lips, then farther down, still holding the gun with its long silencer, pulling down the strap and baring her breast.

"God, you are worth the risk, you really are."

He stood up and pulled her against him, holding her

tightly with his gun pressed up against her back. He had to put Joey down soon, she thought, he had to. That's when she had to go for it, get the gun and turn it on him.

"Look at me, Kate."

Unwillingly, Kate dragged her eyes upward, cringing at the feel of him against her, forcing down the overwhelming urge to shove him away, claw him with her fingernails and sink her teeth into his flesh. He kept her head against his chest but he was looking at her lips. He was going to kiss her, and God help her, she was going to have to let him. She could feel the gun barrel still pressed against her back; all he had to do was twist his wrist a little and pull the trigger and she'd be dead.

She stiffened as she caught a movement above his head at the opening of the cellar. She saw Millie Mae at the top, peeking over the ledge, and Kate tried desperately to hide any reaction. The little girl was wiggling down farther, and Kate saw that she was holding a whiskey bottle in her hands. She was going to throw it down upon Dmitri.

Kate wet her lips and kept her gaze locked with Dmitri's intense eyes, feeling his arousal pressing against her loins, as he lowered his head toward her mouth. Millie Mae lifted her arms high, then hurled down the bottle as hard as she could. It hit Dmitri's shoulder and shattered on the steps, spraying shards of glass and whiskey everywhere. Dmitri jerked to one side and turned to fire at Millie Mae, and Kate grabbed his gun arm before he could pull the trigger. She snatched a heavy quart jar off the shelf beside her and swung it hard, using every ounce of her strength. The glass container smashed against Dmitri's forehead, and he crumpled to his knees, blackberry preserves sliding down his face. His eyes held hers for one awful moment when she thought he was going to lift the gun to her, but then his eyes rolled back into his head and he slid down onto the floor, blood gushing from a gash above his eye.

Kate grabbed Joey from him, thinking only to get away while he was unconscious, grabbing the gun and pointing it down on him. Her hands were shaking, her finger was on the trigger, itching to kill him for all he'd done to her and her family, but she couldn't bring herself to stand there and shoot him in cold blood. Instead, she scrambled up the ladder when Millie Mae cried out for her to hurry.

"That serves him right for killin' poor Pete and tryin' to take Joey away from you. Hurry up, Miss Kate, before the rest of 'em come back!"

Once she gained the upper room, Kate slammed down the trapdoor and threw the bolt tight, hoping Dmitri never saw the light of day again. She hoped he rotted down there for the rest of his life.

"Where are they, Millie Mae?" she asked, quickly strapping Joey's sling across her chest. "Are any of them down at the trailer?"

"No, they're all out huntin' you. Don't know exactly where but they're lookin' everywhere. I think I know how you can get away if you run like the wind."

Kate made sure Joey was secure, then weighed Dmitri's gun in her hand. It felt heavy and unnatural. She'd never fired a gun with a silencer but she'd use it if anyone else tried to get her. She wanted to use it, still felt unclean from Dmitri's hands on her body.

"There, see that fence row that runs off down behind our trailer house. It'll lead you to the river, and if you can get 'cross it before they see you, you can get away. Run, run, before the dogs pick up your scent!"

Kate took off running, down through the tall weeds along the fence posts, heading straight for the most tangled part of the undergrowth. She held tightly to Joey as she flew along but nearly panicked when she saw an old wire fence crossing through the trees and blocking her flight. She stopped and held it down with her good hand while she climbed over, not wanting to risk falling with Joey in her arms. She was looking behind her now, and thank God, she didn't see anyone. But she did hear the dogs. Close, too close. She could hear the men yelling back and forth at each other.

Clutching the gun and Joey, she ran as fast as she could, zigzagging in and out of trees in case they were sighting in on her with their rifles, all the while knowing she had very little chance to escape. The other Russians would kill her if they caught her this time, especially after what she'd done to Dmitri. He might even be dead; the blow on the head had been brutal. Even with a gun, she'd have no chance against so many armed men. The thought sent her ahead faster, her heart thudding like a jackhammer, her breath heaving in and out and burning her lungs. Joey was crying now, struggling in the sling, but she didn't stop, didn't slow down, and barely caught herself from falling when she suddenly burst out of the tangled bushes at the very edge of a cliff overlooking Current River. A sheer, rocky drop-off.

She turned around and heard men coming in the woods behind her, converging on her. Panic stricken, she thought only that she had to get away from them. She stuck the gun in her skirt pocket and started down the rocks of the bluff, grabbing hold of the roots of a mimosa sapling growing out over the edge. She kept herself as flat against the side as she could, inching down slowly, thinking she had to get across the river again to thwart the tracking dogs. It was either that or hand Joey over to them and die.

She got about five feet down from the top when her toe slipped off the narrow ledge where she'd gained a foothold. The vine she was holding ripped out of the ground, and she began to slide. She twisted as much as she could so that she'd go down on her back, clutching Joey against her with one arm, trying to grab something with her other hand. She cried out as the jagged edges of the granite cut into her back like sharp razor blades. Her weight carried her faster and faster until she was shooting toward the water below in a raining torrent of dirt and rocks. She struggled to protect Joey, flailing with her arm to stop herself as she reached the bottom and slid out onto the narrow sandbar. The back of her head cracked down hard atop a flat rock at the base of the cliff. White light imploded behind her eyes and everything faded to black.

Fifteen

KATE HEARD A NOISE, faint, faraway, beyond her ability to reason. She felt trapped on the bottom of a swimming pool, tons of murky water holding her down. She couldn't seem to breathe, couldn't see, couldn't move her limbs. Sheer helplessness plunged her into panic and she flailed upward out of the darkness, spurred by an acute sense of danger.

Jerking up her head she paid an immediate price as a concrete softball crashed around inside her skull. Groaning, disoriented, she focused bleary eyes and realized she lay on her stomach on a narrow cot. The room around her was nearly dark, only a smoky oil lantern flickering on a nearby table. She blinked hard, forcing down fear rising in a vile taste at the back of her throat.

Groggily she tried to remember what had happened, where she was, until suddenly the whole nightmare crashed down on her like a hurricane wave. The little girl, Millie Mae, had hidden her in a root cellar, and then the man named Dmitri had come. She shivered all over, reliving the feel of his hands touching her bare flesh. But she'd gotten away from him, had run away with Joey. Oh, God, where was Joey? Only then did she pull herself together enough to recognize the sound that had roused her, that still came from somewhere in the darkness, the frightened cries of her baby.

"Joey, Joey!" She lunged up, terrified, and that's when she realized her wrists were bound to the bed. She really got hysterical then, jerking her arms, the stone softball wreaking havoc inside her head.

"Stop yelling."

The voice came out of the dark, masculine, deeply pitched, the demand uttered quietly. Oh, God, no, Dmitri had her again, had her tied up and helpless. He wouldn't be merciful this time, wouldn't give her options, not after what she'd done to him. Frantically she searched for him but it was too dark; she couldn't see anything but she could hear Joey crying, and she sobbed, pulling desperately at the ropes. Her body tensed when a tall figure loomed out of the shadows, and she braced herself to suffer Dmitri's wrath. But it wasn't the Russian killer who stepped into the light. Paralyzed with horror, she gaped at the big bearded man who'd accosted her in the woods, and oh God, oh God, he had Joey. Joey was screaming and squirming in his arms.

"Don't hurt him, please, please—" Kate choked on the words and couldn't continue, helplessness overwhelming her. She was at his mercy, and so was Joey. She went rigid, straining back against the wall behind her, as the old man squatted down very close beside the cot. Up close he looked even more terrifying, his camouflage shirt and pants covered with mud and rusty stains that looked like blood. His eyes shone sky blue in the flickering light.

"Look, lady, I'm not going to hurt you. I'm not going to hurt your baby so you can relax. Jerking around like that isn't going to help that head wound."

Relax? Tied to a cot at his mercy? The man was crazy. The Joneses had already told her that, so Kate tried to avoid eye contact with him. Hadn't she read that somewhere? Never lock eyes with a maniac, or had that been growling, rabid dogs? She kept her eyes riveted on Joey who was waving his arms and kicking vigorously in baby rage. She had to stay calm, had to keep her head. God only knew what this wild man wanted with her. How did she get here? What did he want with her? Nausea skittered inside her belly, making her stomach lurch and roll. She squeezed her eyes shut and took a couple of deep breaths, desperate to calm herself.

"Why did you tie me up?" she croaked out in a raspy voice so filled with fear she could hear it herself. Her lips were dry, painfully cracked. She moistened them and tasted blood but forced herself to lie still when every nerve and fiber wanted to pull hysterically against the ropes, to grab Joey out of his filthy hands, and run for her life.

"I was afraid you'd take off if you woke up before I got back."

Oh God, oh God, Kate thought, trying to control the way her chest was bucking. She was shaking, limbs trembling, and she'd never in her life felt so vulnerable. Not even in the root cellar with Dmitri. This man, this horrible-looking, grotesque, filthy creature had tied her up, had her baby. Oh, God, he could make her do whatever he wanted. She nearly went to pieces but Joey's cries ended in pitiful little whimpers, and Kate willed herself, steeled herself to remain in control. Stop, stop and think, think about Joey. He said he wasn't going to hurt them. He had no reason to lie. Cooperate, she told herself, do whatever he says. He didn't kill her the first time in the woods; he let her go then, didn't he? Okay, okay, take a breath, act unafraid, find out what he wants.

Kate opened her eyes and stared at the big hunting knife in his right hand. All the gumption she'd scraped together, all her bravado crumbled into dust. "Please, please don't—"

"If you promise not to do anything stupid, I'll cut you loose."

Kate was so relieved her entire body went limp. She nodded mutely but her breath caught as he thrust the sharp blade under the rope on her right wrist. One sharp jerk and her arm was free. When he cut the other, she scooted back against the wall as far away from him as she could get.

Never taking her eyes off him, she chafed her aching

wrists and tried to ignore the pounding in her temples. She raised her fingertips to the back of her skull and found a gauze bandage wrapped around her head.

"You cracked it pretty good," her bearded captor remarked. "Lost a hell of a lot of blood before I could get you here. You're gonna feel weak."

Kate looked down at herself. Her dress had turned crimson and clung damply to her skin. She felt woozy as if she might faint. No, she couldn't, she couldn't do that. She swallowed down an enormous lump lodged in her throat and gathered all the courage she had left.

"Please give me back my baby, please."

Kate waited breathlessly, eyes locked on his filthy face, terrified he'd refuse and hold Joey as a bargaining chip to force her to his bidding. What in God's name did he want with her? Did he want a wife, or some kind of sex slave? Heaven help her, she'd read about men like him, men who lived alone in the woods and did godawful things to people they captured. Even Millie Mae's big, lethal hillbilly brothers thought he was crazy.

The man said nothing, merely handed Joey over. Kate snatched the unhappy baby against her breast, her heart thumping wildly, holding Joey so tightly that he began to cry again. She laid him on the bed, opening the blanket and examining him for cuts or bruises. He seemed fine. He had on a cloth diaper now, made out of a thin white dishtowel held together with safety pins.

Shocked to find he'd been changed, she enfolded him in the blanket and rocked him, relieved he was safe in her arms. Still wary of the old man's motives, she watched him scrape up a straight chair close beside the bed. He spun it around backward and straddled it. Then they stared at each other, long and hard, until Kate dropped her gaze from his penetrating pale eyes.

"Who are those guys and why are they after you?"

His words were soft, nonthreatening. He had a quiet way

about him, the way he spoke, the way he moved. Deliberate, watchful. He spoke with correct English and no recognizable accent. Neither Russian, nor the hillbilly twang of the Joneses. He observed her steadily without expression. She wondered if she should tell him the truth, afraid if she did, he might believe her the criminal everyone else seemed to think.

"How do you know about them?" she asked fearfully.

"I make it my business to know what's going on in my woods."

Kate examined his face but couldn't see much of it. The beard was long and wiry, very dark, nearly black. Crinkles at the corners of his eyes branded him as an older man, but maybe not as old as she'd first thought. He was big, even bigger than Matty Jones; she'd guess he stood at least six foot five. And he was strong, frightening to look at, especially so near. No wonder Matty and Little John and the others stayed clear of his side of the river. But Dmitri and his men wouldn't be afraid of him; they'd come after her, no matter where she was or who she was with.

"You're trying to decide if you can trust me, I guess," he said.

"I don't trust anybody anymore."

"I have no reason to harm you."

"Neither do they but that doesn't stop them from shooting at me."

Kate watched him cautiously. It suddenly occurred to her, with a sinking feeling, that he could be one of them. What if this was a trick? Maybe Dmitri was in the next room, waiting for this man to interrogate her before he killed her. But why would they do that? If this weirdo guy was in with the Russians, he could have shot her and taken Joey back to them.

"I'm not one of them," he said, as if reading her mind.

Startled she stared at him a moment, not sure what to think. "I can't trust anybody," she repeated.

"I understand."

They sat in silence for a few deeply uncomfortable moments. Kate couldn't hear any sound, neither inside nor outside the room.

"Where am I?"

"My place." He paused, and Kate noticed he had a small crescent-shaped scar underneath his left eye, barely detectable. "Don't worry, they won't find you here. Not for awhile anyway."

"What time is it? How can it be so dark?" She shook her head, trying to think through the jackhammer-thudding headache. "How did I get here?"

"I carried you over my shoulder. You took quite a blow to the head. You're a lot tougher than you look, lady. I've been watching out for you and when I saw you go down, I got to you before they did. Headache?"

Kate nodded, unable to grasp what he was saying. "Watching me? Why? Why did you bring me here when you let me go the first time?"

Something moved inside his eyes, so fleeting she barely caught it. He looked down at Joey who was quiet now, snuffling and sucking on his pacifier. "You were outnumbered. Thought I better even up the odds some."

Kate didn't know what to say. The civilized conversation was an encouraging sign, but Ted Bundy had been a hell of a good conversationalist, too. Still, she felt a little less frantic. She was alive after all. She wasn't in the hands of Dmitri and his cold-blooded killers. This guy had let her go once and he might again. She still had a chance. If she could convince this strange man to take her downriver to Van Buren, she just might make it. One thing she did know. He wasn't the Neanderthal monster grunting monosyllables that he looked like.

"Who are you?" she asked, certain he wouldn't tell her.

At first he hesitated as if he didn't want to answer, then said, "Name's Booker." He held out his hand, the back of which was covered with black grease, the kind soldiers wore to hide their skin at night. Thinking the whole encounter too incredible for words, she tentatively accepted his handshake, not because she wanted to, but because she was afraid not to.

"I'm Kate Reed." She hesitated a few seconds, then decided to tell him the truth. "Those men think I kidnapped Joey out of a hospital in St. Louis."

Kate waited. When he didn't answer, her muscles began to knot up. What if he decided to turn her in to the authorities?

"Did you?"

"No, of course not! I don't know what happened. That's what they're saying on the radio." Her voice quavered as raw emotions bubbled up. "I don't know what's going on, I swear to God. We adopted him. My husband handled everything but it was all completely legal. We signed papers, had them drawn up in the courts. I thought everything was all right, I swear I did. Then these terrible men with guns and Russian accents burst into our house yesterday morning. I got away and hid in the woods but they shot Michael. They killed him."

"Michael's your husband?"

She nodded, catching her trembling bottom lip with her teeth. "They shot him in the head. I saw it. That's when I ran for my life, when I saw you in the woods."

Kate realized tears were streaming down her face. She hadn't had time to mourn Michael yet. Even now her tears weren't just for him but for everything that had come crashing down around her, her marriage, the love they'd shared. All her dreams of being together, having a family, everything they'd been working so hard for, was gone. And she was shaken and emotional because she'd barely escaped the ghastly ordeal with Dmitri, and she was exhausted and injured and scared again, and the only person she had to trust was this horrible-looking dirty old hermit. Angrily, she wiped at her tears and gritted her teeth to prevent more.

"They're going to kill you if they catch you. I guess you know that."

"Yeah, I noticed."

His eyes held hers. "Well, it's me or them. You don't have much of a choice."

Booker was right. She had to trust him. "I need to get to the sheriff's office in Van Buren. If you take me there, I'll pay you anything you want."

"Bad idea."

Kate's heart sank like a barrel of concrete. "Why?"

"You're wanted by the law for kidnapping. They'll arrest you and take the baby and you'll never see him again. Is that what you want?"

"I know the sheriff. He's a friend. He'll help me, I know he will."

"Those copters buzzing the trees are the feds. He won't have jurisdiction on a kidnapping case. The way I see it, you need to get as far away from here as you can before somebody catches up with you. Outside the area where you can find out what's really going on and make some decisions."

Kate was incredulous. This was not your ordinary, hovel-dwelling, run-of-the-mill recluse. This guy had been around the block a few times if he knew about jurisdictions. Who the hell was he?

"Who are you?" she asked again.

"I'm all you've got, lady, and I'm willing to help you get out of here before they find you at my place and come down on me like a load of bricks. After that, you're on your own."

"Why are you doing this?" she whispered hoarsely. "They'll kill you if you get in their way, just like they killed Michael."

"I'm not Michael. They won't find me."

The man named Booker seemed awfully sure, and somehow that made Kate feel more secure, too. She wanted to believe him, really, really wanted to believe him.

"There's four or five of them, I think. They track me down every time I think I'm going to make it. The guy in charge is named Dmitri, and he caught me in the barn alone and tried to make me . . ." She stopped, swallowing down a sick feeling as she thought about the time trapped in the root cellar with Dmitri, what would have happened if Millie Mae hadn't come. "The little Jones girl helped me get away, but her brothers are after me, too. She said they offered them half the money so I guess somebody's put out a reward on my head."

Booker stood up as if he'd heard enough. He looked down at her, too huge and frightening to trust, but for some reason, she did. "Let me worry about them for awhile. Get some sleep while I keep watch. I'll get you out of here and somewhere safe, but like I said, after that you're on your own."

Kate nodded, still clutching Joey against her chest, as he moved across the room, his footsteps barely audible, though he wore heavy black boots. He stopped and turned back.

"There's some powdered milk in the other room if the kid gets hungry and some Bayer aspirin for your head. That'll work for the burn on your hand, too."

Kate leaned her head back against the wall as he left. She shut her eyes when Joey fussed, and she hummed his favorite lullaby as she rocked him gently in her arms. "We're going to get out of this, sweetie," she whispered softly. "Now we've got somebody to help us." She'd do whatever she had to do to get Joey out of danger, even trust a man like Booker.

Long after he'd left the woman cowering on the bed with her baby, Booker sat on the front porch of his cabin, wondering why the hell he was involving himself in her problems. He should have minded his own business as he'd done the first time he saw her. Now he was dead center in Kate Reed's mess, and he wasn't sure why.

Leaning back in the old cane rocker, he looked out over the river. He had exchanged his scoped deer rifle for the M-16 he kept stored in an ammunition box under the bed. It lay across his knees, his finger lightly on the trigger. He had a .45 strapped to his ankle. These men, whoever the hell they were, meant business. Though it was highly unlikely they'd find his place—it was too well hidden in the mouth of a cave—he didn't believe in taking chances.

The riot of tangled vines hid the entrance but gave him a glimpse of twilight mists settling like an ethereal coat on the surface of Current River. He'd been lucky to find the ramshackle gristmill built inside the cave, where decades ago iron miners had dug shafts deep into the mountain. The giant waterwheel was long gone, rotted away and swept downstream in raging spring floodwaters. The protected wood structure had remained relatively stable, though he suspected the cabin dated as far back as the forties. It had made him a good home far enough upriver from Van Buren to keep nosy strangers away. Until now.

Grimacing, he propped a booted foot atop his knee and dropped his head back against the chair. They were still searching for the woman. He'd heard the *thut-thut-thut* of rotor blades as the bird skimmed the trees not an hour ago. Yeah, she was in deep shit. Now that he was playing knight in shining armor, he was in as deep as she was. God knew he didn't need any trouble with the feds; he'd had enough when he was with the Company. He didn't know why he'd brought her here in the first place. He'd never brought anyone here, except for his old friend, Mac Sharp. He had to be out of his mind.

He shook his head angrily, but down deep in his gut he knew the truth. He'd brought her here, followed her harrowing flight through the wilds for two days running, because he couldn't forget how she'd looked when he decided to check her out the first time he saw her. She'd stared at him in utter disbelief, and hell, he must have looked at her the same way since a bloodied-up woman and a little baby had been the last thing he expected to find wandering around in his woods. But it wasn't just that. It wasn't the way she'd looked, all scratched up and filthy, sopping wet and wild-eyed, with her hair straggling down in her face and blood running down the side of her cheek. Nor was it the baby's weak, quavering wails, which was plenty enough.

Booker's fingers squeezed tightly around the arm of the chair. What had gotten to him had been the way she'd fallen to her knees in front of him, utterly defeated, the most awful look imaginable on her face. Utter helplessness. Booker knew how that felt. He felt his jaw begin to clench, tighten so hard that a sliver of pain penetrated his temples. Yeah, he knew how it felt to be hunted down like a wounded animal, thrashing and tearing mindlessly through hot, humid jungles, crawling into slimy, infested holes in the ground, exhausted physically, mentally, all hope gone.

There had been a time when he'd dropped to his knees exactly the way Kate Reed had. But Booker's captors hadn't been so merciful. He squeezed his eyes, clamped his teeth, fighting haunted memories. His throat grew thick, his breathing shallow as a day ten years past welled up in his mind, tormenting him as if it had happened yesterday.

Booker fell to his knees, somehow managing the strength to raise his arms into the air. His lungs were burning, each breath cutting his chest like slashing razor blades. He'd been running hard but he could hear the Sandinistas behind him, crashing through the thick vegetation he'd fought his way through, yelling at each other in Spanish. But it was the man who'd stepped out to block his path at whom he stared. Their gazes were locked, the Sandinista officer so full of hatred and vicious cruelty that Booker knew he was as good as dead, hoped he was dead because he knew now he could never escape, that even if he did there was no American military in Nicaragua to rescue him. He braced for the blow as his captor raised the AK-47 high, then brought the butt down hard. The crunching sound was his collarbone breaking, and the echo of his own scream rang in his ears, the last thing he heard.

"Mr. Booker?"

Booker was on the balls of his feet, weapon trained on Kate Reed before his name had left her tongue. She had the kid in her arms, and she turned slightly to protect him from Booker. She looked terrified again. He lowered his gun, forcing himself to relax his stance.

"Look, lady, don't ever do that, sneak up on me. I'm too jumpy right now." His voice was harsh but he wasn't used to having people around, especially in the cave. He didn't like it.

"I didn't mean to startle you. I'm sorry."

She was wary, very wary, and she had reason to be. Her nerves had to be shredded down to near nothing by now. She didn't know who he was, what he'd done in the past. It was a good thing she didn't. She might prefer to take her chances with Dmitri and the bad guys.

"What do you want?" he asked tightly.

"Nothing, really. I couldn't shut my eyes, sure couldn't sleep. Too wired, I guess."

Booker realized he didn't know what to say to her. God knew how many years it'd been since he'd attempted small talk with a woman. He didn't like it then. He didn't like it now either. "Get some rest. You're gonna need it. I'm taking you out of here in a few hours."

Kate Reed nodded and glanced around. She looked better now than she had when she'd come to and found herself tied to the bed. The look of hysteria was gone. She'd put on the baggy black sweatshirt he'd left lying at the foot of the bed. It swallowed her. She was a real good-looking woman, tall and blond, lithe, slim. She was a good athlete and in very good condition, gutsy as hell, or she'd never have made it this far alone. He was uncomfortable around her, wished he'd never laid eyes on her. He'd had enough sense not to involve himself the first time he saw her, but she hadn't been in imminent danger then. He thought she'd make it out on her own. The second time, when she lay unconscious at the base of the cliff, her pursuers minutes away, had been a different story.

"Would you mind if I sat down for a minute?"

Yeah, he thought, but didn't say anything, so she took a seat on the rocker he'd just vacated, gingerly at the very edge as if she would leap up and flee if he stepped an inch in her direction. He glanced away and perched a hip on the porch rail where he could see the river. He listened for the buzz of boats, but all he heard was the rush of swift currents.

"I never thanked you."

Booker shrugged and kept his eyes focused on the river. He wished she'd go back inside and stay there until he was ready to take her out. No such luck.

"I have to. I really do. You saved my life. And Joey's. I'd be dead right now, if it weren't for you. This man, Dmitri, he doesn't look like a killer, but he is a terrible man, so ruthless . . ."

Booker remained silent at first, then thought that if he answered, maybe she'd leave him alone. "It's okay. Forget it."

"But you saved my life."

"I said forget it."

Quiet for a couple of beats, then she said, "Booker's your last name, right?"

Booker gave a curt nod but didn't look at her.

"What about your first name?"

"What the hell difference does it make? I'm gonna take you out of here, isn't that enough?" He was annoyed, and he sounded annoyed. He didn't like chitchat, especially chitchat about him. It was making him antsy; she was making him antsy. He had enough other things to worry about. Like keeping them all alive till morning.

The woman looked slightly startled by his sudden show of

anger and avoided his gaze. She was afraid of him, her quavering voice dripping with fear. "Sorry. I didn't mean to pry."

His social graces had slipped a notch, hell, a whole staircase, since his self-imposed exile, were nonexistent, in fact. Problem was, he had no desire to rekindle them.

"John," he admitted reluctantly, then wondered why he had. "First name's John."

"Oh, thank God, thank God, I've been looking for you, praying I'd find you somehow. I'd given up all hope, then when I calmed down some and started to think straight I realized you had to be the man Pop used to talk about."

This time she got all of Booker's attention. "You know Pop Macon?"

"He's my grandfather. He passed away a couple of months ago but he mentioned you to me sometimes, said you lived up the river, and I kept thinking that if I could only find you, you'd surely help me."

He hadn't known Pop had died, hadn't known he'd had any family either. But Kate Reed's relationship to the old man put everything in a different light. Pop Macon could have arrested him for squatting on federal land when he'd happened onto Booker a few years back, would have if he'd looked into his past, but the old man had left him in peace, no questions asked. Booker owed him big time. As much as Booker would like to wash his hands of Kate Reed, now he felt a real obligation to help her out.

"He said you were a good man. Said he never had to find you, that you always found him first."

Booker said nothing but had a feeling she was about to start prying into his business now that they had something in common. Women always asked questions, thrived on digging into a man's psyche until they stripped his soul bare. Kate Reed proved him right the next time she opened her mouth.

"What is this place? I've never seen anything quite like it before."

Booker repositioned the gun across his knee, leaning back in a more comfortable position against the rock wall, wishing she'd just shut up. He considered telling her to but decided she'd been through enough without him scaring her some more. Let her chatter, if it helped her get through the night. Her ordeal was far from over.

"This cabin's built inside the cave, isn't it? Except for the porch."

"Yeah."

Quiet again, thank God. But he knew it wouldn't last. Booker could hear the faint creak of the chair when she began to rock. He stole a sidelong glance and found her looking down at the baby. Her expression was so tender that he had no doubt she loved the kid. It seemed unlikely to him now that she'd kidnapped the boy but he couldn't know that for sure. Pop had been an honorable man, an officer of the law, but Booker didn't know his granddaughter from Adam.

Whether she snatched the baby or not, it wasn't his business. His business was to get her out of his woods so he could have some peace and quiet, and the solitude that went with it. He'd make sure nobody hunted her down like some trophy buck, then good luck, lady, just like he'd told her inside. He didn't want any woman hanging around.

"This is the first time I've felt safe since they burst into my kitchen."

Kate Reed talked too much. Booker kept his eyes trained on the mist rolling on the water as dusk deepened, his ears trained for any unusual sounds in the buzzing, chirping symphony going on in the trees. If Kate's pursuers came this way, they'd most likely motor upriver, but he didn't think they'd ever find him. After he'd tied Kate to the bed, he'd gone back to make sure he'd left no trail. Her enemies had been busy hunting her down on the other side of the river, unaware their quarry had taken up with a brand-new, well-armed best friend.

No one but Pop Macon had discovered this cave in the past five years, and Booker had sat on the porch on many a summer day when the river was alive with fishermen and teenagers floating on inner tubes and in canoes. He'd been safe here, to do as he pleased. Once he got Kate Reed and her baby to safety, everything would return to normal.

"The Joneses are afraid of you. They call you Bigfoot. Said they never set foot on your side of the river or you'd shoot them."

Booker looked at Kate. She attempted a tremulous smile. It was the first one he'd seen off her. He glanced away.

"Yeah."

She was trying to be friendly, he supposed, but that's the last thing he wanted. He probably brought it on himself by talking to her so much when she'd regained consciousness. But he'd had little choice for fear she'd go completely hysterical on him. He was surprised she hadn't, as terrified as she'd been. He had to admire her for not giving up a long time ago. Most women would've; most men would've.

"I took some powdered milk for Joey's bottle. I was afraid he wouldn't drink it but the poor little thing was starving. He's a good baby; he doesn't deserve to go through all this."

Her voice broke as if she was going to cry, and Booker watched her out of the corner of his eye. She was dabbing at her tears with the baby blanket, almost angrily, as if she'd cried enough, was mad at herself for getting choked up. Most women he'd known would have fainted dead away right off the bat, and probably gotten a quick bullet in their head like Kate's husband. Betsy wouldn't have lasted two minutes. He pushed thoughts of his ex-wife out of his mind, barely able to picture her face anymore. He hadn't thought about her in a long time. Didn't want to.

"You're gonna be all right. I told you I'd get you out of here alive, and I will."

"I don't want to make trouble for you," she began, voice

urgent, then gave a low chuckle. "Boy, that's a bit of an understatement. I'm surprised I can laugh, though, I mean, it's been pretty terrible. My emotions are just so shot I keep finding myself chattering on when I know you probably wish I'd shut up."

Booker said nothing.

"I ought to get some sleep like you said, but I just can't close my eyes. I keep seeing awful things, the worst of it, you know."

Yeah, he knew. He knew she'd still be seeing her husband shot in the head thirteen years from now, the way he was still reliving the nightmare he'd been through when the goddamn Black Ops OIC left him behind. Yeah, she'd still be seeing it, if they didn't get her first.

"I just feel safer out here on the porch with you. I was really scared of you, too, at first, like with Dmitri, but now I know that Pop knew you, that you're all right and I can trust you—"

"Look, lady, like you figured out, I'm not much of a talker. Why don't you go back inside and get some sleep? I meant it when I said you're gonna need it."

"Okay," she said, quickly rising with the baby. "Okay, whatever you say. I didn't mean to get on your nerves or anything."

Booker didn't watch her go but he heard the screen door give a little squeak. He'd have to oil it. Even sounds like that carried over the water. He relaxed again but kept his eyes on the river. It was going to be a very long night, with his woods crawling with armed intruders out to spill blood.

Sixteen

ALTHOUGH KATE felt safer than at any time since the endless nightmare had begun, she did not sleep. At least the strange recluse knew Pop, she had that much to hang onto, and he'd saved her from Dmitri's deadly games. John Booker was sitting outside with a very big gun, keeping vigil over her and Joey. He was a formidable ally, and she was grateful he'd intervened in her behalf. She'd do nothing to rub him the wrong way.

Pressing her fingertips against her temples, she tried to relax. Her tight muscles would not cooperate. She hurt all over, and nothing alleviated the terrible drumbeat inside her head. Joey squirmed and sputtered on the cot beside her as he began to awaken. Kate turned on her side and checked his diaper. His dark eyes latched on her face, and he smiled and babbled happily, as if they were not fugitives on the run, not in danger of their lives. Her heart clutched with love, and she scooped him up and held him against her breast, wishing she could protect him better than she had, keep all the evil in the world at bay. She nuzzled his soft cheek, then lay him down when he fussed and kicked his feet.

"I bet you're wet, aren't you, sweetie?" She was whispering, afraid to use her normal voice, afraid to make the wrong move for fear she'd be thrust into danger again. She'd been scared so long, so torn up inside, that she doubted she'd ever be the person she'd been only days ago. Joey gooed daintily in his secret talk and tried to grab her nose, and she found herself very thankful that he was with her and all right, healthy and happy.

"Okay, let's go."

John Booker had entered the room so quietly that Kate jumped a foot and would've shot him if she'd had a gun. She stared at him in dread, not sure what to expect. He looked so awful in his dirty, bloodstained clothes. Probably her blood, from when he carried her back to the cave. He was holding a camouflaged field jacket in his hand. A canvas duffel bag was slung over one shoulder; a long rifle hung by a strap on the other.

"All right." Kate obeyed hastily, not wanting to give him any reason to change his mind about helping them.

Booker watched silently as Kate wrapped Joey in a blanket. Then he picked up the lantern and headed out. Kate followed him through a darkened room that acted as a kitchen and held one small table and chair. Through the front door she could see it wasn't yet daylight. She wondered what time it was but didn't really care. Everything seemed meaningless when trapped inside an episode of *The Twilight Zone* with no means of escape.

Ignoring the porch where he'd sat guard, Booker opened a rear door that exited into a cavern that was pitch black and ten degrees colder. The dim light of the lantern reflected on the vast, empty dome, and Booker's heavy combat boots rang off the stone, echoing eerily as he strode off into the darkness. She could hear the steady drip of water and could smell a miasma of vaporous mineral pools and damp earth.

Kate hesitated, overcome by the most awful sensation. She had to be crazy to follow this stranger down into the dark bowels of the mountain, a man who terrified even the tavern-brawling, gun-toting marijuana suppliers across the river. Pop had known him but she didn't know how well or for how long. What if Booker planned to drag her down a deserted shaft and kill her or God knew what else? He could, and no one would ever know. No one would ever find her or Joey. She clung to her baby, fighting the urge to make a wild dash for freedom and fresh air. Quivering with a new kind of fear, she hovered on the brink of pure panic.

A few yards away, headed down a narrow mineshaft, Booker stopped and held the lantern out toward her. "You coming?"

Kate stared at him, her better judgment telling her to distrust the filthy, unkempt man. Yet he hadn't hurt her and he'd had plenty of opportunity. If he'd wanted to harm them, he'd had ample time to do it when she was tied to the bed at his mercy, could have slit her throat with the big hunting knife he wore on his belt. Kate swallowed hard, trying to use reason to control her quaking knees.

"Yes, I'm coming," she got out, but her voice was shaky.

The big man took off again with long, swift strides, not looking back or waiting for her to catch up. It didn't seem to make much difference whether she went with him or not. She considered that a good sign. They proceeded in near darkness down the shaft until it veered to the left and took a decided turn deeper into the mountain. In the cold blackness all around her, she could hear the strange, subterranean echoes their shoes made. Hell must be like this, Kate thought, wondering with a shiver if that's where she was heading.

Suddenly she remembered a California case where two psychopaths had lured innocent families to an isolated farm and locked them in buried torture chambers. Was there another man waiting somewhere below with Booker's other victims? No, no, she couldn't think that way. He would've already killed her, if that's what he wanted. He was saving her, doing her a favor, not leading her to doom. She had to believe that. Still, she kept her eyes riveted on his back, ready to run if he made a suspicious move.

Gaseous, sulfuric odors grew stronger during the descent, and Kate worried about timber rattlers and other scuttling creatures and why Booker hadn't just taken them out the front door. Soon, however, the wonderful scent of fresh air came swirling against her face, carried on a cool breeze that smelled of the river. Booker stopped and set down the lantern, and Kate could see that a low opening led outside. She wondered how many escape hatches Booker had, and why he thought he needed them. Who was he really and why did he hide in a cave out in the middle of nowhere? She wasn't sure she could handle the answer, so she didn't ask.

She waited, rocking Joey back and forth while he gooed in good cheer. Her baby boy had nerves of steel. More than his mother did. She smiled down at him, and his dimples deepened. Tears burned, swift, unbidden, and she knew she could never give him up, no matter what the truth was.

Booker was dragging dead branches away, and she was shocked when he uncovered a four-wheel drive, all-terrain vehicle that looked like a wide, customized motorcycle with four oversized wheels. He pushed the four-wheeler outside into the night, and Kate followed, relieved to be out of the damp, cold place. She breathed deeply and welcomed the rustle of wind-stirred leaves. A full moon rode high in the sky, casting a pearly glow and deep shadows all around them.

"Here, put this on. It'll keep you and the kid warm."

Kate took the jacket and slipped her arms into the sleeves, grateful for the extra layer. She felt cold, inside and out. Booker climbed on the seat and looked at her.

"Okay, get on."

Kate obeyed without a word. She buttoned Joey into the front of the coat and clung to the barred rack attached to the seat. Booker fired up the four-wheeler, the roar so sudden and loud that Joey came unhinged, letting out a shriek that proved his lungs worked just fine. She tried to comfort him, as Booker flipped on a single headlamp and took off through moonlit tree trunks. She held on for dear life, hoping to God that John Booker knew a safe place to take them.

. . .

All Booker had to do was make it to Winona before daylight. He'd visited the small town dozens of times when he picked up supplies at Jumbo's truck stop but never in the dark. Still, he knew the trail by heart and was more concerned about being heard. The four-wheeler gave off a racket that reverberated for miles through the woods. It'd been nearly two hours; they were getting close.

He decided to come out behind the café where Jumbo was likely to be inside alone, preparing for his breakfast crowd. That way no one was likely to see the girl and the baby. If the state police were after them, too, as he suspected, they'd be asking questions in every gas station, restaurant and motel from here to Springfield, a hundred and fifty miles up the road. A lot of highway patrol officers made regular stops for coffee and meals at Jumbo's anyway. But that wasn't Booker's problem. He'd get Kate Reed out of the woods; what she did from there was up to her.

When Jumbo's truck stop loomed into sight—actually café, flea market, motor lodge, gift shop, and gas station—the place was deserted except for a couple of long-distance truck drivers waiting in their cabs for Jumbo to open up for business. Lights glowed at the rear kitchen door and Booker brought the vehicle to a stop there, cut the engine, and climbed off. The girl looked ashen-faced and petrified. He wondered how she looked when she wasn't scared out of her wits. Not likely he'd find out.

"Wait here. If anybody shows up, come inside and get me."

Kate Reed nodded and kept her death clutch on the baby.

Booker wondered how much longer she could take the life-and-death pressure as he opened the door and walked through a hallway to the brightly lit kitchen. His stomach growled in reaction to the mingled aromas of frying bacon, pork sausage and homemade buttermilk biscuits. Jumbo was pulling a long metal baking sheet out of the oven, filled with his famous biscuits the size of saucers.

Jumbo was just shy of three hundred pounds, most of it hard muscle, but the problem was that Jumbo wasn't much over five feet tall. He'd been a fairly good wrestler once, his claim to fame a victory over Gorgeous George in Philadelphia back in the eighties. Now he'd turned his aggression into down-home, country cooking.

When Jumbo saw Booker, his ebony face creased with pleasure and he showed an impressive row of big white teeth. "Well, I'll be damned for a donut, if it ain't John Booker, come to call. What you doin' back thisaway so soon? It ain't been no month yet, has it, Sarg?"

"Hey, Jumbo. I'm not here for supplies. I got me a problem." He glanced around and lowered his voice. "You alone?"

"Yep, Mavis ain't comin' in till five thirty or thereabouts. What's up?" The heavy man wiped his hands on a snow-white bib apron about the size of a small pup tent. Booker had no idea where he'd get an apron that huge. He'd never heard of a Big and Tall Shop apron.

"You heard anything about a girl who was supposed to've kidnapped a baby outta St. Louis?"

"Oh, yeah, been playin' all over the news, every damn channel for two days runnin'. Why? You know her?"

Booker nodded. "She's outside."

That revelation brought Jumbo to attention. He quit slathering globs of butter on the tops of biscuits and stared at him. "Godawmighty, Book, you hankerin' to go back to prison, or wut?"

"Not anymore than you." Booker looked through the round window in the swinging door between the kitchen and the restaurant. Through the plate-glass windows fronting the café, he could see two truckers waiting outside the entrance. "You got a couple of customers out there."

"Let 'em wait. Wut's up with you and this broad?"

"She says she didn't steal the kid. That it was a legit adoption, all signed and legal. There's some real nasty guys after her, guys with guns, guns with silencers."

Jumbo stared at him a moment, then shook his head. "What you gots to do wit' all this shit?"

"She was outnumbered."

Jumbo studied him as he wiped both his palms down the back of his white pants. "Like I say, what you gots to do with her shit?"

"C'mon, Jumbo, what'd you expect me to do? Let them kill her right in front of my eyes? There's more to this than a kidnapped baby."

"Turn her over to the cops and let them earn their pay."

"She's Pop Macon's granddaughter, and I owe him a favor."

"Gettin' kilt over her is a big favor."

Booker remained silent. He probably should contact the police but his gut told him not to. Something about the whole thing smelled, and he didn't want Kate Reed to take the fall for something she didn't do. For Pop's sake, if he had to have a reason.

"She good-lookin' by the by, Book? Is that what's got you so soft and fuzzy and turned your brains to mush?"

"I need a room. Any of the tepees empty?"

"All of them's empty. Nobody comes round much since they opened that damned sissy Honeysuckle Inn up the road. Nobody goes in for genuwine, authentic Shoshone tepees, no mo'. All they care about is havin' a fuckin' Jacuzzi bathtub and a G.E. coffeemaker in the room with lots of them packets of sugar and cream to go in it. Bunch of shit's all 'is, if you askin' me."

"The Honeysuckle doesn't have your biscuits."

"That's right. Nobody makes 'em like me." Jumbo grinned, nodding his head. He was famous in the Ozarks for his mouthwatering biscuits.

"I'll take the one down in the woods. Do you still let people park out front and sell out of their trunks?"

"Yeah, most of 'em come in at daylight and pull out by noon. Watcha need?"

"Some clothes for her and the kid."

"Just got in lots of stuff like that for the gift shop. Plannin' to set up housekeepin' with this chick, huh, Sarg?"

Booker had to grin at his old friend. Jumbo's life revolved around women, like most guys. "You know I leave the ladies to you."

"That's right, you just do that. I'll take as many as I can git hold of."

"Mavis still putting up with you?"

Jumbo nodded, teeth showing again. "Yeah, but she got mad when I hired on Lisa. Said I just hired her cause she's gotta pair on her the size of cantaloupe melons."

Probably true, Booker thought. After Jumbo's biscuits, the built waitresses he hired was his restaurant's biggest draw. "How 'bout fixing me up a couple of breakfasts to go, the works, and some milk for the kid?"

"Comin' right up. Over easy, just the way you like 'em, and a couple more scrambled with butter."

Outside, faintly, he could hear the baby crying. He needed to get them out of sight, the sooner, the better. "I'm gonna take them out to the tepee, then come back for the food. Make the coffee nice and strong."

"You got it, Sarg."

Booker watched his old friend slap down half a pound of bacon on the grill, then turned and headed for the back. He wasn't worried about Jumbo telling anybody about Kate Reed; the two of them went too far back for that. He'd trust Jumbo with his life.

Seventeen

IN A THICK COPSE of pine trees behind the truck stop, Kate climbed off the four-wheeler. Joey was still cranky and crying, and she patted his back soothingly as she stared at a fifteen-foot concrete tepee. Painted blinding scarlet, it made her want to shield her eyes. Three low concrete steps led up to the front door, and several round windows, interspersed with hand-painted running buffalo, rising suns and crescent moons decorated the circular base. The porthole beside the door was set inside a bald eagle with outspread wings and dangling talons. The miniature air-conditioning unit somewhat ruined the effect.

The other tepees they'd passed were equally garish in mustard, chartreuse, and electric blue. Kate had never seen anything quite like Jumbo's Authentic Indian Lodges, even out West where entrepreneurs took full advantage of Indian motif. She wondered why Jumbo didn't just paint them rawhide brown.

"They're all vacant but us. But you still better stay out of sight."

Booker glanced at her as he unlocked the door and shoved it open. That was his longest speech of the day. He wasn't a chatterbox, that was for sure, but it was just as well. She didn't know what to say to him either. She had a terrible feeling he was going to take off, wash his hands of her and Joey, right now, once and for all, before he got shot at. He didn't mind setting her up in a red tepee, but then he'd hightail it back to his cave. She watched him walk back and swing into the seat of the four-wheeler.

He said, "There's a lock on the door. Use it."

"Are you leaving me here alone? I mean, are you coming back?" she asked, trying not to sound as needy and frightened as she was.

Booker stared at her a moment, then said, "I'm going back to the café to get us some breakfast. Go on inside and wait for me. There's a bathtub, if you want to clean up. Don't open the door to anyone but me."

"Don't worry."

The man studied her face, ever serious, and she wondered how long it'd taken him to grow a beard that long and yucky. It straggled to his waist, matted and dirty. And why he wanted to. It did look intimidating with his long hair and intense eyes. No wonder the Joneses were afraid of him. He looked like Rasputin. Or Charles Manson sans the swastika carved into his forehead. For a minute she thought he was going to say something else, maybe warn her again about showing herself, but he just fired up the engine and wheeled onto the road. She watched until he disappeared from sight.

Kate hugged Joey closer. It was very quiet. The sun was rising over the trees, and she could see a patch of blue in the sky. A few bird whistles, the sound of a transport truck grinding through its gears somewhere far away on the roadway. What highway was it anyway? 60 West, perhaps? She'd been up this way a few times, but not often. She certainly hadn't known about Jumbo's Authentic Indian Lodges.

Suddenly she felt utterly exhausted. She'd been awake so long she couldn't remember how it felt to lie down in a bed and drift off to sleep. Her mind wasn't functioning so well either. She couldn't last much longer; she was running on adrenaline. She wished she could go back home to Pop's cabin where Joey had his little room with the rainbow on the ceiling and the yellow crib with navy plaid bumpers, where she could stretch out on the hammock on the back deck with him in her arms and sway in the breeze and listen to the rush of the currents and feel safe.

She wondered if she would ever go home again. What would she do if John Booker didn't come back? And why should he? He didn't know her from a hole in the ground. He didn't owe her a damn thing. And if he did hang around, he had an excellent chance of getting shot at or thrown into jail, if not simply murdered in cold blood, like Michael.

The idea of Dmitri coming after her sent her scurrying inside. She twisted the lock and hooked the security chain. There was a light switch beside the door but she didn't touch it. She'd become nocturnal, afraid of the light, afraid of being seen. Like a bat. Or a vampire. Or a zombie.

The dim room seemed filled with gray gauze, but the interior wasn't as gaudy as the outside. The cabin was divided into a bathroom and bedroom, each a half-moon shape, the bedroom part larger. She could see a sink with a round mirror above it through the open bathroom door. There were two full beds, and the carpet was gold and green shag, vintage Beatlemania—the first one when Ringo and company emerged out of Liverpool in the sixties, before her time at any rate. The bedspreads were red-and-black–checked buffalo blankets, neatly tucked in all around, and there were plenty more cowboy influences in keeping with Jumbo's Wild West theme.

There was a desk beside the door, two bedside tables with matching reading lamps—wranglers on bucking broncos waving ten-gallon hats and hanging on for dear life as they held up fringed tan lampshades. There was a mirrored dresser, and she hardly recognized the poor bruised figure with the frightened eyes staring back at her.

She was tired, that's all. If she could just get some rest, she could start dealing with things again. Even if Booker didn't come back, she'd find a way to get Joey out of this. Gus. Yes, that's who she'd have to go to. Gus was her only hope. If she could get hold of him, he'd intercede with the state police, find out if Joey had really been kidnapped. He was the sheriff, for God's sake; surely they'd listen to him.

More hopeful, she looked for a telephone. There wasn't one. But there was a thirteen-inch television, an old RCA black-and-white job. She flipped it on. A sunrise religious program slowly materialized on the screen. A man was leaning on a lectern talking about the Sermon on the Mount and how the meek would inherit the earth. There was a beautiful blue lake behind him, the sun just coming up behind it with a glory of jagged rays. It looked like Lake Taneycomo near Springfield. That was the only channel.

Kate sat on the bed, staring at the nice calm lake, holding Joey who had finally gone to sleep. She ought to take Booker's advice, draw a bath, give the baby a good scrub, too. She felt filthy and nasty, her mouth stale and sticky. She hadn't brushed her teeth since she'd been chased out of her home. Somehow, that made her want to cry. How stupid. She was going crazy, she thought; the whole world was.

Kate was still sitting on the bed, staring dully at the television when she heard a key scrape in the lock. She jumped up and hid behind the door until the chain caught. She was afraid to say anything, in case it wasn't Booker. She wilted with relief when she heard his deep voice. Thank God, he wasn't going to leave her alone, not yet.

"Open up."

Rattling the chain off, she let it fall, then stepped back. It swung back and forth with a scraping sound as Booker came in with a couple of plastic grocery bags in one hand and some white take-out sacks in the other. He immediately secured the lock and chain. He looked at her.

"Why's it so dark in here?"

Kate shook her head, clueless herself. She didn't know why she preferred to sit in the dark. Booker flipped the light on, then moved to a round table with two chairs positioned in front of the window with the air conditioner. He set everything down, glancing at the television. The choir was now singing high-pitched praises to Jesus.

"Have you heard anything?"

For a moment Kate didn't know what he meant. "What?"

"On the tube. The news mention you?"

She shook her head. "I mean, I haven't seen any news."

His brows knitted slightly. "Are you all right?"

"I guess so." She became aware of food odors emanating from the white sacks. Her stomach rumbled so loudly that Booker heard it.

"I thought you might be hungry. When was the last time you ate?"

Kate tried to remember, couldn't, then recalled stuffing a couple of Millie Mae's biscuits in her pocket about a hundred years ago. "I'm not sure I can keep anything down, not after—" She paused, not wanting to say it or think about it, then finished lamely, "—you know, everything."

He didn't answer but dug out two flat carry-out Styrofoam containers from the white sack and placed them on the table. "You will, once you take a couple of bites. You have to, if you want to keep going." He opened the lid and swiveled the carton around for her to see. Bacon and eggs, a pile of buttered toast, pancakes drenched in maple syrup. "I got a sack of Jumbo's biscuits, too."

Kate watched him get out plastic forks and spoons from another sack. Then he lifted out two huge Styrofoam cups. "Coffee. Black and strong."

He sat down in a chair that gave him a view of the road. He looked out for a second, then gestured her into the seat across from him. "C'mon, eat, before it gets cold."

Kate obeyed, perching on the straight chair, staring at the food in the carton. She found herself unwilling to put Joey down, even to eat. She'd had him in her arms for the most part of two days. He felt like a part of her now, like another arm or leg. Or heart. He was her heart.

"He'll be all right. Put him over there on the bed."

"No, I'll hold him."

Booker shrugged and pried the plastic lid off one of the coffee cups, then placed it in front of her. The aromatic steam rose temptingly to her nose. He removed his lid and took a sip. Now he looked like one of Robert Redford's mountain-men buddies in *Jeremiah Johnson*, incongruously large and out of place at the tiny table, holding a Styrofoam cup stamped with little red biodegradable flags. "Eat, then get some rest. You look out of it."

Kate said, "I'm all right. I'm just all tied up in knots, you know?"

"Yeah."

Booker dove into his breakfast with a hearty appetite more in keeping with his rough-hewn image, while Kate gratefully took a drink of hot coffee. The brew was as black and strong as Booker had promised, and it hit the bottom of her empty stomach and brought it lurching back to life, rumbling and grumbling as she gulped down some more. She got up and laid Joey on the bed, watching him stretch and throw his arms wide. He was more comfortable there, able to move around if he wanted. He was just a few feet away. He'd be safe enough.

Sitting down again, she split the clear plastic encasing her utensils, then forked up a bite of eggs. Hers were scrambled, yellow and fluffy, delicious, wonderful, and she began to attack the food like a starved refugee. She shoveled down her eggs in nothing flat, then plunged eagerly into light brown pancakes, totally, insanely ravenous. She finished up everything on her plate before Booker did and flushed with embarrassment when she realized she must have looked like a wild hyena, wolfing down food before the rest of the pack could steal any.

"Feel better?"

Kate nodded as she wiped her mouth and fingers on a white napkin, then moved back to the bed. She sat down beside Joey while Booker finished eating, more decorously than she had. She wondered if he'd leave her to her fate now. He'd done his duty, after all, saved her, fed her, been more than a Good Samaritan.

"I got you some baby stuff. Didn't know exactly what to get."

He handed her one of the grocery bags he'd toted in. Inside she found a couple of packages of Luvs, travel bottles of Johnson's baby powder and shampoo, and a boxed gift set with a baby towel and washcloth, receiving blanket, and a little sleeper suit made from terrycloth with attached feet and a snap-up crotch. All in blue with St. Louis Cardinal logos. A red rattle was tied on the box with a white bow. In the bottom of the bag she found a bar of Irish Spring soap, a brand-new toothbrush, a small tube of Crest, and a bottle of Tylenol. Tears gushed up her throat, and she was so overwhelmed with gratitude that she couldn't even thank him.

"I got the kid some milk, too." Booker was standing at the window, his rifle in his hand again, obviously expecting trouble to drive up at any moment. "It's in the other coffee cup."

"How can I ever thank you?" All clogged and hoarse.

"Forget it."

"I can't. I can't." Kate choked up and fought back welling tears.

Booker seemed annoyed. "Look, why don't you take a shower? Get some sleep. Nobody knows we're back here. I'll keep watch till you wake up."

She pulled herself together by force of will. She felt better with food in her stomach. Maybe she should take a quick shower and lie down for awhile with Joey. She hesitated, reluctant to leave Joey alone with a stranger, even one who had been so kind. But the baby was sleeping so peacefully. In her heart she didn't believe John Booker would hurt him.

"Will you watch him for me? Knock on the bathroom door if he cries or anything?"

Booker nodded but kept his attention focused outside. Kate picked up the sack of baby supplies and walked into the bathroom. It was tiny but relatively clean, with four thick, white towels and two washcloths folded atop a rack over the toilet. The mirror hung on a nail over the sink and Kate avoided her reflection. She pushed the bolt into place, then swept back the shower curtain with a squeal of metal rings.

She undressed quickly and stepped into the tub. She turned the taps very hot, and for several minutes let the water run down over her face and body, feeling the tension in her muscles finally start to ease. She lathered up with the Irish Spring, then carefully removed the gauze bandage around her head. She poured a palmful of baby shampoo and gingerly washed around the wound on her scalp. She rinsed her hair thoroughly, then twisted off the taps.

Wrapping a towel around her hair and a second one around her torso, she squeezed Crest on the toothbrush and nearly scrubbed the enamel off her teeth. She swallowed down two Tylenol tablets, then added two more to conquer her pounding head before thirstily finishing off the glass of water. Afterward, she felt almost like a human being again.

There was no sound coming from the other room, not even the low buzz of the television evangelist. Worried, she cracked the door and peeked outside. The bedroom was deserted, the outside door ajar.

Joey was gone.

Eighteen

BOOKER JERKED AROUND, rifle gripped in his right hand, Joey riding his left arm. Kate Reed stood in the doorway wearing nothing but a skimpy white towel that barely reached her thighs. Her long blond hair dripped tangled down her back, her face frantic. He reacted as a man first, eyes riveted on her nearly naked body. It didn't take him long to get over that because she rushed down the steps, oblivious to anyone watching.

"What're you doing? Where're you taking Joey?"

The woman was panicked, and Booker put his gun on the seat of the four-wheeler and fended her off with a raised palm. "Whoa, now, lady, wait a minute. I just came out to hide the four-wheeler."

"You didn't have to take Joey! Give him back, give him back now!"

"All right, he's right here, take him." Gladly he handed the infant over, watching her clutch the boy so tightly he let out a shrill complaint. "He was squirming around and I thought he'd roll off the bed. I didn't hurt him."

Kate Reed didn't look as though she believed him, and he tried not to notice how short the damned towel was and how long and shapely her bare legs were. He averted his eyes but not before she'd noticed where he was looking and what he was interested in. Whirling, she ran back inside with the baby. He waited for her to slam the door and barricade it against him, surprised when she didn't.

He wheeled the vehicle to the back and hid it in some bushes. Picking up the yellow plastic baby seat and the rest of the stuff he'd bought, he walked around to the front and peered up the road, hoping no one had witnessed their little public spectacle. He went back inside, not sure what to expect. She was in the bathroom with Joey, and he had a pretty good feeling she had the door locked good and tight. He put down the plastic grocery sacks, turned the lock and chained the front door. He waited a moment, then tapped a knuckle on the bathroom door.

"I got you some clothes. If you want, I'll hand them in."

Silence. Booker asked himself why he was doing this, going to all this trouble, buying the girl a damned wardrobe. He could have left anytime, before breakfast, after breakfast. Now. He could have left her unconscious at the bottom of the cliff and minded his own business. Damn it, she wasn't his problem and neither was the baby. He shook his head. He must be out of his mind to hang around and wait for a bullet to find him.

The bolt rattled, and Kate cracked the door. He stuffed the sack of clothes through the narrow opening, and she grabbed them, shut the door in his face and shoved the bolt home. He shouldn't have gawked at her body like some sex-starved teenager; she was shaky enough. He retook the chair and stared out the window. He should get up and leave. Walk out. That's what he'd told her he was going to do, what he planned all along. She'd made it this far pretty much on her own, hadn't she? But she was hanging on by a strand of gossamer about now. Without his help she wouldn't stand a chance in hell to escape killers as professional as the ones out to get her. That's where the rub came in.

Fifteen minutes passed before she came out of the bathroom. He thought it better not to look at her. She went over to the bed and sat down. He knew that when the bedsprings squeaked like mice in pain. He ignored her.

"I'm sorry, Mr. Booker. I thought you'd taken Joey for the

reward, and I just got frantic. I shouldn't have accused you the way I did."

His eyes focused on the road through the pines, he hunched a shoulder. "You've been through a lot the last couple of days."

Kate moved to the table, picked up the cup of milk, then returned to the bed. Afterward the room grew quiet except for the wind rattling the air conditioner. He thought it better to keep his mouth shut while he figured out what to do with them. He didn't come up with any plan that didn't spell disaster with a capital D, like in DEAD, all of them.

"I gave Joey a bath," she said at length, her voice little more than a whisper. "The sleeper fits him pretty well. There was pacifier with the bottle you bought, one shaped like a clown."

Booker glanced at her, wondering why she found the need to share that little tidbit, and found her feeding Joey with the baby bottle he'd stuck in when he'd bought the clothes. He could remember Betsy curling up on their bed in just the same way, feeding their son, smiling down at him, not long before he left for Nicaragua the last time. An eternity ago. He forced the troubling vision from his mind and didn't say anything. In a little while he heard a belch come out of Joey that sounded more like a three-hundred-pound gorilla. Kate moved around on the bed some more, making metallic music as the bedsprings sang. Then it became completely quiet.

Later when he stole another glance, Kate Reed was lying on her side, her right arm protectively around the baby, both sound asleep. She had on the navy blue sweats he'd bought her, the sweatshirt emblazoned across the front in big white letters with *Jumbo's Famous Ozark Butterfly Biscuits—So Light They Just Float Away*. He stared at them, thinking they both looked pretty little and defenseless, then clenched his jaw in quiet fury when he realized he couldn't bring himself to walk out on them the way he should. She wouldn't make it a mile up the highway before somebody recognized her. And the way her luck was running, it'd be the Russian assassins, or whoever the hell they were. He didn't have the slightest idea what he was going to do with her but he'd better come up with something fast.

After about an hour on watch he decided that he didn't have too many choices. He'd have to go to his old buddy, Mac Sharp. Mac could be trusted and had ties to the police, if she decided to turn herself in. If anyone could get the girl a fair hearing, it'd be Mac. But they'd have to get to Branson first, and that wouldn't be easy. In any truck stop or restaurant along Highway 60, they'd stick out like a family of three in a singles bar.

On the bed the girl and baby still slept like twin logs. For good reason. They'd been through hell and back. With people shooting at them along the route. Outside everything looked fine. Chances were no one knew where they were, at least not yet, and Jumbo was on the lookout for Kate's pursuers out front. He stood up and drew the drapes, plunging the room to near darkness. Picking up a straight chair and swiveling it around, he braced the back under the doorknob, picked up the sack he'd left on the table and walked into the bathroom. He shut the door quietly and propped the rifle in the corner.

He hit the light switch, braced his palms on the sink and stared at himself in the mirror. He didn't like what he saw. God, no wonder Kate Reed was afraid of him. He looked like a deranged hermit. His eyes narrowed and he realized that was pretty much true. His face was still smeared with dried mud he'd slathered on for concealment that first day when he'd become aware of Kate Reed's life-and-death flight through his woods. He'd kept an eye on her after that, more curious than anything, and thought she'd made it out safely when she took up with the boys who grew pot across the river.

The guys chasing her hadn't seen him. The bastards in Special Ops had taught him too well. His mouth tightened. He took a deep breath. One thing was for damn certain, he couldn't wander around looking like Grizzly Adams without drawing attention to the girl. He had to clean himself up and look like an ordinary tourist headed for Branson and its theaters of country stars and twanging guitars. Everything in him rebelled against leaving the sanctuary of the woods, but the sense of honor he'd thought the army had killed off years ago kept pricking him to do the right thing. That, and his indebtedness to Pop Macon. There was another reason, too. Something about Kate Reed had gotten to him, big time, but that didn't mean he had to like it.

Sighing, he reached into the bag and fished out the scissors and shaving supplies he'd bought in Jumbo's gift shop. He grasped a hunk of his filthy, unkempt beard and began to shear it off close to his chin.

Kate came awake, groggy and disoriented. She couldn't remember where she was, only that it was completely dark, tensed up in fear, then relaxed considerably when she felt Joey twisting around on the bed beside her.

"Shhh, sweetie," she whispered when he fussed sleepily. She pushed up and looked around the dark room. It was very quiet. She supposed thick concrete walls did that. Booker was not at the table by the window, but she heard the faint sound of the toilet flushing in the bathroom. He was not gone.

Gathering Joey into her arms she tiptoed to the window and peeked outside. It was a sunny day, the sky bright blue with lots of clouds like shredded cotton. The wind was swaying the pine boughs shading the cabin. She sat down where she could see the road to the café and settled Joey in the crook of her arm. She put the bottle to his mouth and smiled as he sucked eagerly, his tiny fingers squeezing tightly around her thumb.

She glanced at the bathroom door, ashamed of her earlier behavior. John Booker had done everything he could to help them, had put his life on the line, for God's sake. She wondered why but had a feeling she'd probably never find out. He'd go soon, and she had to get word to Gus to come get her.

She hated to involve the old man, but she didn't have anywhere else to turn.

Muffled sounds still emanated from the bathroom, running water, footsteps, creaking sounds in the pipes. The room had grown chilly, and she was glad she had on the navy sweatsuit. She wrapped Joey's new blue blanket more tightly around him. After some time had passed, perhaps half an hour or more, she began to wonder what Booker was doing for so long in the bathroom. He didn't come off like a stickler for hygiene; there were probably cockleburs in his beard older than Joey.

She felt like a new person after getting some rest, then wondered how long she'd slept. Now she felt as though she could go on by herself if she had to. She gazed down at Joey's sweet face, her heart warming at the way he never took his eyes off her. What if the adoption wasn't legal? What if someday somebody came and took him away? She couldn't bear it, couldn't stand to think about life without him.

When the bathroom door opened, Kate glanced up. Her jaw dropped. She stared, couldn't help it. If not for his height and size, she wouldn't have recognized the man who emerged. Clean shaven, black hair cropped short, dressed in khakis and a dark green polo shirt left hanging out, he looked nothing like the man she'd met in the woods. She blinked, wondering if it *was* him, thinking he surely couldn't change his appearance that drastically in so short a time, but he stood there in front of her, a wadded-up bundle of camouflage clothes in one hand.

"I decided to clean up," he told her, a bit unnecessarily.

Kate laughed, rather stupidly, she realized, cutting off abruptly, but her astonishment at his complete metamorphosis staggered her. "Good God, you look like Clark Kent."

"Clark Kent?"

Kate couldn't take her eyes off him. "Yeah, you know, Superman, Lois Lane, Jimmy."

"From the comic books?"

"Yeah, the man of steel who can leap tall buildings with a

single bound, is faster than a speeding locomotive and all that stuff."

"Too bad I'm not. Might come in handy hanging around you."

"Yeah, tell me about it." Kate actually smiled at his dry remark, somehow a lot more at ease now that he looked like a regular, everyday guy and not some woodsy psychopath.

He turned away and stuffed the dirty clothes into an empty plastic grocery bag. She could tell a lot more about him now. He was leaner through the torso and hips than she'd thought, but his shoulders were unusually broad, his arms and back thick with muscle. He had a superb physique, and he looked as strong as an ox, his size still intimidating. He looked like a big, tough normal human being now. She wondered how long it'd been since he'd shaved last and made himself into a clean-cut College Joe. Why now? That was a better question.

"I'm sorry about what happened earlier." She really was, felt she had to apologize. "I feel better now. The Tylenols finally kicked my headache."

"Listen, we need to talk." Booker didn't look at her and she knew it was finally coming. He was taking off. She didn't blame him. She would too, if she was him.

"Okay."

He was toting his rifle everywhere he went, and she watched him walk around the room, lifting the drapes at each window, checking out the sunlit afternoon. He moved slowly, deliberately, like the experienced hunter he was, like a man who knew how to take care of himself. He just looked a lot better doing it now. He was actually handsome, in a rough, taciturn, serious sort of way, actually *very* handsome. She mocked her own thoughts. If anyone would've told her a few hours ago that she'd think John Booker was a cute guy, sexy even, she'd have called them crazy. But he was, he definitely was. She wondered if he knew it.

He sat down across from her, his eyes lingering on Joey an extra moment. When he raised them to her, they shone the intense pale blue as before, more startling now that she could see his face better. He had a square jaw that gave him a powerful look, but his features were clean and chiseled. She noticed again the crescent scar at the corner of his eye and wondered how he'd gotten it. She waited but she already knew what was coming.

"Look," Booker said, "there's no way in hell you'll ever make it out of here alone. I think I can help you, but you'll have to start trusting me more than you do right now. You have to agree to do exactly what I say, all the time, without question, or both of us are bound to get killed."

Kate felt the burn of tears deep down at the back of her nose, but it was gratitude, sheer relief that he wasn't going to leave her alone. Despite her brave thoughts to the contrary, she was still petrified to step outside of the cabin, much less try to find a way back to Van Buren. And she didn't want to give Joey up. As bad as it was to want to keep him if he had been stolen out of his mother's arms, she didn't want to lose him, not if there was any way, any way whatsoever to keep him. He meant more to her than her own life.

"Okay," was all she could manage.

Booker studied her face. He definitely looked skeptical at her easy acquiescence. "You sure?"

Kate nodded. "You've done so much for us already. I can never thank you enough, never."

"Save it until we make it out of here in one piece."

His remark brought the gravity of their situation down on Kate. She said, "I've got a friend. The sheriff of Carter County. You know, I told you about him. I want to call him and see if he won't intervene with the FBI. They'll be involved now, too, won't they? Since it's an alleged kidnapping?" She stopped because Booker was already shaking his head. "No?"

"I can't get involved with the cops, especially the FBI. Not even with your friend."

It was Kate's turn to search *his* face. His jaw and cheeks were unnaturally pale where the heavy beard had been so long. His hair was very dark, jet black, as were his eyelashes; maybe that's why his eyes looked so blue. She wondered how old he was. He looked younger now than he had before, by, say, about fifty years, but she now knew he couldn't be much older than she was, maybe in his late thirties. Why on earth had he let himself devolve into a hideous recluse who hid in a cave? What had driven him to such extremes? She waited for him to tell her why he couldn't involve the police but he didn't elaborate. She felt she had to ask.

"Why not?"

He didn't seem to want to fill her in and that made her nervous about him all over again. She got the definite impression he wasn't going to say anything else. Then he began to speak, but it came out hard.

"I'm wanted, that's why. Does that change your mind about throwing in with me?"

Kate had to admit it did give cause for alarm, but she tried to hide her uneasiness. "What for? Can you tell me?"

Again he made her suffer a long-drawn hesitation. "I broke out of a military prison. They never caught me."

Kate looked down at Joey, whose eyelids were drooping at half mast. He was in what she called his presleep daze, but then he remembered the nipple still in his mouth and resumed his sucking as hard as he could.

"What were you in for?" Kate nearly held her breath while he spent some time deciding whether or not to answer her.

"I shot my superior officer." His voice was extremely quiet, and Kate had a feeling he hadn't often uttered the words aloud. It occurred to her to wonder how often he talked to anyone, for any reason.

"Shot him?" she prompted, closely watching his face.

"He didn't die."

"So you were in for attempted murder?"

He nodded and waited, his clear eyes not showing much remorse.

Kate said, "I guess it's safe to say I don't have to worry about you shooting me, do I? You've had lots of chances to so far and haven't. In fact, you're the only man I've met in the last three days who hasn't tried to kill me." Smiling, she wiggled her eyebrows and held an invisible cigar, performing her best Groucho Marx impersonation.

To her surprise, Booker grinned back. His teeth were surprisingly clean and even for a habitual cave dweller. "I'm always for the underdog in a fight," he told her, his smile quickly fading into a somber expression. "And I reckon you're as much that as anybody I've ever known."

"Why?" she had to know, very serious again herself. "Why are you willing to help us? You might get caught again, sent back to prison, if anyone figures out who you are."

"Hopefully they've closed the book on me. It's been awhile." He laid his rifle across his lap. "Why doesn't matter. It's what I'm going to do."

Kate bit her lip, thinking God had heard the flood of prayers she'd been sending up. He'd sent her a guardian angel of sorts, as unlikely a one as John Booker was. But he was the kind of man who made a woman feel protected, who knew how to handle a gun and could shoot people if he had to, and that was the kind of man she needed. She fought the growing need to get overly emotional and come all apart inside, knowing he also wasn't the kind of guy who'd like a woman to give in to a fit of weeping.

"They know what you look like so you're going to have to change your appearance," he was saying now. "Got any problem with that?"

"I guess I could cut my hair some and dye it another color, or something like that. Does that mean we're leaving here?"

"Yeah, as soon as I can hitch us a ride west."

"We're going west?"

"I've got a friend in Branson who'll help us."

"Okay." Kate was ready to leave everything in his hands. If

he could get her and Joey to Branson and far away from the people trying to kill her, she was all for it. "Then what happens?"

"Then we try to decide what to do about the kid. You can call this guy Gus from Branson if you want. See if he'll intercede. Or I can take off and go home right now, and you can call him and let him come get you. If you do, he won't be able to keep them from taking the kid away from you. Maybe if you get outta here and have time to think things through, you can figure out what's going on, get a lawyer or something, if you need one. Turn yourself in on your own terms."

Kate automatically pulled Joey closer. He didn't seem to mind as he slurped out the last dregs of the milk. "I don't want to give him up."

"Yeah, I gathered that."

He'd said it seriously, but somehow the drollness of the remark struck Kate funny. She laughed. Booker gave a slight smile, as if unaccustomed to levity of any kind. He wasn't a jolly kind of guy. She wondered just how hard it was for him to step out of the woods and his Bigfoot persona in order to help her.

"I need to see if anyone's come in the café looking for you," he said, scraping out his chair and standing up. "I'll try to find you some hair dye and maybe a hat and some big sunglasses that'll hide most of your face. I already bought some scissors. Anything else you want?"

Kate shook her head and followed Booker to the door. The minute he was outside, she shut and locked it, then moved to the back window to watch him fire up the four-wheeler and head up the road.

"I think we're going to make it, sweetie," she whispered softly against Joey's black curls that smelled like Johnson's baby shampoo. "Booker's going to help us get away. He's gonna take us somewhere safe."

She lay down on the bed with Joey and closed her eyes, feeling better about her chances of escape than she had in a very long time.

Nineteen

JUMBO'S CAFÉ was busy with the hungry noonday crowd. Booker parked in back but entered through the restaurant front door as if he'd pulled off the highway. The tables and the red vinyl booths edging the plate-glass windows were full of loggers, state highway maintenance men and truckers, and the clatter of silverware and clink of glass mixed with the low rumble of conversation.

No one reacted negatively and moved away from him as on prior occasions when he came in for supplies wearing camouflage and long hair. Now he fit in so well that he was ignored. He realized that for the first time in years it mattered to him what other people thought, not for himself but for Kate Reed. He walked to the back and pushed through swinging doors into the kitchen, immediately buffeted with savory aromas of fried chicken and cinnamon apple pie. Jumbo stopped whipping potatoes and stared at Booker as if he had just flown in from the rings of Saturn.

"Holy shit, that you, Book?"

Jumbo shook his shiny bald head, then gave a big, booming laugh. "I ain't seen you so spiffed up and shiny since you left Leavenworth for your court martial." Jumbo kept grinning as if fondly remembering the seven years they spent together as cell mates before Booker had climbed over the fence and said goodbye to prison for good. "Jesus, you know who you look like?"

"Clark Kent?" Booker glanced around but the cooks and waiters were too busy sweating over the stoves and deep-fry vats or clattering dirty dishes into the soaking sinks to pay attention to what he was saying. He was amazed at how easily associating with other people was coming back; he'd kept to himself a long time.

"Nope, I was thinking more on the lines of Lurch on that old Munster show we used to watch when we was in the pen." Jumbo nodded sagely, then showed his huge white grin and great appreciation for his keen wit.

"Yeah, right. Listen, Jumbo, I need a ride outta here, pronto. Got any ideas where I can get one?"

Jumbo frowned and wiped floury hands down the front of his grease-stained apron. Both men had to step aside to let Mavis, Jumbo's bosomy waitress, squeeze out the swinging door with two heavy white platters of butter-drenched biscuits. She was pretty and petite, her hair braided with about a million white beads, her skin almost as black as Jumbo's. She and Jumbo'd been an item for at least five years running.

"Like your haircut, Book," she called over her shoulder, then let loose with her piercing cackle. "'Bout time, man. You was gettin' a mite mangy there lately."

Booker waved a hand. He liked Mavis a lot, hoped she'd someday agree to marry his friend the way Jumbo wanted. Another girl walked by him with several hamburger platters, and Booker realized how long ago breakfast had been. He followed the food with hungry eyes until the girl disappeared into the front.

"I dunno. Where you headin'?"

Booker hesitated, reluctant to draw Jumbo into Kate's mess but having little choice. "Mac's place in Branson. I'm gonna call him in a minute outside at the pay phone."

"Hell, use the phone back in the office. So Mac the Knife's still pickin' and playin' up there, huh?"

"Yeah, far as I know. Anybody been poking around about the girl?"

Lowering his voice to match Booker's, Jumbo shook his head. "Not yet but I'm keeping my ears open." He paused, thinking about it. "I tell you what, though, I got an old friend comin' in here tomorrow morning. We used to ride bikes in the old days with the Fightin' Tarantulas out of East St. Louis. He's droppin' by to see me and score some pot, then he's goin' on up to the Do-Duck-Inn, you know, the tavern up past the Mountain View Wal-Mart store. He might bring you along wit' him, if I let him know you okay. He had some run-in with the law down in Nashville a few months back. Got a drug warrant out so he's movin' out to Kansas City. Want me to say somethun to him, just say the word."

"Can he keep his mouth shut?"

"Put it this way, I wouldn't be barin' my soul to him if I was you."

"Don't worry."

Jumbo guffawed as if amused by the idea of Booker running off at the mouth. He flipped over a couple of hamburgers sizzling on the grill and slapped squares of American cheese on them, and Booker told him to fix a couple of cheeseburger specials to go, with a carton of milk on the side. Jumbo nodded and plunged frozen french fries into hot grease with a huge hiss and spatter.

"My money still in the freezer?"

Jumbo nodded. "Safe as a flat-chested virgin."

"I'll leave enough to pay for all this stuff."

"Sure, I trust ya, Book."

Booker started off, but Jumbo stopped him and brought his voice way down. "Don't be comin' out here 'round closin' time. Couple of state cops, friends of Mavis and me, like to come in and fill up their thermos jugs, y'know, to keep 'em awake out on the road till mornin'. Another thing, Book, heard tell they was setting up roadblocks lookin' for the woman and kid all up and down the highways outta Van Buren. Thought you oughta know."

"Yeah, thanks."

Booker frowned on his way to the rear storeroom, thinking all they needed was roadblocks. He pulled open the lid of the big chest freezer. He kept his cash there, wrapped in tinfoil in a Folger's can. Back pay he'd earned and stockpiled in the service and never needed until now. He took out most of the thick wad of folded twenties and stuffed them in his pocket, then shut the top. He headed to Jumbo's private office and tried to get through to Mac Sharp but got no answer. He'd try again later.

While Jumbo cooked his order, he sauntered into the adjoining souvenir shop where he'd picked up Kate's sweats and baby stuff earlier that morning. There were a few customers browsing around but no one paid much attention to him as he idly swiveled the sunglasses rack and cased out the joint. He didn't see anybody he knew or who was chasing Kate Reed, so he picked out a wire-rimmed pair of green-tinted aviator's shades for himself and large, owl-eyed black plastic ones for Kate.

He also chose a couple of Kansas City Royals baseball caps, the kind with adjustable straps, got some more shirts and T-shirts for Kate and him both and a package of Hanes For Women cotton underwear and socks he thought would fit her. He browsed the grocery shelves until he found a box of hair color called Nice and Easy. He chose it in dark auburn brown. He turned to leave, hesitated, then went back to the pharmacy aisle and got a tube of red lipstick and some makeup out of the spinning Cover Girl display rack. Maybe Kate could use it to hide the bruises on her face.

Booker glanced up as a tall man moved up beside him and picked up a bottle of burn ointment. He recognized him instantly. The big blond-haired kid chasing Kate. Booker's first impulse was to get out of there ASAP but the guy paid no attention to him. Booker slid the Nice and Easy under the clothes he carried and backed up a step or two. He picked up a *Sports Illustrated* off the periodicals rack. There was no way the young Russian would recognize him or suspect he'd taken up with Kate Reed, but having their pursuers right on top of them did not bode well for Kate.

The boy killer was younger than Booker had expected, and Booker noticed how one side of his face was mottled red with a blistered burn. Booker watched him pick through the medicines, choosing a bottle of Caladryl lotion to go along with the burn salve, probably for the guy who'd blundered into the yellow jackets. Kate had left them licking a few wounds along the way. The boy was intent on choosing the medicine, giving Booker plenty of time to size him up. He had on a black windbreaker, unzipped and hanging loose, probably to conceal the weapon he had tucked at the back of his waistband. Booker could see the bulge underneath his coat.

Booker casually made his way to the next aisle but kept an eye on the kid who had stopped at the jewelry counter beside the cash register. He held up a dangly earring to his pierced right ear and bent down to look into the mirror. Booker realized the guy was vain as well as deadly, which would distract him from the hunt. A definite sign of inexperience. Pros did not draw attention to themselves, not with jewelry or anything else. Booker waited until the Russian finished checking out his purchases, then carried his own stuff to the female clerk.

According to the plastic nameplate pinned to her black uniform, the girl's name was Charlie. He remembered her from past excursions to Jumbo's but she didn't recognize him, smiling and chatting about what a nice day it was, warm and sunny with a cool little breeze to keep a girl from getting too warm. Unusually friendly, Booker thought, more interested, however, in where the Russian with the ponytail was headed.

The youth entered the adjoining restaurant, which had cleared out some, and sat down in a booth by the window with two other guys. Booker recognized them as the men who'd been tracking Kate in the woods. He'd not seen them earlier when he'd come in, so they must've just arrived. In the booth next to them, Matty Jones sat with two more men, both sporting welts from yellow jacket venom. Alarmed they'd picked up Kate's trail so quickly, Booker decided to see if he could find out what they were up to.

As Charlie bagged Booker's purchases, a young couple with two little kids got up from the booth beside the Russians, blithely unaware they'd just munched burgers next to a team of cold-blooded killers. Booker strolled across the restaurant and took the vacant table, sliding in with his back to the blond youth and a handsome man with a close-cropped goatee and ugly cut on his forehead.

Booker had a feeling that he might be Dmitri, the fresh wound another of Kate's calling cards. They were speaking together softly in Russian, a northern dialect somewhat different from the Moscow one he'd studied at the Company. Linguistics had been his specialty, and though a little rusty after so long, Booker could understand most of what they said. When a waitress named Bobbie arrived with a menu and a smile, he told her he was waiting for an order to go.

"One of us will remain here and keep an eye out for the woman. The rest of us will check out every damn place along this road if need be. If we offer a big enough reward to anybody who sees her and calls us, somebody will eventually get greedy."

"I don't see why you trust this farm boy," the kid muttered sullenly. "He is a stupid man. He cannot know she took up with the hermit."

"Yes, he is a stupid man but he knows this area better than we do. If he says there's an old man across the river who could've helped her vanish into thin air, then I'm inclined to believe him. Matty and his brothers were right behind her when she fell and injured herself, and Yuri found traces of blood on the other side of the river. There's no way she could have outrun us on her own if she was dazed and bleeding." He paused, waiting as Bobbie refilled their water glasses, then continued when she moved to the next table. "All of us heard a vehicle somewhere across the river last night, and Matty says this restaurant's the only place he's ever seen the hermit go outside the woods. Maybe he doesn't have her, maybe he's been here and gone, but if he does show up with or without the woman, we can force him to tell us what he knows. Obviously he's not a hard man to pick out of a crowd."

Misha was not convinced. "What if the farmer's wrong?

What if we're wasting our time looking for this strange old man?"

"Then we'll search every single stop along this highway. There aren't that many places to look in this godforsaken wilderness, so we'll split up and leave snitches in the most likely places. Misha, you ride with Nikolai and Andre. Yuri and I will take the farm boy with us. He's got his brothers offering rewards to their drug buyers for information on a woman with a baby. Somebody will see or hear something eventually. I want her, do you understand, and I'm going to get her."

"We've been driving up and down these roads all night," the boy complained in a whining tone. "I need sleep. We can't go night and day without fucking up. You are obsessed with this woman, uncle."

"Shut up, Misha, and do what you're told. We don't rest, any of us, until we get her. And I want the bitch taken alive, you hear me, Misha? Kill her, and you answer to me."

The third guy spoke up, very quiet and reasonable. "The boy is right, Dmitri. We cannot function well without rest. This place has cabins in back, well hidden in the trees. It'd be a good base of operations where we can regroup without drawing undue attention."

Dmitri was obviously calling all the shots, and his obsession with finding Kate had probably turned personal after she'd escaped from him at the farm. He remembered her trembling voice and how scared she was of Dmitri and wondered what he'd done to her in that barn. Booker sipped from the glass of ice water the waitress put down as the killers' conversation ended and Mavis brought their food. When Dmitri spoke to her, his English was flawless. Where the hell had these guys come from?

"Beg your pardon, miss, but do you have lodgings available for tonight?"

Booker grimaced when he heard Mavis's eager reply, apparently willing and able to rent Jumbo's prize tepees. He hoped Jumbo hadn't told her he was staying in one. He breathed easier at her next words.

"Oh, yes sir, the whole bunch is vacant at the moment. You can have your pick."

"We need two units for the night."

"Yes sir, you just tell Charlie over there at the checkout counter when you leave, and she'll write you up and get you your keys." Unaware of whom she dealt with, Mavis sounded pleased as punch.

Booker cursed under his breath as the men lowered their voices and lapsed back into Russian. "Give out my cell phone number to anybody you find along the road who'll agree to watch for Kate and the kid, Misha. Tell them we'll pay them a hundred dollars cash and double the sum if we get there before the girl gets away."

"I don't understand how she always escapes us. She's got the saints on her side." Young Misha again, feeling abused by his victim.

"The saints have nothing to do with it. We have been clumsy and incompetent, starting with you bungling the hit in her kitchen. But that won't happen anymore. Understand me, Misha? No more carelessness or you'll find yourself on an Aeroflot flight back to Moscow and your mother."

Misha made a disgruntled sound but didn't argue. They concentrated on their meal, and a few minutes later Booker eased out of the booth, intent on getting back inside the room with Kate before they finished their meal and checked things out. They barely paid attention to him as he walked past, then paid for his carryout at the register and left through the front door.

As he passed the plate-glass window he saw Dmitri watching him. Booker walked on casually, fairly confident he wouldn't be recognized. Matty Jones had looked right at him and not made the connection. He headed for the kitchen, stopping inside long enough to inform Jumbo he was about to rent rooms to a gang of killers. Unfortunately it was too late to refuse them lodgings without raising suspicion. He and Kate needed to lay low and make sure nobody saw them until Dmitri cleared out. He locked the four-wheeler in Jumbo's shed out back, not daring to fire it up in hearing distance. He walked back in a hurry, knowing now that he and Kate couldn't get much deeper in trouble.

Booker found Kate waiting on pins and needles. She tried to hide her nerves but he knew good and well she thought he'd taken off on her. He had a feeling she was going to think that every time he got out of her sight from here on in.

"I brought burgers and fries. Got some cokes and some more milk for the kid."

"Did you find out anything?"

Booker hesitated, looking down into her worried face. "Yeah. I got some good news and some bad news."

Kate did not look encouraged but she mustered a thin smile. "Anything the least bit good would be a change for the better, I guess."

"One of Jumbo's friends is coming through in the morning and can give us a lift, but there's a bunch of roadblocks where they're looking for you so we'll have to think of a way around them."

"That's the good news?" Kate attempted a laugh but it didn't come off well. Booker thought it took guts to have any sense of humor after what she'd been through.

"The bad news is *really* bad news."

"Oh, God, I'm not sure I'm up for *really* bad news."

"Dmitri and his men are staying next door tonight."

Kate's smile faded big time. "Dmitri's here? Oh, God, we've got to get out of here! I've got to get Joey away from them!"

She ran to gather her things, and Booker had to grab her arm to stop her. "No, Kate, now calm down a minute and think. They don't know we're here, and they sure as hell aren't going to see us because we're not stepping foot out of this cabin till they're gone."

"But we can't stay here! He'll find me! He always finds me! He'll kill me this time, I know he will! He won't give me any options this time."

Booker didn't know what she meant by options but she was edging toward hysteria now, and he had to calm her. "Stop it, Kate, and listen to me."

Kate was shaking her head frantically, trying to pull loose. He held her firmly, but he could see panic welling in her eyes. She was terrified of Dmitri. "We can keep an eye on them if we stay here. We'll know where they are all the time so they can't sneak up on us. They think these cabins are empty. They'll never expect we're right next door. They're looking for me here and plan to search for you along the highway. I overheard them talking in the restaurant."

"But they'll kill me if they see me, they'll kill us both and take Joey!"

"That's not going to happen. You've got to trust me on this, Kate."

"What if they recognized you?" Kate was starting to calm down a little but had her fingers over her mouth, horror stamped all over her face.

"Matty didn't even recognize me. They've guessed I might be helping you but they don't know we're back here. You need to change your looks, too, the sooner the better."

"You sure it was Dmitri? A man with a beard and very dark eyes. I hit him in the head so hard I thought I might've killed him."

"Yeah, it's him. You got a good shot in but he's alive and well."

Her eyes darted to the windows. "He could've followed you just now. He could be outside with his gun ready to come in for me."

She was trying hard to regain composure; he could see her struggling with her terror of Dmitri. He admired that about her, how she could bring herself under control by force of will.

Not just anyone could do that, not without training, and that was probably the reason she'd made it so far on her own.

Kate pulled away and sat down on the bed beside the sleeping baby.

"I got you more clothes. And dye for your hair. They're setting up informants in truck stops and gas stations along the highway, so you better make yourself look damn different."

Kate nodded eagerly. "Yes, yes, I will, I'll change the color and cut it short." She absently touched her long hair. Booker followed her hand. Her hair had dried out now, looked silky and soft, the color of sun-shot honey, real curly down on the ends. He found himself wanting to reach out and touch it, too. He stifled that impulse before it got out of hand. He found the woman appealing, more than he should, more than anyone he ever remembered, and a hell of a lot more than he wanted to.

"Yeah, whatever. Just keep quiet and stay out of sight."

She was wringing her hands, nerves showing again. "Yeah, I will, I promise. You sure they're going to stay here tonight? Maybe they'll change their minds."

Booker shrugged. "They'll be back here after they eat, and I'll never let them out of my sight. I won't let them surprise us, believe me."

"Well, okay, I guess I can believe you. You've never lied to me before."

It took Booker a minute to realize she was kidding, but her faint smile faded quickly and she became stone-cold sober. She studied his face, then said, "You've got to be exhausted. Let me watch for them awhile so you can get some sleep."

Booker welcomed the suggestion. He needed to rest so he could stay up through the night on watch. He told Kate they wouldn't suspect her to be so close but things could go wrong, especially if the baby started screaming its head off. They were taking a chance staying so close to the killers, but his gut told him they'd be safer here than striking out on foot without a clear destination in mind.

He ate and watched for them to show up. They drove up within fifteen minutes. He could see them clearly through a crack in the drapes. Dmitri, Yuri and Misha took the blue tepee; the others stayed in the yellow. It wasn't long until they loaded back into a black Cadillac Seville and a dark blue Jeep Grand Cherokee and drove off in search of people greedy enough to rat out Kate and the baby. Once he was sure they were gone, he lay down on the bed, fully dressed, his rifle beside him. He still had the .45 strapped to his ankle and he left it there for the time being.

Kate had relaxed a little once the Russians had driven off, and now seemed thrilled with the yellow baby seat he'd brought in that morning. She had Joey sitting in it on the table beside her while she watched the blue tepee a good distance down the road. She was holding the bottle to the baby's mouth with one hand and eating french fries with the other. The woman was damned adaptable.

Booker shut his eyes. He could will himself to sleep, when he had to. Could get by on three or four hours a night, sometimes less. Just like all GI alumni graduated out of Special Forces. He'd been trained to exist on little or no food and a couple of hours of sleep. And to kill on command. Without question.

Sweat ran down and stung Booker's eyes, eyes riveted on the man directly across from him. Donald Horne looked back at him, face contorted with agony, lips drawn back over clenched teeth. Horne wouldn't be able to stand it much longer. Booker knew it and tried to prepare himself for the few minutes he had left before the pain slammed into him again. He dropped his eyes to the arms of the wooden chair in which Horne was strapped. His wrists were buckled down; his right forefinger just able to reach the bell that would end his agony. The bell was the kind on reservation desks in hotel lobbies, the kind rung to summon bellhops. When Horne went for it, their torturer would take the live electrical wire off his genitals and use it on Booker. Soon, very soon now.

It'd come any second now, the awful jolt of electricity that would send every muscle in his body rigid. When the bell dinged, when Horne couldn't stand it anymore, it would be Booker's turn. The Sandinistas were not laughing anymore, watching curiously now, wondering how long the two Americans could pass the current back and forth without killing each other. Booker wished they'd just kill them like the others and be done with it. He watched Horne's finger, watched it tremble, quiver, couldn't take his eyes off it. It had only been seconds but it would seem like hours. Horne was yelling now, couldn't stand it much longer.

When it came back, Booker had to hold on, give Horne time to recover before he sent it back to him. He had to brace himself for the first excruciating shock, then ride it out. He was stronger than Horne, physically, mentally; he could bear the pain longer.

Ding.

Booker ground his jaws together as Horne went limp against the straps. Booker heard the corporal sobbing and trying to catch his breath; then the current hit Booker just above his right nipple, so hard in the chest that his body spasmed. Electricity seared and burned until he could smell his own flesh burning, until he heard his own scream, long, loud, terrible. Across from him, Horne ground his teeth, waiting for his turn. Hold on, hold on, hold on. . . .

Booker came off the bed fighting, hearing the insistent ding, ding, ding of the bell, yelling for it to stop. He found himself on his feet, rifle clenched in one fist, eyes wild with hatred and horror, body drenched with sweat, before he realized it was not real, Corporal Horne wasn't there; the Sandinistas with the electrical power box weren't there. He was panting, his chest heaving as he glanced around the room, his hands trembling so badly he couldn't control them.

Kate Reed stood cowering against the wall beside the door, eyes wide and confused, holding the baby tightly against her. She looked petrified, and the terrible look on her face brought him back to his senses faster than anything else. Beside him on the table the insistent dinging of the clock radio's alarm went on unabated. Booker slammed his fist down on the button and it stopped. Thank God, it stopped.

Kate still hadn't moved a muscle. Still shaky, Booker moved into the bathroom and splashed cold water over his face and back of his neck. He stared down into the sink, trying to get rid of the adrenaline still rushing through his veins. God help him, how many years would it take before his mind healed enough to forget the atrocities done to him and his men in that goddamn, stinking jungle camp in Nicaragua. He stood there for several more minutes, trying to regain enough self-control to reenter the bedroom. Kate still hadn't moved away from the door. Her eyes were wide and watched him as if he was some kind of freak. Maybe he was.

"Are you all right?" she asked after several seconds of tense silence. "Is there anything I can do?"

"Go to bed. I'll take watch. Have they come back yet?"

She shook her head, and Booker moved to the chair by the window. It had gotten dark while he'd been asleep. He could see a light in the window of the blue tepee. A few stars in the sky. On the other side of the room he could hear Kate recline on the bed. She probably thought he was crazy. She wasn't the only one who did.

He settled back in a chair, propping his feet on the seat of another one. He was still shaky, nerves raw, jumpy as hell. He would be for awhile. He always was after he relived it. Now he'd think about Horne, have him on his mind for days. Horne and McClellan. Ramirez, Johnson, all tortured to death in front of his eyes. All because of Denton's betrayal. He was sorry he hadn't killed Denton when he'd had the chance. He wished him dead and burning in hell.

Twenty

KATE AWOKE early the next morning and found Booker still sitting guard in the chair. Surprisingly, she'd slept fairly well after Booker's disconcerting episode the night before. She gathered her things and headed straight for the bathroom, taking Joey with her. She didn't think Booker would hurt them but neither was she sure he was completely stable. She bathed and changed Joey first, dressing him in the yellow terrycloth sleeper with a little brown bear on the collar that Booker had brought in the second time he'd visited Jumbo's gift shop. The baby was in a good mood, so she fed him his bottle and then placed him atop a folded blanket where he could kick and stretch while she set to work altering her appearance.

Following the directions on the box, she mixed the Nice and Easy and applied the pungent solution to her hair, carefully avoiding the cut on the back of her head. She couldn't stop thinking about how Booker had thrashed around in his bad dream. When his fists clenched and his face went rigid, she'd grabbed Joey and moved to the door, but he'd rocketed off the bed like a madman, scaring her half to death. It had taken all her willpower not to run, get out before he attacked them. He'd seemed embarrassed and gotten himself under control immediately, but Kate now understood the nature of nightmares. She was living one.

When the color was set she washed it out and gently toweldried her hair. Gazing intently in the mirror, she did look different but the disguise wasn't nearly good enough yet. She needed a drastic change. Gathering her hair into a ponytail atop her head, she took the scissors and cut it off several inches above the rubber band. When she pulled out the rubber band, layers fell around her head, short and shaggy, reminiscent of seventies hairstyles. Add a hat and sunshades, and she didn't think anyone would recognize her, especially from a distance. Joey had begun to fret by the time she was dressed and ready to go, and she got down on her hands and knees to tend to him.

"Hi there, little punkin," she whispered, checking his Luvs. "You know it's mama, don't you, squirt?"

Joey squirmed around, his knees drawing up as he puckered up and let out a unhappy wail. She removed his soiled diaper and realized he wasn't tolerating the whole milk.

"Now, now, sweetie, don't cry," she said soothingly, but became alarmed when he started to yell as if his tummy hurt. If Dmitri's men heard him, they'd check it out; she knew they would. That's how Dmitri had found her in the root cellar. She couldn't get him to calm down, even when she lifted him against her shoulder, crooning softly and patting his back.

Kate jumped when Booker suddenly banged on the door, his voice urgent. "Keep him quiet! They're outside getting ready to leave!"

Kate rocked the baby against her, trying to keep the frantic quiver out of her voice, but Joey'd have none of her comforting. She searched desperately for the pacifier in the grocery sack and put it in his mouth. He wouldn't take it at first, tossing his head from side to side and screaming louder, but he finally took hold of it, and she whispered baby talk and settled him in the crook of her arm. He sucked on it eagerly but still whimpered as if in pain. Relieved he'd grown quiet, she waited tensely, glad Booker was outside her door with a gun.

"Okay, they're gone. Come on out."

Cautiously Kate opened the door. Booker was at the window and seemed edgy over the close call but apparently suffered no ill effects from the nightmare gruesome enough to cause him to yell and fight imaginary enemies. Without a word, he stared at her, critically examining her appearance.

"Well, do I meet muster? I must look different because when Joey saw me he screamed bloody murder." She attempted a thin smile at her joke, but instantly regretted her unfortunate choice of words. Bloody murder could very well be in the cards for all of them. In any case, Booker wasn't amused. He'd been nothing but somber since he'd crashed free of his nightmare. He'd been sitting up awake ever since, guarding someone he barely knew, and Kate suddenly realized that falling asleep might be the last thing Booker wanted to do.

"Put on the cap and glasses I got you and get ready to go. Jumbo's sending his friend down here as soon as he sees the Russians pull out of the parking lot."

Kate was glad to oblige, desiring nothing more than to get as far away from southern Missouri as she could. She stuffed her new possessions in the white plastic bag. Joey was relatively content at the moment, his stomachache better, or maybe it was only gas pangs. Within ten minutes a vehicle pulled up outside. Booker cased out the windows, then stood waiting at the door as she picked up Joey and joined him. He kept his voice low.

"The guy we're riding with's name is Miller. He's Jumbo's friend, not mine, and I sure don't know him well enough to trust him. So I'm gonna go by the name Smith, and you're gonna be my wife, Betty Lou. Got it?"

"Betty Lou? Where'd you come up with that?"

He scowled at the way she was smiling, in no mood this morning for screwing around, not that he ever was. But she felt better now that they'd actually made it through the night with Dmitri on their doorstep. She was mighty pleased she was going to go on breathing for awhile. But Booker was right. They weren't out of danger yet, and she was willing to let Booker take charge for awhile. Get her out of here and give her some time to get her shattered nervous system under control. Then she'd be all right. Then she could figure out a way to keep Joey with her; that was the important thing, the only thing she cared about.

"Mornin'," Booker said as they stepped outside into the bright sunshine where their ride was waiting for them in a brand-new brown Ford pickup with one doozy of a Harley Davidson strapped in the bed. Miller turned out to be a big biker with lots of tattoos and wild, wiry black hair that stuck out from under a black felt Stetson with a silver-studded band. He wore a black sleeveless T-shirt with a glow-in-the-dark silver webbed spider on the front, black jeans and hand-tooled black cowboy boots. He stretched out a hand with a tattoo of a hairy, rearing black tarantula on its back.

"Name's Smith." Booker accepted the handshake, then presented Kate without much ado. "This here's my old lady, Betty Lou."

"Ma'am." Miller actually doffed his hat like a real southern gentleman. She kept wondering how he was going to get all that hair under the motorcycle helmet dangling from his forefinger, a black one with lots more homemade silver spiders and skulls painted on it.

Nodding and smiling, agreeable as pie, Kate decided the less she said, the better, and the less likely she'd say something wrong.

Miller gave her and Joey a long, interested look, then returned his attention to Booker. "I been thinkin', Smith, and the truth is, I'd sure like to put a few miles on my bike 'fore I take it on up to Kansas City. You know, burn out the kinks and get 'er broken in some." He paused, and Booker merely waited for him to go on. "How 'bout this? How 'bout you and your old lady take my truck and let me follow you on the Harley 'til we get up to the weddin' reception at the tavern? How 'bout it? What you say?"

"Sure. Ain't got no problem with that. You doin' me a favor, Miller, least I can do back to you."

Kate turned and looked at Booker with not a little surprise, thinking he'd metamorphosed again, this time into a good ole boy biker. He had taken on the mannerisms and speech patterns of their new buddy, Miller, as if he were a chameleon, or a member in good standing with the Hell's Angels Motorcycle Club.

Again, Kate conjectured about his past. What else had he done in his life except try to kill a superior officer? Which was bad enough, mind you, but still, he seemed awfully well versed in donning disguises and handling guns and evading killers. Who the devil was John Booker anyway? She was dying to know more about him yet scared to ask, but that didn't stop the questions from whirling around inside her head. Who had he been before he decided to hide in a cave? Why was a good-looking man like this living alone in the woods disguised as Rasputin for so long? Or had he been alone? It occurred to her that he could've had a woman out there in his cave with him, maybe even a wife. Like most men, he probably had a significant woman somewhere in his past.

"Yeah, man, and there's somethin' else, too." Miller looked around as if afraid of being overheard. Booker glanced around in turn, probably searching for Russians sneaking up on them. The mere idea sent a cold chill up Kate's spine. "Jumbo says they got a roadblock up the road. Jumbo's cop friend told him he was gonna work it today when he was in the café last night to fill up on coffee. Mind if we kinda avoid it, y'know? I gotta stash in the truck I ain't wantin' nobody to find. Jumbo told me 'bout this loggin' road that goes up through the woods that'd take us round it. Jumbo told you 'bout the warrant out on me? They'll bust me good if they search the truck."

"Sure. Just lead the way. We'll follow."

Kate didn't think Booker looked exactly thrilled to be transporting drugs for a wanted felon, but he didn't have much choice. At least Miller had as good a reason as they did to avoid the roadblocks. While the two men unloaded the motorcycle from the bed, she went ahead and climbed inside the cab with Joey. The front seat was wide, covered with red velour, and it smelled heavily of beer and marijuana. There was a sticker on the rear window with yet another black skull and crossbones. The words around it said SUCKIN' GAS AND HAULIN' ASS. She put her bag on the seat and pressed down the door lock. She was anxious to get out on the road, get going, get out of the state if it came to that. Maybe she should just flee the country, start a new life with Joey somewhere far away where nobody could ever find them.

Booker got in beside her and pulled the door shut. He turned the ignition and the truck purred. Miller took good care of his engine. "I don't trust this guy. He stinks of marijuana and he seemed a little too interested in you and the baby. Get down out of sight until we get on the road. I have a bad feeling about this, but we don't have much choice because it's too dangerous to stay here."

Kate was not glad to hear his misgivings. She hunkered down on the floor with her back against the door where she couldn't be seen. She watched Booker drive the truck down the narrow road through the pines, marveling at how different he looked. His profile was classically cut with strong, even features, and she could see how his chest muscles molded the green polo shirt. She could not believe he was the filthy, frightening man in camouflage she'd seen that first day in the woods. He seemed very tense today, on edge in a way he hadn't shown before. But why wouldn't he be; they were outside now, in plain daylight, vulnerable to their enemies. She was nervous and wanted to talk, ask him questions about where they were going, but she wasn't about to distract him, not until he'd gotten them all to safety.

About five minutes later they were on the highway, Miller riding their tailpipe on his gigantic Harley. It wasn't long before the biker lost patience with Booker's adherence to the speed limit and shot past them with a roar and gleam of polished chrome.

"You can get up now, if you want."

Kate obeyed and sat close against the passenger door. The scenery flew past outside the window, and she kept looking behind them, expecting to see a black Cadillac or blue Jeep Grand Cherokee coming up fast on their tail, men hanging out the windows with machine guns like in *Godfather* movies. But this wasn't the movies; it was real and there was no guaranteed happy ending. She swallowed hard and took Joey out of the plastic seat. She put him down on top of her knees and found his diaper dry, so she let him lie there on his back. He sucked rhythmically on the clown pacifier and stared at her, a tiny frown marring his brow as if he still didn't feel good. She thought about his chortling laugh the day of the timber rattler and wished he'd do it again. She guessed he didn't have much to laugh about either.

They rode in silence, and the traffic was light. Each time a vehicle came abreast of them in the passing lane, she turned her head and stared at the passing forest tracts. Booker had left his rifle behind but he had a loaded pistol now, and he kept it in reach, on the seat between them. She had no doubt he'd use it, if he had to. She was relieved when Miller turned off onto a gravel road to circumvent the roadblock.

"Do you mind if I turn on the radio? Maybe we'll hear something."

Booker shook his head.

Kate switched it on. Miller had it set on a Country and Western station that was playing an old Johnny Cash tune about a ring of fire. She began to roll the tuner, encountering lots of static as she tried to locate KWOC in Poplar Bluff. When she finally found it they were in a commercial about First Midwest Bank, then cut to the local K Mart store where they were having some kind of spring-fling sale. When they finally got around to the news, she listened eagerly.

"More news on the Kate Reed investigation. According to FBI sources, Kate Reed of Van Buren, is purportedly still on the loose. Alleged now to have killed her husband, she is being tracked in the Ozark Riverways north of Van Buren but has yet to be apprehended, despite a three-county manhunt and roadblocks on highways leading out of the area. The authorities are still warning people not to approach her. She is armed and dangerous. More news later but now back to Bill Steiger at the front of K Mart. . . ."

Kate stared at Booker. "Good God, now they think I killed Michael."

"Yeah, and you'll get the blame for anybody else they knock off along the way."

"Do you think they'll kill Matty Jones when they don't need him anymore?"

"He sure better watch his back. He shouldn't've joined forces with those guys. They're way out of his league."

Kate bit her lip and stared out the window, fighting a new emotional upheaval, not sure why except that things kept getting worse and worse. She ground her teeth together so she wouldn't go to pieces. She wanted to wake up, wake up like Booker had and find out that none of this was happening to them.

"You okay?" Booker glanced over at her, then put his eyes back on the road.

Kate nodded, forcibly shutting off her feelings. Booker didn't try to comfort her, didn't say anything else for a long time. Kate hummed a lullaby and rocked Joey to sleep, more to soothe herself than him, wondering how much more of this she could take without cracking up.

After an hour's ride, Booker followed Miller into a rustic log tavern called the Do-Duck-Inn. Kate estimated that perhaps fifty ornate, oversized motorcycles, some with sidecars, were propped together at one side of the parking lot like a herd of bison corralled on a concrete prairie. Like Miller's, all the bikes had black skull-and-crossbones pennants emblazoned with a fighting red tarantula. They fluttered gaily on the aerials, making this look like the grand opening of a car dealership.

Miller had climbed off his hog and was directing them to pull his pickup alongside the other bikes. As Booker did so, Kate said, "Do you think it's safe to go in? There's a bunch of Hell's Angels here."

Booker braked and shoved the gearshift into park. "If Miller vouches for us, nobody'll mess with us."

"You're sure?" Kate had enough troubles to deal with without antagonizing a motorcycle gang, fifty strong.

"Yeah, I need to use the phone." He turned to look at her. "We'll be safer inside than out here in plain view of the highway."

"Okay, if you say so." But she intended to keep a close eye on Joey. She hoped none of them had heard about her on the KWOC news bulletins. Maybe they'd all be on good behavior today; after all, it was a wedding reception. She eyed the long, log building with its multitude of Schlitz and Coors signs and pitied the poor bride.

"End of the line, pal," Miller was now saying to Booker. He took off his helmet and his bristly hair sprang up like an unruly Brillo pad.

"No problem," Booker said. "Thanks for the lift. I owe you one."

Miller looked at Kate for a moment. "Where you headed now?"

"West, I guess, not sure where we'll land yet."

"Hey, wait a minute," Miller suddenly exclaimed as if he'd just had an epiphany. "Why don't you guys mosey in wit' me and down one wit' Panther and Sugar? I got enough pot for all of us, bought it this mornin' at Jumbo's place. The Do-Duck'll be runnin' over with booze, and all the beer you can drink, if I know Panther. Maybe we can find you a ride west, if you hang around till the fun's over."

With extreme reluctance Kate followed the two men to the front door, glad Booker had stuck the .45 in the back of his waistband under his loose shirt. She wished she had one, too. In her hand. Cocked. She had a feeling there were probably a hundred weapons inside the Do-Duck-Inn. None registered with the police.

Inside they discovered what was best described as a drunken orgy going on. Well, maybe that was overstating it, but it was safe to say Kate had never seen so many empty beer bottles in her life. Miller was greeted like the long-lost spider he was with lots of grizzly-bear hugs that would have crushed a lesser man. While he was slapping high fives with somebody named Killer Boy, who unfortunately bore a striking resemblance to Saddam Hussein, mustache, dead black eyes and all, Kate glanced around and kept very close to Booker's back. Even among the burly wedding guests, Booker stood taller and bigger than most of the other men.

The interior was dusky, most of the light filtering down from a few high windows and three dozen neon signs touting various beers and cigarette brands. Square tables with black Formica tops were positioned around the perimeter, with a couple of deserted booths along the back wall. A long table set up in front of the mirrored bar to accommodate the actual wedding party was littered with enough brown beer bottles to outfit a recycling center. The jukebox was ablaze with a rainbow neon, and *Wild Thing* blared over the yelling and laughing. Kate readily admitted to herself that she was terrified. Booker acted as if he felt more than comfortable with the drunken outlaws in black leather and gold jewelry.

Miller was keeping a close eye on them, and he motioned them across the floor to the head table, guzzling a Coors Light with one hand and walloping friends up the back of the head with the open palm of the other. Kate was pleased when

Booker put his arm protectively around her waist like any good husband leading his wife into the den of an inebriated motorcycle gang. Joey was looking around as if he was in the middle of a riot but he wasn't crying. Kate hoped the pall of cigar smoke didn't choke him.

"Hey, Panther, congrats, man, didn't know you had it in ya!"

Panther was another bristly specimen, tall, husky, scary. Was that a prerequisite of membership? Surprisingly, he had crew-cut blond hair but his huge, bushy muttonchops made up for it, along with the mat of blond hair peeking out of his unzipped black leather vest. He was missing a tooth in front when he beamed at his old bud from Tennessee, and Kate stifled the urge to search the floor for his missing canine. There was already one fight going on in the corner by the bathrooms, but no one seemed to be paying much attention to it. She heard a bottle break and watched one of the antagonists go over backward like a felled oak. The other guy crowed victory and dropped the broken beer bottle on the floor. Kate averted her eyes. Don't make eye contact with anyone, she told herself firmly.

"Sugar, doll, you look as fine as Heather Locklear in that weddin' getup," Miller enthused to the blushing bride, who wore a short, white leather miniskirt and matching bra. The picture of a panther was tattooed above her right breast, and white lace stockings covered her legs down to her black combat boots. She had hair bleached out snow white with rather noticeable red roots, but she was happy and laughing, and about as drunk as any woman Kate had ever seen. So was the proud bridegroom.

"This here's Smith and his wife. Betty Lou's'r name. Bummed a ride off'a me so I brought'm on in fer some fun. Didn't think you'd mind any if they shared yer big day."

"Hell no. Any sonofabitch's a friend of your'n, is a friend of ours!" bellowed Panther, a very loud, loquacious sort. He shook Booker's hand, pumping it while slapping him repeatedly on the back. Kate quailed in her tennis shoes, afraid he might want to grab her and kiss her.

"And Betty Lou, wow, you got yerself a looker there, man. She's lookin' good enough to eat, ain't she, Miller?"

Sugar doubled her fist and gave Panther a good jolt to the right temple in mock outrage, but he thought it cute and guffawed good-naturedly and took to nuzzling Sugar's deep cleavage. When he came up for breath about five minutes later, he was still indulgent of her transgression. "Don't mind her none. She's as jealous as a stray cat. Cain't look at nobody no more without her popping me one up the side of the head." He nodded and gave a gap-toothed but pleased grin.

Kate nodded agreeably as the couple dissolved into another slurpy kiss that never did stop. When he started groping Sugar's anatomy right then and there, she transferred her attention elsewhere and decided they truly must be in love. Booker was glancing around now, too, totally forgotten by everyone, including Miller, who had another guy in a stranglehold around the neck while he rubbed his knuckles on his bald head hard enough to make the man scream for mercy. When his friend finally began sputtering and turning red in the face, Miller let him go and they shared a good chuckle over their shenanigans.

"C'mon," Booker said aside to Kate. "There's a booth in the corner."

Gratefully she let Booker lead her out of the fray. Another scuffle was commencing at the bar but she tried not to notice. Joey was grinning up at her, as if he thought it all very amusing, as if they'd taken him to Disney World. Booker sat her down, his eyes continually scanning the place. He sat down on the opposite side of the black vinyl booth.

"Look, I've got to make that phone call. You be all right here alone a minute?"

"You're kidding, aren't you, Booker? Tell me you're kidding, please." Kate glanced around. The melee was proceeding on all sides with lots of sound and fury.

"They're having too much fun to hassle us. They only pick fights when they're bored. Sit here and don't start anything." As if she would, Kate thought, wide-eyed.

"The phone's at the end of the bar, over by the door, see it?" Booker jerked his head to show her. "I'll keep an eye on you. If any of these guys gets too close, I'll come back."

"Sure, don't worry about me. I'm a sucker for weddings. Maybe I'll catch the bouquet."

Booker looked at her a second, unsmiling, and she decided he didn't get her sense of humor much, but hey, you had to have one in a place like this, scared out of your wits the way she was. She watched him walk off as the jukebox died at the end of a song. Yelling, screams of laughter, screams of pain, breaking glass, and pure pandemonium rocked the Do-Duck-Inn to the rafters.

Joey chuckled and waved his arms happily, and Kate knew he really did have to be the bravest baby in the whole wide world, as one of the bridesmaids—at least Kate assumed she was because she had a nosegay of yellow daisies hanging around her neck on a black leather belt—climbed atop a table and began a striptease for a ring of admiring Tarantulas. *Devil in a Blue Dress* blared suddenly and seemed to give the woman all the incentive she needed to bare it all. Luckily, someone grabbed her down in a fit of amorous zeal before she took much off. Booker was still on the phone but he was watching her, thank God. If possible, the wedding reception was livening up.

"Oh, boy," Kate whispered under her breath as someone threw someone else over the bar with an awful crash and splintering of glass, "I *really, really* wish I wasn't here."

Twenty-one

BOOKER LISTENED as the phone rang at the other end, wondering where the hell Mac was. His old friend rarely worked mornings, never this early. Booker's recollection was that Branson theaters didn't open their shows till three in the afternoon, with a second evening performance. His initial plan had been for Mac to drive down and pick them up at the Do-Duck, but now he'd have to think of another way.

One thing Booker did know, he didn't want anymore to do with Miller. There was something about the guy; he was a bit too interested in Kate and the baby. Booker had caught him watching her since they'd arrived at the tavern and that worried Booker. He'd have to keep an eye on the guy, and he wanted to get Kate out of the tavern before the rowdy wedding reception got too wild or was raided, whichever came first. They could probably hitch a ride with a trucker, but that was even more dangerous with roadblocks and frequent radio reports about Kate.

Booker glanced at Kate's booth to make sure she was all right. She looked petrified. Her brown eyes were wide, watching the goings on as if she'd been beamed down from the *Enterprise* to an alien convention. Still, she was holding up fairly well. Booker was damn sure she'd never stepped foot in a biker bar in her entire life. Too classy a lady for that. Even with her hair whacked off and dark, she looked good. He scowled, cursing as the phone continued to ring off the hook at Mac's place. He'd try again later. He had a feeling they'd be forced to stay put awhile, at least until everyone passed out. The bikers were nowhere close to that point yet. Most were stumbling around table to table, only a couple of guys already unconscious on the glass-strewn floor.

The Tarantulas were trying their best to get down, Booker'd give them that. Jumbo was missing quite a bash with his good ol' buddies. Near the back door unopened beer cases were stacked, waiting to be noticed. The bartender was keeping out of sight and letting everyone fend for themselves. Booker thought he was a smart guy to make himself scarce. Panther's guests were definitely not guys to wait in line for booze.

Deciding he'd left Kate and Joey alone long enough, he hung up the receiver and wound his way across the crowded room. An amorous couple was making out beside the jukebox with no thought to the laws of decency. Others, including the bride and groom, were stamping around on the littered dance floor to *Unchained Melody*, obscenely groping each other to beat the band.

"I'm sure glad you're back," Kate whispered as he slid into the booth opposite her.

Booker nodded, searching the crowd for Miller. He didn't see him at first, then caught sight of him at the pay phone. Instantly he was alert. Who the hell would an out-of-towner like Miller be calling?

"Did you get hold of your friend?"

Booker shook his head but kept his eyes on Miller.

"What are you going to do, call again later?"

He nodded. Miller talked a minute or two and hung up, but Booker didn't like it. His attention was diverted briefly when a table full of bottles crashed over on a guy holding a girl on his lap. Glass tinkled and curses resounded. Everyone laughed uproariously 'cause gee whiz, accidents happen when you're having fun.

"That's my favorite song," Kate told him loudly over the racket. "I love the Righteous Brothers."

Booker watched Panther pick up Sugar and carry her back to the table, her legs wrapped intimately around his waist. Oh, boy, and things were just getting started.

"Wanna dance?"

A biker who gave the word *hideous* new and greater meaning was leaning over Kate. She cowered away from him as if he were a fire-breathing dragon, but all things considered, a fire-breathing dragon was tame stuff up against a drunk-out-of-his-mind Fighting Tarantula.

"Well, thank you very much, Psycho Man," Kate was replying politely to her new suitor, reading his name off the black leather cap he wore. "I'm flattered you asked me, really I am, but I'm here with my husband and baby—"

The guy grabbed her by the arm. "Let yer old man watch the kid then. I wanna dance so come on, git up, now don't go gettin' me pissed off."

"Shove off, pal."

Booker kept his voice low but he wasn't in the mood to prolong the confrontation. He stared unflinchingly into the guy's bleary blue eyes. Booker could see Psycho Man's fighting spider tattoo through his ripped black T-shirt, and it looked as if some drunk had inked it on free of charge.

Psycho Man really got pissed off then but hesitated since Booker made two of him. Fortunately, somebody grabbed his arm and dragged him off to look at a Penthouse pinup poster, one of Panther's favorite wedding presents from Sugar. He went eagerly to adore Miss March.

"My hero."

Kate smiled at him but it looked forced. Booker had to admit the situation was ludicrous. He wished he could hurry up and get them on their way but he wouldn't let her come to harm. He'd been around the Tarantulas a couple of times when Jumbo was hosting their knock-down-drag-out reunions in his café. They were drunken, disorderly, profane, crude and given to brawls, but all in all, they weren't bad guys. Not like some more murderous biker gangs he'd run across. The Outlaws came to mind.

"I can't tell you how much I hate to say this but I need to use the ladies' room," Kate said after half an hour watching the fracas grow rowdier. "Is it safe?"

"If there's a lock on the door, it is."

Booker went to check it out for her and found the women's bathroom vacant with a sturdy slide bolt on the door. Incredibly, it looked halfway clean, too.

"It's not a McDonald's, but it'll lock," he said when he got back to the table. "I wouldn't touch anything if I were you."

"As if I'd want to. You better keep Joey here, don't you think? Where he'll be safe." She lowered her tone so as not to offend the guy staggering past.

"Yeah. I'll watch until you get inside."

"Thanks."

Kate rose, took a bracing breath and started off as if she was navigating an armed minefield. Booker eased in beside the baby, who was reclining comfortably in his yellow infant seat and grinning as if he owned the place. The wedding party was involved with jumping around and yelling to the strains of *YMCA*, and Kate had a fairly easy route to the restroom amidst loud, slurred voices drowning out the Village People. The Tarantulas did go for the Oldies.

Booker sat watching the bathroom, thinking Kate Reed was holding herself together pretty damn well. Most women would have crumbled to dust by now, and he'd frightened the wits out of her last night. He frowned, forcing the nightmare from his mind. He had bigger things to worry about at the moment. He realized how true that was when Matty Jones and Misha walked through the front door like Tarantulas in good standing.

Booker crouched down and shielded Joey with his body.

His gaze went to the bathroom, only a few yards from where the two were standing, and he prayed Kate wouldn't come out. They were searching the room, and Booker eased lower when two more of them showed up. The Russians were no longer dressed in the black sweats and nylon windsuits they'd worn in the woods. Now they were dressed redneck à la Matty Jones.

Misha wore his new dangly earring, his long blond hair pulled back in a low ponytail. All of them wore flannel shirts and jeans with St. Louis Rams football caps. All obviously had been shopping at the same K Mart; all looked like Mafia hitmen dressed up as lumberjacks.

Most of the spiders hadn't noticed them yet, but Miller had. He hastened to Matty's side and talked urgently a moment. Then both men turned to pick out Booker through the gloom and hazy cigarette smoke. Goddamn it, Miller must have gotten his pot that morning from Matty and heard about Kate and the kid. Booker cursed himself for not putting it together sooner. He pulled his gun and glanced at the ladies' room. Don't come out, Kate, stay put, stay put just a few minutes longer.

Two seconds later Kate walked out and stopped as if to gauge her chances of making it to the booth. When she looked in his direction, Booker pointed at Matty. She followed his warning, then froze when she clashed eyes with Misha. The Russian recognized her at once, and Kate darted away but not fast enough. Misha grabbed her arm and brutally jerked her back.

Booker was up and heading toward them as Misha dragged Kate toward the front door. Booker couldn't cut them off in time, and he looked around frantically, saw Panther dirty dancing with Sugar a few feet away. He stepped forward and grabbed Panther's arm, yelling at the top of his lungs.

"Hey, Panther, that guy said Sugar's legs open up more than Jumbo's refrigerator door!"

That insult shocked most of the gang out of their boozy daze. For the first few seconds only the loud strains of *Born to Be Wild* rocked the room. Everybody knew how Panther doted on his Sugar.

"What'd he say? Who said that shit 'bout Sugar?" a guy demanded from a table nearby, smashing a full beer bottle on the floor to show his dismay.

"That guy at the door," Booker shouted in outrage. "Now the bastard's got hold of Betty Lou. Get him, boys!"

That got the job done. Enraged wedding guests rushed the hapless Russian backing toward the door. A burly biker grabbed Misha around the neck, and the kid made short work of his half-drunk attacker but not before Kate had jerked free and fled back to Booker. The rest of the Fighting Tarantulas descended in a bellowing mass upon Sugar's detractors with a zeal that gave new glory to their club name.

Panicked, Kate reached Booker and grabbed Joey, and Booker pulled her toward the back door as the rumble developed rapidly into a full-fledged, all-out brawl with the sickening thunk of fists on bone, grunts and screams, and the shattering, crunching sounds of breaking glass. Booker and Kate burst through the storeroom and out the rear of the tavern. The back parking lot was clear and they raced around the side of the tavern. The black Cadillac the killers had been driving was parked by the front door, and Booker headed for the driver's seat and jerked the door open. No keys. Shit!

"Hurry up, get in!" he yelled at Kate.

Kate ran around the front of the car with Joey, and Booker leaned inside and worked frantically to hot-wire the ignition.

"Hey, there, what the hell you doing?"

He looked up and saw Dmitri heading toward them, his hand inside his coat.

"He's got a gun, Booker, get it started, get it started!" Kate thrust Joey down on the seat on the passenger's side and grabbed up the Glock nine millimeter that she found on the floorboard. Booker hoped to hell she knew how to get the safety off the pistol as he fumbled with the wires.

Phut. Phut. Phut.

She knew how to get the safety off, all right. The ignition revved, music to Booker's ears. "Get in, get in!" he yelled, jumping and slamming the gear into drive. Kate was braced outside the door, a perfect police stance with arms extended, forearm supporting the gun barrel.

Phut. Phut. Phut.

Booker yelled at her again, looking over his shoulder just as she blew out the front tires on Dmitri's Grand Cherokee. Another *phut*. The windshield exploded in a shower of glass, and Dmitri dropped for cover behind the driver's door. Kate jumped inside, dropping the smoking gun and grabbing Joey's yellow plastic seat. Booker peeled out, throwing gravel all over the place, the back end fishtailing wildly as answering gunfire hit the trunk with staccato little pings. He swerved out onto the highway in a screech of burned rubber and stomped the gas pedal to the floor, heading west.

Panting for breath, eyes glued on the rearview mirror, he kept the accelerator floored, bringing the big luxury car up to seventy in nothing flat. Kate had done a job on the Jeep, so no one was in pursuit, not yet. Maybe they'd get lucky and the Tarantulas would finish them off. Neither of them said a word, Booker concentrating on driving and Kate comforting the baby. Joey was whimpering a little but obviously under the impression that gunfire and squealing cars were everyday occurrences for him and his mommy.

"Where the hell did you learn to shoot like that?"

"My grandpa was a sheriff."

That's all the explanation he got, so he kept his eyes on the road, aware they'd have to ditch the car as soon as possible. A brand-new black Seville didn't exactly blend into the Ozark countryside, especially a stolen one.

The chance to hide the car came about sixteen miles up

the road. At the junction of 60 West and 63 North out of West Plains were a couple of big combination gasoline station/restaurants that catered to tour buses heading to Branson. One was called Gramma's Kitchen and the other one was Hillbilly Junction. Hillbilly Junction was the closest and had the most crowded parking lot, so Booker pulled in and stopped near the gas pumps. Three tour buses were parked outside waiting for their passengers, and he could see the dining room was chock-full of people.

"Take Joey inside and wait for me. I'm going to find a place to dump the car, then I'll be back."

Kate seemed reluctant but she obediently opened the door.

"You gonna be okay?" he asked, but he knew she would. She was tough, no question about it.

"Yeah. I'll wait inside for you."

"Find some people and act like you're with them. I'll be back in ten minutes or less."

Kate nodded and headed for the entrance, carrying Joey's seat tightly against her chest. Booker found it hard to leave her there alone but he knew he couldn't keep her in the car. He doubted if Dmitri would call it in as stolen, but the sheriff's department would reach the Do-Duck-Inn eventually and might get a description of the Cadillac fleeing the scene. He waited until Kate was safely inside, then drove down the access road in search of woods thick enough to conceal the Caddy from cars passing on the highway.

Shit, shit, shit! Dmitri cursed violently in his own tongue as the Cadillac disappeared up the highway at incredible speed. He could hear the commotion inside the tavern, an ugly fray by the sound of it. Misha and the others were outnumbered by the trash on the motorcycles. He turned as a man ran out from behind the tavern and barreled into the front seat of a white Isuzu Scout.

"Yuri! Get that car! We don't have time to change tires!"

Yuri ran to obey, brandishing his gun at the frightened man as he jerked open the driver's door and pulled the hapless fellow out onto the gravel. He pistol-whipped him about the head and when the man fell, he jumped in and revved the engine a few times.

Rock-faced with anger, Dmitri ran to the front of the Do-Duck-Inn, wanting only to get the hell out of there before the cops showed up. He raised his silenced Beretta and fired at the high windows under the eaves. The panes imploded with a loud splintering, which no doubt got the attention of those scuffling inside. Within minutes a tide of bleeding, drunken humanity came flooding out the door, Misha at the forefront, his nose bloody and swollen. Matty Jones burst out right behind him and sprinted for his own pickup truck, obviously wanting no trouble with the law.

"Yuri's in the Isuzu," he ground out to Misha, turning toward it as Nikolai and Andre fought their way out of the tavern.

Within minutes they were pulling out of the parking lot, amidst the pulsing roar of dozens of motorcycles. Vehicles were pouring onto the highway in both directions while the distant whine of sirens pierced the din. Yuri turned west, the way Kate and the big guy had escaped, and Dmitri turned his wrath on the rest of his team.

"Jones said that guy Miller was going to turn her over to us for cash. What the hell happened to screw things up?" Dmitri was furious, almost as much as when he'd awoken bleeding from the head inside the goddamned root cellar. Kate Reed would pay for that humiliation as well as this one. It was personal now, a vendetta, just him and her. With effort, he controlled the rage roiling inside him, and said through gritted teeth, "Well, Misha?"

Misha was holding a handkerchief to his nose, muffling his answer. "They were too many, uncle. Drunken animals.

Jones told us not to use our guns because some of them were friends of his."

"Since when does Jones give you orders, nephew?"

Dmitri's voice was so lethal that no one offered further explanation but sat sullen and uncommunicative. Dmitri strove to get himself under control. He rarely allowed himself the luxury of showing rage, which he considered stupid and unproductive. But never had he been so frustrated, as Kate Reed continued to slip through his fingers time and time again. He took a couple of deep breaths while Yuri slowed to the speed limit. A dark blue Missouri Highway Patrol car sped past heading east, followed by another a few seconds later. Muttering an oath beneath his breath, Dmitri flipped open his cellular telephone.

"Yes, please give me the highway patrol. I want to report a stolen car."

He gave the operator the make and model of both the Cadillac and the Grand Cherokee Kate Reed had busted up with her incredible marksmanship. He shook his head. No wonder she'd taken his Beretta when she'd fled the cellar. It had been sheer luck that Yuri had found it where she'd fallen by the river.

And Jones had been right about the guy helping her. He'd obviously changed his appearance from the way Matty had described him, but Dmitri had gotten a good look at him this time. He was a big man with black hair, strong looking, and he'd been at Jumbo's yesterday when they'd been there. Dmitri had seen him leave the restaurant himself. He wondered why the man was putting his life on the line for Kate, unless they were lovers, unless Kate had been going to him all along. The idea of them together made him livid, and he hung up the phone without giving his name. They couldn't trace the cars to him. They'd rented both vehicles in St. Louis under false names.

"Now that you've let her make fools out of you," he said,

twisting slightly to look at the trio in the backseat, "anybody care to tell me what happened in there?"

Misha answered in Russian. "Kate Reed has changed her looks. Cut her hair and dyed it brown. She wore a shirt from the truckstop that said Jumbo's Famous Ozark Butterfly Biscuits. The man with her was big. Taller than me."

Misha sounded as if he took personal offense to that.

"Yes, Misha, and he's obviously smarter than you, too, by the outcome of your first encounter with him."

Anger burning through him like a hot current, Dmitri turned to Yuri, thinking he'd do well to send the other three back to St. Louis and let them face Vince's wrath, which was growing with each passing hour.

"Find the first big petrol stop so we can ditch this car and get another one, Yuri. We have no choice after this royal screwup but to go back and have a little talk with the black man who owns the truck stop. I saw the guy Kate's with hanging around there yesterday. He seemed to know his way around the place, and something tells me he knows this Jumbo character as well. If we can't get anything out of the fat Negro, then we'll have to check every goddamned place along this highway until we find her. Vince is losing patience, and so am I."

No one replied. Everyone knew what that meant.

Twenty-two

KATE ENTERED Hillbilly Junction as if it was the Roman colosseum and she, a Christian martyr. She was still pumped up with fear and a dreadful adrenaline rush from firing the gun, but it felt good to fight back. She was fed up with running scared; she had to play their deadly game if she was to survive.

Inside the door she hesitated and glanced around the crowded souvenir shop. This was the most convenient place to stop when heading west, and she feared she might run into someone she knew from Van Buren. She had before, on several occasions when she'd driven to Springfield on shopping excursions. Thank God, she didn't see a familiar face, and she decided that most everyone in the place had come off the big tour buses. She had a bad feeling that the unpleasant biker odors of beer and cigarette smoke permeated her clothes. Nobody seemed to notice her, so she kept her head down and tried to look inconspicuous.

The counters were filled with myriad souvenirs stamped with The Ozarks or Missouri or Hillbilly Junction, lots of toys, sweatshirts and teensy little spoons and shot glasses sporting the official seals of every state in the union, just about anything a tour bus traveler would want to shell out money for. A white sign with red letters advertised the snack bar as Moonshine Joe's and offered popcorn, soft drinks, hamburgers and hot dogs.

Through long, heavily laden souvenir racks was a nice big restaurant designed for more leisurely meals; it touted the

Ozarks' Finest Chicken and a complete food bar. The tour bus clientele had migrated there, eating lunch and making a whole lot of noise. The gas pump checkout was near the front door. It had a glass case that displayed big luscious sheets of homemade fudge in every conceivable flavor from peanut butter to amaretto chocolate swirl.

Pretending to browse through T-shirts adorned with lanky hillbillies wearing big straw hats, Kate made her way toward the restaurant proper, deciding to melt into the busy lunch crowd. She soothed Joey who was getting fussy, sputtering angrily and twisting in his baby seat. She hoped he wouldn't start crying and bring every pair of eyes in Hillbilly Junction down on them. He was bound to be hungry, and Joey never minded letting her know when he wanted a bottle. She stopped for a moment and tickled his bottom lip with the clown pacifier. He watched her face as he pulled on it like crazy for a minute, then got mad, spit it out and let out a furious cry.

The restaurant hostess was waiting at her station, a wonderfully bright smile on her face. She was young, probably late teens, her long brown hair twisted up under a peaked white waitress's cap, which Kate suspected she hated to wear. She had lots of brown freckles across the bridge of her nose and braces on her teeth.

"How many will be dining, ma'am?"

"Two, please. My husband will join me." Kate thought of Michael and her heart dropped a beat. She couldn't believe he was really dead, and now it seemed an eternity ago, a bizarre hallucination that couldn't possibly be true. She forced his face from her mind, unable to think about it.

A church pew sat beside the door, and on the right was a private Victorian room with mauve walls, lace curtains, a crystal chandelier and a fireplace. The girl led Kate into a more spacious room with a cathedral ceiling, knotty pine floors and native stone walls, and at least two hundred senior citizens enjoying themselves immensely. Kate knew that the elderly flocked in droves to Branson for clean, wholesome fun. By the looks of it, most of them went there via Hillbilly Junction.

Avoiding eye contact with the diners, she felt as if every soul in the place was comparing her with wanted posters and television bulletins, especially now that Joey was having such a fit. She was led to a teal-blue corner booth alongside a window that gave her an unimpeded view of the parking lot.

A pint jar filled with dry beans and dried flowers was the centerpiece, and the silverware was tied up in bright kitchen towels. Kate accepted the large green menu handed to her, smiled and politely thanked the hostess but watched anxiously for Booker to show himself outside. Give him time, she told herself, but panic was just beneath the surface, especially when she thought he'd gotten smart and left her to fight her own battles. She wouldn't blame him. She wouldn't blame anyone for getting out of this mess. It was hard to believe he had put himself in the line of fire for her in the first place.

Ten minutes crawled by, then fifteen, and Booker didn't show. Kate ordered fried chicken, iced tea, and warm milk for Joey. The baby was still crying for his bottle, causing lots of people to stare at them. She tried helplessly to soothe him but he wouldn't have any of it. She worried again that he might have a stomachache. She'd been feeding him milk he wasn't used to, dragging him around in godawful places. No wonder he was mad; he'd been through enough and wanted to go home. As soon as the waitress brought the milk, she poured it into his bottle, praying he'd be content to take it.

"Sure got a cute baby there," the waitress noted, stopping and gazing intently at Joey. She was older than the hostess had been, graying dark hair pulled severely into a bun atop her head. She wore black slacks and a white dress shirt, topped with a black bib apron with a moonshine-swilling hillbilly logo. Her name tag said Gail. Her face was pleasant but heavily lined, tired and beaten down. She appeared overly interested in Joey, and Kate was instantly suspicious. Dmitri and his men were placing informants along the highways, and Gail could very well be one. Kate tensed up, very frightened again.

Fearing the woman might be on the lookout for Dmitri, she tried to act normally and said, "Thanks. She's ready for her bottle, that's for sure."

"Oh, a little girl. What's her name? She's a tiny little thing, isn't she? Can't be more'n a month or so, huh?"

"Jennifer," replied Kate off the top of her head, but the waitress was snooping after Joey's age, maybe putting two and two together.

"Your food'll be out shortly, ma'am. We're real busy. You know, the lunch bunch."

"I'm in no hurry. My husband isn't here yet anyway." Kate smiled at Gail, hoping to God she was wrong and the woman was just friendly.

Gail nodded, turning away as a man nearby, obviously irritated, called out for a bottle of catsup. Kate breathed easier when the waitress got busy again, but she'd keep a close eye on Gail, just in case. She tried to give Joey his bottle but he wouldn't take it. He wailed louder, and Kate's nerves quivered until she wanted to roll up into a ball and hide. More and more diners were turning to stare at her. She checked Joey's diaper to see if he was wet. Slightly damp but not messed, thank God. She'd change him as soon as they got on the road again. *If* they got on the road again. She tried to banish increasingly negative thoughts and kept her face averted, desperately soothing Joey, but she was getting worried. Booker should have been back a long time ago. Where the devil was he?

She shot a worried look past diners sporting white hair, eyeglasses and polyester pantsuits, appalled when she saw two uniformed highway patrolmen waiting at the hostess station. Oh, God, were they after her?

Kate turned toward the wall, lifting Joey out of his seat and cradling him against her chest. She searched for a rear exit. There was probably a back door out of the kitchen; she debated getting up and leaving while she still could. Where in God's name was Booker?

When she glanced at the cops again, they were coming toward her. She froze in dread, then melted with relief when the hostess merely seated them at a nearby table. Both officers were tall and held brimmed hats in their hands. They both looked at Kate when Joey let out an angry yell. She cringed, waiting for recognition to flare in their eyes. They sat down and chatted with the waitress. She hoped her apprehension wasn't written all over her face.

Joey would not stop crying. No matter how she held him, how she whispered to him, nothing worked. She had a terrible feeling he was sick, the stomachache she'd been worried about, maybe, or an earache from the plunge in the river. Panic surged, nearly overwhelming her; Joey had never been ill since she'd gotten him. What was she going to do? They couldn't take him to a hospital. The police would surely have alerted emergency rooms to be on the lookout for them.

As Joey's cries turned into screams, everyone in the place watched her. One of the cops leaned close and said something to his partner. Kate patted Joey's back, searching the parking lot for Booker. The patrolman stood up. Oh, no, no, he was coming over to her table.

"Good God Almighty, Katie? That is you, isn't it?"

Jumping as if jabbed with a fork, Kate jerked around, then nearly fainted. Heaven help her, it was Henry Hinkley from Van Buren. His bushy white brows were drawn together in consternation, apparently nonplussed by her new look. She wished she'd stuffed all her dark hair inside the baseball cap so she wouldn't have to explain her change in appearance.

To her relief, the seated highway patrolman called out a greeting to the man who had materialized in front of her, obviously old friends, and the other officer sat back down as Henry turned and said hello. Kate braced herself as Henry slid into the booth across from her.

"Hi, Judge," she managed as brightly as she could. She noticed the nosy waitress standing beside the salad bar, watching them. "What're you doing way up here?" Inside she had disintegrated to a basket case. Why did she have to run into him now, of all times? And why did Joey have to pick this moment to get sick? And, for heaven's sake, what had happened to Booker?

"I'm on the way to Branson," the judge answered, examining her face with narrowed eyes. His gaze lingered on the darkening bruise on her cheek. Kate turned her face slightly and hoped it didn't look too bad. "Driving a busload of folk up to see the shows. Already been down to Hot Springs and the horse races. Spent most of last week there. Lost a dadgum bundle on the ponies."

Kate remembered then that Henry had bought himself a bus and had taken to guiding tours. Judge Hinkley had been Pop's best friend when he'd been the circuit judge at Van Buren. In his seventies now, Henry was retired but had been voted out of office a decade ago for abandoning his loyal wife of thirty years and eloping with a seventeen-year-old assistant law clerk by the name of Gwennie Briggs. She, in turn, had run off with his young law partner, Mel Lance, Jr., before her marriage to the judge was hardly consummated. Judge Hinkley had become the laughingstock of the legal community afterward, lambasted by the decent citizens of Carter County. He had never lived the scandal down.

"What's the matter with Joey? Colic or something?"

The judge liked babies and had come to visit Joey just after Michael had brought him home, armed with a dozen packages of disposable diapers and a silver rattle. He'd stayed long enough to rock Joey to sleep. A month ago, which seemed totally inconceivable to Kate. The last few days alone seemed like a year.

"You all right, honey?" the judge was asking now.

Kate stared at him like a felon facing the executioner. Henry had known her too long and too well. She felt she could trust him with anything, but involving him in this mess would get him thrown in jail as an accomplice after the fact. Or murdered by Dmitri. That sobered her quickly enough. There was no way she could tell him the truth. She plastered a big, happy smile on her face, but she had a feeling she looked as plastic as a Malibu Barbie. "I'm fine, really, just worried about Joey. I'm going to Branson, too, with a friend of mine."

Kate watched Gail move past their booth and stop to wipe off the next table, but she had a feeling the woman was really eavesdropping on their conversation.

"Is that a fact? Who you here with?" Henry was eyeing her intently as he helped himself to the glass of water the waitress had left for Booker. His hair was thick and wavy, white as chalk, with a cowlick at midforehead that sent a natural wave above his right temple. His mane was his pride and joy; he loved comparisons with Kenny Rogers.

"Just a friend."

"Where's Slick? Still getting sleazebag junkies off up in Clayton?"

Slick was what Henry had called Michael. Needless to say, he hadn't cared much for her husband. But the judge obviously hadn't heard what had happened to her during the last few hellish days, or he wouldn't be asking such questions. Momentarily she considered telling him everything, baring her soul and asking his help, but discarded the idea at once. She could trust him but she couldn't bring herself to endanger the kind old man.

Henry set down the glass. He shook his head and leaned forward, lowering his voice as Gail walked past them yet again. "Why are you lying to me, Katie girl? You think I haven't heard all the newscasts about you? It's all over the media. Did that sonofabitch beat you up? Is that why you had to shoot him?"

Oh, God, he did know. Kate glanced around nervously, not wanting the cops to overhear them. It seemed now that everyone must know who she was, who Joey was. She searched for Gail but couldn't see her anywhere.

"I didn't shoot Michael, Judge, I swear to God." She hesitated a moment, as Joey squirmed and fought in her arms. She patted his back, thinking that if she could get him to burp, it might help his stomachache. She was so jittery; she heard the tremor in her voice. "I can't tell you what's going on, Henry, I really can't. You've just got to trust me on this. I need your help, I need it desperately. The baby and I both do. Something's wrong with Joey, I think he's sick, and I've got to get him out of here." She scanned the parking lot for Booker but didn't see him. Didn't see Gail, either.

The judge was frowning.

"Please, Henry, don't ask any more questions, just hear me out. I haven't done anything wrong, none of the things the news people are reporting. I need to get to Branson as soon as possible, and I don't have a ride."

When she kept glancing anxiously at the door, Henry finally followed her gaze. He spoke softly. "You've got to tell me more than that. You're in big trouble, Katie, bigger than you obviously realize. Maybe I can help you."

"I don't want you getting involved. Can't you just trust me, just this once, Henry? I need help, and I don't have anywhere else to turn. Please, please help me." Joey had stopped crying to heave in a shaky breath, and Kate tried to interest him in the bottle, but he still wouldn't take the nipple. He was sick, something was terribly wrong, and Kate didn't know what else to do for him. She put his pacifier in his mouth and he sucked on it a moment, then stiffened and cried as if struck by a gas cramp.

"My God, Kate, what's going on? What have you gotten yourself into?"

"All I'm asking you for is a ride to Branson. That's all. Please, Henry."

Henry wasn't finished with the questions. After all, he was a lawyer. "Who're you traveling with?"

"I told you, an old friend of mine," she lied with not a lot of finesse. "You don't know him, I'm sure. He's not from Van Buren."

"I might. What's his name?"

Booker chose that moment to show up at the hostess station, and Kate nearly wilted with relief. He was scanning the tables for her and didn't look thrilled when he saw her talking to Henry with a couple of police officers sitting right beside them. In fact, he looked as if he might turn around and walk back out. He hesitated there until Kate beckoned to him. Reluctantly, it seemed, he strode across the busy restaurant toward them, looking too big and strong and vital to be a noonday patron of Hillbilly Junction. His eyes were locked with hers, asking a ton of questions.

"Here he is now, Judge. This is my friend."

"Does he have a first name, or do you just call him *friend?*"

"Of course," she said, laughing falsely at the judge's sarcasm as if he were just so silly. Then she lied to him some more. "Smith. His name's Jack Smith."

The judge looked Booker up and down, then got to his feet and offered his hand. Henry was a little man, only five foot five. Booker veritably dwarfed him. "Jack Smith, is it?"

"That's right."

"I'm Henry Hinkley. Old friend of Katie and her grandpa."

Booker didn't comment on that, or anything else, just sat down, turned where he could keep an eye on the door and the cops. His guarded body language was telling enough. He did not like having Henry at the table with them, not a bit. He wanted Kate to get rid of him.

"Henry knows about Michael. He heard about it on the news," she said, very low. "He's here with a tour bus. Headed to Branson."

Booker looked more wary now, if that were possible, all tensed up, she could tell that, too, though his facial expression didn't change. But there was something else that moved inside those pale blue eyes of his, a warning. Believe it or not, could it be she was actually learning to read him a little?

"I told him I can't explain anything right now and asked him to give us a lift. Have you decided if you can do that, Henry? You'll never know how much it'd mean to me."

Judge Hinkley was looking at Booker through slitted, openly suspicious eyes. "How'd you get this far, Smith? You wouldn't want to be leaving a vehicle behind, would you?"

"Car broke down a few miles back."

The two men stared distrustfully at each other.

"Katie's like a daughter to me, especially since Pop died. She's in an awful lot of trouble all of a sudden. Wouldn't want to see her get hurt."

If Henry only knew, Kate thought, but she said, "Henry, please. I've asked you to trust me on this. To help me out. If you don't want to, fine. Jack's been trying to help me get out of this mess, so quit looking at him like he's going to pull a gun on you."

Booker threw her a startled look, not amused. Henry wasn't laughing either. It had been a bad choice of words. The two men looked as though they were going to grab each other by the throat and take to grappling at any minute. Joey spit out his pacifier and let out a shrill wail. Nearly everyone in the restaurant turned in unison to look at them. They had to get out of there.

"Well, I'd be a lot more comfortable with all this if you'd just explain the part about Joey being kidnapped," Henry demanded very low, distracted momentarily when two women with whom he'd been dining gathered up their purses ready to leave. "I just might be able to intervene with the authorities, you know. Especially if Slick's the one who got you involved in all this."

Kate simply shook her head. Booker said his usual nothing.

"Well, you've always been a good girl with a damn good head on your shoulders, and I'm not surprised in the least that Mike got you involved in some of his St. Louis shit, through no fault of your own."

Kate nodded, encouraged. Booker didn't comment. Joey slacked off, thank God.

The waitress finally showed up with their food. As she set down the plates, she eyed Booker with undue interest, then moved on. Henry pushed back his chair and got to his feet. "Well, I'll ask the others and make sure nobody minds you two tagging along. Got a few seats empty. Go ahead and eat, then come on out to the bus. I reckon we can find room for the both of you."

Booker watched the starchy old man wend his way through the tables and join two old ladies at the cash register. He looked at Kate. "Are you crazy?"

"We need to get to Branson, don't we? I got us a ride."

"Are you crazy?" Booker repeated. "The man knows we're running from the law."

"Do you have a better idea?" Obviously Booker didn't, because he didn't offer one. "I tell you we can trust him," she whispered, putting Joey back in the baby seat. He didn't like that either. He'd never cried so much before. "I've known the judge since I was a little girl. He's not going to do anything to hurt me. I didn't tell him anything anyway. He already knew I was in trouble."

"You sure he's not out there calling the cops right now?"

"He'd never do that. He's like a grandfather to me. I trust him completely." She looked for Gail, didn't see her. "Did you ditch the car?"

"Yeah, in a patch of woods about a mile up the road behind Gramma's Kitchen. I hid it as well as I could but they'll find it eventually." Booker glanced at the patrolmen at the next table but they were enjoying T-bone steaks, their suspicions obviously blunted by Judge Hinkley's friendship with

Kate. His eyes darted from table to table. "Let's hurry up and get out of here before somebody shows up we don't wanna see."

Kate nodded. "There's a waitress here, one who's showing a lot of interest in us."

"She could be trouble. Which one is she?"

"That's her, standing by the door."

Both of them watched her pick up the phone at the hostess station. She fished a small piece of paper out of her apron pocket and punched in a number.

"She's calling them," Booker said, turning his head as the waitress glanced in their direction. "Come on, let's get out of here, now."

Kate nodded, sneaking a surreptitious glance toward the woman again. The hostess was coming down on Gail for being on the phone, frowning and gesturing her toward the kitchen. Gail headed back to work. As soon as she entered the swinging kitchen doors, Kate said, "Okay, let's go while she's in the back."

Booker threw a twenty on the table, and Kate picked up Joey and followed Booker out of the restaurant. Joey was sniffling again but not yelling, so they didn't attract much attention as they moved outside into a warm sunshiny day and air that smelled like diesel exhaust. Judge Hinkley was waiting beside his bright blue bus with dark-tinted windows as elderly passengers pulled themselves up the steps at the door beside the driver's seat.

"Everybody agreed it was okay for you to board since I could vouch for you," he said with a pointed look in Booker's direction. "Hope you won't make me regret this, Smith."

"Appreciate the ride," Booker said, every bit as uneasy as Henry.

Kate was just glad to step aboard Henry's bus where she felt a little safer, at least for the two hours it'd take them to reach Branson.

Twenty-three

BOOKER FOLLOWED KATE into the tour bus. They were getting plenty of attention from the senior citizens already aboard, all of whom seemed collectively thrilled to the gills to have a baby to make a fuss over. Nothing like forty or more grandparents to help Kate dote on the kid. The windows were heavily tinted, dark gray, which was very good. The people inside were pretty much invisible from outside; Booker had checked that first off. The seats were upholstered in soft crimson plush. Recliners. With two bathrooms in the back. A luxurious coach in which to escape. Kate probably felt like Cinderella. Still, he was increasingly uneasy. By getting on board they were endangering the life of every single person smiling and welcoming them so eagerly.

"Try to get a seat by the emergency exit," he said close to Kate, who seemed to be enjoying showing off Joey to every admiring gramma along the aisle. There were a couple of husbands along for the ride, but not many. The judge obviously catered to the ladies. Henry Hinkley was watching Booker like a hawk beaded in on a field mouse. The old man wasn't stupid. He knew there was a lot they weren't telling him but he had no idea how bad it really was. Booker hoped to God Hinkley didn't act on his suspicions. There was a CB radio up front at the driver's seat. Booker had seen it. It wouldn't take two seconds for Hinkley to bring the police down on them. Thanks to the waitress, Dmitri and the gang were probably already on the way.

Two women, with tightly curled white hair frozen into place with enough hairspray to wax a car, generously offered to move so that he and Kate could sit near the bathrooms. Kate smiled warmly; man, she did have one hell of a nice smile, and thanked them, and introductions fluttered around like happy canaries. As Kate included Booker, he tried to remember that he was Jack, supposed to be Joey's proud papa. He put on a stiff, skeleton's grin that probably frightened the elderly women more than disarmed them. They gazed curiously at him as they transferred their large straw purses and busting-out-full souvenir bags to the next empty seat. Joey started crying again, and Kate tried to comfort him while the busload of grammas and grampas gave a sympathetic oooh, aghast by his discomfort.

"Oooh, you poor little thing, don't you cry now. You're just pretty as a picture, yes, you are," crooned a woman who'd christened herself Louise. She wore black slacks and a black-and-white–striped silky-looking top with a sailor's collar. She smelled good, like red roses, and was really getting into the cooing, mewling mode now, saying things like *ah goo, ah goo, peeky pie, pooky poo*. To Booker's surprise, Joey immediately responded big time, pausing his building little tantrum and gazing up at her with utmost interest. When he let out a chortling little laugh, Louise absolutely glowed.

"I just love babies, all children, really," she informed them merrily. "They just take to me. My daughter says babies know instinctively who loves them. I think that's true, don't you, Frances?"

Her seat partner nodded, beaming about it, too. She wore a charcoal gray jogging suit with lots of silver ornaments and tiny mirrors around the neck and down the sleeves.

"Could I hold him a minute for you while you get settled?" Louise offered, brown eyes glowing behind her glasses. She couldn't wait to get her hands on the baby. "My grandchildren are all grown up. Julie has her own baby now. Trey's his name. He's my very first great-grandchild. He's a little doll but all babies are, now aren't they?"

At first Kate seemed reluctant to hand Joey over. She'd hardly had him out of her arms since Booker first laid eyes on her. But it didn't take her long to decide she could trust Louise. So would Booker. Louise loved children, there could be no doubt. When Kate acquiesced, Louise lifted Joey out of his yellow seat, very gently and cautiously, as if he were made of crystal, then quickly proved herself adept at cuddling infants. She stood in the aisle, tenderly gazing down at Joey while Frances hung over her shoulder, remarking what a sweet little face Joey had, what dark eyes he had, so bright and intelligent as if he understood everything they were saying.

"I bet he's got a tummyache," offered a lady seated across the aisle from Louise and Frances.

"Novella's got a new little great-grandbaby," Louise informed them, but all her attention was zeroed in on the child she was adoring. "If you like, I'll hold him for awhile. Sometimes if you put them down on their tummies on your knees, it helps relieve colic."

Kate told the ladies she wasn't sure what was making him cry, and Booker stood waiting impatiently until Kate moved into the seat beside the window. He examined the parking lot for signs of trouble. He didn't see the waitress who'd used the phone, or any hoods with guns or highway patrolmen with arrest warrants approaching the bus, so he considered himself lucky. The exit door was just across from him, which made him feel more secure about trapping himself and Kate inside a bus with lots of innocent people in their sixties and seventies. On the other hand, who in their right mind would expect Kate and him to board a tour bus?

Kate leaned over the seat and checked on Joey but the baby had quieted considerably. Louise knew what she was doing. Booker peered out the back window for any cars pulling off the highway. He had no doubt they'd come after them, especially if the waitress had snitched. If they could just get out of Hillbilly Junction and on their way without any trouble, they might luck out and lose Dmitri and his Russian cronies for good. Hell, what was Hinkley doing up there? Why didn't he fire up the bus and get the damn thing rolling? The last thing he wanted was a shoot-out on a senior citizen bus full of sweet, affectionate little grammas.

For about ten minutes Hinkley stood outside the front door shooting the breeze with another driver and waiting for his last, wayward passenger to wander back to the bus. Apparently a lady named Margaret decided she had a yen for some vanilla walnut fudge, simply had to have a piece to munch on until they arrived at the motel. Hinkley had agreed indulgently, obviously a tour guide who aimed to please.

Come on, come on, Booker muttered under his breath, then decided Kate might be better off in the restroom where nobody could recognize her. If Henry Hinkley had heard about the kidnapping, so had a lot of his passengers. Kate nodded and excused herself, and Booker sat watching the parking lot, nervous as an expectant father outside a delivery room. Louise cooed like a pigeon and rubbed Joey's back, charming the kid out of his little baby mind. Joey was actually trying to answer her, making happy little grunts that sounded a little like *ah goo*. Louise was indeed a natural-born granny, but Booker was more interested in natural-born killers as a white Isuzu Scout pulled into a parking place beside the bus. Misha of the dangling earring opened the door and got out of the backseat.

Booker slid down in his seat and put a hand alongside his face to hide his profile, no longer comforted by dark-tinted windows. He propped his left foot on his knee and put his hand on the .45 he'd strapped to his ankle before entering the restaurant. He unsnapped the holster. *Come on, Margaret, forget the fudge and get on the damn bus*. Two other men got out of the Scout while Misha ran inside, nearly knocking down poor Margaret who was exiting the place with several boxes of goodies.

Out the corner of his eye, Booker watched the men only feet away, his heart thumping against his breastbone as Margaret stopped at the door to chat with the judge. *Shit, shit, get on, just get on*, he wanted to stand up and scream at her. Dmitri had wasted no time hijacking a new vehicle, and Booker watched Kate's nemesis, wondering why the man was so hell-bent on killing her. She was right; Dmitri didn't come off as your everyday bloodthirsty assassin. He looked to be in his early forties, slim, muscular, standing about five ten or eleven. He had on sunglasses and was talking intently into a cell phone. His eyes never stopped searching his surroundings. Booker pressed back into the seat and averted his head as the Russian killer scanned the dark windows of Hinkley's bus. Booker hoped the waitress hadn't seen them board the bus.

Finally, finally, Margaret hopped aboard and came rushing down the aisle, handing out pieces of fudge to anyone who admitted having a sweet tooth, which was nearly everybody she passed. It turned out she was great friends with Louise, Frances, and Novella and plopped down in the seat beside Novella. They all chose different kinds and went on about the deliciousness of each flavor as Hinkley moseyed aboard and took what seemed an hour getting himself settled satisfactorily in the driver's seat before he finally whooshed the doors shut with a hydraulic hiss. He spent the next few minutes telling everybody to sit down, it was time to be off. Booker muttered an ugly oath to himself and slid the .45 out of the holster and onto his lap underneath Joey's blue baby blanket.

"Here, try a piece," Margaret offered Booker, looking over the back of her seat. "It's rich but almost as scrumptious as my own recipe." She winked, every bit as friendly as the rest. These women were the stuff Super Grammas were made of, and remarkably well preserved for their ages if they were great-grandmothers.

Booker nodded stiffly, keeping his eyes on the men outside, compelled to take a piece for fear she wouldn't stop offering until he did. He chose a piece of plain milk chocolate from a little white box replete with a plastic knife with which to cut it.

"Thank you, ma'am."

Novella peered around the seat. "My, aren't you a polite one? Not many youngsters have manners any more." *Youngsters*, Booker thought, then wondered how polite Novella would think him if she knew he had his finger on the trigger of a gun hidden in his lap.

Booker realized he had to come up with something to say. Problem was he hadn't had much practice with inane pleasantries. "This is good fudge."

The ladies agreed enthusiastically while Booker watched the killers. They were having a heated discussion at the front of the car, then one was dispatched to search the cars in the parking lot. Another hurried inside the café, and Dmitri bent over a road map spread over the hood, still talking on the telephone. *Start the motor, Hinkley, turn the goddamn key*. Booker's jaw clenched hard, and he shifted the gun to a better position. The men were looking at the tour buses now, gesturing toward the one in which he now sat eating fudge like a sitting duck.

The ladies in front of him chatted innocently, and Booker went rigid as Joey let out a loud cry about the time the judge fired the engine and revved it to near B-52 roar. The Russians didn't hear the baby's wail, and never in his life had Booker felt better when a set of wheels began to turn and his window slowly slid past the white Isuzu full of hired killers.

Minutes later Kate made her reappearance. Booker glanced back and relaxed some when he saw the men still leaning over the road map, which probably meant they thought they'd lost them and were trying to figure out their next move. As Kate stopped beside his seat, her new auburn hair shone with all kinds of reddish highlights under the ceiling light. She looked good, but he liked her better blond.

Once Kate was seated the coach gradually grew quiet as people settled down to their Mary Higgins Clarks and John Grishams. Joey finally went to sleep in Louise's lap, and Booker kept his guard up, watching both lanes of traffic, front and back. The white Isuzu was not in sight.

"Did you see them?" Kate whispered.

"Uh huh, they parked right beside us while you were in the bathroom. They're driving an Isuzu Scout now, a white one."

"Oh, my God, no. Was it Dmitri?"

Booker nodded. He wondered again what Dmitri had done to Kate when he had her under his control. The fear was back in her eyes, the way it always was when Dmitri got too close.

"You're sure he didn't see us?"

"No, but I was sweatin' it there for awhile." He lifted the blanket and showed her how much he'd sweated it.

Kate was leaning against the window, trying to see the cars parked at Hillbilly Junction. When she turned back, she looked pale and frightened. It had obviously occurred to her what a firefight aboard Hinkley's bus would have been like. "Thank God they didn't see us."

Booker examined her face, frowning at all the scratches and bruises. She had really gotten roughed up during her ordeal.

Kate leaned her head on the soft cushion, as if she was exhausted, and Booker checked out the back for pursuers. As far as he could tell, they were still parked where they'd left them. There was chitchat going on around him, and it was getting on his nerves. But he might as well get used to it. That's what normal people did. They talked to one another. Ate fudge. Traveled. Laughed together. Enjoyed themselves. He had a bad feeling it'd take him a long time to relearn those things, much less interact with other people. He'd been uncomfortable merely accepting a piece of candy.

Kate was staring out the window at the passing scenery, looking a little more relaxed. They'd had a close call at the truck stop, too damn close for comfort. Joey was sleeping, and he hoped Kate would get some rest, too. Hinkley continued to watch him for the felon he was through the rearview mirror. Aviator sunglasses still on, Booker furtively slid his weapon back into his ankle harness and snapped it in place. He leaned back and shut his eyes. He was tired. Maybe he should try to get some sleep, too, when he knew he wouldn't get jumped. He had gotten himself into quite a mess this time with Kate Reed. He just hoped he could get them both out of it alive. Now Mac was their only chance. Their *only* one.

Twenty-four

ALTHOUGH SHE KNEW Dmitri was somewhere behind them, coming, always coming, Kate felt relatively safe as long as the motor hummed and Louise and her friends cooed and cuddled Joey. Surprisingly, she was able to relax, even doze, grateful for a respite when her head didn't ache and muscles weren't knotted in a constant fight-or-flight dilemma.

Later, about the time they hit a sprawling cloverleaf outside Springfield, Kate sat up and looked around as the bus took an off-ramp in a long curve to 65 South and Branson. In front of Kate, Joey was still being adored by the kind ladies. He seemed to feel better, had even been coaxed to take a bottle from Louise. Kate leaned back, deciding that the more crooning voices he heard, the more gentle hands that touched him, the better. He'd been through a hellish ordeal that nobody should have to endure, much less an innocent baby. Kate hoped fervently the worst was over now that they'd evaded the Russians at Hillbilly Junction. How could Dmitri possibly deduce their destination was Branson? There were hundreds of other towns in the area.

Her head resting on the velour cushion, she turned and studied Booker. He looked halfway relaxed for a change but sat so perfectly still she thought he was asleep. Dark sunglasses covered his eyes, and his face was turned to the window. Momentarily he shifted a bit, awake after all, and Kate wondered how he continued to make do with so little rest. She recalled his night terrors and thought how awful it would be to fear sleep every night.

John Booker was such an enigma. She was grateful, owed him an unbelievable debt, but he was turning out to be a completely different man than she'd first thought. He'd shown strength and courage, of course, in a hundred ways, but it was his kindness that intrigued her, the small, thoughtful things he'd done for Joey and for her. She had never met a man like him, and she certainly didn't understand why he had decided to become their protector.

"Booker?"

Slowly he turned his face toward her. His jaw bristled black with a heavy five o'clock shadow. He studied her face questioningly, and she wished he would smile and reassure her. If nothing else, it'd make her feel better, even if it weren't true. She leaned close to him and spoke in a whisper.

"Do you think they'll figure out where we're headed?"

Booker shrugged a shoulder. "Maybe. If they find out who I am. Dmitri got a pretty good look at me at the tavern but I suspect they'll wanna check out Springfield first. They'll probably think we'd feel safer losing ourselves in the nearest big city."

"Do you think your friend will help us?"

"He'll help us. If he can." Obviously done with the conversation, Booker turned back to the window and examined the cars passing on their left.

Kate wanted to ask him more about himself, about this unknown friend of his, about why he lived the bizarre life of a hermit until her own plight had flushed him out of his woods. The Joneses had called him Bigfoot but he wasn't anything like what Matty and his brothers believed him to be. Now the Jones family was after her, too, except for poor Millie Mae who'd saved Kate's life not once, but twice. She hoped nothing bad happened to the little girl.

Her thoughts turned to her husband and what he'd done

to them. How could she have fallen in love with a man who could betray her so completely? With some guilt she wondered if she and Michael had ever been right for each other in the first place. He had tried to make a go of their marriage, she supposed, they both had, especially after they'd gotten Joey, but she wondered if they'd been kidding themselves. She doubted now their marriage could have lasted.

There had been something different between them, something wrong for well over a year. Michael had become withdrawn, had distanced himself from her emotionally and physically. She'd known it but hadn't been certain why, had ended up blaming herself for wanting to conceive so badly that their intimacy became nothing more than a chore to Michael.

But she wouldn't blame herself for his involvement with criminals. He'd put Joey and her in such terrible jeopardy. How could he have brought this down on her head? When he knew all along that everything he told her about Joey had been a pack of lies? What had gone so wrong that he would treat her in such a way? He'd been a good man when they married, kind to her, loving enough, and she'd thought he'd become that man again during the last month. But something had been terribly wrong; something had driven him to the awful things he'd done.

Their marriage had been doomed from the moment he'd begun defending thugs and gangsters, refusing to discuss his work and clients with her. She hated being lied to, wanted an honest man who'd treat her as an equal, a partner in life. She wondered if Booker would be such a man. She wondered how it would've been if she'd met him years before he hid out in the woods. She wondered if they'd met another way, another time, they would've gotten together, become more than friends. They were certainly friends now. She trusted him with her life.

Kate shut her eyes, wishing she had met him first, before he'd become embittered and isolated himself from the world.

She wondered if he laughed back then, enjoyed little pleasures like everyone else. He loved Current River as much as she did, obviously loved the out-of-doors, the simple life. They'd probably have been good together, if they'd ever gotten that chance, but the truth was that Booker didn't seem to need anybody in his life. He was doing just fine all by himself. And she supposed she didn't either. If she got out of this, got to keep Joey with her, she could make it on her own. Would have to make it on her own.

She blew out a sigh, wondering if Joey really had been kidnapped. Maybe it was a ruse made up by Dmitri to take the baby from her. Michael had plenty of faults but she couldn't imagine him kidnapping someone's baby. He'd been distraught that day at the Picketts' cabin but he'd given his life helping her escape with Joey; at least he'd done that much for them. Surely at that moment he was too frightened to make up lies. Joey could be a black-market baby as he'd said, perhaps obtained outside the country, but illegally. And if he was, Kate would never give him up. She couldn't, just couldn't. She'd fight for him, go through every court in the land to keep him. Once she turned herself in to Gus or to the Branson police, she'd get herself a lawyer, the best one she could find. Or, if worse came to worse, maybe Booker could take Joey, keep him somewhere safe for her until the whole mess got straightened out before a judge.

The drive to Branson took them through thirty miles of beautiful scenery. Great forested hills rolled into the distance as they journeyed deep into the Ozark Mountains. The billboards advertising Branson theaters appeared along the road. The first one was for the comedian, Yakov Smirnov. His huge red and white sign proclaimed: *From Red to Redneck*. She looked away; she'd seen enough Russians to last her a lifetime. The Laurence Welk show appeared soon with the logo: *Bring the kids. Oh, heck, have them bring their kids, too.*

Little more than a decade ago Branson, Missouri, had

been a sleepy little resort town perched on the shores of Lake Taneycomo and Table Rock Lake, where fishermen rented rustic little cabins vintage 1950. Vacationing families swam in ice-cold lake water at places called Rockaway Beach, visited a tiny theme park called Silver Dollar City, and enjoyed the idyllic panorama of the wooded Ozarks.

Pop and Grandma had brought Kate when she was a little girl. They'd fished and swum and cooked cornbread-coated crappie in a kettle of crackling deep fat. She'd loved it then, the peace and quiet, the mist caught like cobwebs in the hilltops, but now it seemed as if mighty Zeus had waved his hand from atop Mount Olympus and changed the sleepy hamlet into a virtual Hillbilly Las Vegas, minus the gambling. Now as she watched countless signs go by—Shoji Tabuchi, The Osmonds, Barbara Fairchild—she wished the gods could put it back the way it was.

On the right, a huge billboard advertised outlet malls, one with ninety stores. She hadn't seen those yet, hadn't been to Branson since she and Michael had driven down from St. Louis for a weekend not long after they'd wed. She bit her lip, remembering that trip. Now everyone believed she'd killed him, her own husband. How could any of this be happening?

The divided highway dove more deeply into valleys, leaving cars to scurry up the next high hill like ants in a trail. Kate's ears began to pop as they passed road construction sites with the giant yellow caterpillars, bulldozers and dirt haulers covered with rust-colored dirt that devastated natural rock mountains in the name of progress. Rubble lined the road, tons of rocks from dynamite blasting that left the hills sculptured into what looked like the red mesas of Arizona.

More construction met them at the city limits, and Kate was shocked at how much the place had changed since her last visit. The first theater offering was already visible, *The Promise*, its religious content heralded by a gigantic picture of Jesus Christ, aglow in white raiment, arms outstretched.

Dozens of vehicles were already in the parking lot, glittering like jewels as they awaited the three o'clock performance.

As the judge braked and took the exit to the main thoroughfare of Branson, she caught sight of a roadblock at the end of the ramp. Booker got out his gun, and Kate quickly retrieved Joey from Louise.

"If they do a search we'll go out the emergency exit," Booker whispered. Kate nodded, ready. She was always ready now, for anything. She was not going to give up Joey.

The judge brought the bus to a stop, and she could see his eyes on them in the rearview mirror. A Branson policeman walked to the front door, and Henry swooshed it open. The officer gripped the boarding rail and stepped inside, and Kate sank down deep in her seat. So did Booker. The bus got quiet, everyone curious as to what was going on.

"Howdy, judge. How's it goin'?"

"Fine, Ken. Got some kind of trouble?"

"Kid was abducted outta St. Louis. Can you vouch for all these people?"

"You bet. I screen my customers before I accept them."

"Okay, have a good time. You got some good weather for it."

The doors shut again, and the judge glanced back at them before he put the bus in gear. Kate and Booker looked at each other, and Kate was glad Henry knew so many area law-enforcement officers from his time on the bench. They turned onto Highway 76 and soon found themselves moving at a crawl in bumper-to-bumper traffic. Everyone called the road the Strip, and the people on the bus stirred and readied themselves for fun in the Ozarks.

Silver-haired senior citizens walked along the sidewalks, and lots of young families holding tightly to the hands of their children, all swarming among a hodgepodge of T-shirt and souvenir shops that boasted Buy Two, Get One Free. Country crafts shops with names like The Gingham Goose or Apple

Tree Mall lined the street, along with every conceivable fast-food place from Burger King to Pizza Hut. Quaint motels like the Rockin' Chair Inn, Dogwood Inn, and Hillbilly Inn offered low rates, crowded along the curbs like viewers on a parade route.

"Man," said Booker, shaking his head. "What the hell hit this place?"

Kate laughed, surprised he'd been there before. "When were you here last?"

"In the eighties."

Good Lord, she thought, wondering if that had been the last time he'd been out of the woods. "Before you went in the army?"

"Yeah."

That dismissed that subject. Kate had a feeling he'd never discuss the military with her, or with anyone else. It'd scarred him enough to drive him underground. She wondered if the government was still looking for him. Surely not after so many years. She hoped to heaven that she wouldn't be the one to get him caught. She couldn't imagine a man like Booker caged up inside a cell. Her eyes lingered a moment where Booker's hand rested on the ankle where he kept his gun. She wondered what Louise would think if she knew Kate had a big gun affixed with a silencer in the sack with Joey's Luvs. Probably pretty much appalled.

The bus rolled slowly past a shopping center or two, one with a busy Wal-Mart and Consumer's grocery store. Bobby Vinton's theater was on the right, its marquee advertising the Glenn Miller Orchestra. A Shoney's loomed, a place called the Garden of Eatin'. You name it, Branson had it. Kate wondered which motel the judge had booked for his tour. The Strip ran atop a high hill, and she could see other massive white theaters and hotels on other green hills, with shopping centers and restaurants nestled in the valleys between. Ancient Rome must have looked similar on its seven hills crested with gleaming white temples and villas.

"Where's the Shoji Tabuchi show?"

"Down there somewhere." Kate pointed downhill to their right, surprised by Booker's question. "At the end of the Strip, you take a right." She smiled a little. "You want to catch his show while we're here?"

"Yeah."

Kate waited for further explanation but got none. She didn't demand answers, pleased to think Booker might have a plan. He'd gotten her this far. She sure as the devil wasn't going to nag him. They passed the Baldknobber's Theater, the Riverboat Motel shaped like an old-fashioned paddle wheeler, the Osmonds place, the Roy Clark Theater, and Lodge of the Ozarks before Judge Hinkley finally nosed the motor bus into a brand-new Hampton Inn, built in dark glass and sleek, contemporary lines. He pulled up underneath a gigantic front canopy.

Everyone was gathering their belongings. The ladies they'd met bid them a warm good-bye and filed toward the front. Kate was just glad she and Booker had not embroiled them in a gunfight. Booker let her precede him to the front exit where the judge was helping the passengers to disembark.

"I sure wish you'd tell me more 'bout what's goin' on, Katie," he muttered beneath his breath, his eyes keen on Booker. "C'mon inside. I'll get you and Joey a room and we can figure all this out. Whatever it is, it can't be that bad."

Kate wished it wasn't that bad. But it was worse. "Remember, Henry, no matter what else you hear about us, it's not true. I didn't do anything wrong."

"Dadgumit, Katie, let me help you."

"You did, more than you know. Just keep on trusting me."

Booker shifted impatiently, glancing around at cars pulling in and out of the parking lot. Diesel fumes hung thick in the air. She knew he wanted to get out of sight before somebody recognized her.

"Gotta go now, Henry, but thanks for everything. I'll never forget it, I mean that." She gave him a hug and kissed his wrinkled cheek.

"Where are you going now? At least tell me that much," Henry demanded, grasping her arm, still reluctant to let her go.

"Oh, Jack wants to see a couple of shows while we're here, you know, all the usual touristy stuff," she said for the benefit of the nearby passengers. "Maybe we'll go out to Silver Dollar City or somewhere."

Henry didn't believe that for one minute. "Do you need some money? You don't even have any luggage, do you?"

"I'm fine," she told him, hoping Booker did have more cash to throw around. "Gotta go now, bye, Henry."

"Call me as soon as you can," he said, as she and Booker moved off toward the front sidewalk.

"Okay, tell me how to get to this Shoji place," Booker said, as soon as they were out of earshot. "Can we cut down through this parking lot and get there?" Booker was gazing down the back of the Hampton. A theater called the Remington had been built behind the hotel, a beautiful building with lots of brown wood and arched windows.

Kate nodded. Booker took the baby seat from her, then held her arm as they walked swiftly around the back.

"You think Joey's okay now?" he asked her.

"Yes. It must've been gas."

"He's a tough kid."

Kate was incongruously proud that Booker thought so. He hadn't really touched Joey much since she'd jumped his case for taking him out of the tepee when she'd been in the shower. Now she was ashamed she hadn't trusted him. Well, she trusted him now. Without reservation.

Twenty-five

THE SHOJI TABUCHI THEATER was indeed a sight to behold. The huge building, facing a corner, was tan trimmed in purple, mauve and forest green with enough neon to light a small town. The Japanese violinist had spelled out his first name in gigantic letters crowning a picture of himself and his pretty blond wife. The parking lot approximated the size of Rhode Island. Apparently, Shoji was an entertainer to be reckoned with.

At the moment, however, Booker was more interested in getting inside without being nabbed by some citizen wanting the reward offered on Kate, so was particularly pleased to see the large crowd milling around the front doors and spilling into the interior lobby. Several bored-looking security guards were directing the parking of diesel-belching tour buses and corralling a whole herd of shiny new Continentals and Cadillacs. No one paid a bit of attention to one more couple with a baby hurrying across the street so as not to miss the three o'clock show.

Inside the lobby was an absolute mob scene. In the middle of the uproar was a big-screen television playing tapes of a prior live performance by the man of the hour, Shoji Tabuchi in the flesh, absolutely playing the hell out of a violin. Booker had to admit the guy was good, more than good. There was a two-sided snack bar shaped in a V with concession counters on each side, mirrored brilliantly to show the ornate decor, where awestruck customers bought popcorn and jujubes to eat while the master fiddled.

"The ladies' powder room has gold fixtures and fresh flowers on every wash basin," Kate whispered. "It was featured once on *60 Minutes*."

Booker looked down at her. "They put Shoji's bathroom on *60 Minutes*?"

Kate laughed softly. She looked good when she laughed but she sobered self-consciously and glanced around, remembering their peril. "It was a piece about Branson and how it had become a boom town for country stars. Surely you've seen *60 Minutes* with Ed Bradley and all those guys?"

Booker hadn't watched much television in the last fifteen years and didn't want to start now, especially if they were featuring the lavatories of stars. The ticket booths were lined up to the left of the entrance, five abreast, with long waiting lines at each one. A pink neon light on the wall spelled out the word *tickets* in script with a curlicue under it for emphasis. He took hold of Kate's arm and led her to the one farthest from the front door.

"You think it'd be okay if I changed Joey in the bathroom before the show starts?" Kate asked in a low voice, brown eyes scanning the lobby for enemies. Booker had been doing the same thing.

"Looks like I'll be here awhile. But make it quick. I don't like us being separated."

"Me either. Believe me, I'd rather be joined at the hip with you more than anyone I know," Kate said, taking Joey's seat back from him. The baby smiled when she leaned close, apparently feeling chipper now, his dimples deepening as if Kate made his day just by looking at him. Booker was beginning to understand that. "If you get the tickets before I come back, wait outside the ladies' room door where I can find you. I'll hurry, I promise."

Booker nodded, trying to look less anxious than he really was and like all the other carefree tourists gawking at the purple-and-mauve–medallioned carpet and wrought-iron balconies festooned with hanging artificial vines entwined with purple Christmas lights, but he didn't think he carried it off too convincingly. People glanced at him, then took a second look, not a good sign. He didn't want to be noticed. He tried to slouch a little so he wouldn't seem so tall.

The ticket lady was regretful that there just weren't any great seats left, but that didn't really matter, sir, you see, because all the seats are good because our theater is built so every person can see the stage just fine. Booker bought two at twenty-five bucks a pop but Joey got in free, if his mother could hold him on her lap.

Booker shelled over three twenties from the stack he'd cashed out of a bank circa nineteen eighties, then asked the woman, keeping his voice quiet, "Mac Sharp still work here, ma'am?"

"You know Mac?" She smiled, a real friendly sort with half-glasses perched on the tip of her nose and attached around her neck on a necklace of big fake pearls. She had dangly earrings that looked like something Hopi Indians would dance around their ceremonial fires wearing, and a fire-engine red jogging suit with silver half-moons all over the jacket. Her nametag said Myrtle. Everyone seemed to wear nametags nowadays. Booker wondered why.

"Yeah, a little." He didn't feel the need to chat about his life history with Mac. He just wanted to know if he was around. "He workin' today?"

"Oh, yes, he's in the show, but you'll probably have to wait until after it's over to find him. They'll be starting the first act any minute now. You'll have to hurry to be seated before the lights go down. You don't want to miss Christina. She's Shoji's daughter, you know. Sings like a nightingale, truly does. And the prettiest little thing, pretty as a picture, but so's Dorothy, that's Mrs. Tabuchi, you know."

"Yeah? Well, thanks, Myrtle," he said, gathering up the blue tickets and pocketing his change. He glanced at the doors again, feeling fairly certain they hadn't been followed but never quite comfortable believing it. And there were always the news reports and reward to worry about.

"Tell Mac I said hi when you see him. He's just the nicest man, always wearin' that big smile and a howdy, always talkin' about the Cardinals and Mark McGwire. Thank goodness, I get to go home now for a spell. Have a nice day, y'hear? And enjoy the show. It's really something to see."

"Yeah, thanks."

Booker felt he was getting better at making the eternal small talk everybody seemed to require, not good, but at least he was carrying on conversations that he wasn't used to. He moved past a seven-foot-high flower arrangement with lilies and every other conceivable kind of flower to where Kate had disappeared earlier. There were double French doors of cut and beveled glass that led into the entry foyer of the ladies' room. The LADIES transom sign above the door was of stained, jeweled glass.

Booker could see inside well enough to make out a big chandelier and a long marble table with a gilt-edged mirror over it. Little red lights glittered under glass insets on the table, and a pair of two-foot-high, rectangular crystal vases held pink and white irises. Lots of women were standing around eyeballing everything, no doubt oohing and aahing over the magnificence. And that was only what he could glimpse through the doors. Nope, Kate wasn't kidding about Shoji having glitzy bathrooms.

Most of the crowd had swarmed and pushed their way into the auditorium at the rear of the purple lobby by now, just a few hungry old men left loitering around the refreshment counters and Booker hanging around the ladies' room like some kind of pervert. He didn't like standing around in the neon glow, for anyone to pick out and stare at. He wished Kate would hurry the hell up. She came out a couple of minutes later, looking refreshed with lipstick on her mouth, baseball cap off and hair fluffed up some. Booker looked at her full red lips a second too long and remembered how she'd looked in that damn little white towel. His body reacted.

"You wouldn't believe that place. Real orchids in crystal vases at every sink and a huge chandelier in the ceiling with purple crystal teardrops, and the changing table had a teddy bear."

"C'mon, let's get inside before the show starts."

Booker had a feeling Kate felt a little too safe all of a sudden. They were not out of trouble, not by a long shot. They weren't on a damn vacation here. He told her to put her hat back on as they were led down the side aisle by a retired man wearing a green blazer. As they took their places the lights flickered, then went down, and the curtain went up. They were seated about halfway down the huge auditorium, more toward the middle, seats not too bad, actually. Booker was more interested in their proximity to the exits.

Row upon row of silver heads faced forward, the glow of the stage lights on their eager, lined faces. Christina, the Tabuchi offspring, was on stage now, greeting everyone and telling them they were in for some FUN TODAY. A rumble of approval greeted her proclamation. Get it on, get it on, they all seemed to say in a way reminiscent, if the truth were known, of the gladiator duels of ancient Rome. He wondered if Shoji ever got bum crowds who booed him, or just sat there and looked bored. Probably not, the way he made his instrument sing. For the most part, senior citizens seemed to remember how to be polite.

For awhile they were entertained with various tour groups shouting out like high school cheering sections as the name of their state was mentioned. After Kentucky, Arkansas, Kansas, Michigan, Florida, and Mississippi, Booker was afraid they'd have to suffer the entire lower forty-eight, but luckily the show finally got started with Shoji's daughter belting out a song and dance that really got everyone's blood pumping.

Booker scanned the performers backing her for Mac, especially during a portion of the show where a sixteen-piece orchestra sat on a tiered stage to accompany Shoji Tabuchi, who was turning out to be quite the showman. A glance told him that Kate seemed to be enjoying herself. She had turned Joey, too, his back against her chest, both proving to be ever adaptable. But Kate leaned close to him most of the time and kept a tight hold on Joey. Joey seemed to enjoy, gurgling now and then with appreciation for some of Shoji's high notes.

At one point, Shoji showcased his home country with an incredible rendition of Gene Krupa that looked like the Japanese equivalent of three giant bongo drums. They were called taiko, according to Shoji's introduction, and were the instruments of the ancient Japanese art of drumming. Booker had seen the real taikos once in Tokyo on a mission, and the beating throb of the drums quickly enthralled the audience.

When suddenly two drummers were spotlighted being lowered from the ceiling in slings about ten yards in front of them, Booker was first stunned, then relieved to find that Mac Sharp was the one on the right, closest to them. He looked pretty much the same as he had the last time he'd come down to the river to visit Booker, the only person who'd ever been inside the cave, besides Kate Reed.

Booker watched his old pal, thinking he looked good to be almost forty, a hell of a lot better than Booker did. They'd served together in the Green Berets, though Mac had enough sense to get out and enter the police academy. Booker had been recruited by the CIA, and that had cost him his wife and son and sent him to his own brand of personal hell in a steamy, stinking jungle hut.

The drumbeats filling the air suddenly took on another meaning, the sound of guards having fun around their cook fires while he and his men were starving and filthy, arms crossed over their chests and shackled tightly to the next man's wrist so none of them could move. He began to tense up, feel the stifling, close heat of Central America, the jungle rot eating away the flesh between his toes and fingers, the dinging bell, the shrieks of pain that always followed.

When Kate touched his hand, Booker jerked back as if she

was the sadist with the electric wire. She started in surprise, her eyes shifting to the sweat beading his forehead. "What's the matter? Are you sick?"

"Nothin'. That's Mac up there." He pointed toward the man suspended from the ceiling.

"You're kidding." Kate stared up at Mac beating the drum with his sticks as if he'd been born in a pagoda at the base of Mount Fujiyama. "He's really good."

The Japanese spot ended with an abrupt blackout. Somehow the two drummers in the ceiling were hoisted away without much ado. The show went on, spanning every kind of music known to man, from jazz to show tunes to another Japanese number where the women dancers wore white porcelain geisha masks and twirled parasols to a tune from *Madame Butterfly* or something like it. Booker caught sight of Mac a couple more times, once playing a guitar in a fifties dancing number on a soda-shop set, again after the intermission, during a disco number. He was glad when the three-hour show came to an end.

The crowd filed out in an orderly, pleased-pink hush, and Booker led Kate and the baby outside an exit located low in the sloping parking lot. The freight entrances were there, all locked and deserted, and they hung around, conspicuously he feared, near a wooden stair that led up to what Booker determined was the stage door used by the performers, while buses idled with more acrid fumes and the parking lot gradually emptied.

When a young kid wearing a Mickey Mouse shirt finally showed up at the top of the steps, Booker inquired after Mac. The kid had strange designs carved into his burr cut, a phenomenon new to Booker, and he grinned and ogled Kate's figure openly for a minute, then said they could wait inside while he found Mac for them. They stood just inside the door beside the time clock and card slots, the air-conditioned hallway cool and dim after the hot tarmac on which they'd been standing.

Ten minutes later Mac Sharp walked through a locked steel door at the far end of the hall. He stood about five ten, and he kept himself real buff, had ever since he'd been a detective with the St. Louis police. He was as muscular as he was agile, and Booker wondered if he still ran five miles every day and swallowed down multiple vitamin tablets like M and M's. His hair was cut short, its light brown color now bleached out white for some reason. He wore a Cardinals T-shirt, which didn't surprise Booker because Mac was the most fanatical sports enthusiast he had ever met, especially about the Redbirds. Mac didn't recognize Booker at first, peering at them curiously as he strode toward them. He was paying more attention to Kate, but Mac had always appreciated a good-looking woman, and Kate was certainly that, more than that.

"Are you the people looking for me?" Mac asked, looking at them quizzically, obviously not as used to fans swarming him at the stage door as Shoji no doubt was.

"It's me, Mac."

Mac took a double take right out of a Charlie Chaplin skit, looked startled, then laughed. "Good God, Book. Don't tell me you've finally decided to join the human race?"

It must've occurred to Mac then that Booker was actually in the company of a good-looking female. He grinned knowingly and looked to Booker for explanation. Booker didn't see any point in keeping the guy in suspense, but he kept his voice down.

"This is Kate Reed, Mac. We're in trouble and need your help."

Mac stared at him, Kate's name obviously registering at once and with some impact. "If she really is Kate Reed, you're in deep shit."

"She is, and I am."

"Jesus Christ." Mac glanced at the baby seat Kate was holding, then at the closed door behind them. He lowered his voice even more than Booker had. "Every goddamned cop in the state's after her. The news is full of all that shit about her husband and her kidnapping the kid."

"She didn't do it."

"Is that the kid in the baby seat?"

"Yeah."

Mac frowned and swiped a hand through his spiky bleached-out hair. "Okay, okay." He dragged his palm down over his face. He was trying to think what to do with them without getting thrown in jail for his trouble. "Man, man, you got yourself a shitload of a mess now. Let me think a minute."

Booker let him think a minute. Kate looked nervous again.

"Okay, okay, listen, I've got a couple of hours before the next show. I'll take you down to my place. Nobody'll notice you guys there." Something troubling suddenly occurred to him. "Anybody know you're here? In Branson?"

"Don't think so. Not yet."

"Good." Mac was obviously extremely relieved. "C'mon, let's get the hell out of here before somebody does recognize her."

Pleased to do just that, Booker took Kate's arm and followed his old friend out onto the parking lot. Mac had a brand-new, silver-gray Mustang convertible with a black top. Booker had to fold his legs up like an accordion just to get in the front seat. Kate sat in the back with Joey. Mac had the wherewithal to keep the convertible top up, as well as the black-tinted windows. He turned the key, glancing at Booker as the engine settled into a soft, well-serviced purr, lots of unanswered questions behind the wire-rimmed spectacles he'd put on to drive. Booker would fill him in later, when Kate wasn't there to listen. He was asking a lot from his friend but Mac would come through for him. He always had. He would this time, too.

Twenty-six

DMITRI KAVUNOV stood alone in the darkness, waiting. He could hear the soughing wind in the trees, whispering pine boughs so reminiscent of the forests near St. Petersburg. The lonely sound of a car whooshing at high speed down the deserted highway came to him, and he listened to make sure it continued on its way. Yuri and Misha were in place, in the shadows near the front of the restaurant, waiting for the Negro named Jumbo to close up for the night.

He shifted his eyes to the man's upstairs living quarters. It was still dark. The last waitress had left about fifteen minutes before, well past eleven o'clock. The parking lot was empty and had been since the woman had driven her beat-up black Nissan out of the place. He tried to pick out Misha's place near the front door but couldn't see him. Yuri was on the other side somewhere. Andre and Nikolai had returned to St. Louis to mollify Vince Saracino, who was threatening to jerk Dmitri's contract on the woman and do the job himself. Dmitri found that amusing, considering how Vince relied on inept, untrained soldiers out of New York to do his dirty work.

On the other hand, he didn't want Saracino to get his hands on Kate. Dmitri had chased her too long, had held her in his arms, caressed the satiny softness of her skin and hair. She was his now, whether he decided to kill her or not, whether he decided to bed her or not. He had wanted to let her go, still did at times, had given her a chance to live, to be with him.

Increasingly, however, he was thinking she should pay for clubbing him in the head and taking up with the big man. He had no doubt she was free enough with her favors with him, whoever the hell he was. His jaw tightened. Kate shouldn't have spurned Dmitri's attempts to be merciful; she wouldn't find him nearly so accommodating to her feelings when he caught up with her again. As they liked to say in the American films Misha enjoyed so much, the time had come to play hardball.

He found his jaw clenched hard and relaxed it, forcing down the anger he felt. He was not a man used to failure. Or having to track down his targets more than once. His methods didn't account for that, and it galled him that Kate had humiliated him so deeply, then slipped through his fingers yet again today. The trail had grown cold after the waitress had spotted them at Hillbilly Junction and called Dmitri's cell phone. His instincts told him that this place, where he'd seen her companion, was the key. Jumbo of the biscuit fame knew where she had gone, Dmitri would bet on it.

Dmitri had begun to believe that Kate and the big man had probably been there the same time they were, had probably changed their looks there as well. It all made perfect sense due to its proximity to the river and the hermit's habit of trading there. Matty had sold hashish to the motorcyclist named Miller on the parking lot the very morning they'd left Jumbo's cabins to continue the search. Yes, the pieces all fit.

How they must be laughing at him as they lay abed together, making love. It galled Dmitri to think Kate might be telling this man about Dmitri's desire to let her go, his hunger for her so strong it blinded him to his duty. No, this was no longer merely a hit commissioned by Vince Saracino and paid for with a coveted Fabergé egg. This was personal now, between Kate Reed and Dmitri Kavunov. This time he would offer her no quarter.

Dmitri shifted his stance, angry inside, increasingly impatient. He glanced around the empty parking lot, tired of waiting for Jumbo to close up. He was eager to know who the man with Kate was and if she had known him before, if he was her lover, as Dmitri suspected. How else could she have hooked up with him so damn fast? Despite her ingenuity at escaping them, if not for him, they would've caught up with her by now. This guy knew what he was doing. He wasn't some random fisherman she'd stumbled upon.

All the lights in the restaurant were still on, sending a faint glow onto the tarmac. Someone moved into sight inside, at the front of the restaurant where the booths were. He saw Jumbo, a short, obese black man wearing a long white chef's apron, moving slowly toward the entrance to lock up for the night. A moment later he secured the door and headed back toward the kitchen, switching off lights as he went. Dmitri waited a moment after the restaurant was plunged into darkness. When the giant neon sign out by the highway went dark, he gave the signal to proceed.

Misha jimmied the lock within moments, more than facile with breaking and entering, then went in first, Yuri right behind him. They moved quickly, hunched down, guns drawn. Dmitri moved inside and reset the lock as his two companions burst through the swinging door into the kitchen. He could hear pots and pans clanging and hitting the floor in the struggle, but by the time he'd nudged open the swinging door, Biscuit Jumbo was spread-eagled atop a high cutting-block table, Misha atop him, one knee driven hard into his back. His nephew had the restaurateur's neck caught with a thin wire, holding his head up by pulling back hard on the tight ligature.

"Turn out all the lights except the one over the table until we finish with him."

Yuri moved off while Dmitri walked around to where the black man could see him. Jumbo's eyes were squeezed shut, his teeth gritted with pain as Misha forced his head up another notch.

"What'da you want?" the black man choked out, trying

to swallow through his constricted throat. Misha shoved his knee harder into the man's back. Jumbo grunted with the pain. "Today's take's in the strongbox," he managed hoarsely. "There in the cabinet by the door. Take it all."

"We don't want your money, my friend," Dmitri told him calmly. "We have a few questions. Answer them and we'll leave you alive. Refuse and we'll cut out your tongue before we go."

Jumbo's eyes were open now. He stared at Dmitri. "Who the hell are you?" Jumbo's eyes darted to Yuri as he reappeared and put the end of his silencer against his temple.

Dmitri had a feeling that Jumbo knew exactly who they were, had helped the woman evade them. "Where is the woman, Kate Reed?"

"I don't know what the fuck you're talking about . . . aaaugh . . ."

Misha jerked the wire so tight the man's eyes protruded to a dangerous degree. Dmitri frowned. His sister's damned kid was going to strangle the man before the interrogation was successful. "We know she was here. We know a man was helping her. A big man, a man who we suspect is a friend of yours. Tell me about him, Mr. Jumbo, and maybe we'll let you live."

"Go fuck yourself."

The man was obviously very stupid. A pity. He didn't realize yet who he dealt with. He would have to die, the fool. But first he'd give up Kate Reed to them.

"Do you really wish us to kill you, my fat friend?"

Jumbo stared silently at him but he was beginning to sweat. His white shirt was damp with it.

"As you please. Tie him down."

Jumbo began to struggle but Misha's hold was too tight. Misha was still humiliated by his failure at the tavern and would no doubt release his frustration on poor Jumbo. Yuri took the coil of rope off his belt and quickly lashed their victim to the table, hands and feet secured to the table legs.

"Break his forefinger."

Jumbo's eyes widened but he couldn't move. He tried to double his right fist as Yuri spread his fingers out against the table. Misha smiled and picked up a meat tenderizer off the counter. It was heavy, made of steel, shaped like a hammer. Without a moment's hesitation, he brought it down hard against the knuckle of Jumbo's forefinger.

Jumbo's scream was shrill and awful to behold.

"Bind his mouth."

Yuri yanked a white apron off the table and jerked it tight across Jumbo's open mouth. The man continued to groan, his eyes rolling back into his head.

Dmitri found the task distasteful, a little crude for his sensibilities. Cold war stuff that he never should have had to resort to. Again, he was incensed at Kate for making him use strong-arm tactics. "I suggest you make this a bit easier on yourself. Where's the girl?" He motioned for Yuri to loosen the gag.

"I dunno, I dunno, damn you fuckin' Russian commies. . . ."

Dmitri sighed, annoyed by the man's stupidity. Why should the man choose to suffer at their hands when all he had to do was answer one goddamn question?

"As you wish."

As soon as Yuri had replaced the muffle on Jumbo's mouth, Dmitri nodded for Misha to proceed. He did, bringing the hammer down on Jumbo's middle finger. The scream came again, muffled, full of agony. The man thrashed against his binding ropes like a juicy rabbit caught in a steel trap.

Dmitri leaned against the counter and took a moment to light his meerschaum pipe, waiting patiently for Jumbo's groans to die away. Unfortunately, this might take some time. "Use your head, Jumbo, we have all night, you know."

Jumbo's face was livid with anger and pain, and he began to curse them, the profanities indistinguishable but the sentiment unmistakable. Dmitri had a feeling this man wouldn't talk, no matter how long they worked him over. He'd seen such subjects before, unfortunate victims of trained KGB interrogators. Like Alina. He thrust the thought of her out of his mind.

"Do his hand, Misha."

Misha raised the hammer high but before he could bring it down on the back of Jumbo's hand, Dmitri heard something. The scrape of a key in the locked back door.

"Keep him quiet," he told Misha as Jumbo tried to yell a warning. Misha quieted him with a brutal elbow against his jaw. Jumbo's head thunked against the table. Dmitri motioned Yuri over behind the door that led down a narrow hallway to the back entrance.

The door finally opened with a loud jingling of keys. The overhead lights came on, one at a time, and a few seconds later a big-busted black woman in a short red dress appeared, her white purse tucked under one arm. Jumbo moaned and tried to twist free when he heard her voice.

"Sweet stuff, you still down here? Forgot my damn house key again," she called, about that time turning toward the table where Jumbo was strapped. She froze when she saw him, until Yuri grabbed her from behind. Then she fought like a demon out of hell. He got his forearm around her neck and flexed his biceps hard. She dropped her purse and clawed at his arm, choking as Yuri dragged her back to the table.

"Well, now, Mr. Jumbo, look who's come to visit. Mavis, I see, from her nice little plastic nameplate. Maybe she's a more cooperative person than you seem to be. Look at her lovely long fingers, and those scarlet fingernails. Very pretty, very pretty indeed."

Still groggy from the jolt to his head, Jumbo tried to wrench free, and Mavis's large brown eyes grew enormous as she stared in horror at Jumbo's purple, rapidly swelling fingers.

"Strap down Miss Mavis's arm. Let's see what kind of gentleman is Mr. Jumbo here."

Mac Sharp lived in a relatively quiet section of Branson, in an RV park located along the bank of Lake Taneycomo that edged the older, so-called historic downtown area. From where his trailer was set up, it looked more like a river than a lake, but the wide expanse of cold green water that fed directly into the larger reaches of Table Rock Lake held great appeal for fishermen and young vacationing families alike. There were dozens of other campers and RVs lined along the graveled shore on the north side, just below the Highway 65 bridge.

Mac had dropped them off at the old but spacious Gulfstream he called home, a vehicle that resembled a giant bullet out of the Lone Ranger's holster. He'd found himself a plum spot, however, set apart from other seasonal hookups, being as he was the sole year-round tenant. His place was sheltered by a thick grove of oaks and willows, and he'd built his own private dock where he could moor his prized bass boat under a roofed overhang. The craft was the best of its kind, purchased new at the Bass Pro Shop in Springfield several years ago, a boat that cost three or four times as much as everything else Mac owned, with the exception of the shiny new Mustang. Mac took his fishing seriously, almost as seriously as his collection of St. Louis Cardinal memorabilia.

Mac told them to keep out of sight until dark, then promised to see what he could find out from his old friends still working homicide on the St. Louis force before he hightailed it back to beat his taiko drum in Shoji's late show. They'd been relieved to find a place to lie low, and after examining some of the white game jerseys, signed baseball bats and balls hanging on the walls in polished oak racks, Kate fed Joey and put him to sleep. She fixed a couple of omelets by raiding just about everything inside Mac's health-food–laden refrigerator, and Booker found that she could cook as well as she could shoot and evade enemies.

Afterward she said she was tired, and when Booker cracked open a Miller Lite and went outside to wait for Mac, she crashed next to Joey in the sardine-can guest room with its built-in bunk beds and gigantic poster of Ozzie Smith. Last time he checked, she was still out like a light, and Booker was glad she could sleep. He sure as hell couldn't but he needed space to think anyway. Besides, he wanted to talk to Mac alone when he got back.

There was a scarred-up, ancient redwood picnic table on the dock, and Booker sat on top of it, where he could keep an eye on the trailer as well as the gravel road leading in from the highway. It was after midnight, real quiet outside in the cool, damp air, with just the sound of frogs and crickets and somebody's radio playing Frank Sinatra's *New York, New York*. No one was about, but he could see a couple of fishermen night-fishing out on the lake, up under the bridge, their small lights bobbing in the blackness. He felt they were fairly safe at the moment, but now that they were in Branson, he wasn't sure what their next move should be. He supposed that depended on what Mac found out. Too many things about Kate's story just didn't add up.

It was almost one in the morning when Mac finally drove up and parked his Mustang under the metal canopy covered with lattice and purple clematis plants that acted as his carport. Booker whistled softly as he got out. Mac turned and Booker could hear his footsteps crunching against the rocks as he walked down the path. He took a seat beside Booker on the table. He was smoking a cigar, and the aromatic scent carried on the soft night breeze.

"Never knew you were so good on taiko."

"Shoji's got a thing about those drums."

"He ought to, if the big one cost a million dollars like he told the audience."

Mac laughed and glanced up at the trailer. The lights were all on. "Where's the girl?"

"Inside. Asleep."

"Kid, too?"

"Yeah."

"Good God, Book, you stepped in it this time. Every goddamned cop in the state is after her."

"We're more worried about the hard-asses with Moscow accents that shoot first and kill second."

"Yeah, well, I made those calls and you're in shit up to your eyebrows, pal."

"Not exactly what I wanted to hear, Mac."

"You sure you can trust this dame?"

"Why? What'd you find out?"

Mac took a deep drag on his cigar, exhaled, sighed heavily, then spoke. "I got hold of a buddy of mine, a detective at metro. You know who that kid belongs to?"

"I know the cops think he's kidnapped from some family up there, straight out of Barnes Hospital. Kate says she got him nice and legal, and has papers to prove it. If her husband was mixed up in something dirty, she didn't know anything about it."

"Not only was he kidnapped outta Barnes, man, but Jimmy says the kid's Vince Saracino's boy, and in case you don't know, he's the guy who runs rackets up there for his bosses in the New York Mafia. I mean, this guy's straight out of *The Godfather*, Book, except he's a screwed-up mother who'd make Michael Corleone look like a Carmelite nun. Jimmy said he's nuts and gets off on killing people."

Booker frowned. "That makes the rest of it make a little sense. So he's the one who sent those guys after her?"

"Yeah, and Jimmy says they're probably his wife's bodyguards. She's a Russian, too, the daughter of one of Vince's business cronies in Moscow. He says the guy named Dmitri is ex-KGB. Bad news all around, Book, real bad news. These guys won't quit. Even worse, the rumor is that Vince's raging around like a bull and has put out a universal kill on her, and that means he'll pay anybody who brings her down and gets his kid back unhurt. He wants her stone-cold dead, no questions asked."

"Jesus Christ."

"Yeah, Book, she's as good as finished. It's a miracle you got this far without getting cut down."

"What about Michael Reed? Did Jimmy know anything on him?"

"Just that he was dirty. One of Saracino's mouthpieces."

"Kate's not in on this. She's thinking of sending the baby into hiding, then turning herself in until she gets things worked out."

"Bad idea. Vince has more people inside the court system than out. She'll get whacked before they snap her mugshot."

They sat in silence for a moment. "Got any ideas, Mac?"

"Yeah, but she sure as hell won't like it."

"Tell me."

Mac began to talk, softly, and the more Booker heard, the more he dreaded putting the idea in front of Kate. There was no way she'd agree to it, not a chance in hell. But if she didn't, and she didn't fast, Kate Reed, and probably the rest of them, too, weren't going to see too many more days before they were gunned down.

Twenty-seven

KATE AWOKE to the faint murmur of male voices. She lay still a moment, recognizing Booker's slow drawl at once. The other one was Mac, Booker's friend. The men spoke quietly, calm and low, probably so as not to awaken her. She was still safe, at least for the moment. The small, windup Lenox alarm clock on the built-in bookshelf behind her head read eleven thirty. She had slept deeply, without dreaming of Michael or Dmitri, for the first time since it all had begun. She felt better, ready for whatever the coming day had in store.

When she sat on the edge of the mattress to check on Joey, the pulled-out drawer in which she'd made his bed was empty. Her heart lurched but she relaxed almost at once, confident that Booker must have him. But she had to know for sure. She already wore a T-shirt so she grabbed her jeans and pulled them on, then stood up, only taking the time to run a brush through her sleep-tousled, dark hair. She stepped out of the tiny bedroom into the hallway. She could see Booker at the kitchen table. Joey was in the crook of his arm taking a bottle. She smiled, pleased despite the incongruity of an infant perched on the lap of a big, rough-looking man like Booker.

"Good morning," she said as she joined the men. "I see Joey got up early."

"Yeah. This is his second bottle. When you didn't wake up the first time he fussed, I figured you needed more shut-eye so I brought him out here."

"Thanks." She nodded and smiled again, but he looked uncomfortable, worry written all over his rugged face. She sobered. Mac had that same look. Something was wrong.

"There's a fresh pot of coffee. Over there by the stove. Mugs are hanging on the wall right behind the coffeemaker."

"Thanks, Mac."

Although she'd already sensed they had bad news, she didn't ask. Didn't want to hear it before she got some caffeine in her. She poured the strong, black brew into a heavy white mug with a Cardinal logo and scraped up a chair next to Booker's. She liked to stay close to him, just in case. His .45 was lying on the red Formica tabletop beside Joey's clown pacifier. Somehow, extraordinarily, that didn't seem an appalling sight to her anymore. She shut her eyes and took a bracing sip, wondering at what she'd become in so short a time. Joey was dozing, the nipple loose in his open mouth. Every once in a while he'd rouse and suck vigorously, then gradually nod off again.

Mac's coffee was so strong with chicory, or something Kate wasn't used to, that her eyes watered. The two guys remained silent, neither looking at her. The milk carton was on the table, so she stirred some milk into her cup. They had to be waiting for her to ask and she finally did. But she didn't want to.

"Bad news, right?"

Booker nodded, then looked down at Joey who was sucking again. It must be very bad. He was definitely not wanting to meet her gaze.

"Tell me then."

Heaving out a sigh, Booker took the nipple out of Joey's mouth and shifted the baby to a more comfortable position, as if he was used to holding and feeding babies every morning of the world. Joey sure didn't seem to mind being cradled in his muscular arms. "Mac's got some friends in St. Louis. Guys who work homicide at St. Louis PD. One of them filled him in on the investigation."

"Yeah? And?"

"Joey was kidnapped, Kate. From Barnes Hospital, just like the news said. Somebody took him out of the mother's room while she was sleeping. The police think Reed did it. So do the baby's parents."

Kate shook her head. "No, that can't be true. I'm telling you the adoption papers were legal." She spoke slowly, searching Booker's face, then turning her entreaty to Mac Sharp.

"There wasn't any adoption. Your husband must've faked it." Booker met her eyes, pausing momentarily before he went on. "Joey's family wants him back. They said the mother's close to a nervous breakdown since he's been gone, blaming herself for not waking up when he was taken. Apparently they've got her under sedation some of the time because she's so distraught. And that's not even the worst part."

It was for Kate. She began to shake her head, not wanting to hear more, not wanting to believe any of it. "Michael said he got Joey off the black market just before they killed him. He wouldn't've lied to me then, he had no reason to, Dmitri and his men were already after us. He said he was supposed to pay them and didn't have the money. That's why they're chasing me. They think I'm in on it, Dmitri told me they did."

"No. That's not the way it went down." Mac looked as though he was really sorry about it, but his eyes were intense, his voice firm. "I'm sorry, Kate, I really am, to have to be the one to tell you this, but it's worse than you think, a lot worse."

Kate couldn't speak, just waited, staring at one man, then the other, wanting one of them to give her some sign of hope. Inside she rebelled about where all this was leading. She wouldn't give Joey up, not now, not after all they'd been through together. He was hers, her son, her baby, nobody else's.

"Mac found out that Joey's father is Vince Saracino," said Booker at length. "Have you heard of him, Kate?"

"No."

"He's real bad news, the head of the crime family in St. Louis. He's put a contract out on your head, Kate, you and

Reed both. They got him but they want you, too. This Dmitri guy is a hired assassin, and he's not going to stop until you're dead and Joey's in his hands. Saracino wants you six feet under, no matter how long it takes. As an example, if nothing else, to anyone who might wanna screw around with his family."

For a moment Kate couldn't believe her ears, couldn't fathom that she was the target of that kind of man. A criminal, a Mafioso. It had been Michael, of course, Michael who had been involved with those people. He ran with criminals, defended them, but even he knew better than doing something so self-destructive. "Michael isn't that stupid," she said, remembering then that he was dead and that she should've used the past tense. She couldn't bring herself to do it yet. "He wouldn't have the guts to take the baby of a Mafia boss. Why would he do it? It would be sheer suicide. It doesn't make sense. None of this makes sense."

Booker hiked a shoulder. "Who knows why he did it? Maybe he didn't know who Joey was. Maybe whoever kidnapped the kid told Michael it was a black-market baby like he told you. Whatever the hell happened, it doesn't matter now. They think you did it, and they won't stop until they get you and make you pay."

"It doesn't matter. I can turn myself in. If I have to, I'll find a place to hide Joey until the real truth comes out . . ."

"You don't understand how the mob works," Mac told her, locking his gaze on hers. "I know Saracino personally, went to school with his cousin Dave for awhile, played football with him. He told me some stories about his Uncle Vince that curled my hair, and I found out the rest when I was on the force up there. Vince came out of the New York branch of the family, and he's one cold mother. He's got people in his pocket just about everywhere in the state, cops, judges, prison guards. If you turn yourself in, Kate, here or anywhere else, trust me, you'll be one dead lady before the sun goes down. And if you don't give yourself up, if you keep running the way you have been, they'll track you to the ends of the earth and cut you down, I don't care how far they have to go or how long it takes."

Kate looked back at Booker. His blue eyes looked calm but she knew what they were telling her, both he and Mac. She didn't want to listen to it. She stared down at Joey, who slept so peacefully in the crook of Booker's arm, and her heart twisted until she actually felt it might stop beating.

"My friend at police headquarters said the mother's due to give a public plea for her baby's return. It should be on any minute now." He gestured at the small television in the corner. The screen was on but the sound had been turned off. "If you don't believe what we're saying, maybe you ought to listen to it out of her own mouth."

Kate watched him walk over and turn up the volume. Two commentators were talking about the case, a guy named Beeson and a woman with short blond hair. Both worked for KY3, a channel out of Springfield.

"Although the family has wished to remain anonymous up until now, the child's mother has decided to make a plea to the kidnapper, who is purported to be Kate Reed, a woman renowed for winning an Olympic bronze medal a few years ago. At the family's request we will not reveal their name, but they have now offered a five hundred thousand dollar reward for the baby's safe return, no questions asked. . . ."

Kate sat frozen with dismay when the station suddenly cut to a film clip. She watched herself crawling over the finish line in the downpour, red-faced, exhausted, the cameras pushed in her face. Then the television cut again to a postevent interview where she was smiling and talking excitedly, her knee in a cast, holding up the medal beside her face as the photographers snapped their pictures.

"You are watching a film of the primary suspect, Kate Reed, taken three years ago. We have been informed that she may have darkened her hair color and disguised her appearance. The public is being warned that she is armed and dangerous, perhaps traveling with a male accomplice. Kate Reed is also suspected in the shooting death of her husband, Michael Reed. If you have

any information about this woman call your local authorities or contact the St. Louis Police Department. . . ."

Kate turned horrified eyes to Booker.

"I'm sorry, Kate. This is bad for you, I know that, I wish things were different."

Kate thought that he couldn't possibly know how it felt to have your heart ripped out. She couldn't speak, but she quickly returned all her attention to the television set when the blonde announced that the mother was about to speak. Every muscle bunched in hard knots, Kate waited for them to show Joey's mother.

It was a remote shot, on what looked to be a private driveway. She could see a barred gate, open now but usually a formidable barrier into the grounds. A magnificent Tudor mansion could be glimpsed in the background behind some trees. The woman was sitting at a small wrought-iron table, alone, and the rowdy group of cameramen had been cordoned off some distance away, well outside the gates away from her. She looked extremely young and vulnerable, and the purple rings underneath her eyes revealed her exhaustion. She got a terrified look on her face as the camera zoomed in for the first close-up. She was very beautiful, with long, straight black hair and striking light blue eyes, a lot like Booker's. Hers were swollen and red from weeping. About fifty microphones were clustered in front of her, and she kept darting glances to one side of the driveway, where Kate supposed her husband was standing. He was not in the picture. The woman had been left alone to face the wolves.

"Please, please, whoever take my baby, please give him home to me."

Her voice was heavily accented with Russian, the broken English a pitiable quaver, and Kate saw that she had a wad of tissues in her hand. She dabbed her eyes amid a thunderous amount of clicking and whirring of cameras as anxious photographers got their still shots.

"I beg you bring son back to us. He is little and helpless, he much frail and we miss him much. . . ."

The mother wept again, openly, tears running down her cheeks, and the news people zeroed in with glee. Just like them, Kate knew there could be no faking such genuine distress.

"Please, please, give back our baby, do not hurt, I beg you not hurt him, please, please . . ."

When she covered her face with her open hands and sobbed into her palms, a voice came from outside the picture, one heavy with a Brooklyn accent, ordering the interview to stop. As the gate swung shut, slowly blocking off the sight of the crying woman, Kate could see a stocky, deeply tanned man with silver-blond hair stride across the driveway and take the weeping woman into his arms. The picture returned to the studio and the two suitably sober commentators with sprayed-stiff coiffures.

"I think we can all appreciate that poor woman's anguish, so please, please, if you have any information about the suspected kidnapper, Kate Reed, immediately get in touch with the authorities. The number to call will be repeated until this ordeal is at an end. Please call day or night and operators will be on hand to take down any information you might have concerning this terrible crime."

The television duo eventually moved on to other, less dramatic news. Kate continued to stare numbly at the screen, stunned by a churning conflict of emotions. The two men sat unmoving behind her, saying nothing. Her breast began to ache, so much so that she couldn't stand it, couldn't stand knowing the things she'd just been told. She stood up so hard she nearly knocked her chair backward, then turned and stared at Booker. He looked up at her, and she couldn't bear the pity she saw on his face.

"Give him to me, Booker, give him to me!" she cried, snatching Joey up from Booker's arms, blanket and all. She clutched the baby tight for a fraction of a second, tears filling up her eyes so fast she couldn't stop them from falling. She turned blindly for the door, only wanting to get him outside, get him away from the truth that would take him far from her forever.

Booker watched Kate flee out the door, leaving it standing open behind her. He began to feel a little sick inside. He looked at Mac, who said, simply, "Well, shit."

"Guess I better go talk to her," Booker said. Which was the last thing he wanted to do. What could he say that would make her feel any better? Nothing. She was about to lose her boy, the son she had gone through hell on earth for already. God help him, Booker sure as hell didn't have any words that would comfort her. There weren't any.

Picking up his .45 and tucking it in his belt at the small of his back, he left Mac sitting at the table. He stepped outside into the sun and looked around. Kate had run down to the dock to the picnic table where Mac had first given him the bad news last night. He hadn't gotten much sleep after that, maybe a couple of hours, dreading the moment they'd have to lay it all out in front of Kate. She'd taken it just about the way he'd expected her to.

He glanced around, up the road behind Mac's trailer in both directions, but he found no suspicious-looking parked cars or people loitering around. It was unlikely Dmitri had found them yet, but if the hit team was as good as Mac intimated, it was only a matter of time before they picked them up again. He walked down the path to the lake.

Kate was sitting at the end of the bench, facing the calm, dark green water of the lake, clutching Joey up against her chest as if she'd never let go of him again. He sat down directly across from her, not quite sure what to say. He finally repeated what he'd said earlier, but it was heartfelt. "I'm sorry, Kate. Wish I could do something to make this turn out different."

Kate was crying, silently, but it was the first time he'd seen her shed many tears, despite all they'd been through together. He set his jaw, hating to see her suffer, wanting to touch her but not wanting to touch her. He didn't know what to do.

"Oh, God, oh, God, Booker, what am I going to do? What am I going to do? I can't give him up, I can't, I can't. . . ."

Sobs ended her words, and she lifted Joey up and buried her face against his dark curls. Joey felt her anguish and started to cry uncertainly himself, unsure what was wrong with his mommy. Kate pulled herself together a little, but not much, and tried to soothe him, rocking him in her arms. She couldn't seem to stop crying, though.

"It's a bad situation, Kate, that's for damn sure. I don't know what to tell you." He paused but he knew she didn't have any choice, and so would she, after she got over the initial shock.

"Tell me I can keep him," she whispered, turning to look at him, her brown eyes swimming with tears. "Tell me that, Booker, please."

"They'll kill you if you try to keep him. Mac says Vince's opened up the contract. Anyone who gets you gets the money, but only if you're dead and the baby's left unharmed."

"We can hide him! We could go back and stay in your cave, couldn't we? Nobody can find us there! You've lived there for years without any trouble, haven't you?"

Booker knew she didn't believe that so he didn't answer.

"Or we could leave the country, go far away, to Hong Kong or South America, Paraguay or somewhere, anywhere."

"They'd find you, Kate. Five hundred thousand dollars is a lot of money. The Mafia has a long memory. Vince wants blood and he won't rest until he gets it. They say he's crazy about his young wife, and you saw the way she looked just now. She's a basket case."

"I can't hand him over to them, to a monster like Dmitri," Kate whispered hoarsely. She shivered. "They're nothing but murderers, criminals, all of them. How can I send Joey back into that kind of life? I can't do it, I'm telling you I can't, Booker!"

Booker let his gaze wander out over the water. A fisherman sat in a small jon boat about fifty yards away. He'd hooked a crappie and was slowly reeling it out of the sun-spangled lake. Booker watched him put the catch on a stringer and rebait his line. Kate was still crying, but not as hard. She was thinking now, trying to think how to save Joey, using her cleverness to overcome this turn of events as she'd evaded everything else they'd thrown at her. But she was fenced in this time. There was only one way out.

"Whether you like it or not, Kate, that is Joey's kind of life. Those two people are his real parents. The luck of the draw, I guess. It seems like his mother loves him. That's pretty hard to ignore."

Kate lowered Joey and looked down at him. Her tears dropped onto his chest. When he gave that little grin he was always giving, the one with the dimples showing, Kate burst into tears again. Booker shifted uncomfortably, feeling he should take her in his arms and try to comfort her but not sure she'd want him to. He blew out air, angry that everything had come down to this.

"But he's mine, Booker, I've held him and nursed him, I've changed his diapers and rocked him. How can I bear it if they take him back, if someone else raises him?"

"I reckon that's how his mother feels, too, since Reed, or whoever it was, stole him out of her hospital room. You saw her face, how she's suffering, just like you are. She gave birth to him. She loves him, too."

Kate turned her face toward him. Booker knew then that she knew every bit of that, that the knowledge of the mother's agony was what was killing her the most. The Saracino woman was Joey's real mother and she wanted him, needed him, just as much as Kate did. He'd been snatched away from her. She was as much a victim as Kate was. Kate was the kind of woman who would feel the other woman's pain, no matter how worse off it made things for her.

They sat in silence until Kate finally got up and walked around the table to where he sat. Booker stood up, too, and she came into his arms. She pressed herself in close against his chest, still holding Joey. Booker put his arms around her and held them both tightly, his eyes fixed on the glittering water. They said nothing. There was nothing to say.

Twenty-eight

DMITRI WAS ASTONISHED by the bright lights and bustling tourist atmosphere of Branson, Missouri. Good God, the tiny town was out in the middle of nowhere, carved from high stony hills but filled with theaters, hotels, restaurants and souvenir shops. It reminded him of Atlantic City in miniature, countrified with a lake view rather than an ocean vista.

He sat in the backseat of the new white Suburban they'd rented in the city of Springfield, one chosen for dark-tinted windows that gave him privacy to watch the throngs on the street. Yuri found a map of Branson at a petrol station in a tiny hamlet called Ozark some miles down the road, one with the names and locations of all the shows and motels. The Shoji Tabuchi show was the one they were interested in and shouldn't be hard to find. How many Japanese shows could there be in the Ozark Mountains?

"Look there, uncle. Yakov Smirnov." Misha spoke in their own language, pointing a finger toward the left side of the street. "You will appreciate his humor, I think."

A large marquee encircled with lights identified a giant theater down the sloped parking lot as Yakov's American Pavilion. Another billboard said *From Red to Redneck,* and Yakov had commissioned twin pictures of himself—one wearing a huge white cowboy hat that made him look like a simpleton, the other a traditional Russian fur hat. His telephone number was 33-NO-KGB.

"Yeah, real fucking funny," he muttered sourly, but Misha and Yuri thought it was humorous and laughed together at his expense.

"America—the land of opportunity," Yuri said, turning back and grinning at Dmitri. "You have only to look at us. Do we not make a good living killing off unwary Americans?"

"Just find this guy Shoji's theater before Kate gets away again. I'm tired of chasing her. I want her. Do you hear me? And I want her taken alive. Nobody touches her but me. Not a single hair on her head."

His companions nodded, well aware that the contract hit had gradually turned into Dmitri's own personal vendetta. Yes, he was anxious to get his hands on Kate again. She needed to be punished, to suffer a little, a good deal, in fact, for the things she'd done to him. He found himself craning his neck to spot the theater, his eagerness to capture the woman growing rapidly into an obsession that stunned even him. Only moments after they'd turned at a red light onto the Shepherd of the Hills Expressway, the Shoji show turned up on the left. Yuri pulled into the parking lot and was directed by a man in uniform to parking places facing the street. There was a restaurant next door called Contrary Mary's Garden Restaurant. Dmitri thought that a stupid name to call an eating establishment.

"Go inside, Yuri. See what you can find out," Dmitri said, but as Misha made to get out the passenger's door, he stopped him with a curt order. "You stay here."

"I want to see this place. Yuri's brochure says a billiard table's in the men's room."

"Shut up."

Annoyed with his nephew, with the whole stinking mess, Dmitri watched a pair of elderly couples get out of the shiny white Lincoln Continental parked next to them. Every one of them reeked of money. He wondered where they were from and how much they had invested in the American stock market. Or if any of them had the taste to acquire a Fabergé masterpiece, had ever visited an art museum in their lives. He was tired of this po-dunk part of the country but getting his hands on Kate would be worth everything he'd been through. He planned to enjoy making her pay; maybe he should prolong her punishment, keep her locked up somewhere for his amusement, but only after he'd gotten the baby safely back to Vince and Anna.

Dmitri grimaced. Furious, Vince had called Dmitri on the cell phone and yelled incoherent curses for a good ten minutes before he'd calmed down from his insane temper tantrum enough to listen. Anna was upset over the baby's disappearance, was on the verge of a total nervous collapse, and he wanted his son found, and found now. Vince hadn't even gotten to see his kid before Reed snatched him because he'd been in New York facing racketeering charges when Anna went into labor. He was fucking going to open up the hit to anyone with a goddamn, fucking gun in their hand since Dmitri was screwing around while he had to sit there and watch his poor wife suffer and cry.

Dmitri had almost hung up the receiver and headed back to Moscow, not willing or used to taking verbal abuse from anyone, not even Vince Saracino. He would have returned to Russia, if they weren't closing in so quickly on Kate Reed. Now it was a matter of principle and pride. Kate would be his, and her lover, John Booker, would die a painful death before her eyes. Maybe he should make Kate kill him herself. If Dmitri held a gun to her baby's head, Kate would do anything he said, anything at all. His smile was cold, his eyes hard. They'd been worthy opponents, he'd give them that much, more than most of his targets, but now time was up. He'd finish the hit, then take his time deciding what to do with Kate.

"Mac Sharp lives in a trailer park on the lake called Taneycomo." Yuri was back, sliding into the driver's seat. He turned and rested his forearm on the back of the seat. "It's just below the bridge. The lady in the ticket booth said it's got a boat dock and a lattice screen covered with purple flowers."

"Was she suspicious of you?"

"No, she was friendly like all the people here. She asked if I knew Yakov Smirnov. Said we talked with the same accent." He grinned. "I said I was Yakov's brother and he wanted Mac Sharp to work for him."

"Very clever, Yuri."

"She was most eager to tell me where he lived and what he drove. A silver Mustang convertible with a black top. These Americans, they are much too trusting."

"Lucky for us. Let's go."

"She also said he started his vacation this very day."

"That probably means they're ready to take off. Step on it, Yuri. I'll be damned if she'll get away this time."

As Yuri started the motor, Dmitri spread the map of Branson atop his knees. A moment later he stabbed his finger on the bridge that spanned Lake Taneycomo just south of the historic downtown area of Branson. If the silver Mustang automobile was parked at this man's trailer, they had them cold.

"Mac has an idea how we can do this, if you want to hear it."

Kate nodded, but inside she felt dead, as if her heart had shriveled up and crumbled to dust. Joey was her heart; she'd have no life if they took him away from her. She fought the burn of tears, fought the intense compulsion to run, to keep the inevitable at bay. Earlier on the dock she'd wept until she hung limp and weak against Booker's chest, hard, racking sobs, despair such as she'd never felt before. But he was right. She had little choice but to return Joey to his family. She'd known that the minute she'd watched his mother's face twist with agony and loss. Kate had seen the woman's terrible pain, felt complete and total empathy because she knew how she felt. Oh, Lord help her, what would she do without Joey? He was all she had, all she'd ever wanted.

Mac was outlining his plan for dealing with Saracino, and Kate stared dully at him, thinking he was crazy if he believed they could deal with such people. She finally blurted it out. "He's a cold-blooded murderer. How can we trust him? Trust any of them?"

"We can't, of course. But it's our only shot at getting you out of this mess alive. Besides that, we'll be telling him the truth."

"He'll kill us, no matter what we do," Kate insisted, thinking the two men surely must see that. The man was insane, evil, had ordered Dmitri to hunt them down and shoot them like ducks in a carnival gallery. "Why wouldn't he? He's holding all the cards."

Booker had been sitting silently, listening to them discuss the situation. He leaned back in the kitchen chair and propped his foot atop his knee. "Mac's right, Kate. It's worth a try. Otherwise, we have no chance. If they don't get us now, it's only a matter of time until they do. We've been lucky to make it this far."

Kate searched Booker's serious face. She had begun to wonder if she really cared if she lived or died, but Booker and Sharp were different. Both of them were involved because they'd tried to help her. They'd put their lives on the line to save her and Joey. She couldn't just stand back and let them die for her. She didn't have any choice but to go along with their plan. Her mind had accepted that already but her heart hadn't, and never would.

"I'll do whatever you think is right," she said at length, rising as she spoke. She carried Joey to Mac's Lazy Boy rocker beside the television set. Booker and Mac glanced at each other, questions in their eyes, but she didn't elaborate, really didn't care how they did it. All she could think of was that Joey would be gone soon, out of her life forever. She'd never rock him again, never warm to his melting smile that carved the dimples under his eye, or hear the chortling little laugh that so delighted her. She wouldn't see him crawl or take steps, or call her mommy. A gigantic lump rose at the bottom of her throat, expanded until she lowered her head so the men wouldn't see the tears filling her eyes.

"I've already asked for time off so I can drive you to St. Louis. We've got to decide on a place. Somewhere full of people so they can't work an ambush or hit us without a lot of witnesses around. Whatever we do, we've got to do it right. Vince's crazy; everybody knows it. He's got a hair-trigger temper, and he's pissed off as hell right now, insulted that anybody'd dare mess with his kid. Who knows what he'll do?"

So Joey's father was crazy, a crazy murderer who'd involve his son in his Mafia lifestyle. How could she hand an innocent baby over to a future with the mob, a life where he might be cut down in some bloody gun battle before he reached manhood?

The shrill ring of the telephone startled them all. Booker sat forward as Mac came to his feet. Kate held Joey closer.

"It's probably somebody at the show. Take it easy."

At Mac's words Booker relaxed a little but his nerves were quivering on the brink. They'd been at Mac's place too long. They needed to move on, get out of Branson. Kate was so stressed out she was ready to snap. They needed to end this, get it over with, once and for all.

Mac picked up the receiver and was talking. He immediately turned to Booker and held out the phone. "It's for you. Some woman who won't give me her name."

"Nobody knows I'm here except Jumbo."

Mac shrugged and waited. Booker hesitated, then walked across the room.

"Hello."

"John Booker?"

"Yeah."

"It's Mavis."

Booker frowned, immediately aware something bad had happened. "What's wrong, Mavis?"

"Jumbo said to call. Said to tell you some guys paid us a visit."

Tensing up, Booker's fingers squeezed more tightly around the receiver. "Is he all right?"

"No."

"How bad is he?" Booker asked tightly but inside he could feel rage already beginning to build. A kind of anger he hadn't felt in a long time.

"They beat the shit out of him. Broke his jaw and all the fingers on his right hand." Mavis's voice caught and she stopped talking.

"Goddammit."

"He's in Mountain View, at the hospital. He can't talk much but he told me to make sure you know that he didn't tell'm nothin' till I walked in and they grabbed me, too. When they started in on me, he said he had to tell them who you were and where you were headed. He said you gotta get out of there quick."

"He told them we're in Branson?"

"Yeah, with a guy named Mac Sharp. He told them he worked at the Shoji show but only after they got hold of me, Booker. He wouldn't've told'm shit if they hadn't been hurtin' me."

"Are you hurt bad, too, Mavis?"

"Not like Jumbo. They broke some bones in my hand. Hit it with Jumbo's steel meat tenderizer."

Booker shut his eyes, fighting the fury that was roiling around inside his gut, building, building, streaking through his blood like a torched stream of gasoline. "I'm sorry. Tell Jumbo that, tell him I didn't mean for him to get hurt, you either."

"The doc says he's gonna be all right. They got his jaw wired up and all his broken bones set."

"Which one of them did it, Mavis?"

"A kid with blond hair and blisters peeling off his face. The guy givin' the orders called him Misha or something like that. He grinned when he hit us like he was havin' lots of fun. There was three of 'em, but the one in charge had a beard. He was real calm and business-like, eyes cold as ice, just watched and told the kid where to hit us. They would've killed us both, Book, if some cops hadn't knocked on the door wantin' to fill up their coffee jugs. They took off out the back and got clean away."

Booker's jaw clenched and his knuckles whitened around the phone. "Thanks for warning us."

"Yeah. Well, gotta get back to Jumbo's room and help him with his dinner. A malt's all he gets. Hasta eat through a straw. Good luck."

"Yeah."

The line went dead. Booker hung up, turned and found both Mac and Kate on their feet. Mac looked wary. Kate looked alarmed.

"We gotta get Kate out of here. Right now. They know we're here, Mac. They know your name and where you work."

Mac needed no further encouragement. "Okay, let's get going, but let me call the theater and see if anybody's nosin' around up there."

Booker watched Kate run into the bedroom to gather her things, then withdrew his .45. He pulled back the curtains and watched the road while Mac spoke briefly on the telephone. He looked back as Mac hung up. "They've already been there. Talked to a friend of mine at the ticket counter. They're coming."

Booker nodded but said nothing as Kate rushed out with Joey. He took her outside and waited until she was in the backseat with the baby before he spoke quietly to Mac. "Take her and wait for me on the bridge up there." He jerked his head downstream. "I can make my way there on foot easily enough."

"Why, man? We gotta get out of here."

"They busted up Jumbo and his girlfriend. Hurt them bad."

Mac shook his head but he knew better than to argue. "All right, but be careful. These guys don't mess around."

"Get going. I won't be long. If I'm not there in half an hour, go on without me."

Mac got in and started the car, and Booker could see Kate motioning to him from the backseat. He watched them pull up the road onto the highway and out of sight. Then he went back inside the trailer to wait.

Twenty-nine

BOOKER DIDN'T have to wait long. He squatted down behind the front door, back against the wall, and watched through the curtains as a big white Suburban turned off the access road. It stopped about thirty yards up the graveled road from Mac's place. Two men sat in the front seat, and Booker set his teeth as Misha, the psychopathic punk who'd accosted Kate in her kitchen, who'd had a jolly good time busting up Jumbo and Mavis, got out of the car.

Something terrible moved deep inside Booker, visceral emotions lain dormant for years, stirring again, struggling for life, for release. His muscles flexed, went completely rigid, trembled with leashed power. He clamped his jaw until he feared his teeth would crack. Rage, the deadly, helpless anger he'd suffered in the Sandinista camp was bubbling free, heating up, hotter, hotter, lethal, all-encompassing, uncontrollable.

Propping his head against the wall, he shut his eyes and fought to keep himself under tight control. The moment was at hand. He had to be patient now that he'd made up his mind to act, now that Kate and Joey weren't around to get hurt. Flight was over; the time had come to fight back. He was ready. He took a deep, steadying breath but the tugging, twisting urges inside him would not stop, the eagerness to strike back like an atrophied muscle learning to flex again. He had taken down men before, kill or be killed, a concept he knew only too well, at times more than one enemy at a time and nearly always under worse conditions than he faced now.

He'd been trained by the best, he thought bitterly, taught to murder at eighteen by the best killers the United States Army had to offer. He'd be rusty but it'd come back and he felt deathly calm, mind cold and detached from what was about to go down. He knew what to do and how to do it. He thought of Jumbo and Mavis, the pain they'd endured at the hands of the snot-nosed sadist who liked to smile as he tortured people. But Misha'd chosen the wrong people this time. He'd chosen Booker's best friends.

Through a crack in the drapes he could see that the Russians knew exactly where Mac lived. Misha was coming in alone. Booker was surprised by that, wondered if there were others, if they'd split up to surround the trailer. He moved quickly, silently to a rear window with an open view of the access road but saw neither men nor vehicles approaching the trailer. Then he was back in place, watching Misha come down the gravel path into the shade of Mac's metal carport. Now Misha was behind the lattice privacy screen shielding the front door, out of sight of his backup man in the car.

The guy sitting in the driver's seat had yet to emerge but Booker recognized him as Dmitri, the boss man who wouldn't give up on killing Kate and taking her baby. Dmitri didn't know it yet but he wasn't going to get another chance to hurt her. Booker supposed he was letting Misha secure the place before he followed him in. Through the dark window glass he looked to be speaking on a cellular phone but Booker couldn't be sure.

Misha stopped by the front steps and examined Mac's trailer for signs of life. Booker had a feeling the kid was salivating at the idea of hurting Kate, payback time for the pan of boiling water. He wondered how tough the kid would be when he met up with a man his own size instead of helpless women and unarmed men.

Booker stuck his gun into his waistband and took down

Mac's pride-and-joy Stan Musial bat from its shelf, one the famed Card used to crack homers during the sixty-six season. He kept his back flat against the wall behind the door. His senses had sharpened considerably; he could smell the sweet scent of baby powder and realized Kate had left a can of it and a box of Luvs on the floor beside the door. That alone would bring Misha inside for Kate and the baby. He got the bat handle in a good, comfortable, two-handed grip. He was ready.

Within minutes he heard a knock, which probably meant they thought no one was at home because the car was gone. If that was true, he'd get the jump on Misha. Scratching sounds came next as the kid slipped the lock with a credit card. He was inside seconds later, quickly and quietly, bent low, efficient killer with silenced gun out and ready to kill an innocent woman. Booker saw red and gave him no time to go looking for him. He swung Mac's baseball bat down atop Misha's forearm so hard he heard bone crack. Misha let out a scream as his weapon hit the floor and went skittering into the kitchen. Booker got him in a brutal uppercut under the jaw that cut off his cry and sent him down hard.

Finished with the bat, Booker propped it against the wall, then checked to make sure the guy in the car hadn't decided to join the party. He hadn't. He glanced down at the man lying on the floor. He lay unmoving and bleeding from the head. Only a few seconds had elapsed. Booker shut the door and locked it. He wasn't finished with Misha yet.

Booker moved into the kitchen and picked up Misha's weapon. He stuck it at the small of his back, turned on the tap and filled a glass with cold water. He walked back to the unconscious Russian and flung the contents into his face. Misha roused with a sputter and moan but he was aware enough for Booker's purpose. Booker grabbed his ponytail and a fistful of his blue denim shirt and dragged him bodily to the door that closed off the hall. Misha groaned and tried to open his eyes as Booker pushed the kid's right hand into the crack of the door just beneath hinge.

"Hey, Misha? Can you hear me, Misha?" he said softly, jerking him up by the shirt and holding his hand in the door with one knee. He spoke to him in Russian, so he'd be sure to understand.

The kid opened bleary eyes but his vision cleared quickly enough when he recognized Booker. "Think back, tough guy. Remember my friend named Jumbo? A black guy wearing a white apron? Remember him, Misha, my friend? Him and the pretty lady you messed with the other night?"

Misha stared bug-eyed at him, apparently stunned that Booker was speaking his own language. Booker watched fear steal across his face like a stalking black cat.

"Don't kill me, I follow orders, I follow orders. . . ."

"I heard you enjoyed your work, Misha," he said, very low. "I really dislike guys like you who get off hurting people." Still holding him by the shirt, Booker jerked out his gun and pressed the nose of it hard into the hollow of the man's cheek.

Misha's obsidian eyes bulged, then got moist as he realized the extent of his peril. "Don't kill me, please don't kill me."

Booker ignored his tears. "It's a little different now, right, Misha? I don't see you smiling much so I guess you're not enjoying this little show. You're nothing but a stinking coward without your gun or a steel meat tenderizer, isn't that the truth, Misha?"

"I'm sorry, sorry about your friends."

"Doubt if that'll make their broken bones heal any faster, punk, but I know what would make them feel better, Misha. This is from my friends, Jumbo and Mavis. I want you to remember that. This is from them, got it?"

When Misha gave a slight nod, Booker put his shoulder against the door and shoved hard. Misha screamed as his fingers smashed flat against the jamb, one high-pitched, horrible shriek that died abruptly when Booker grabbed him up again, the gun against his temple.

"But this is from me, understand? Say hello to hell, Misha."

Misha struggled but before Booker could pull the trigger, he caught a movement out the corner of his eye. Senses screaming danger, he lunged to the side, holding Misha as a shield as he got off a couple of rounds toward the bedrooms. He got a bare glimpse of the man firing back from the hallway, heard the muffled *phuts* of a silenced gun and felt slugs tearing into Misha's body. Booker rolled away toward the front door, scrambling behind the couch and letting loose a barrage of shots that pierced the thin trailer wall and felled the guy coming after him. He couldn't see him but heard him go down, the loud blams echoing in the confined space. He cursed at his own stupidity, angry he'd let the third Russian sneak up on him, but well aware Dmitri would've heard the shots.

Dmitri was outside the car now, moving in, gun in hand. Booker came out firing, getting off a couple of shots at him before jumping off the steps and into the bushes behind the lattice screen. The Russian blasted back, the percussion muffled by the silencer, but his attack shattered a big section of lattice and clematis just above Booker's head, raining wood splinters and torn leaves down on him. The Russian kept shooting, bringing down more of the screen, but Dmitri was at a disadvantage out in the open with nowhere to take cover.

Booker moved, keeping low to evade Dmitri's constant gunfire, making it to the end of the trailer and flattening himself against the wall. Dmitri didn't waste any time getting back to the car. He jerked open the driver's door, a good distance away now, but Booker ran at him, firing as the Russian slammed the car into reverse and stomped the gas pedal, throwing gravel all over the place. Booker stopped, took aim at Dmitri's head behind the windshield and squeezed the trigger, then cursed as his gun clicked, the clip empty. He jerked

Misha's 9mm out of his waistband and took off after the wildly careening car.

Dmitri had already made the access road, swerving out onto it in reverse, stopping with a screech of brakes, then gunning the car toward the bridge. Too far away now to stop him, Booker took off on a parallel course along the rocky beach, realizing that Dmitri's desperate escape would take him straight across the bridge where Kate and Mac were waiting. Booker sprinted harder in an attempt to cut the killer off, ignoring the people who'd come out of their campers at the sound of gunshots. They screamed and scattered as he raced among them, pistol in hand. Dmitri would be on top of Kate and Mac before they knew what hit them. They wouldn't have a chance.

Kate was terrified Booker wouldn't make it back in time. She held Joey in her arms, trying to quiet his fussing, but kept her eyes glued on the bridge behind them. Mac had parked the Mustang at the side of the road, under some shade trees about fifty yards from the bridge. She bit her lip, afraid Mac would take off before Booker got there.

"Do you think he's okay?" she asked Mac, sounding as nervous as she felt.

"Yeah, don't worry, Book can take care of himself. He'll be here in plenty of time."

"But he's taking so long."

"Well, there's probably more than one of 'em." Mac laughed as if he thought that was funny. Kate's eyes accused him, and he sobered at once.

"Look, Kate, Booker knows what he's doing. I've known him a long time. Seen the guy in action. I'm telling you he'll be okay."

"What do you think he's doing?"

Mac met her worried gaze. "Letting those guys know he doesn't take kindly to people messing with his friends. Book's always been that way. You know, real loyal to people he cares about."

Kate glanced at the bridge again. "Were you in the army with him? Is that how you met?"

"Yeah. Green Berets. I had enough sense to get out. Book didn't."

"Why not?"

"He thought he was fighting for America. For the land of the brave and the home of the free, all that crap. He was as idealistic as the rest of us then, more, I guess."

Kate put Joey down on the backseat where he'd be more comfortable. He quit fussing and kicked his feet, glad to be able to move around, but she was thinking about what Mac said. She had wondered about Booker's past and the suffering he still seemed to endure. Maybe this was her chance to find out more about him. She wanted to know him better, understand him.

"He has terrible nightmares," she told Mac. "Really bad ones. I was there once and saw how it got to him. I assumed it had something to do with the army."

"Yeah, well, he's not the only one who can't put that shit behind him."

"It must've been something really horrible."

Mac was sitting sideways in the driver's seat, his back to the door while he watched out the rear window for Booker. He nodded and she thought he wasn't going to say more. Then he focused his attention on her face. "Book had it worse than most. I don't suppose he's told you anything about it?"

Kate shook her head. "He told me he was wanted for shooting an officer. He said he served time for it." She hesitated, wondering if Mac knew Booker was still wanted.

"I know about him escaping from Leavenworth, if that's what you're thinking," Mac said.

"Why'd he feel he had to escape?"

"He got twenty-five years for attempted murder, served seven in minimum confinement and then went up for parole.

They denied it to him when Denton, the guy he shot, came to the hearing and argued against him. Book climbed the fence the next day. I guess he felt like he'd spent enough time caged up in Nicaragua."

"He was in jail in Nicaragua?"

Mac darted a quick look at her. "Guess he wouldn't tell you about that either."

"About what? Please tell me, Mac. I think I should know. He's done so much for us that I'd like to help him, if I can. I can't understand why he's put his life on the line for me and Joey."

"He must've had a reason." Mac hesitated as if uncertain if he should continue. Kate was glad he did. "He was captured by the Sandinistas, held in one of their hellhole camps a long time before he escaped. God only knows how he managed it."

"Oh, my God, I had no idea." She tried to absorb that knowledge, felt her stomach turn over. She'd heard about cruelties in South American prison camps, read about atrocities committed by guerrilla fighters. "How long was he there?"

"A little over a year. Had a real rough time. The bastards."

Kate felt sick but she had a feeling she knew what Mac was talking about. He was talking about torture. Again, she felt she had to ask. "I noticed that Booker has a thing about bells, you know, buzzers, stuff like that. Is that why? Does it remind him of what they did to him down there?" Her breath caught and she was almost afraid to hear Mac's answer.

"He wouldn't like me telling you this stuff. He doesn't talk about it, not to anybody. I only know because it came out during his court-martial. All the ugly details how he and his men were tortured and starved. It's ugly, Kate, real ugly. The Sandinistas ended up killing every one of them except Book. The whole squad died under torture. It was a damn miracle Book survived all the shit they did to him."

Kate swallowed hard, gruesome mental images welling up inside her head, pictures she didn't want to think about. "Do you know what they did to him?"

"I wish I didn't. They liked to use electricity on the Americans, you know how it works, don't you? They put live wires on him, different parts of his body. That's where he got the aversion to bells. They played games with our guys, mind games. At the court-martial Book said there were some Russian advisors at the camp, you know, assigned to train and arm the Nicaraguans. The Russians were the ones who started the Pavlov shit, you know about his theory of conditioned response, don't you? He's the guy who rang a bell every time he fed his dogs, or something like that, and they began to lick their chops and salivate when they heard the bell ring. Well, the bastards always rang it right before they hit the switch and jolted him." He looked down, shook his head, blew out his breath. "That wasn't even the worst part." He locked eyes with Kate and she could read the horror in them. "Sometimes they'd put Booker and one of his men face to face, tied down in chairs. They'd let them ring the bells themselves to stop the current but the only thing was, when they rang the bell to stop the pain, it got sent to the friend in the chair across from them. They had to sit there and watch them take it until they reached for the bell and sent it back."

"Oh, dear God." Kate shut her eyes, felt emotions flood into her throat. It was so horrible, so cruel. She couldn't bear to think of Booker enduring that kind of hell.

"What's really bad is that none of it had to happen. You see, Book and his men had been working with the Contras. The U.S. was backing them then. They were out on a night reconnaissance mission. Book was one of the best. He speaks eight languages, you know that? He's an army brat, and his dad dragged him all over the world when he was a kid. That's how he learned a bunch of them. He was born down around where you're from, Poplar Bluff, or somewhere."

Kate shook her head, trying to absorb it all.

"Anyway, they went out on a Black Ops mission. Their commanding officer, a major named Denton, just pulled out lock, stock and barrel and left them behind in the jungle to fend for themselves. He was a real bastard. That's why Booker went after him. I've always said if Book really wanted him dead, the guy'd be dead. Book doesn't make mistakes like that. He's too good, and he can shoot the eye out of a gnat. He's that good a marksman, he really is."

"How did he get home if they pulled out and left him there?"

"He found his way to the San Juan River and crossed it into Costa Rica. Some of the Contra supporters there helped him get back to the States. That's when he made his way back to LA, then tracked down Denton and put a bullet in him."

Kate stared at him, shocked, but a lot of things made sense now, especially Booker's self-imposed exile. Trusting people wouldn't come easily to him. She'd seen that herself. But God knew he had reason to be distrustful.

"I wish he'd hurry up. It's almost half an hour now." She turned and gazed worriedly at the bridge. Fear was rising inside her, stronger and stronger, and deep down in her heart, she knew why. Booker had become important to her. She couldn't bear to think of anything else happening to him. She cared for him, more than she should, more than she ever could have imagined. It hit her hard, took her breath, the knowledge that she already cared so much for him, a man she hardly knew. She cared about him more than anyone else in her life, except for Joey. How could that be possible?

"There he is," Mac said to her, turning around at once and starting the motor.

Kate's heart leapt and she jerked around to look out the rear window. Booker had appeared on the bridge but he wasn't coming toward them. He was standing at the far end, his arms outstretched in front of him. Oh, God, he was shooting at somebody!

"They're after him, Mac! Hurry, hurry, go back, do something!"

Mac shoved the car into gear just as a white Suburban

came into view at incredible speed, swerving over toward the edge of the bridge where Booker stood. He dove to one side as the car nearly ran him down but was up on his feet almost at once, firing at the back of the car. He must've hit a tire because the rear end suddenly fishtailed, sending the Suburban into a roll off the embankment at the end of the bridge.

Mac gunned the Mustang around in a sliding turn, the traffic along the highway squealing to avoid him as the Suburban slid down the hill on its side and slammed up against a tree. Booker was at the end of the bridge now, firing down at the smoking wreckage.

"Shit, shit, shit," Mac was saying as he hit the accelerator and brought them up alongside Booker in nothing flat. He reached over and slung open the passenger's door. "Get in, get in, before the cops get here!"

Kate held tightly to Joey, frightened eyes on Booker as he jumped in and slammed the door. Mac took off like a race car at Indy, weaving through the halted traffic as if he did it every day of the week. Booker was panting hard, had blood trickling down the side of his head, but he was there, he was all right, they hadn't got him. She was so glad he was alive that she felt the urge to reach up and hug him, but when he turned around to look behind them, she saw how tight his face was, how hard the expression in his eyes. He looked like a different person from the man who'd stood watching them leave Mac's trailer less than an hour earlier.

"What the hell happened back there?" Mac asked as they sped down the access road onto the highway that would take them to Springfield. They could already hear the high-pitched whine of sirens.

"Slow it down now, Mac," Booker said, still watching the road behind them. "We don't want to get stopped before we get outta town."

Mac eased on the brake, slowing them a good bit. "Did you get them? How many were there?"

"They're out of commission, I figure."

"For good?"

"Yeah. Unless Dmitri crawls out of that crash."

Mac glanced sideways at Booker, then nodded. He put his eyes back on the road.

"Good deal," he said, hooking his seatbelt for the drive to St. Louis. "Best news I've heard all day."

Booker was leaning down, putting something on the floor in front of him, guns, Kate saw, craning up to look. She wondered what happened back at Mac's trailer, knew the killers were probably dead but felt only a sense of relief. They were the animals who'd killed Michael, who wanted to kill her; they deserved whatever Booker had done to them. She was just glad Booker was back with them, alive and unhurt. She thought of the things Mac had told her and wondered how Booker had managed to get away from Dmitri's men, how he dealt with the terrible things done to him in the past. No wonder he couldn't sleep at night.

"You okay?"

Booker was turned around again, looking at her. She realized that tears shone in her eyes but she blinked them away. "I'm just glad you got back okay. I was worried."

Booker nodded. He seemed perfectly normal again, as if nothing out of the ordinary had happened. "You can relax now. Get some sleep, if you can. It'll be awhile before we get to St. Louis."

"Are you hurt? Your head's bleeding."

"It's nothing. Just a scratch."

Kate watched him wipe blood away with the back of his hand, then turn around and slump down in his seat. He pulled his baseball cap low over his eyes and leaned his head against the seat, but she knew he wasn't going to sleep. He never seemed to sleep. Wearily she laid her head back and tried not to think about what the next few days might bring.

Thirty

ON I-70 across from Lambert Airport they found a high-rise Marriott busy enough to ensure they wouldn't be noticed. The parking lot was packed with cars and airport shuttles arriving and departing every few minutes, while jets took off overhead in thunderous roars that shook the place. Mac went inside and paid cash for two adjoining rooms under the name Jack Smith. They needed a place to hole up for awhile, lie low until they contacted Vince Saracino and got the ball rolling.

Booker made sure Kate was comfortable and secure in a spacious room with two queen beds—a chair pushed under the doorknob just to be cautious—before he joined Mac in the adjoining room to finalize their plans. There wasn't much to discuss once they found out the Cards would be playing a doubleheader the next afternoon and evening. That would give them plenty of time to get inside the stadium and set up the exchange with Saracino.

While Mac tracked down the street address and telephone number of his old friend, Dave Saracino, Booker took a shower and dressed in fresh khaki shorts and a blue cambric shirt they'd purchased in a Wal-Mart store just west of St. Louis. They'd gotten everything they needed, baby stuff and toiletries, and lots of shirts and caps stamped with the Redbird logo to wear to the game. They made another stop, too, at Mac's favorite gun dealer, who quietly sold them from his basement storeroom three bulletproof, Kevlar vests and enough ammunition to start a small war. Yeah, they were as ready as they could get.

Booker scrubbed down well in the shower, washing his hair, shaving and generally cleaning up, doctoring the flesh wound on his temple with a Band-Aid. He was becoming accustomed to daily showers, clean clothes, even interaction with other people. Kate had given him that by dragging him out of his self-imposed banishment. He felt better than he had in some time, almost normal, and fairly confident they were safe at the moment. At least from the Russian hit team, who wouldn't be murdering innocent victims anytime soon.

Dmitri's fate was still unknown, but the two he'd left inside Mac's trailer were either dead or soon would be. Dmitri used surprise so that his kills would go swiftly, his victims unsuspecting and easy to take down. Not anymore. At least Kate had one night when she didn't have to worry about bloodthirsty thugs bursting in her door with loaded guns. The way Booker figured it, that was the one thing he could do for her. Sure as hell wasn't much else he could do to raise her spirits.

"Okay, I got Dave's number. He wasn't there so I talked to his wife. She said he'd be home all day tomorrow," Mac informed Booker when he came out of the bathroom. "We'll call him tomorrow night from Busch Stadium and tell him Kate will hand Joey over to the mother, no questions asked, just so we walk away free and clear. Right?"

"Yeah. Does his wife know what's going on?"

"She said Vince's on a rampage and his wife, her name's Anna, by the way, is a candidate for the funny farm. She can't stop crying and Vince is scared she's gonna crack up. It's their first kid, and Vince's been hungry for a son since they got married. It seems Reed, or whoever the hell snatched Joey, got him before Vince got a look at him, which makes things even worse."

"How come he didn't see the baby?"

"He was up in New York facing some kind of criminal hearing and the kid was kidnapped before he got home."

"You think Vince's gonna go for this, Mac? You know him."

Mac took off his shoes and leaned back against the headboard. "Yeah, I think he'll do whatever it takes to get the boy back to his wife, but who knows? Vince doesn't compute like everybody else. He's nuts, and ruthless as hell."

"No kidding."

Mac grinned and watched Booker pull back the drapery and check the parking lot. "You think the girl's gonna hold up tomorrow?"

"I don't know. She's shaky."

"Think you oughta tell her how it's gonna go down?"

"Don't know." Booker had been trying to figure out a way to deal with Kate and found himself anxious to see her again, make sure she was all right. Watching over her had become a habit, and he felt uneasy when she was out of his sight, even though Misha and the gang weren't around for their games of bust-in-and-slaughter-everybody.

On the other hand, they were in St. Louis now, Vince Saracino's turf, and given the time, he had the resources to find them. Down deep Booker was afraid Kate might run again, on her own since he and Mac were against it. She was desperate enough. He'd seen the agony in her eyes when she looked at Joey, all warmth and pleasure robbed from her. "Think I better check on her. Make sure she's all right."

"Okay. I'm gonna order up some room service. Want some?"

"Go ahead. I'll order for Kate and me next door. I don't think she'll like being alone in there."

Mac nodded and turned to pick up the motel telephone on the table between the beds. Booker opened the connecting door and tapped a knuckle on Kate's locked one. Within seconds she was there, opening it and looking up at him. She had Joey in her arms. She hadn't showered or changed clothes. She'd been crying. Her eyes were red and puffy. She didn't look so good.

"You okay?"

"No."

"Thought I'd get us something to eat from room service. You hungry?"

"No."

"Want me to come in?"

Kate stepped aside and let him enter. She shut the door behind him and locked it. He had a feeling she would never enter a room again without turning the locks and throwing the bolts. She had been robbed of peace of mind forever; he'd lost his a long time ago. Her curtains were drawn, and a second chair was jammed underneath the knob alongside the first one. He had a feeling she'd been sitting in the dark, holding Joey tightly in her arms, already mourning his loss. Watching her carefully, he sat down on the bed beside the phone.

"What sounds good to eat, Kate?"

"Nothing." She shrugged, then roused up some as if she realized she was taking her misery out on him. "Whatever you get's fine with me. Joey's gonna need some milk."

Booker watched her lay Joey on the bed closest to the bathroom, propping pillows around him. She moved to the closet, took down the extra blanket on the shelf, then pulled out the top dresser drawer. She set to work making the baby a bed as she'd done at Mac's trailer. She looked and acted absolutely numb, moving around in a trance. She'd fought the good fight, had shown guts few women had, but having to give up the baby had broken her. He dialed the number for room service.

"Yeah," Booker said when the restaurant picked up. "I'd like a couple of T-bones sent up. Yeah, that's room 107. With the works, french fries, salad, whatever kind of pie you've got. Yeah, well done. Send up a couple of Coors Light in the can. And two large milks, in the carton, if you've got it that way." He paused, raising his eyebrows at Kate for confirmation, but she wasn't paying attention to him. She was sitting on the bed beside Joey, staring down at him, looking ready to cry again.

"And a bottle of wine. Yeah, chardonnay's fine. Thanks." He hung up. Kate still wasn't looking at him.

"She said it's gonna take half an hour or so."

Kate nodded absently, picking up the sleeping infant and placing him gently in his drawer-bed. The baby didn't stir. Joey was a good little baby, Booker had to give him that. Kate just stood there staring down at him, and Booker frowned, not sure Kate could go through with this, no matter how sorry she felt for Joey's mother.

"Why don't you take a quick shower before dinner comes?" he suggested. "You'd probably feel better. I do."

"Maybe later." Kate finally met his gaze, her expression so sorrowful that something twisted in his heart and made him feel a little sick. Then she said, "I guess you're right. I should wash my face and clean up a little. You'll watch Joey, won't you?"

"Sure."

Kate picked up a blue plastic Wal-Mart sack from the table, one with toothpaste and soap, and carried it into the bathroom. Booker waited until she shut the door, then switched on the TV set with the remote control, keeping the sound low so as not to awaken the baby, but Joey wasn't moving a muscle. When the kid slept, he really slept. Booker got up and stood looking down at the little baby in the drawer in much the same way Kate had done.

Joey slept on his back; Kate said it was safer to put him down that way. Both his arms were thrown over his head. One hand was tangled loosely in his silky black curls. Kate must have bathed and changed him while Booker had been with Mac. He had on a new blue terrycloth sleeper. The clown pacifier that Booker had bought for him was in his mouth but he wasn't sucking on it.

A deep-rooted memory rose wraithlike from the dark, hidden places in his heart, and anguish hit him when he saw the face of another child, another tiny baby boy. He swallowed hard, felt his throat grow thick with emotion. He was going to miss the little guy, too. He didn't know how the hell Kate was ever going to get through this.

Not wanting to think about losing Joey, he lounged down on the bed beside the picture window. It was time for the evening news and that's what he wanted to hear. When Peter Jennings came on, he talked about the latest political scandal for awhile, another investigation of the presidential past, then moved on to an air crash outside Mexico City. They had it on film, a ghastly nosedive into the side of a mountain that gave anybody watching cold chills. He turned off the sound for awhile, waiting for the local news to come on.

A knock on the door sent him to his feet. He pulled his gun from the back of his waistband, moved to the door and used the peephole. A young woman in a black waitress's uniform stood outside holding the handle of a wheeled cart. He opened the door a crack and made sure she was alone, then shoved the gun in the front of his waistband under the loose fabric of his shirt.

"I can get it," he said, not wanting her inside the room. If she saw Joey asleep in the drawer, she just might put two and two together the next time she heard a news flash about the kidnapping.

"Sign here, please." She smiled up at him, a pretty girl with long blond hair woven up in a French braid, about the color Kate's used to be. "You look familiar," she said, studying his face. "You stay here a lot?"

"Yeah," he answered, adding a tip then scribbling Jack Smith on the ticket. She was still smiling, and he had a feeling she might be coming on to him but was too out of practice with that sort of thing to be sure.

"Have a nice evening, Mr. Smith," she said, looking up into his eyes. "There's a really good band playin' down at the bar tonight, if you like dancin'."

"Never learned," he said.

"Too bad. It's fun. I'm gonna go with my girlfriend. We'll be there till late if you wanna come."

"Yeah? Well, thanks but I gotta turn in early," he said, handing the ticket back.

Booker waited until she turned the corner and headed toward the front lobby, then pulled the cart inside and locked the door. He realized how hungry he was when he lifted the warming dome and the aroma of charbroiled beef wafted up and wreaked havoc inside his empty stomach. He pushed the cart toward a round table with two comfortable, black-and-white–floral armchairs set beside the window.

When Kate came out a few minutes later, he said, "Food's here. Looks pretty good. I thought we'd listen to the news while we ate."

"Joey didn't wake up?"

"Hasn't made a peep."

"I gave him the rest of his bottle just before you came in." Kate checked on the baby anyway, tenderly stroking his cheek before reluctantly leaving him and joining Booker. He set the plates across the table from each other. He poured wine into a stemmed wineglass. He had a feeling Kate needed a drink.

"I rarely drink," she said, shaking her head and pushing it away, but almost immediately changed her mind. She picked up the goblet and took a deep swallow. Booker didn't comment when she drained the glass to the bottom and poured herself some more.

"The steak looks good. Hope it is," he said for the sake of conversation. Something he hadn't worried about much until lately. In the woods, weeks had gone by without an uttered word.

Kate nodded, and as Booker cut a bite of the thick, juicy steak and forked it into his mouth, she watched him silently, holding her wineglass but barely touching her food. She kept looking at the baby, then started visibly when she glanced at the television. Booker turned quickly and saw that ABC was broadcasting Kate's picture again. He picked up the remote and unmuted the sound.

". . . is still at large. Authorities are asking for help in locating the woman and missing child. The baby's mother made a heartbreaking plea yesterday from her home in Ladue. . . . Here is Robin Latham with that report. . . ."

As soon as the mother's face appeared on the screen, Kate spoke sharply. "Turn it off, Booker. I can't listen to that again."

"Okay."

He muted the sound and they sat in silence. Kate finished the wine and poured herself a third glass. Booker wasn't sure what to say, knew good and well nothing he said would make any difference anyway. Maybe getting drunk would make her feel better.

"You think we're safe here, Booker? You're sure Dmitri won't come after us again?"

"Even if he survived the crash, it's unlikely he could track us here. You can sleep without worrying. Mac and I will be right next door, if you should need us."

Kate's eyes darted up and locked on his face. She was alarmed. "No, please, Booker, stay with me. I don't want to be alone tonight. I can't, I just can't."

"Okay, if that's what you want. No problem. I'll stay in here."

Kate relaxed visibly and leaned back against the cushions. She stared at her untouched plate, deeply lost in her own morose thoughts. Booker pulled the tab on his second beer. It was going to be another long night, but this time he had hope they might have found a way out. One where Kate didn't end up with a bullet between her eyes. He started to tell her about the ball game, how they planned to hand Joey over to his father's cousin, but couldn't quite bring himself to do it. He didn't want to see the look on Kate's face when she realized Joey would be gone for good the very next day.

"I gotta talk to Mac a minute," he told her a short time later. "Then I'll come back and stay here with you till morning so you can get some rest."

"Okay."

Booker unlocked the door and found Mac's side ajar. His old friend was enjoying a huge chef salad and an egg-white omelet, his usual health-food fare that to Booker was most unappetizing. "Did you get the tickets?"

"Yeah, everything's set up. We pick them up at the gate, and once we're inside we contact Saracino. You hear tonight's news?"

"Kate didn't want to listen to it. What happened?"

"They're saying the parents aren't cooperating with the police or the FBI anymore, or the media, either. They're probably hoping the open contract out on Kate'll get the baby back sooner than the cops can."

Booker nodded. "I'm gonna stay in there with Kate tonight. She's not doing so good."

"Can't blame her. She's sure crazy about that kid."

When Booker went back to Kate's room, she was changing Joey's diaper. The baby was wide awake now, doing his usual gooing, gurgling, chuckling routine. Kate held his hands and baby-talked to him but she looked so distraught Booker found it hard to watch. When she sat down to feed Joey a bottle, Booker stretched out on the bed, his back against the pillows. He flipped through the channels for awhile, finally settling on a movie where some guy had just jumped off the roof of a glass skyscraper at the end of a fire hose while some guys were shooting at him from a helicopter. The whole top of the building went up in a pyrotechnic panorama, then the chopper went spiraling to the ground in a big, fiery explosion. The hero was trying to bust out a window on the side of the building by swinging at it with his bare feet. Yeah, right, Booker thought, where do these guys get this stuff? The guy finally had enough sense to shoot out the glass and came through in a crash that probably would've cut him to shreds in real life. He did end up with a lot of blood all over him.

When Joey finally went back to sleep, Kate lowered him into the drawer and covered him with a new white baby blanket. She leaned down, kissed the top of his head, then came back and sat down on the opposite bed. She looked at the television as a firefight began with lots of automatic rifle fire, ending up with another guy dangling out a window holding on for dear life to a woman's wrist.

"Good grief, what are you watching?" Kate asked.

Booker frowned at the screen, where the hero was now kissing the woman and getting her face all bloody as the guy who'd been holding her hostage fell about fifty stories and hit the ground. The hero was barechested, showing lots of muscle, and covered with about three pints of fake blood. Booker grinned a little and looked back at Kate.

"He doesn't have much on us, if you ask me. You've been through more than he has the last few days."

Booker had wanted to worm a smile out of her, and he succeeded because she laughed out loud. Only problem was, she didn't stop. She laughed almost hysterically for a couple of minutes, then burst into tears. Booker stared at her in concern, not sure exactly what to do. She had her face buried in her open hands now, sobbing hard. Booker got up and laid a hand on her back.

"I know how hard this is on you, Kate. I wish I could do something."

"Couldn't we just take a plane out of here? I've been sitting here all afternoon listening to the jets. They're right across the highway. All we'd have to do is get on one. I have a friend named Elsa in Sweden, a girl who ran marathons with me. We could go there, she'd take us in, or go anywhere, I don't care. Anything would be better than giving Joey to those monsters."

"His mother's not a monster." Booker hated to remind her but he had to make her understand, see reason, or she'd end up six feet under. "They'd find you, Kate, they would, trust me on this. No matter where you went. The Mafia doesn't forgive people who've wronged them. If we don't give him back, we're finished, all of us."

"Oh, God, Booker, I can't stand it," she whispered, her voice hoarse, so clogged he could barely understand her.

When she pulled him down and wept against his chest, he put his arms around her. He stroked her hair and tried not to think how soft it was, how good she smelled, like Johnson's Baby Powder. He was not exactly unaware of her breasts pressed against his chest, either. This wasn't the time to be thinking like this. He needed to get a grip on his own desires but she was making it hard on him.

"C'mon, now, Kate, why don't you go take a shower? Get ready for bed and get some sleep," he said, pulling her up and pointing her toward the bathroom. He needed to get her out of his arms, the sooner the better. She was much too vulnerable at the moment. So was he. "You'll feel better, trust me."

Kate nodded wearily, wiping tears away as she left his arms, and Booker kicked himself for not knowing how to handle her grief without being so aware of her as a woman. He'd been celibate too long for this kind of forced intimacy with a woman like Kate. She was just too damn desirable.

Kate stayed in the bathroom for nearly an hour. Booker kept thinking about how she'd looked in that skimpy white towel and hoped for his own sake that she got dressed before she came out. He was only human, for God's sake, and he wasn't sure he could handle seeing her almost naked again. He had admitted to himself a long time ago that he desired her. Hell, he wanted her about as much as he'd wanted anything in his life, but he knew it was the wrong time for them, the wrong place, wrong decision, wrong everything, for both of them. He wouldn't think about her that way, not until all this was over, when and if they both came out in one piece. About the time he'd persuaded himself to do just that, Kate opened the door.

She stepped outside, her face flushed from steam that swirled out the door behind her. She wore a thigh-length T-shirt nightgown she'd picked off the rack at Wal-Mart, a yellow one with Snoopy playing badminton with Woodstock. She was barefoot, her hair wet and combed straight back off her face. She wore no makeup. She looked unbelievably beautiful to Booker.

"You're right. I do feel better."

She moved across in front of him, towel-drying her hair, and Booker glanced away from those long, bare legs of hers. Christ. He turned around and punched the pillows, just for something to do. Unfortunately, Kate sat on the edge of the other bed and stared at him.

"I guess I want to thank you. For everything you've done. I don't know why you've put yourself on the line for us, but they would've gotten Joey a long time ago if it hadn't been for you."

"Don't worry about it. Want me to turn off the light so we can get some sleep?"

"I guess so."

Booker did, gratefully, but he watched her where she sat on the edge of the bed, looking very small and vulnerable in the light flickering off the television. There was silence now except for the low sounds of explosions and gunfire from the movie and the occasional roar of jet engines going overhead.

"I don't want to be alone tonight. Not tonight."

"You're not. I'm right here."

"I want more than that."

Booker knew what she meant but couldn't believe she really meant it. "You're upset. You don't owe me anything."

"I need your arms around me. I need you to hold me, I really do."

Booker still hesitated but she moved first, came to him, crawled across the bed and snuggled in close beside him. She took his arm and pulled it around her. He shut his eyes at the feel of her body pressed full-length against his, pulling her closer and sighing when she lodged a silky thigh between his legs.

"You know," she whispered, her lips moving against the side of his throat. "I feel so close to you. I feel closer to you, I feel more for you now, I think, than I ever felt for Michael, even in the beginning when things were good between us. I loved him, I did, but then he got into trouble in his work, he changed, and everything started going wrong. He betrayed me when he lied about Joey, betrayed my love, our life together, but I trust you, Booker. I know you'd never do that to us. I'd trust you with anything, my life, Joey's life. I already have. I'd do anything for you, anything at all."

Booker felt a little thrill inside, but when she started unbuttoning the front of his shirt, he put his hand over hers and stilled it against his chest. His heart was beating hard, too fast; they both could feel it. "Look, Kate, I haven't been with a woman in a long time. I don't think this is the right thing to do now when you're so upset. Not for either one of us."

"It is right, it's the only thing that is. I want you. I want you to want me."

"I can't offer you anything. I'll be looking over my shoulder for a long time to come, you know that."

"I'm used to running now."

As she whispered that, she worked on the buttons, and as soon as she had his shirt open, she pressed her lips upon his chest. He felt a shudder rise from somewhere deep inside and a shiver coursed over his flesh. She slid her arms around his waist under the shirt and pressed herself tightly against him.

"Make love to me, Booker, make me forget tomorrow."

Booker didn't need more encouragement and didn't have it in him to resist the woman he wanted, admired, respected, desperately craved. He found her mouth with a greedy hunger he could barely control, buried his hands in her damp hair as he turned over with her. He was tentative at first, exploring her slender body, giving her time to change her mind, but the point came when he could hold back no longer, his feelings for her running wild, his blood rampant with need, and Kate accepted all he offered, clung to him, responded to his touch, gave herself freely, eagerly, without hesitation.

Maybe it was the moment, maybe it wouldn't last but it felt so good, sliding his hands over her satiny skin, her body soft and small and warm in his arms. He made love to her for a long time but not long enough, never long enough, and it was so good between them, they cried out together, bodies left quivering and spent, sated in a way neither had ever experienced before.

When they finally lay entwined, comfortable in their intimacy, able to breathe normally again, her back cupped against his chest, his arms tight around her, Kate sighed, then asked him a question he didn't want to hear.

"Tell me why you helped me out there in the woods. I need to know. Even if you knew Pop, you didn't have to get as involved as you did. You were safe in your woods but you put yourself in danger for me. You didn't even know if I was innocent or guilty. You didn't know me at all."

Booker heaved out a deep breath as she twined her fingers through his. She was hard to resist, this woman he'd gotten caught up with. She wanted to know all his secrets, and he wasn't sure he was ready to give them up. He'd been a loner too long.

"I have a son," he admitted finally and felt her start with surprise. "He was about Joey's age the last time I saw him. Just before my last mission with the Contras."

Kate squeezed his hand, her voice gentle. "Where is he now?"

"His mother divorced me when I went to prison, and I haven't seen either one of them since. Last I heard, she'd remarried and moved to Rome. I guess seeing those guys trying to get you and Joey made me think of Billy."

Kate turned in his arms until their faces nearly touched. She put her hands up and tenderly cupped his chin. "You know how I feel about losing Joey, don't you, Booker?"

"Yeah, I know."

Kate kissed him then, a sweet, loving kiss, and they settled into silence. She cried softly for awhile, and he held her against him until he heard her breathing even out and soften as she found solace in sleep. A long time later, he fell asleep, too, one arm around Kate, the other on the .45 under his pillow.

Thirty-one

AT HALF PAST SIX the following afternoon Booker sat in Mac's field box seats at Busch Stadium, four rows up from the home dugout. The Cardinals were warming up, stretching out, working out nerves before they met the Braves. The stadium was full, a sellout of fifty thousand yelling, screaming, fanatical Redbird fans. The perfect place to hide.

Kate was beside him in Mac's other box seat, holding Joey on her lap. It was a promotional night, the first five hundred people to arrive presented with a small Busch Beer cooler free at the gate. Kate had removed the lid and laid Joey inside, hoping the baby wouldn't be as noticeable as he would in his baby seat. She was right. Few people paid attention to them.

In front of them the St. Louis Cardinals' mascot, a big goofy-looking, red-feathered cardinal in a white St. Louis uniform jersey known by the initiated as Fredbird, was cavorting for all he was worth. He stood seven feet tall with yellow hands and skinny yellow legs ending in big clawlike feet. He was atop the dugout at the moment, dancing around, flapping his wings and making an idiot out of himself. The crowd loved it.

Kate realized that Booker was looking at her and put on a tentative smile, but her brown eyes were shadowed with sorrow. He had a feeling she was secretly hoping she wouldn't have to go through with it. When she laid her hand on his thigh, he entwined her fingers and squeezed reassuringly. He thought about how they'd made love, how good it had been, how easy the intimacy had come. It felt right and natural between them, without guilt or regret or embarrassment. He'd made love to her again when he'd awakened and found her in his arms, slowly and tenderly, and although Booker feared that Kate's vulnerability, her need for comfort, might have brought her to his bed, he was only too glad it had happened.

He jumped and let go of Kate's hand when the cell phone in his breast pocket activated. The well-groomed woman with tortuously teased, ash-blond hair sitting on his right glared at him as if the phone had committed a felony. Unlike Booker and Kate, who wore red satin Cardinals' warm-up jackets over T-shirts with St. Louis logos, cut-off jeans, and tennis shoes in order to blend in with the other fans, she wore a black silk blouse and matching slacks with stiletto heels. She looked hot, overdressed and pretentious. He ignored her outrage and flipped open the phone before it could ring again. Mac's voice came through the wire, as clear as if he were sitting beside them.

"I'm in place. Got me?"

"Just a sec." Booker picked up the small military binoculars hanging around his neck and peered through them at the bleachers over center field. Busch Stadium had recently replaced eleven sections of the upper deck in center field with a giant manually operated scoreboard that could track every major league game in progress with a full line score. At the very center of it, underneath a huge neon sign sporting two red cardinals perched on a bat, he zeroed in on Mac standing at the mouth of an exit tunnel, looking nervous as hell. Mac had insisted Dave Saracino could be trusted, but in Booker's mind, the man was still Vince Saracino's first cousin. Booker damn well didn't trust him.

"Okay, I see you." He watched Mac cup his hand over the receiver to shield his conversation from the people milling around in the nearby tunnel.

"I just hung up with Dave, caught him at home in Florissant. I figure it'll take him thirty or forty minutes to make it downtown and find a parking place. You're on the lookout for Vince's goons, right?"

"If I see anybody suspicious, I'll ring the phone once and hang up. You got the plan down?"

"Yeah. God, I hope Dave doesn't bring Vince in on this."

"You warned him not to, didn't you?"

"You bet I did, first thing. Told him all bets were off if he told a soul. He liked the idea of being the one to get the kid back. Thinks it'll put him in real tight with the boss man."

"When you see Dave come out of the tunnel, let me know, take off your cap or something."

"Okay. Jesus. I wish this was over."

"Yeah."

Booker closed the phone but not before taking a second to poke in Mac's cell phone number so that if he had to get hold of him in a hurry, all he had to do was punch the *send* button. Then he focused on Mac's position with the field glasses and stayed there. He was on edge, jumpy as a mosquito, feeling as if he had a bull's-eye plastered to his head, despite the hundreds of people surrounding him. He didn't know this Dave guy at all, had never laid eyes on the man, but his familial blood ties with a homicidal maniac didn't particularly recommend him as trustworthy. He hoped to God Mac was right about him.

"Is he going to do it?"

Kate had leaned close to whisper in his ear, and he caught the sweet fragrance of baby powder. He doubted he'd ever get a whiff of the stuff again without thinking about last night and the way she'd felt against his chest, her skin as soft and warm as velvet, her lips opening underneath his mouth. He met her gaze, saw how worried she was. He hoped his eyes didn't reflect his own foreboding. "He's on the way now. Be ready to go whenever I tell you."

Booker winced at the look of despair that crept over her face. She stared down at Joey, both arms wrapped tightly around the cooler. "You sure this man can be trusted with

Joey? He won't take off with him, or do anything stupid, will he?"

"Not if he knows Vince as well as Mac says he does," he answered, but the truth was he didn't have a clue what the guy might do. "All he has to do is take Joey and drive him up to his parents' house in Ladue."

The plan for the transfer was fairly simple. Once Mac was sure Dave was alone, he would direct him to drive his car around the stadium. He was to pull to the curb at every stop-light and wait several minutes. Eventually someone would run to the car and place the baby on the backseat floor. Dave was to take off without looking back and drive Joey straight to Vince Saracino's estate. It wasn't the most brilliant plan in the world but it made it hard for Dave to double-cross them or follow them once they gave the baby back. But that only held if things went according to schedule.

Over the loudspeaker a man was announcing the Cardinals' lineup. Mark McGwire, the St. Louis home-run icon, got an ovation that wouldn't quit. Booker glanced at him, never having seen the powerful hitter before, but mainly watched Mac, who still waited under the scoreboard. Mac's arms had been folded across his chest but he couldn't resist applauding his homer-hitting hero. Mac was completely fanatical when it came to the Cards and thought McGwire the greatest thing alive; Booker just hoped he didn't forget what he was doing. The game got under way with the singing of the National Anthem. Booker and Kate stood up with everyone else, and Booker glanced incredulously at the blonde next to him when she started belting out the Star Spangled Banner as if she thought she was Whitney Houston or somebody. He wished she'd go get a hot dog.

Dave took his time getting there, so much time that Booker became extremely nervous. It was well past dark, the game moving fast, well into the eighth inning, 2–1 Cards, before Mac took off his hat and fanned his face with it. Booker scanned the guys loitering around the tunnel, searching for

Dave Saracino. Mac had described him in detail—tall, skinny, always dressed to the nines in fancy Italian-made suits. He had long black hair usually full of gel and slicked straight back off his forehead. He was supposed to be a part-time boxer, wiry with a quick, light step that'd probably be the best way to pick him out of a crowd. It didn't take Booker long to spot him. He moved like a dancer.

Dave came quickly across to Mac, and the two old friends met, clasped hands and began to talk, their heads close together. Booker played the binoculars down the walkway around the exit tunnels, searching for anyone who looked out of place, or was paying undue attention to Mac. He didn't notice anything unusual. He began to feel relieved, was about to tell Kate it was time to head outside when he spotted a vendor moving toward Mac. The guy had his cap pulled down but there was something about him. When Booker saw the man's goatee, his heart took a nosedive. Shit, it was Dmitri. He'd made it out of the crash alive and deadly.

He hit the *send* key, cursing inside, still watching Mac and Dave. It was a setup, goddamn it. Mac was in big, big trouble. The minute the phone rang at the other end, Mac tried to take off but didn't have a chance. Dave Saracino stepped back as Dmitri grabbed Mac and shoved him face-first against the wall. Another man, a stranger, suddenly showed up and crowded in on the other side of Mac. Then Vince Saracino himself stepped into view. Booker would have recognized him anywhere, if only by his silver hair and dark tan.

Heart vaulting into his throat, Booker scanned the other tunnels, focusing in at the top of each ramp. He hoped to God they didn't have the exits covered, but that hope died a quick death when he saw a beefy, heavyset guy loitering at the top of the next section. He was searching the crowd with his own set of binoculars. Every exit Booker went to had similar lookouts on guard. Cautiously he turned around and peered up through the rows behind him, spotting the man posted at the exit ramp he and Kate had to use to get out of the stadium. He was dark and burly, too, and had his right hand hidden inside a black nylon jacket. They were trapped like rats.

His phone buzzed, and the woman beside him said, "I do wish you would attend to your business calls elsewhere. I'm trying to enjoy the game."

Booker ignored her as Mac's voice came from the other end, breathless and scared.

"They got me. Sorry, man."

Booker saw they had Mac sandwiched between them, one in a sideways stance indicative of a gun pressed into Mac's ribcage. "Let me speak to the guy with the goatee," he said to Mac and watched him hand over the phone to Dmitri.

"You made a very big mistake killing Misha and Yuri. Get ready to die, you bastard. I'm going to enjoy killing you and Kate both, as slowly and painfully as possible."

He'd spoken in Russian, his words iced with rage, and Booker answered in the same language. "Listen up, Dmitri, and listen good. Don't hurt Mac. He's not involved in this. He's just doing me a favor."

"That's his bad luck, Booker. Mr. Saracino's had a gutful of you. You want your friend back alive? You do exactly what we say."

Booker still watched them through the binoculars. "I want a trade. Mac for the baby. On our terms, but only if Mac's still alive . . ."

Before he finished, Vince Saracino grabbed the telephone. "You're a dead man, you hear me, you fuck? You're dead and so is anyone else who had anything to do with taking my boy."

"If you want to see your son again, you better make sure Mac stays alive and well, got it, Saracino?"

Beside him Kate was alarmed. She was looking all around, craning her eyes toward the scoreboard. She twisted in her seat and grabbed Booker's arm. "Oh, my God, Booker, they've got him, don't they?"

Mark McGwire chose that moment to hit his first home run of the evening, one with a couple of men on, and the crowd around Booker stood up and went absolutely bonkers.

"You're right. He's somewhere in the stadium," he heard Vince say to Dmitri.

Booker cursed and hung up. He glanced behind him and found the guy guarding the tunnel talking on a walkie-talkie. While Booker watched he began to move down the steps among fans still on their feet and jumping around in celebration. It was only a matter of time before he spotted them. Booker turned around and tried to think. He looked to his right and gauged the distance to the next exit ramp. It was too far and was probably covered anyway. The stadium was crawling with Saracino's men. They'd made a major miscalculation contacting Dave Saracino.

He watched McGwire round third and head for home plate where a bunch of his teammates were waiting to congratulate him. The crowd was still on their feet, pandemonium prevailing. This was their chance to get out. He looked at McGwire as the grinning player came toward the dugout, met there, too, with plenty of high fives and back slapping. He looked at the roof of the dugout directly in front of them and searched out the nearest security guard who was paying more attention to the celebration on the infield than to what the fans were doing.

"C'mon, Kate, we gotta get out of here. Follow my lead, and do what I say."

Kate looked scared but she stood up, clutching Joey's cooler as Booker pulled her out into the aisle among cheering, excited fans and down the steps to where the roof of the dugout met the seats. Fredbird was still hopping around on top, bending over and shaking his tail feathers to the delighted crowd. Booker boosted Kate up on the roof where the big mascot was gyrating, then jumped up himself. He glanced at the thug searching for them, and their eyes met. The guy started down the steps toward them.

Booker grabbed Fredbird's wing and yelled in his ear, his

voice barely audible over the roaring crowd. "I got a gun under my coat, you hear me? Do what I say or you're dead, got it?"

"Huh, man? Whassa matter with you, you crazy?" Fredbird's voice was muffled by the big, beaked Cardinal head and he kept trying to pull his wing free.

"Act like you want us up here. Dance around like you were, ham it up."

Fredbird awkwardly raised his wings and flapped some more, and the crowd roared with laughter. Booker glimpsed at least three security guards coming down the steps to arrest them. "Jump down, Kate, hurry up." Under his shirt he kept the gun pressed against Fredbird's feathers, grimacing when he realized they were being featured on the huge video screen in left field. As Kate hit the ground with Joey, Fredbird broke Booker's grip, lunged away and dove headfirst off the dugout roof into a knot of players congratulating McGwire.

Boos and catcalls began, gained momentum as Booker dropped to the ground. A bunch of the players were gathering around the fluttering mascot, helping him up, laughing, thinking it a new part of his act.

"Go for the tunnel," Booker told Kate, dragging her along as Fredbird grabbed one of the Cardinals' shirts and hysterically pointed a wing at them.

They jumped down into the nearly empty dugout, making it to the door of the locker-room ramp before they were accosted by a huge black security guard.

"Hey, you? What the hell you think you're doin'? You can't come down on the field!"

"I gotta get my kid to the hospital, he's sick! C'mon, man, the security guard up there told us it'd be quicker to go out this way!"

Kate held out the cooler and Joey cooperated by yelling bloody murder, obviously deciding to join the crowd.

"He ain't got no authority to send you down here," the

guard grumbled, but Kate grabbed the front of his shirt with her fist, displaying panic that was extremely real.

"Please, sir, please let us through, we've got to get him to the doctor. He'll go into convulsions if he doesn't get help."

The man didn't hesitate long. "Okay, I guess you can go in but don't be touchin' nuthin'. The locker room's at the far end. The team physician's in there. Maybe he can do somethin' for the kid."

"Thank you, thank you so much!"

Booker didn't waste time on conversation. He and Kate ran like hell for the locker room and found it deserted except for the doctor and a couple of team trainers sitting on a bench eating hot dogs and drinking cokes. They didn't say anything, just stared at them, as Booker and Kate ran past them and headed for the exit door.

Outside, plenty of people were wandering around, hoping to catch sight of their favorite players. Kate was glad Booker slowed to a walk, giving her time to catch her breath. He pulled her along with him, his hand gripped tightly around her upper arm, his eyes searching the sidewalks for Saracino's henchmen. They crossed the street, jaywalking at midblock, evading the honking traffic until they reached the other side. They'd left Mac's car in a parking garage, one chosen because it didn't have a nosy attendant who might recognize Kate and the baby.

Fortunately there weren't many people returning to their vehicles as Booker rushed Kate through the parked cars on the bottom level, most fans wanting to see the end of the game. Kate's heart was beating like crazy, and she kept turning back to see if anyone was after them. She didn't think so but she knew Saracino had to have people outside the stadium, too. They had to hurry, do something to help Mac. The parking garage was lit by yellow vapor lights, sending a sickly pall over the ugly gray concrete walls and low ceilings, and Booker chose to use the ramps instead of the stairwells, no doubt afraid of getting trapped in one.

They reached the third level without a problem, but when

they were almost to the Mustang, a man with a gun suddenly stepped out from behind a black van. She recognized him at once as one of the men with Dmitri down on Current River. Booker pushed her aside as the man opened fire but Booker managed to get him first. Hit in the chest, the man went down between the cars, and Booker wasted no time, grabbing her arm and sprinting for the car.

Clutching Joey in the cooler, Kate ran for the passenger's side of the Mustang as Booker headed around to the driver's door. Before she could get inside, another man materialized behind Booker. Kate screamed and Booker ducked and swiveled but not before the killer fired twice into his chest at point-blank range. Booker was thrown down hard and didn't get up, and Kate ducked behind the concrete pillar in back of the car as the assailant turned the gun on her.

Heart in her throat, sobs choking her, she crouched down and darted behind the next parked car. Joey was crying, and she could hear the man's running footsteps echoing hollowly off the walls. Surely someone would come, would've heard the shots, and she dropped down to hide, desperately scrambling underneath the bed of a white pickup truck, pushing Joey's cooler in ahead of her. Panting hard, she squirmed on her stomach to the other side, trying to conceal herself behind the rear wheel. Booker was hit, oh, God, he was dead, but how could he be? He'd had on a Kevlar vest like the police wore, both of them did. Why hadn't it worked? Had one of the bullets penetrated it, or hit him above it, in the throat? Oh, God, God, the man would find her any minute now; he'd find her and kill her.

She couldn't hear his footsteps anymore. Where was he? Had he stopped? Or was he just moving around more stealthily, stalking her? Her heart was slamming like a trip-hammer, so hard she shook with it, and she peered out from underneath the truck, trying to see anyone walking between the cars. She couldn't stop seeing the way Booker had been cut down. She lay still, holding her breath, trying not to give in to wails of grief and fear, but Joey was scared, crying louder. They'd hear him, find him. It was over. She was going to die.

She shrieked shrilly when someone grabbed her foot and tried to kick him loose but he had too hard a grip on her ankle. She let go of Joey, left him under the car in the cooler, clawing hysterically at the killer's hold as he jerked her out. He was too strong, and he grabbed her up by her T-shirt as if she weighed nothing and forced her back against the hood of the next car. He got her by the throat, his fingers clenched around her gullet, squeezing, squeezing, until she choked and struggled for breath.

"We aren't in the woods anymore, are we, bitch? Aren't any yellow jacket nests up here for you to play tricks with. You got my friends killed, and you're going to die for it. I'd do it right now if Dmitri didn't want you for himself."

Kate fought wildly but the Russian was strangling her to death, his thumbs pressing harder and harder into her windpipe. Kate struggled frantically, trying to use her legs to kick him, but he was too big and strong, and he was leaning against her, pinning her down. She could see his face, red with exertion, still swollen from yellow jacket venom, eyes alive with hatred. Her vision began to dim, blacken around the edges, oh, God, she couldn't breathe, was going to pass out. She went limp, unable to fight anymore, and he must've decided to obey his boss because he suddenly let loose of her throat. She dropped to her knees on the pavement, weak, gasping for breath, trying to crawl away.

"I'm not finished with you yet," he growled, leaning down and grabbing her jacket. He raised his hand, and his palm cracked hard across her cheek, brutally slapping her head to one side. She broke his hold and scrambled away from him, screaming for help, but her cries echoed eerily inside the deserted parking garage. He had hold of her again, dragging her back toward him by the back of her jacket. She turned, jabbed at his eyes with her thumbs, but he easily evaded her attack. He was going to beat her unconscious, was enjoying her terror, as she could see from the excitement in his eyes.

She grabbed his arm when he came at her with another blow, held on with all her strength and sank her teeth into his wrist. He yelled in pain and ripped loose, backhanding her hard enough to knock her on her side. Dazed, she lay unmoving, groggily watching him approach until suddenly he was jerked back, choking and struggling. She blinked and tried to back up as someone dragged him away from her. Sobbing, holding her bruised throat, she watched the men grapple at the front of the car until a shot rang out and the Russian crumpled to the pavement. Then she saw Booker, oh, God, thank God, it was Booker. He came to her, dragged her onto her feet, but she was shaking so hard, trembling so much, he had to support her.

"I thought you were dead. I thought you were dead," she sobbed hysterically, as he got an arm around her waist and tried to calm her.

"I would be if it weren't for the vest. The slugs knocked the wind out of me, nearly stopped my heart, cracked a couple of ribs, I think." He winced, his hand rubbing his chest, but his voice got urgent as he heard a car start up somewhere on a lower level. "C'mon, get Joey and let's get out of here before we get jumped again. Hurry it up, Kate! There's got to be more of them watching the parking lots."

Kate pulled herself together somehow, knowing she had to. She slid underneath the truck and pulled Joey out, then ran back to Mac's Mustang. She jumped in the front seat as Booker jammed it in gear and took off toward the exit. He gunned the car down the ramp, didn't stop at the booth but slammed through the wooden barrier and out onto the street where crowds of people were emptying out of the ballpark, yelling and celebrating the Cardinals' victory. He took off toward the I–70 ramp, going around the car waiting at the stoplight and into oncoming traffic, causing a Dodge minivan to throw on its brakes and swerve sideways to miss them. Then they joined the heavy traffic speeding west toward the airport, whipping in and out of cars, Joey's screams filling the car, both of them knowing there was nowhere left to run.

Thirty-two

NEITHER OF THEM said much, couldn't say much, until they were well away from the downtown stadium. Kate finally pulled herself together enough to lift Joey out of the cooler and try to calm him. Booker exited onto a down ramp that led to the University of Missouri at St. Louis. The campus was relatively quiet so late in the evening, and he pulled up in front of a dark classroom building and killed the engine.

"Are you all right?" he asked her.

Kate nodded. "What about you?"

"I'm sore where the slugs slammed into me. Thank God Mac insisted we get the vests, or we'd both be dead."

"What are we going to do now?" she asked him as he stared straight ahead.

"I don't know."

They looked at each other a moment but both knew they couldn't allow Mac to die, no matter what else happened.

"They'll kill him." Kate thought of Michael and the terrible way he'd died, the way Booker had catapulted backward when they'd gunned him down so mercilessly, and now they had Mac. They wouldn't hesitate to murder him.

"We can't trust them," Booker muttered, running both hands through his cropped hair. "Vince wants our heads, and he's not going to stop until he gets us."

Suddenly it dawned on Kate that there might be another alternative, *was* another alternative. One no one would expect. She thought about the idea for a moment, bringing Joey up against her shoulder and patting his back. He gave one last whimper, then nestled his head into her neck. He was tired, poor baby, tired of running, tired of being dragged around. He didn't deserve this, had never deserved it.

"I know what we have to do," she said, gently touching her fingertips to her cheek where the man had struck her. It ached, already felt swollen.

Booker looked at her. "You do?"

"Yes, and it's the right thing, too."

"Lay it on me, Kate. We don't have time to screw around. They're gonna make Mac tell them where we're headed. Torture him like they did Jumbo and Mavis." Booker sounded tired, too, Kate realized. He shifted in the seat, groaned a little, but didn't take off the heavy vest that had saved his life. She had put so many people through hardship, jeopardized lives. It shocked her how many people had helped her, mostly total strangers who'd been willing to make the sacrifice. Especially Booker. Booker had done so much. But it was time for it all to stop, she knew that now.

"We've got to go to Joey's mother. She's the only chance we've got."

"What do you mean, go to her?"

"We'll make the deal with her instead of her husband. Offer her a chance to get her baby back, no strings attached. Tell her the whole story, the truth, and beg her to intervene with Vince in our behalf and save Mac's life."

"Are you completely out of your mind, Kate? There's no way in hell Vince'd ever let us get near her, especially now, after his son's been kidnapped."

"Think about it, Booker. Vince dotes on her. You could tell when they were together on the newscast. She was obviously distressed, beside herself with worry. I can talk to her, woman to woman, I know I can. I can make her understand how I felt, how I wasn't sure Joey was hers because of the adoption papers until I saw her plea on television and knew she couldn't be faking that kind of pain. I knew then how she felt, because I was feeling it, too, when people were trying to take Joey away from me." Her voice got all gruff and scratchy from forcing down the regret, the grief. She steeled herself against the flood of heart-wrenching loss. "I'm telling you she's the one who can help us get out of this. I would, if I were her. If I thought I could keep Joey, I'd do anything, talk to anybody, just to keep him with me. You know that, Booker, you know it."

Booker propped his forehead against the steering wheel. She heard him blow out air, and she knew he didn't like it, not at all, that he saw a hundred things that could, and probably would, go wrong. She saw them, too.

"I don't like it," he finally said, as she knew he would. He turned his face toward her. Under the dim illumination of the streetlights, his blue eyes were lost in shadows, his mouth set in a tight, grim line.

"Do you have a better idea?"

Silence for one beat, then another. Then, he said, "If it weren't for Mac, I wouldn't go for this in a million years. I'd say we go on the run again."

It was Kate's turn to sigh. She leaned her head back against the seat and felt Joey shift his position. He was calm now, almost asleep. He was an incredible little baby. "But there *is* Mac. They're going to kill him."

"How the hell can we contact the woman? Vince's house'll be as secure as Fort Knox."

"Mac told us where she lives. I know the street, I went to dinner parties in that area with Michael, at clients' homes. I can find it, I know I can. We'll just walk up to the door and ask to speak to her. Then we'll tell her we have news about her baby but we'll only talk to her about it."

"This is crazy, Kate. They'll nail us before you get a word out."

"Maybe, but it's our only choice." She leaned over and placed a hand on the lean contour of his cheek, tenderness welling up inside, gratitude for everything he'd done for her, her newfound love for him. "She'll help us if we give Joey back. I know it, Booker, I know it as a woman, as a mother. I feel it in here." She touched her breastbone, tears filling her eyes.

Booker didn't look convinced. He shook his head and stared silently out the driver's window. Then he turned back and started the ignition. "Which way is Ladue?"

Kate was right about what Booker thought of her idea. He thought it was absurd. Only problem was, he didn't have a better idea, any other ideas, period. They were about as deep in trouble as they possibly could get. If they did explain everything to the wife, showed her how well Kate had taken care of Joey, how much she loved the kid, it'd be hard for Vince to explain away shooting them down in cold blood. If anyone held sway over the psychopathic killer who was her husband, it had to be Anna Saracino. Kate was right about that, too. Booker had seen the way he'd embraced his wife when she wept in front of the cameras.

Ladue was old money; it stuck out all over the quiet residential streets lined with immense, colonnaded houses hidden behind ancient oaks and lush, well-groomed beds of flowering azaleas and hydrangeas. The Saracino estate was not hard to find, had probably been two or three lots once, now a walled-off, hidden enclave with lots of yard, lots of privacy, and lots of armed guards. They recognized the wrought-iron gate from the clip of Anna's plea on the KY3 newscast.

The house was some distance up the concrete driveway but there were lights on in every window, and there were rows and rows of them. A small brick guardhouse stood outside the locked, motor-driven iron gate. One man was inside it, sitting in a swivel chair at some kind of control panel. Two more men, no doubt armed, stood just inside the black rails, chatting together and smoking cigarettes. They all wore matching olive-drab security uniforms but that didn't disguise the fact that they were hoods. Booker tried to tamp down the certainty that they were committing suicide by walking inside. The feelings roiling around inside him gave a whole new meaning to the phrase *Daniel entering the lions' den.*

"You sure you want to do this?" Booker asked Kate after they'd circled the block twice and in so doing, drawn the attention of Saracino's guards.

"I know it's going to work." She didn't sound as certain as her confident words intimated.

Booker pulled the car in and stopped at the gate. All three guards looked at them like rottweilers ready to jump a couple of toy poodles. The guy in the little sentry box came out and looked them over for awhile. He wasn't dressed as a security guard but looked buff enough to go more than a few rounds with Mike Tyson. Booker had a feeling he'd be the one who ended up with Tyson's ear in his mouth.

"May I help you, sir?"

Very polite for a murdering henchman, Booker thought. He started to respond but Kate spoke up first. "Yes, you can. We're very sorry to disturb you so late but we need to speak to Mrs. Saracino. It's very important."

"I'm sorry, miss. Mrs. Saracino isn't receiving callers. She's not well. Are you guys reporters?"

Kate hesitated, and Booker thought she was considering saying yes as a ruse to get inside. "No, sir, but we've got possible information about Mrs. Saracino's kidnapped baby."

That got the thug's attention. "What information might that be? If you'd like to tell me, I'll pass it along to her and her husband."

"I'm sorry. I can't tell anyone but her."

"I'm sorry, too. I can't let you in. Mr. Saracino's orders."

"Look, mister, we'll take off if you want us to." Kate's voice had grown a sharper edge. Booker was amazed she had regained control so quickly after what she'd gone through in the parking garage. She was some woman, yes, she was. "But if I were you, I wouldn't be so hasty about turning us away. We may know where her baby is. Call up to the house and ask her if she wants to talk to us. Let me talk to her over the phone, if nothing else."

The guy's eyes were on Booker now, crawling all over him, more than skeptically, downright suspiciously, but Kate's words had obviously given him pause. He was no doubt having vivid mental pictures of what Vince'd do to him if he passed up a lead about his baby boy.

"Okay, I guess it'd be all right to call up to the house and see if she's still awake."

"Yeah, buddy, you do that," Booker said, tired of being eyeballed. He rubbed his chest, thinking how close he'd come to death, glad they both still had on the vests. At least they had a little protection.

Kate and Booker sat silently, watching him walk back inside his hut and lift the receiver to his ear. He punched in a few numbers and waited.

"If we get inside, you're going to have to get rid of your gun," Kate told him. "Put it under the seat now before they frisk you."

"I'm not going inside without my gun."

"Then I guess you'll have to stay out here."

Booker grimaced, thinking things were getting a bit too far out of his control. It was crazy what they were doing. They were putting themselves in Vince's hands like coins tossed into an offering plate. They'd just seen what fate Vince and his goon, Dmitri, had in store for them, lots of pain with dying hard at the end. "How do you plan to get Joey inside without anybody seeing him and taking him away from you?"

"In the cooler, I guess."

"You think they're not going to look inside the goddamn cooler, Kate?" Booker broke off their conversation as the man came up to the window again. He held a portable phone in one hand. His other hand was on the butt of the .38 snub-nosed revolver encased in a black leather holster attached to his belt.

"She wants to talk to you."

Kate took the phone, then waited while Booker put his finger on the button and watched his window roll up in the guard's face.

"Hello, Mrs. Saracino?"

"Yes."

Kate thought Anna's voice sounded weak and tired, maybe even a little frightened. That's why she'd agreed to pick it up. She was as desperate to get her baby back as Kate was to keep him. But she couldn't let herself think that way.

"Please, just hear me out, Mrs. Saracino. I want to talk to you. I know where your baby is. I know everything that's happened. Please, just let me come in and talk to you. Please."

Anna's hesitation lengthened until Kate's nerves began to dance.

"Who is this?"

Kate hesitated, knowing full well what a chance she'd be taking if she told her the truth. "My name is Kate Reed." She heard the woman's gasp and hurried on before Anna could sic the guards on them. "Please don't hang up! I didn't kidnap your baby. He's safe, he's just fine, I swear he is. He's a wonderful little baby." Her voice left her, emotions going ragged, and she felt Booker put a comforting hand on her shoulder. "He's out here in the car with me, Mrs. Saracino. Let me bring him inside. I want to give him back to you. This has all been a big mistake, I swear to God it has."

Anna Saracino began to sob at the other end, quickly dissolving into a full-fledged fit of weeping that took several moments to subside. Then her voice came again, choked, more heavily accented than before. "He's out there with you?"

"Yes. He's perfectly all right, I promise. I've taken good care of him for you. I didn't know who he was, Anna. You've got to believe me. Michael, that's my husband, told me we could adopt him, told me everything was legal and aboveboard. I had no idea he'd been taken from his family. I swear that to you."

"Oh, my God, oh, my God, I can't believe this."

"It's true." Kate could see that the two guards standing on the other side of the gate now had their guns out. So did the guy beside the car. "I beg you to just listen to me. Call off the guards, Mrs. Saracino. They've got their guns pointed at us out here. Let me and my friend come in with your baby. We've come in good faith, I swear to God, we have."

"All right. I'll tell them to let you come in. My son's there with you? Now? You got him there, he safe?"

"Yes. He's fine. You'll see."

"Let me talk to Tommy."

"And, Mrs. Saracino, your husband's got a friend of ours. A man named Mac Sharp. Promise me you won't let Vince hurt him. Or us, either. Can you promise me that?"

"I don't know. I can try."

"Please try. Mac's innocent. He was just trying to help us get your baby back to you. We're all innocent, you've got to believe me."

"Let me talk to Tommy," Anna Saracino said again.

Kate assumed Tommy was the guard with his gun pressed up against Booker's profile. "Roll down the window," she said to Booker. As the glass slid down, she said, "Are you Tommy?"

"Yeah."

"Mrs. Saracino wants to talk to you."

The guard took the gun and the phone and wandered off a couple of steps, no doubt wanting some privacy. Kate had a feeling he was arguing with his employer's wife because several minutes passed before he came back and leaned down to the window.

"Okay, we're gonna let you go in but I'm warning you people. One wrong move and believe me, I'll be happy to put a bullet in your head."

"Yeah, join the crowd, Tommy. We just left a couple of your friends who felt the same way," Booker said sourly, shifting the car into gear as the gates began to roll open with a soft electronic whir. They drove through them and up a dark, winding driveway lit on each side with small lights hidden in the shrubbery. Near the front of the house they were redirected by another pair of guards, these two carrying automatic rifles, to a curve that led underneath a side portico supported by big white pillars. Light blazed inside it, and Booker pulled up out of the darkness where three more guards were waiting to escort them inside.

"Get rid of your gun now before we get out," Kate told Booker.

"I don't think so."

"They'll shoot you down the minute they get a glimpse of it. Do you want that to happen?"

Booker looked outside into the barrels of three M-16's and decided Kate might be right. "Okay."

Booker slid it out from the back of his waistband and held it up, dangling the trigger guard off his left thumb. All three guards zeroed in on him as he slowly laid the .45 up on the dashboard. He was glad he still had on the bulletproof vest. "Put the cover on the cooler," he told Kate as he opened his door.

Kate did so, watching Booker get out. He was immediately swarmed and slammed up against the hood of the car. They frisked him roughly, holding his arms behind his back while one of them kept a gun at his head. Fear came slithering up into her throat, but she opened her door. She sat still for a moment, afraid to get out.

"Let him up."

The soft words came from Anna, Kate recognized the Russian accent at once. The woman was standing at the top of a flight of marble steps. Kate peered into the shadows that half hid the woman and watched Joey's mother descend toward them.

"Wait a minute, Mrs. Saracino," one of the men called out. "We've got to make sure the woman isn't carrying a weapon. Vince's orders."

Anna stopped halfway down and waited, apparently unwilling to overrule her husband's commands. That was not a good sign, Kate feared. She climbed out of the car, leaving Joey asleep in the cooler on the floor of the passenger's seat. One of the men grabbed her, made a quick search of her clothing, then released her.

"She's clean, ma'am, but they're both wearing vests."

Kate watched Anna walk the rest of the way down, her hand trailing along the smooth marble balustrade. As she stepped from the shadows into the light, Kate realized how young she was. She looked little more than twenty. She wore a long white robe, shimmering satin, belted tightly around her waist, with matching high-heeled slippers. Up close and despite skin blotchy from crying, Kate thought she might possibly be the most beautiful woman she'd ever seen, but she looked as scared as Kate felt. She was trying to see around Kate, see inside the car. She was looking for her son.

"Inside the cooler," Kate said softly.

The man pushed Kate back against the fender with his gun barrel as Anna bent and leaned into the car. Everyone watched silently as she lifted a corner of the lid off the small red cooler. She made a strangled, muffled sound, then picked up the cooler and held it tightly against her chest, the same way Kate had been carrying it.

"Won't you please come inside?" she murmured, not bothering to wipe away the tears rolling down her cheeks. "It's all right, Sammy. You can let them come with me."

"That's right, Sammy boy, back off," Booker said, jerking his arm loose from the man holding him.

Kate looked at Booker as Anna started up the steps. Two guards came with them, still toting their guns. Anna ignored them all. They entered the house into a wide hallway, painted beige with white trim, a beautiful modern house with expensive furniture and damask draperies. Ornate sconces lined the walls, flickering crystal fire as they walked across the shiny black marble floor.

They followed Anna to an absolutely gigantic interior staircase that wound up in twin spirals from a front foyer with the same polished marble floor and a matching black marble fireplace beside the front door. Vince had spared no expense in making a home for his lovely bride. The young woman went up to the second floor, cradling the cooler, her unlikely retinue following in her wake. At the top of the steps she turned down another impressive corridor that ended in front of two double French doors with mirrored insets. She opened one of them and turned to her overly attentive guards.

"I'll be all right now. Please wait here while I talk with these people."

"But Mrs. Saracino, your husband said not to . . ."

"Please, do as I say. You've found no weapons on them. I be all right. Call my husband and tell him he must come to home at once. Tell him I need him, that Kate Reed has come to bring our son home to us. And Sammy, tell him I say he is not to harm man named Mac."

Her voice had not changed a bit, was just as soft and agreeable as ever. Sammy looked at her, mouth agape, as Anna invited Kate and Booker to come inside, then drew the doors together behind the three of them. She said nothing but walked across the spacious bedroom to a large four-poster bed draped in some kind of filmy white fabric. She laid the cooler atop the white satin comforter, took off the lid and then very, very gently lifted Joey into her arms. She looked at him a long moment before bringing him tenderly against her breast. When she turned around, her cheeks were wet with tears.

Kate clenched her jaw until it ached, struggling not to fall apart now, not with so much at stake, but God help her, she wasn't sure she could bear this, just handing Joey over to Anna as if he meant nothing to her. There was no doubt the woman in front of them loved the child she now cuddled and wept over, but that didn't make it any easier for Kate to lose him. She felt her own tears coming on, fought to control them, looked at Booker who looked sorry for her, but apprehensive, too, very apprehensive indeed. She had a feeling he was casing ways out of the room.

"Will your husband kill us?" Kate asked, bringing the most pertinent concern out into the open.

"He'll want to," Anna replied, as if that was an everyday question around the happy Saracino household, "but I think I can make him not do it."

"*You think?*" Booker said. "That's not very reassuring, Mrs. Saracino. I don't know if you know it or not, but your husband's not exactly the most stable guy around."

Anna looked up from Joey's face, the warmth of her smile slowly fading away. Her pale blue eyes turned hard. "I know what my husband is. He is a filthy, murdering animal. I loathe every single thing about him."

Thirty-three

BOOKER STARED at Vince Saracino's wife, shocked by her admission, then slowly slid his eyes to Kate, who looked as stupefied as he felt. Anna Saracino sat down on a tufted pink satin rocker beside the white marble fireplace.

"Is he not the most beautiful baby?" she murmured, rocking Joey and speaking to them as if they were old school chums come to admire her newborn. "It was most difficult decision of my life to give him to Michael but I knew I had to. I didn't have choice, none at all, you do understand that, don't you?" Suddenly she bit her lip, lapsed into silence, her vivid blue eyes brimming with unshed tears. "Surely you know how I feel, don't you, Kate? How hard it is to give up beloved child?"

Speechless, Kate and Booker stared at her. Bewilderment written all over her face, Kate shook her head, trying to make sense of what Anna was saying. "I don't understand. What do you mean? Why would you give him to Michael?"

Anna contemplated her for a few moments in silence, then admitted, very low, eyes downcast. "I gave him to Michael because Michael is his real father."

Kate jerked physically as if she'd been slapped and staggered back a step. Booker steadied her with a hand on her shoulder.

"What?" Kate finally breathed out. "What are you saying?"

Joey began to fuss, squirming in her arms, and Anna crooned softly to him while Kate and Booker stood frozen in disbelief. "I know Michael's dead. Vince had him murdered," she said in a hollow voice. A tear rolled down her cheek, and she wiped it away with her fingertips. "I loved him, and he loved me."

Booker scowled, not liking the way this was going. Kate stood shock still, blood draining from her face. She looked as white as Anna Saracino's satin canopied bed.

"I'm sorry, Kate, so sorry you had to find out truth like this. We never want to hurt you, never meant for these terrible things to happen. It just did, is all. It just did." She stopped, and put her hand against her mouth as if she felt sick. "Michael cared about you, respected you, he really did, but he said you'd grown apart. He said you didn't love him anymore, not like I loved him."

"You and Michael?" was obviously all the response Kate could manage.

Anna nodded, stricken eyes latched on Kate's face. "He was one of Vince's lawyers, but you know that. He spent time here at house, joined us for dinner. Vince has been under indictment in New York last few years and had to go back and forth for court hearings. Michael and I fell in love; he was so kind to me, so thoughtful of my feelings. We had to be very careful but we became lovers. It was foolish, madness, but we truly loved each other."

"Oh, my God, I can't believe this." Kate sank down in an upholstered wing chair beside the door.

"It's true, every word of it. Then I know I was pregnant and was absolutely frantic. I did not know what to do. I did not know if it was of Michael or my husband. I was terrified Vince would find out. Vince would kill me if he ever found out I'd been with another man. He'd kill Michael and me both. He'd even kill the baby, if he knew for sure it wasn't his. I know him, he would've killed my baby if he'd found out."

Anna's words had spilled out faster and faster, her accent growing thicker, but she saw the revulsion on Kate's face. "You must believe me. He'd do something that horrible in blink of eye. He's a terrible man, a devil. I didn't know until after we married. He courted me in Moscow, was kind, always kind, bought me fine presents and treated me like queen. My father is Ilie Kafelnikov, very powerful man in Russia but also into criminal affairs like Vince. They are partners in illegal activities, here and in Moscow, and when Vince showed interest in me, I became my father's bargaining chip. But we had no idea the kind of man Vince was. He's crazy, he kills people for any little thing."

Anna gazed down at Joey, who sputtered until she stopped rocking and laid him on his back atop her knees. Her voice was threaded with horror when she spoke again. "I saw him kill man who'd crossed him, shoot him in head out on lawn below my balcony." She gestured at a pair of French doors that led to an upstairs porch. "He was dressed for dinner, in formal evening clothes, and afterward he came upstairs for me, as if nothing happen, and took me out to eat. There was spatter of blood on his sleeve. I never forget that drop of blood, how red it looked against his crisp white cuff. I can see it now. I see it all the time. It haunts me." She screwed her eyes shut and shook with a delicate shiver.

"So you were in on this all along," Booker said. "You planned for Michael to steal your own child?"

"Yes, yes, but I had to! Don't you understand this?" The young woman rose and began to pace, cradling Joey against her chest and growing more agitated and upset. "My son has Michael's blood type. That's the first thing we checked when he was born. It was only matter of time before Vince realized he was not his. We thought of running away together, far away where he could not find us. But we knew he could, he would, he'd never stop until he find us. He's obsessed with me, treats me like prized possession." She stood still and looked at

Kate, as if begging her understanding. "He calls me that, his trophy, his little Russian prize."

"How in God's name did you pull this off? Without your husband finding out?" Kate asked, her face now uphill from incredulous.

"We were lucky that Vince was in New York for court when I went into labor. He was not here, and we had to figure way to get baby away before he found out truth. It was Michael's idea to take our son to you." Her fear-shadowed eyes returned to Kate. "He said you wanted baby, that you could not conceive and would jump at chance to adopt. He said you'd never guess truth. You see how perfect it seemed? Michael would raise our son with you, and Vince would never find out. He was going to move to those Ozark hills where you live. He was going to tell everyone, how do you say? That he wanted his roots back? That he wanted his marriage to grow strong. He was going to let me see the baby when he could. It almost worked but then everything went all wrong."

"How did your husband find out about Reed?" Booker heard a car outside and had a feeling by the way the tires screeched to a stop on the driveway that it was Vince Saracino come home to kill them.

"Somebody on street, you know, the ones they call snitch, told Vince he saw Michael with baby and Vince sent Dmitri after Michael. You were not supposed to be hurt. Michael never wanted to hurt you. We were desperate."

Kate and Anna stared at each other silently until the bedroom door was thrown open and Vince Saracino burst into the room. Dmitri was right behind him, and a couple of Vince's goons dragging Mac between them. Mac had been pistol-whipped. Beaten badly. His nose was bleeding, one eye nearly swollen shut, but he was walking on his own two feet, and that was a hell of a good sign around this murderous bunch. Booker breathed easier until he saw the look on

Vince's face. His eyes looked black, black and deranged. Dmitri was staring at Kate, a triumphant smile on his face.

"You're dead, you piece of shit, for coming to my house like this," Vince ground out, getting up close and glowering into Booker's face. His rage rolled off him like waves of heat. "You and the woman are both dead."

Anna rose at once, clasping Joey against her breast. Her voice was soft, sweeter than it had been, but she wasn't trying to hide her tears. Booker was very glad to hear her next words. "You've got to let them go, Vince. All of them. They did nothing wrong."

Vince turned on her, red in the face, nearly foaming at the mouth. "What the goddamned hell are you talking about? They took my kid, came into my fucking house. Nobody's gonna do that and live, nobody."

"No, no, Vince, you are wrong, you don't understand. Somebody made horrible mistake." That got everyone's attention, even Dmitri, who was mighty bruised up from his near-death experience in the car wreck but glaring at Booker now, no doubt salivating with the fantasy of killing him with his bare hands.

"What are you talking about, Anna? Kate Reed kidnapped our son. She and Reed took him . . ."

"No, Vince, no, she was trying to bring him back but everything's all mixed up," Anna cried, looking down at the baby, then tearfully meeting her husband's furious eyes. "It's not our baby, Vince. It's not him."

Vince looked as if she'd cold-cocked him with a two by four. So did Kate and Booker.

"That's bullshit," Vince barked angrily, striding across the room to his wife. "That's my son. They said it was him themselves. They wanted to trade him to me, my own son."

"No, he's not our son, he's not," Anna cried desperately. "Our son has birthmark on his right arm, just above wrist. You know that, I told you about it, did I not?" She sobbed, very convincingly. "He does not have it, Vince, look, see, he does not have it. Michael told her he got this baby from Philippines, and he must have been telling truth. He's not ours, he's not."

When Anna dissolved into tears, Vince pulled up Joey's sleeve, shaking his head and looking as confused as everyone else. He stared helplessly at his weeping wife, but Anna turned away and walked sobbing across the room to where Kate had risen unknowingly from the chair.

Booker watched Anna stare into Kate's eyes, and it dawned on him what the woman was doing. Vince had never seen his son, had been away in New York when Joey was born. There was no way in hell that he could contradict his wife on the baby's identity, no way. Good God, Anna was giving up her son all over again, giving up all claims as his birth mother. To save Joey from the kind of life he'd know as the son of a Mafioso, Booker realized, the miserable life she endured as Vince's wife. A thrill went through him when he realized Kate might get to keep Joey after all, and he saw the same joyous emotions flickering across Kate's face.

Anna handed the baby into Kate's arms, and Kate cuddled Joey close to her heart, both women weeping for completely different reasons. Anna backed away, turning and running into the arms of her stunned husband. She wept against Saracino's chest, her words muffled but full of anguish, "It's not him, Vince. It's not him, it's not, oh God, what are we going to do now? Where's our baby, Vince? Where is he?"

Booker watched Vince slowly dissolve to the consistency of a melted marshmallow, holding tightly to the wife he obviously adored, unaware of the undercurrents of her despair, seeing only her grief and her tears, and how much she needed him. "We'll find him, sweetheart, we'll find him. I'll search every goddamned inch of this earth before I give up." His eyes clashed with Booker's, but fortunately no longer filled with the murderous insanity of moments ago. "Get them the hell out of here, Kavunov, and make sure they keep their mouths shut."

"Promise me you won't hurt them, Vince, promise me," Anna begged, clutching the front of her husband's shirt, her voice growing slightly shrill. "They're innocent, I tell you. They did not anything but try to give my baby back, but he wasn't mine, he wasn't mine. Please, I can't bear it if you hurt them, I can't bear it."

"Hush, my prize, don't cry, they won't be hurt, I promise." He patted her back when she buried her face in his shirt and looked at them over Anna's bowed head. "Unless they do something stupid. Like go to the cops."

"No, no, we won't," Kate hastily assured him. "You'll never see us again, I swear to God, you won't."

"I better not," Saracino muttered, cold eyes latched on Booker's face. "Kavunov, take them outside and let them go."

"You're going to let them go?" said Dmitri in disbelief. "Just like that?"

"That's right. You idiots've been chasing the wrong goddamned people for the last week. Let them go and then find out who the hell's really got my son."

Booker took Kate's arm and led her toward the door, wanting to get off the property before Vince could change his mind. Mac was just as eager to get the hell out but Dmitri moved out of the room behind them, eyes narrowed, just itching to get at Booker. Booker grinned into the man's bruised face.

"What happened to you, Dmitri, have a little fender bender?"

Dmitri's eyes turned rock hard with hatred but he controlled himself. "You got lucky this night, friend," Dmitri muttered in Russian, very low. "But it's not over between us yet."

"You're scaring me to death, Dmitri." Booker moved past him, glancing back to see that Saracino had shut the bedroom door. Two guards stood outside while he consoled his distraught wife. Booker turned back and said in Russian, "By the way, *friend*, if you ever lay a finger on Kate again, if I even see you down in my neck of the woods, I'll kill you just like I killed your two buddies. Got that, Dmitri?"

Kavunov did a slow burn, his face darkening, a tic working in his cheek as he ground his teeth in rage. He said nothing but followed them all the way out to the car. He stood at the bottom of the portico's steps as if waiting his chance, and Booker helped a woozy, disoriented Mac into the front seat and buckled him in, noting that Saracino's guards had confiscated his gun from the dashboard. He wished they hadn't, especially with Dmitri lurking around like the Grim Reaper. He turned back to help Kate and the baby into the backseat, then froze, his eyes locked on the Beretta Kavunov now held against the back of Kate's head.

"You killed my sister's boy and the best friend I ever had, Booker, you and this bitch. You aren't going to get away with it, I don't care what Vince says."

"You're out of your mind pulling this stunt on Saracino's property. He'll have your head if you go against his orders."

"Shut the fuck up and get in the car, or I'll shoot Kate, right here, right now. Believe me, I'd like nothing better."

Booker stared at him, saw the fear in Kate's eyes. Dmitri would do it. His face was alive with hatred and the thirst for vengeance. Eyes locked on the Russian's gun, Booker got in and started the Mustang. Dmitri pushed Kate and the baby into the backseat, and Booker contemplated taking off, but Dmitri kept the gun trained on Kate's temple until he was settled in beside her. Booker couldn't take any chances, not with a killer as cold-blooded as Dmitri Kavunov.

"Okay, Booker, drive through the gate as if nothing's wrong. I'll kill her if you don't. Make one wrong move and I'll show you how her brains look spattered all over the window."

Booker watched him in the rearview mirror, aware he'd

eventually have to make a move against Kavunov because the man was definitely going to kill them, all three of them. The Russian just didn't want to murder them at Saracino's house and risk facing the Mafioso's wrath. He probably wanted to take them somewhere more private, an isolated country road where he could torture them to his heart's content with no one to interrupt. Booker's best chance was to make a move right here and now but he couldn't without Kate taking a bullet. He'd have to think of something else, some way to overpower the Russian before he got a chance to kill them. He put the car in gear, backed up, turned the Mustang around and headed for the front gate.

"You okay back there, Kate?" he asked, slowing to a stop and waiting for the entrance gate to swing open. He had an idea, a bad one, true, one that was risky as hell, but the only one he could think of. He turned around, catching her eyes and holding them, as he made a show of strapping on his seatbelt.

"I've been better," she murmured, but took the hint and snapped her own restraint across her chest. She was holding Joey tightly against her with both arms. She looked terrified.

Booker glanced at Mac. His head was lolling against the window. They'd roughed him up good before they'd gotten Anna's call. Mac wasn't doing so good at the moment.

"Don't try anything with the guards, Booker. I'll shoot her, and they'll shoot you because they'll think you're firing at them."

Dmitri was right, that's exactly what the hoods would do. They had their guns out already, pointed at Booker. He sat still, both hands on the wheel, his mind racing. The iron gates opened slowly and Booker drove through them, watching the barrier close behind the car. He turned left and headed down the dark, deserted residential streets. It was well past midnight now, most decent folk already safe in their beds. He wished they were safe in their beds.

"Where to, Kavunov? Got somewhere special in mind to kill us or you gonna play it by ear?"

"Shut your mouth or I'll just do it right here, starting with the woman and the baby."

Booker shut his mouth but he pressed down harder on the accelerator. The Mustang jumped ahead and quickly gathered speed. Dmitri was sitting sideways on the seat behind Booker but his gun was still point-blank against Kate's head. Booker had a feeling he'd done this before, lots of times. Housecleaning hitman-style, mopping up all the messy details, getting rid of any pesky witnesses before he flew away home, but this time the Russian had extra incentive. Kate had spurned him. Booker had killed his friends. Mac had helped them escape. It was definitely payback time for everybody at the party.

"The interstate's about three blocks up, take it and head south," Dmitri said conversationally, in total control of the situation at last. He sounded really happy about it.

Booker pressed down harder on the gas pedal. They were doing close to sixty already, and he could see a traffic light flashing to red at the next corner. He didn't slow down.

Kavunov was becoming downright chatty. "I'm going to enjoy killing you, Booker. But first I'm going to kill your friends so you'll know how I felt when I walked into that trailer and found Yuri and Misha shot to pieces. I'm going to rape Kate, let you hear her scream for mercy, then you can listen to her last agonizing gasps for breath as I strangle the life out of her. Then I'm going to blow your head off."

Booker's fingers tightened on the wheel but he forced his voice steady. "You really shouldn't mourn so for Yuri and Misha, Dmitri. They were nothing but murdering cowards who deserved to die. Just like you."

Kavunov forced a cold little chuckle. "Don't think you can goad me into doing something stupid. I'm not stupid. But I always avenge the wrongs done to me. It's a funny little quirk I have, one of my idiosyncrasies, if you will."

They were up to eighty now, the speedometer still climbing, faster and faster. Booker took them through the stoplight without flinching, causing a car entering the intersection to throw on its brakes in a screech of rubber tires.

"Goddammit, slow down," the Russian yelled as Booker took the on-ramp without braking and shot out on the interstate like a launched rocket. "I'll shoot her! I will!"

"You shoot her and I'll take this car off the road into the nearest concrete wall, and we'll all die together. What do I have to lose, Kavunov? You're gonna kill us anyway, right? Go ahead, pull the trigger but you're gonna die if you do."

Dmitri took his gun off Kate's head and rammed the nose hard against Booker's temple. "Slow the fuck down, do you hear me, Booker? Slow it down!"

Booker jerked the wheel and shot around a semitruck, doing well over a hundred miles an hour. The trucker honked and gestured obscenely, and Booker hoped to God the driver had a CB radio he could use to alert the authorities. If he could get a motorist on the interstate to call 911, make them the target of a police chase, they might have a chance. He'd be damned if he'd sit docilely while Kavunov took turns putting bullets in their brains.

"You shoulda done your murdering back there when you had the chance, Kavunov," he told him, trying to sound calm and wondering how fast the Mustang could go. They were edging up on a hundred and ten, and Kavunov was the only one who didn't have a seatbelt on.

"Stop, stop, you stupid fuck!" Kavunov yelled as they forced a pickup truck off the road, "I'll shoot, I'll shoot!"

"Go ahead, and see how long you last going this fast."

Mac had come to his senses a little now, enough to get the drift of what was going on around him. He was pressing back into his seat, bracing both hands on the dashboard as they roared up behind another car and went around it in a blur.

"God, God, oh, God, we're going to crash, we're going to crash, Book . . ."

Suddenly Dmitri jerked back from the seat and shoved the gun into Kate's face. "I'm gonna kill her, I'm gonna kill her, slow the car down, goddamn you!"

At that point Kate acted, knocking the gun up and away from her and jerking to one side. Booker slammed on the brakes the same instant Dmitri pulled the trigger and blew out the back passenger window. The car shimmied and shivered, went into a skid, the brakes locking and burning, but the sudden deceleration flung Kavunov forward over the seat into the windshield. The top of his head hit the glass, sending out spiderweb crackling from the point of impact.

Booker grabbed the Russian around the neck with his right arm, squeezed it back against him as hard as he could as Mac grabbed for the gun, desperately trying to wrest the weapon away. It went off again, hitting the front windshield and shattering the glass. Still holding onto Kavunov and clamping his foot down on the brake, Booker fought the shaking steering wheel with his left hand, bringing the car around in a sliding, screeching U-turn that left them facing the traffic behind them.

A car honked and veered off to the left, barely missing them, as Kavunov struggled, getting off another shot, but Booker was pummeling his head now with his fist while Mac was trying to get the gun away. More traffic was slamming to stops with blaring horns and squealing brakes all around them, ramming each other with rending metal and smashing glass. Mac finally wrenched the gun out of Kavunov's hand, but the Russian somehow jerked free and was out the back door before they could stop him. Booker fumbled with his seatbelt and jumped out, thinking only that he had to get him. His blood was rushing hot, his mind sharp, and he thought about only one thing, getting to Kavunov, killing him so he wouldn't come after them again.

Dmitri was heading for the overpass about twenty yards up the highway, running hard and jumping down into a ditch that ran alongside the road. Booker could see him in the smoky lights thrown from the headlights of the stalled traffic jam. Kavunov was moving more slowly now, bleeding heavily from where his forehead had slammed into the windshield. Booker bolted after him, his mind and body filled with a red haze, his blood beating with adrenaline-pumped rage.

He caught Kavunov on top of the overpass where an old Buick was slowing down as the bleeding Russian ran toward it and tried to force open the driver's door. The woman driver screamed and took off, tires squealing down the road to safety as Booker tackled Dmitri around the waist. They went down together on the pavement, and Booker drove a doubled fist into the man's face. He grunted as Dmitri kneed him in the groin and wrestled away.

He only got a couple of feet before Booker had him again, this time getting him around the neck with one arm, jerking him to a stop, trying to squeeze off his carotid artery. Kavunov struggled fiercely, then somehow, someway, he had a small gun in his hand. He turned it into Booker's side and pulled the trigger.

Booker moved but not quickly enough and felt hot lead rip like fire across his hip. It spun him back against the concrete barrier, high above the honking, smoking accident scene. Then Kavunov was on him again, leaning over him, the gun muzzle against his cheek. Dmitri's lips stretched out over his teeth in a feral grimace.

Booker grabbed at the gun and they grappled a moment until Kavunov's grip on him went slack, his eyes looking vaguely surprised for an instant. Then he fell to his knees, and Booker saw the gaping wound in the back of his skull. Heaving in great gulps of air, Booker rolled away and glimpsed Mac at the end of the overpass, both arms extended, the Russian's silenced Beretta still smoking in his hands.

Kate was behind Mac, holding Joey in her arms, and when Booker took a step toward them, she rushed past Mac and into Booker's arms. She wept against his chest and he held her, trying to calm her but knowing how very close they'd all come to dying.

"It's okay, Kate, it's over. It's over for good."

Kate nodded, somehow managed to pull herself together. Booker kept his arm around her as Mac walked up.

"You hit bad?" Mac asked him.

Booker glanced down, hardly feeling the pain. "No, I think he just nicked me. He had a gun hidden on him somewhere."

"Well, I'm gonna shoot you myself if you screwed up the brakes on my new Mustang."

Booker managed a shaky laugh, then shook his head. "I owe you a big one this time, Mac."

"You sure as hell do, those guys beat the hell out of me back there."

Booker stared at his old friend's battered face, and they shared a serious look before Mac glanced down on the roadway below, where a lot of yelling and screaming was going on, as people pulled off the road to make way for the police cars roaring toward them through the stopped lanes of traffic. Shrill sirens splintered the night.

"You better get the hell outta here, man, both of you, before the cops catch sight of you. I'll tell them I was alone in the car, that it was a carjacking. I know most of the guys on the force, they'll believe me."

"Can't let you do that, Mac," Booker said, watching several officers streak to a stop behind the Mustang and jump out of their patrol cars.

"The hell you can't. You'll go back to jail if they find out you're involved in all this shit. There's gotta be a motel somewhere down this ramp. Find it, check in and I'll come back for you when I talk myself outta all this. Go on, get going, hurry it up."

Booker shook his head. "I'm tired of running. This is where it's going to end."

"Oh, man, you sure that's what you wanna do?"

Booker nodded as half a dozen police officers rounded the end of the overpass, guns drawn.

"Police! Drop the gun, drop it, drop the gun!"

Mac immediately tossed the Beretta aside and raised his hands. "Take it easy, take it easy, I'm St. Louis PD retired. The dead guy was trying to kill us."

"Get on the ground! Get on the ground *now!*"

Booker and Mac both dropped to their stomachs, arms spread wide, and within seconds were surrounded by cops, knees in their backs as their arms were dragged behind them and handcuffs snapped into place.

"You, too, lady, get down, get down!"

Booker lay helplessly and watched as they forced Joey out of Kate's arms and got her facedown on the ground. While they were cuffing her, she looked at him, her cheek against the pavement, eyes afraid.

"It's going to be all right, Booker, we can explain everything, tell the truth," she cried, as they patted her down, then pulled her back to her feet.

"Mac's got a lawyer he can call, name's Dick Graysen. Don't say anything until you talk to him, you hear me, Kate, don't say anything until you talk to him," he told her as he was jerked roughly to his feet and hauled with Mac and Kate toward the waiting police cruisers. Despite Kate's words, he knew it wasn't going to be all right. Kate had a lot of explaining to do before she could get herself out of trouble, but she had a good chance to walk free if Saracino backed up her story. Booker wouldn't be so lucky. He was on his way back to prison for a very long time. No question about it.

Thirty-four

KATE MASSAGED grainy, bloodshot eyes and tried to estimate what time it was. It seemed hours on end since she'd been closed up in the police interrogation room. Surely it was getting close to daybreak. Sometimes she'd been left alone in the unventilated, windowless room, subjected to endless waiting after she'd told her story to Mac's lawyer friend, Dick Graysen, who'd sat at her elbow through an endless grilling session by detectives. She'd told them the basic truth, omitting only the fact that Joey really was Anna Saracino's baby, starting from the moment Misha had burst into her kitchen until Mac had shot Dmitri dead on the overpass. The cops had seemed skeptical, to say the least, but on Graysen's advice Mac and Booker were telling the exact same story.

Rubbing her stiff neck, she stretched her arms over her head and tried to stay alert. She stared into the mirrored wall directly in front of her. There were people behind it, of course, watching her. She'd seen enough episodes of *NYPD BLUE* to know that.

The primary detective who'd done the questioning had been an older man named Lieutenant Piedmont, and her eyes still watered from his habit of chain-smoking Marlboros. The white ceramic ashtray in front of her was overflowing with ashes and butts, and a stale odor emanated from the thin, gray haze lingering near the ceiling. But he hadn't gotten rough with her, probably because of Graysen's presence. Kate took a sip from the Styrofoam cup that had been brought in to her an hour before. The coffee was cold and tasted as if Piedmont had put out his cigarettes in it.

Kate wondered if they were still questioning Booker and Mac, working them over, meticulously comparing their stories. She'd asked if Booker was all right, if he'd been taken to the hospital for his gunshot wound, and Graysen had told her he was in the next interrogation room. He'd also assured her that Joey was being well taken care of for the night, safe and sound in the home of a city foster caregiver.

Pressing her fingertips into her aching eyeballs, she rubbed them a moment, trying not to worry about the baby, about Booker, but that's all she'd done, all she'd been able to do. She needed to talk to Booker, be with him; she didn't feel safe without him anymore. She'd come to depend on him. She sighed miserably and propped her forehead in her open palms. When in God's name was this ever going to end?

It seemed as if hours had crept by before the door opened again. Kate jerked her head up, hoping she'd get some news. Graysen appeared, a diminutive man in an expensive brown plaid sport coat and silk tan tie knotted neatly at the collar of a crisp white linen shirt. He was dark of skin, eyes, and hair, unshaven from being awakened in the middle of the night but ever relentless in the protection of his clients. He spoke rapid-fire and expected everyone else to do the same. He'd pounded home every conceivable question time and again during his first, private interview with Kate. Her low spirits leapt like a startled gazelle when she glimpsed Mac Sharp behind Graysen in the doorway. Then Booker moved into sight, and thank God, he looked all right. Kate shot to her feet and rounded the scarred wooden table, eager to talk to them.

"They're gonna give you a couple of minutes," Graysen told Booker.

"I owe you for this, buddy. How about I buy you a steak

and eggs breakfast as soon as you get us outta here," Mac was saying as they closed the door and left Booker alone with her.

Kate couldn't take her eyes off Booker. He looked as weary as she did. He had on his red satin Cardinals jacket without a shirt, and she could see the gauze wrapped around his torso and several huge black bruises where the slugs had impacted the Kevlar vest. Without a word she walked into his arms and put her cheek against his bare chest, uncaring who might be watching them through the mirror.

"Thank God, you're all right," she whispered, wincing as she took in his bruised, battered face. His bottom lip was split from the fight with Dmitri, and there were a couple of butterfly Band-Aids on a cut on his chin. "I've been so worried about you." She gently touched the tightly wrapped bandage around his waist. "Does this hurt much?"

"No. The bullet barely grazed my side. The EMTs fixed me up in the ambulance, then turned me over to the cops to bring downtown in the cruiser."

Booker pulled her with him to the table and dragged two chairs close together. Kate gripped both his hands, glancing at the mirror and speaking very softly. "Are they watching us?"

"Graysen said he'd make sure no one was in there while we talked so we have some privacy."

Kate felt herself relax. "Then they've finished questioning you and Mac?"

Booker nodded. "Yeah, all night long, but our stories apparently jibed with Vince Saracino's version of what went down. We got a real break when Mac got hold of Graysen. He knows how to handle the detectives and managed to persuade them to take the Saracinos' statements tonight instead of tomorrow. Graysen called a couple of Mac's old friends on the force to come down, too, and that probably helped us get a fairer shake than we would've otherwise." He'd been looking closely at her as he spoke. "You don't look so good, Kate. Were they rough on you?"

Kate shook her head. "No, not really, I'm just tired. Graysen made things fairly easy, I guess. I just told them the truth in as much detail as I could remember."

"Vince and Anna told the detectives the same story we did about Kavunov coming after us, said as far as they were concerned we had nothing to do with the abduction. That pretty much gets you off on the kidnapping rap. You're gonna walk as soon as they get the paperwork done. Graysen's even agreed to give a press conference to the media exonerating you from any wrongdoing."

A great tide of relief rolled over Kate's mind as Booker continued.

"Vince played dumb and told the cops he didn't have a clue why his wife's personal bodyguards came after you and your husband so hard, said he didn't even know they were after you until Mac contacted his cousin about exchanging the baby. The cops are conjecturing there was some kind of vendetta between Dmitri and Reed, and when Dmitri heard Michael had a baby, he decided he was the kidnapper and went after him."

So that was the story they were using, noninvolvement, which would fly since the Russians were all dead and unable to dispute their version. But Kate was more concerned about the baby. "Then they don't suspect the truth about who Joey really is? They'll start looking into the adoption now, won't they, to see if it's legal?"

"They already have." Booker smiled a little. "Your sheriff friend in Van Buren came through for you big time, Kate. When they called down there to find out what he had on the case, he'd already done a search of your cabin and had Joey's signed adoption papers in evidence. Faxed them up here within the hour."

"Thank God."

"Michael must've gone to a lot of trouble making sure the adoption was signed, sealed and delivered by a judge out of St.

Charles. Graysen had to wake him up to verify the signature but he did inform the cops it was legitimate."

Kate was surprised to learn that the false adoption papers had stood up to scrutiny, then wondered why she doubted Michael's expertise. He'd always been slick, always won his cases one way or another. Of course he would've covered his tracks well, in case Vince got suspicious and checked out Joey's true identity. Thank God he'd bribed the judge or done whatever illegality was necessary, because those false documents were going to save her from losing Joey.

"So it's over? For good?" Kate shut her eyes and felt raw emotion burn its way up the back of her throat. "When can we get Joey back? I need to hold him in my arms, Booker. I want you to take us home. Then I don't think I'll ever leave the river again."

Booker's gaze slid away from her face and stayed fastened on their entwined hands. Fear streaked through her like fire, and Kate cupped a palm on his bruised jaw and forced him to look at her. His blue eyes were shadowed, hiding the truth, but she knew, she knew, and her heart sank like a granite gravestone. "Oh, my God, Booker, they aren't going to let you go, are they?"

Booker lifted a shoulder, tried to shrug it off. "They ran my name and came up with the military warrant. It's not exactly a surprise. I figured it'd happen sooner or later."

Kate stared at him, sick inside, afraid for him, afraid of losing him. She thought of visiting him in prison, seeing him locked behind bars, and it made her sick to her stomach. "What's going to happen to you? Tell me."

"They've got MPs on the way to pick me up. I'll probably end up back at Leavenworth."

Tears brimmed up before she could stop them. "You wouldn't be in this trouble if it weren't for me. This is my fault. Oh God, I can't bear for them to take you."

"It's not your fault so don't start blaming yourself. I didn't go into this blindly. You're gonna get Joey back, that's the important thing."

"But I want more than that, Booker, I want us to be together, I don't want to lose you . . ."

Booker let go of her hands, stood up, raking his fingers through his hair. "Look, Kate, don't feel obligated. You don't owe me a thing. My advice is to get Graysen to make sure Joey's adoption is ironclad legit, then go on with your life. I'm gonna be locked up for a long time, you can bet on that."

"Graysen's good, he can get you out of jail and back on the river with us where you belong." They stared at each other, neither able to speak. "I'm going to get you out, Booker, I don't care how long it takes. . . ."

Booker suddenly got agitated. "You need to get on with your life, raise the kid. You don't owe me a damn thing."

Kate stood up and faced him, her own temper flaring. "Will you quit saying that! Of course I owe you. I owe you my life, and Joey's, quit acting like that means nothing, like you don't care if you ever see us again, I know better, I *know* better."

A beat passed, then another. Booker pulled her against him, one hand in her hair, his words muffled against her ear. "Don't you understand, Kate, I don't know how things are gonna turn out so we can't make any plans. I don't know if we'll ever be together again. All I know is that I don't want you wasting your life waiting around for me to get out when I know full well they're gonna throw the book at me. I may be locked up for another twenty years, Kate."

"I don't care if it is twenty years," she whispered stubbornly. "I don't care if it's forever."

They broke apart when someone tapped on the door. Graysen poked his head in. "Sorry, Mr. Booker, but they're here for you."

"Please, can you give us a few more minutes," Kate asked quickly, "to say good-bye?"

Graysen hesitated but he finally nodded. "I'll try but make it quick."

Kate said nothing, couldn't say anything, just pressed herself against Booker, her arms clasped around his waist. Though she struggled not to cry, knew he wouldn't like it, a sob caught in her throat. His arms tightened, and she could feel his pain, hear it in the hard pounding of his heart. Booker held her a moment longer, then stepped back. "You take good care of Joey. He's a good little kid. Go on with your life like before, you'll be fine."

Kate looked into his eyes, eyes that had seen too much, had suffered too much. She raised her chin. "I'm going to get you out, Booker, no matter what it takes. I'm not going to rest until you're free."

Kate smiled at him but her eyes were swimming with tears when he pulled her back into his arms. He held her wordlessly until Graysen showed up again a minute later.

"Okay, Booker, time's up."

Kate gripped Booker's hands, hanging on as if that would keep him there, squeezing his fingers as two tall uniformed MPs moved across the room. She had to stand back as they cuffed Booker's hands in front of him and led him away. At the door Booker stopped and turned back.

"Take care of yourself, Kate. Everything's gonna be okay now, you'll see."

Kate nodded and watched the door shut behind him. Her legs crumpled and she sank down at the table. *I'll get you out, Booker*, she thought, *I will, no matter what it takes*. She forced a swallow over the giant lump in her throat, then found the wall holding back an ocean of suppressed emotions begin to crack. She'd fought so long, held herself resolutely in control throughout the long, horrible ordeal. But she couldn't do it any longer, not without Booker there to bolster her courage and help her get through it. She put her head down on her folded arms and wept with the fear she'd never see Booker again.

Epilogue

BOOKER STOOD on the front porch of his cabin and stared out through the scarlet and gold trees lining the riverbank. Afternoon sun streaming through the branches made the colors glow with such vivid beauty that his breath caught in his throat. It had been a year and a half since he'd stood in this quiet place and enjoyed the serenity of the river. The last time was the night he'd stood watch over Kate and Joey, the day he'd carried her unconscious and bleeding into his life. In the distance the river rushed and swirled and he shut his eyes, inhaling the familiar, long-coveted scents of fish and mud and fallen autumn leaves. God, he'd missed it. All the months in Leavenworth he'd thought of this moment in this place, visualized it in his mind as he tried to lock out the constant noise of prison life, the yelling and screaming, the clanging of heavy iron doors.

Booker had come home well after dark the evening before, but Kate had already been there. She'd left a vase of yellow roses on the front porch beside the cane rocker. He could smell their sweetness in the air. She'd left him food in a cooler, fried chicken, potato salad and apple pie, a pile of clean, neatly pressed clothes on the cot, and a six-pack of Coors Lite. He shook his head. He'd never met anyone quite like Kate. She was indefatigable. After he'd been taken into custody, she had pursued his release with the same dogged determination she had displayed when she'd saved herself and Joey from Dmitri Kavunov. Kate Reed was a woman like no other, no question about it.

Booker had spent the morning sitting in the chair, watching leaves flutter down into the splashing currents, thinking about Kate and everything awaiting him downstream at her cabin. He had stubbornly told himself for months he was no good for her, that she didn't need an ex-con in her life, but he hadn't been fooling anyone, not himself, and especially not Kate. He would be with her again if he was lucky enough to get the chance; he knew that now and he'd known it then.

Suddenly compelled to see her again—it'd been a month since she'd visited the prison—he stepped over the railing and shuffled through the leaves on his way to the riverbank, his thoughts on Kate and what she'd done for him since his incarceration. She had marched into his military hearing, pumped up and outraged that the army would dare jail a war hero, much less a prisoner of war. She had testified articulately and passionately for his release, had brought in Jumbo, Mavis, Mac and everyone else she could think of as character witnesses. She had been magnificent.

To Booker's shock, the court had decided to show leniency, perhaps because of Kate's relentless campaign for his freedom, or more likely due to the fact that Denton had succumbed to heart disease since Booker's last trial and hadn't been there to press as the victim for maximum punishment. The judges had given him two years, but he'd gotten off six months early for good behavior.

Kate's letters had begun as soon as the hearing was over, one every single day. She had come to visit him once a month, always with Joey in her arms, but seeing her and being unable to touch her had tortured him as much as life in an eight-by-eight cell. She had baked him dozens of chocolate chip cookies, sent him photos of Joey and her fishing or swimming or dozing together in a giant hammock on her back deck. And he'd been grateful, so grateful to have that lifeline to the

world, to the river he loved, that even now his heart clutched to think what it'd meant to him.

The canoe she'd left for him was pulled securely onto the bank. Big red letters spelling out *Pop's Bait Shop* emblazoned the side. Kate's invitation to float down the river and join her. Booker didn't need an invitation. He stepped in the canoe and pushed off with the paddle, caught the swift current and dipped his paddle deep into the clear blue-green water. She had wanted to drive up for him at his release but he had asked her not to. Mac had come instead, and Booker was glad. He had needed time to acclimatize himself, to get his mind in order.

Raising his face to the sun, he let the warmth invade his skin, savoring the joy of freedom, of sun and wind and rushing water. He'd done his time for good this time; no one would hunt him down; he had nothing to fear. Kate was waiting for him just as she'd promised. Unlikely, unfamiliar emotions began to stir inside him, and he stroked steadily, kept the boat on course, eager to see her again, be alone with her, without guards watching and listening to everything they said and did. He had hated seeing her and Joey inside the ugly, barred buildings surrounded by razor-wire fences; it had seemed obscene for them to be there.

And Kate had done more than wait. She had flown to Rome and gotten permission to visit Betsy and his son. She had brought home their address and insisted Billy was eager to hear from him. She had browbeaten him in every single letter until he agreed to write the son he'd thought lost to him forever and found it the hardest thing he'd ever done. Now Billy was here on the river, staying with Kate, waiting to meet his father. Sometimes Booker couldn't believe it. He felt nervous inside, at a loss for what he'd say. The kid was a teenager, for God's sake. His letters had been friendly enough, but what did the boy really think of a father who'd abandoned him, who'd done time for attempted murder?

Booker fought the cowardly urge to turn the canoe around, fight his way back upstream, the urge powerful but not as much as his desire to see Kate and meet Billy. In his wallet he had a picture Billy sent him, taken at his American school in Rome. He had on a black soccer uniform, and Booker thought him a fine-looking boy with Booker's blue eyes and his mother's big smile.

The river flowed onward, swift, eternal, the trees along the banks bright and alive with October brilliance, the wind spiraling down leaves all along the shoreline. A chill in the air cut through his blue flannel shirt but caused everything to seem brighter and fresher, more beautiful, and he felt a burn behind his eyes with the sheer pleasure of being back where he belonged. He dipped the paddle faster, deep, even strokes that would take him home to Kate.

When the bait shop appeared on the left shore, he steered the canoe straight toward it, his heart in his throat. It scraped against the sand and he laid down the paddle and stepped onto the bank. He stood looking up at the log cabin on the hill, where Kate had fled one night a long time ago. Yellow ribbons decorated nearly every tree in the backyard, and he could see Kate playing with the two boys, his son, and her son. He swallowed hard, just seeing them all together, laughing and having fun. God, Billy was so tall, taller than Kate. He had a baseball glove and was playing catch with Kate. Joey was toddling around, pushing a little toy lawnmower. He fought down a surge of raw emotion.

When Kate caught sight of Booker, she squealed with delight, then ran down the lawn to meet him. He could see her smile; he loved that smile, was pleased at how happy she was to see him. A thrill went through him when she threw herself into his arms, laughing, hugging him.

"I didn't think you'd ever get here! I've called Mac a dozen times asking him when you were coming. What took you so long?"

Booker examined her face, touched her nose. "You're sunburned."

"Billy and I went fishing this morning." She smiled at him, eyes alight with happiness, and his gaze strayed up the hill where his son was waiting to meet him, slapping the ball in his glove while Joey mowed the grass around his feet.

"Come on, Booker, you've got somebody to meet."

Booker let her lead him by the hand, and he watched his boy walk toward him with the awkward, loose-limbed stride of adolescence, and wondered if he was filled with apprehension, too, with fear he wouldn't know what to say.

"Billy's a great kid," Kate whispered. "I've loved having him here. Joey's nuts about him. See, just look at them together."

Joey was clinging to Billy's leg, being dragged along, squealing the whole way. As they approached, Kate laughed and scooped Joey up into her arms. Billy looked at him, and Booker couldn't speak, searched for the right words, didn't find them.

"Hi, Dad. We've been waitin' for you."

"Hello, son."

Billy truly had Betsy's smile, and he used it now. "Wanna see the bass I caught this morning? Kate put him on ice so I could show you. Got him on a purple plastic worm 'cause Kate said they hit the best on them. I reeled him in myself. Kate says he's a big sucker."

Booker laughed. "Sure. Bring him on."

Billy turned and headed at a run for the bait shop. Kate pushed Joey up into Booker's arms. Joey stared him in the face a moment, then decided Booker was too big and scary for him. He puckered up.

"You better get used to him, kiddo," Kate said with a laugh. "He's here to stay."

Booker held the squirming toddler but he watched his son pull a stringer out of the river and hold it up as high as he could. He waved an arm, then found Kate's eyes.

"I can't begin to tell you how grateful I am, Kate. I owe you."

"Good. That's the way I like it." She smiled, but her eyes were serious. She understood what he was saying, how much he appreciated her smoothing the way for Billy and him.

"You grateful enough to quit stalling and marry me?"

Booker laughed again, twice now, more than he had all the months in prison. "Plenty enough for that, I reckon."

"Then come on, let's go check out Billy's fish. Maybe I'll fry it up for supper. How's that sound?"

"Good," Booker said, entwining his fingers with hers. "That sounds just about perfect."